MEAD MOUNTAIN

AUTHORITATIVE

*We want to hear from you. Please visit **www.BKDell.com** and reach out.*

1.00

This novel is dedicated to my beautiful wife Eleasha, the precious gift that God chose for me.

Mead Mountain by B.K. Dell

Chapter One

January 2

Riley Ellison was in love.

He studied the woman as she took a drag from her lipstick-stained cigarette. Her tiny halter top was covered with gold sequins. It was flashy and sexy, but the hem and the straps were starting to tatter. The narrow strip of spandex wrapped around her hips barely qualified as a skirt, and the black garter she wore on her leg had a silver skull pendant.

Everything about her—the sharp angles of her aging hands, the contemptuous way she flicked her ashes, the ever-present tension in her expressions—all seemed to echo the same sentiment: *Back off.*

Riley Ellison found her beautiful, and in that moment, she was the only thing he cared about in the entire world. He zipped his windbreaker closed around his body, protectively, and hoped she would not catch him staring.

"Poison to the DJ booth. Poison to the DJ booth." An announcement came over the club's sound system.

The black-gartered woman rolled her eyes and turned around. "I'm right here!" she snapped.

The DJ didn't laugh at his error. He curtly asked, "What's your music?"

"You know my music. Tim McGraw."

"Can't do it. Wyatt said no more country."

"Well, *Junior* doesn't run the place," Poison insisted, hoping he would catch the veiled threat contained in her statement.

"Just pick something else," he grumbled. "How 'bout I put on some Bell Biv DeVoe?"

"You're not funny," she snapped. "Just play the music I tell you."

The DJ's head lolled to one side as he groaned in disapproval.

"Junior doesn't run the place," she repeated her threat forcefully. To punctuate it, she leaned into the booth and pressed her cigarette out in the DJ's ashtray, trenchantly adding, "Mr. Holloway does."

The DJ finally understood her meaning, and made it clear by the irritation on his face.

"Track three," she said and turned her back on him.

As she walked away, she took a second to congratulate herself on her last comment. One, she knew full well he wasn't still using CDs, but she liked the way the obsolete reference highlighted, rather than ran from, the truth that she was *slightly older*. Two, the fact that he would be unable to look up the track by number put the lie to the whole charade of him asking for her music. *He knows my music. He just doesn't want to play the song... but he will.*

As the current song playing reached its end, Poison went to help Ecstasy down from Stage One, then climbed the stairs to replace her. The time for Poison's song to start came and went, but *track three* was yet to play. Poison shot the DJ a dirty look, but to no avail.

It was a rare moment in such a club to have no background noise, and the half dozen indecent conversations in the room came to an abrupt stop. The whole place was eerily silent as Poison stood center stage, feeling her cheeks begin to burn with rage, and awkwardly tugging at the bottom of her tiny skirt.

Finally, the first notes of "It's Your Love" played through the sound system and Poison could hear a few distant groans, not from the patrons, but from the other dancers.

The gentle melody helped Poison forget all about the DJ. Her hips began to sway as she halfheartedly mimicked the moves generally understood to turn men on. As usual, the handful of perverts in the place ignored her in favor of the younger girls. She leaned the top of her spine stationary against the polished steel pole as her pelvis continued its hypnotic undulations. Her lips moved, almost imperceptibly, in sync with the lyrics. She tilted her head back and could feel the cold metal tingle her scalp.

She closed her eyes and tried to escape. The music entered her soul, and for a moment, she was well-loved. She lived a romantic life most women would envy. She was desired and sexy and was dancing for a man to whom she belonged and to whom she was proud to belong, a loyal and deserving man.

But she couldn't keep her eyes closed forever.

When she opened them, she was surprised to see a man standing at the foot of the stage. He had a full head of dark hair that was starting to grey around the temples. His eyes were a bit too clear, and his relaxed confidence was incongruous with the surroundings. He wore a red windbreaker, conspicuously zipped all the way up.

Poison took one look at Riley Ellison and knew his whole story. He probably just had a big fight with his wife. He had come to have a few overpriced drinks, tip two strippers one dollar each, then return to his buttoned-down, henpecked life and give in to all his wife's demands.

Poison sauntered over to where he stood. The strap of her top fell off her shoulder as she began to perform some of her A-moves for his benefit. Ellison fidgeted nervously, and Poison noticed that despite her very best gyrations, his eyes never left hers. She looked back at him sweetly and touched a warm hand to his cheek. She liked him. She might've even thought he was handsome, if only his face had a few scars.

Finally, she pulled her garter far enough away from her leg for him to slide a tip through. He left a twenty on the edge of the stage instead and nodded to the table where he had been sitting. All he said was, "Come and see."

The song ended and Desire was approaching the stage to take Poison's place. Poison reached out her hand for the younger stripper to help her down, but Desire ignored her and stormed up the stairs that Poison had been trying to descend. This was not only against club rules, but it nearly caused Poison to trip over her high heels.

No matter how often the new girls acted rude, Poison would never get used to it. She could feel her blood beginning to boil. To top it off, the music switched back to Hip Hop—vile, misogynistic lyrics over primal beats. She saw the DJ smirk and could hear Desire laughing. Poison put her clothes back on in a fit. She had almost forgotten about the aloof patron who'd cryptically invited her to *come and see.*

Poison approached Ellison's table and, without even a handshake's worth of introduction, slid her slender body down onto his lap. "Hi sexy," she laughed.

Ellison looked away blushing, unprepared for her mischief.

She flashed a coquettish grin. "You don't come to places like this much, do you?"

"You'd be surprised," he said.

Being this close to him, she could see his face better. She said, "Yeah, I think I recognize your face." She looked again. "Hold on..." She was searching her memory. "Yeah, I've seen your face. I don't think it was around here though."

"I've been on TV," he said with a dismissive gesture of his hand.

"What's your name?"

"Riley Ellison."

"What?" she asked because the music was loud.

"Riley Ellison," he told her.

She showed no indication that she recognized the name.

"What's your name?" he asked.

"Poison."

"What's your real name?"

"My real name is Poison." She didn't laugh. Her words came with no delay. It was an evasive line she had used for years. "You seem uptight," she said as she teasingly tugged the zipper of his windbreaker. "Why don't you take off your jacket?"

"I get cold," he said, flatly. It was an evasive line *he* had used for years.

"Yeah, what's up with this weather recently?" she asked. "I thought California was supposed to be famous for its weather."

He shrugged. He had only heard enough to know she said something about the weather.

"So, you want a dance or what?"

"Do I want to what?"

"A dance. Do you want a lap dance?"

"Is there a place we can go that's quieter?"

"There's a VIP section in the back," she said.

"Okay, let's go."

"You've got to be a member."

"How much does that cost?"

"It's a thousand dollars for the year."

"How much just for the day?"

She shook her head. "It's a thousand dollars for the year."

Ellison sat bewildered for a moment. This was a curve in the road he hadn't anticipated. He looked down at his right hand; there was a piece of twine tied around his finger. He asked, "Do they take Visa?"

"Sure. I'll go get Mr. Holloway."

While he waited, Ellison wondered just what Mr. Holloway would look like. He pictured a young punk, tattooed out, smoking a menthol. But he didn't have to wonder for long, because an elderly man soon rounded the corner to greet him. His skin was weathered by sunshine and cigarettes, and he was wearing an old, faded blue cowboy shirt—the kind with pointy flaps on each pocket and metal snaps holding them shut.

Mr. Holloway shook Ellison's hand cordially as if he wanted to set him up with a high interest loan. He asked him to fill out a few forms, then disappeared with Ellison's Visa.

Ellison's phone buzzed. He pulled it from his pocket and discovered he had missed several texts, which the music had been too loud in the main room to hear. His wife, Deborah had been texting him photos she took of herself: one of her in her drab, faded blue kitchen apron... and one of her with a whisk, mixing ingredients in a large bowl... and one of her wearing a large oven mitt. She gave an exaggerated, cartoonish sexy face in all of them.

Ellison's face flushed. *She's just so stinking funny.* He was about to text her back when Mr. Holloway returned.

Mr. Holloway handed Ellison a black laminated card, still warm, that read "Boys' Club" on the front, and "Riley Ellison" on the back. Mr. Holloway secretly did recognize the name, but was able to maintain his professional discretion.

Poison reappeared at the table, and the avuncular Mr. Holloway made his exit, silently tipping the hat he wasn't wearing. He took one last look at the two of them and told Ellison, "I say, that Poison's just as pretty as a picture."

"Yes, sir," Ellison agreed.

As Mr. Holloway turned away, he mumbled, "And mean like a bull."

Ellison wasn't sure he heard him clearly, but still chimed merrily, "Yes, sir. I'm sure she's very likeable."

Poison couldn't help but laugh. She grabbed Ellison's hand spritely and led him back. The VIP area had sectioned off private rooms and the two of them were able to find one unoccupied. There was a table surrounded by chairs in the middle and a long sofa in the corner. The whole area smelled like carpet shampoo, which was reassuring to Ellison, and disconcerting at the same time.

Ellison seized a chair and pulled up close to the table. He left Poison no room to welcome herself onto his lap again, so she sat in a chair across from him. The room was much quieter and he thought it was perfect.

With her no longer on his lap, he was able to get a more complete look at her. He saw a complicated woman. The slender slope of her neck befitted a young girl wishing to one day be a bride, but the tension in her jaw befitted a grown woman wishing she never had been.

She wore the years of bad decisions, loss, and regret on her face. Her soul still carried the pain—visible to anyone with the special ability to see it—of every man who had neglected her, rejected her, hit on her, and spit on her. Her posture, however, told a different story; her straight spine said she was a fighter, *yes, a survivor.*

Ellison noticed Poison tense a little when a waitress entered their room. As she walked closer, Poison drew her arms in to her sides. It wasn't a typical defensive gesture; it was a habit that she'd developed subconsciously, meant to hide the part of her halter-top that was missing the most sequins.

"Would you like to order some drinks?" the waitress asked Ellison, ignoring Poison entirely.

"No, ma'am," he said reflexively.

"I'll have a shot of Patron," Poison said to Ellison, not to the waitress.

"A shot of Patron," Ellison nodded to the waitress, but looked back at the stripper. "Salt and lime?"

"Of course," confirmed Poison.

"Thank you," he said to the waitress as she left.

"Now how does this work?" Ellison turned his attention back to Poison. "I pay you twenty dollars and you dance for the length of one song?"

She laughed. "Yes, that's how it works."

"So twenty dollars a song. And a song is about what, three minutes?"

"Yeah, about." Poison laughed again.

Ellison opened his wallet and pulled out a twenty. The current song was ending, so Poison dutifully rose from her seat to make her way over to him.

He raised his palm and said quickly. "I don't want you to strip for me."

"Huh?" Poison froze.

"I don't want to pay for a dance," Ellison reiterated.

Poison drew her elbows in again and even crossed her arms in front of her. Before she could respond, the waitress returned with Poison's shot. Ellison handed her a bill, and hoping to dismiss her quickly, told her to keep the change.

The waitress saw the forlorn expression on Poison's face and was prompted to ask, "Everything okay in here?"

"Yes, ma'am," Ellison quickly answered for the room.

As soon as the waitress left, Poison asked firmly, "What do you want with me?"

Ellison noticed her eye the door, so he warmly implored, "Please, sit back down."

Poison returned to her seat. She tilted the shot down her throat without effort. Her *back off* face had returned and even the burn of the alcohol couldn't disrupt it. Again she asked, "What do you want?"

Ellison summoned his most calming voice. "I'm willing to pay you for your time. Twenty dollars for three minutes, right? I want to talk."

She sucked some juice from the lime and tossed it fiercely into the empty glass, then demanded, "About what?"

Riley Ellison did not sit up taller. He did not clear his throat. His manner was casual when he responded, "I want to tell you about our Savior, Jesus Christ."

His tone was as unremarkable as if he had just made a comment about the weather, but her response was as explosive as if he had just asked her to have his children. "What?" she exclaimed. "Get out of here!"

"I'm quite serious."

"You're crazy. You must be some kind of..." She trailed off. Poison didn't know how the sentence would end at the time she began it. Frustrated, she just repeated, "Get out of here!"

Riley Ellison was indeed one of those able to identify the hurt behind her eyes. He understood the pain and dark confusion that had led her to this life. He saw everything that Jesus loved about her and he asked God for the humility to, himself, love her that deeply.

He slid the twenty across the table. He said, "Please. Twenty dollars for three minutes." He cracked open his wallet. "If we need more time, I have more money."

Poison looked at the twenty, then at his wallet bursting with twenties, considering his bizarre proposition. Her face was frozen in an expression usually reserved for watching eye surgery. Finally, she slid the twenty back and said, "This is... this is... this is... *weird*."

"You mean you'd rather spend the same three minutes shaking your moneymaker, instead of—"

"Moneymaker?" scoffed Poison. Even though their ages were only separated by a few years, his slang was out of step with hers by a generation at least.

"Poison, wait. Please listen." Ellison did not want to be diverted from his point. "Are you really telling me you are prepared to dance naked on a total stranger's lap, and that you'd rather do that, than simply listen to what I have to say about God?"

"Well …yeah!"

"And you don't think *that's* weird?"

"It's part of the job," she protested.

"Twenty dollars for three minutes! *That's* part of the job," he insisted. "Here." He pulled out his stack of twenties. "We could sit and talk all night."

Poison gazed at the mass of bills. It was enough to give her pause, even while faced with the looming threat of hearing this man go on about Jesus.

"All you'll have to do is listen," he pleaded.

"No." She shook her head. "No, it's weird."

Like a Martial Arts master trained to never completely commit to a single strike, Riley Ellison knew when to abandon one approach and flow seamlessly into another. He said, "Then at least take the money."

"What? Really?"

"How much money do you estimate you'll make for the rest of today?"

"I work a double." Her words were flat, but still jagged.

"How much money?"

"Nine-hundred." She spat the sum in his pious face.

Riley's groan was concealed by the music. He pulled out the entire contents of his wallet. "One-thousand dollars," he said. "Um... minus forty." He gestured to the waitress and the stage. He remembered he had also paid a cover charge. "Minus sixty. Nine-hundred and forty," he settled. "It's my money; I earned it. Take it and go home. Have the day off."

"Why?"

"Because Jesus doesn't want you here. And therefore I don't either."

"I don't believe in Jesus."

Ellison knocked the money forcefully down onto the table, trying to make it sound heavy. It was. He tried his best to show concern and not pity, and to Poison's surprise, he hit his mark. He said, "Don't you ever worry about coming into work? Don't you ever worry that today might be the day that the wrong guy brings you back here, that you will meet the man of your nightmares, the man your brain will never let you forget?"

"I've met him," she snapped.

Ellison winced. He looked down at the money, pleading, "Take it and go home. In Jesus' name. Let today be a day that... " He searched for words.

"That what?" she snapped.

"That no one disrespects you."

She looked at the money. Her lips drew in tight. She said, "I'll take the money and work anyway."

Riley shook his head forcefully. "That's not the deal."

Her jaw seemed to hover slowly as she fought to not clinch it.

He said, "Go home and have a bubble bath. Go home and eat a pint of ice cream. Put on your favorite music, or binge watch a TV show. Go home and enjoy the life He's given you."

It sounded nice to her: one day to breathe. But still she snipped, "Why do you care?"

"Because He cares. I love you because He first loved me. There is nothing in this world I love right now more than you."

"I've heard that before. I heard that from the *nightmare man*."

"I don't mean it like he did." Ellison drew his wedding ring out of his pocket and put it back on. "I love you because I see you as a masterpiece creation of God, a work of art, delicate and precious and mistreated by the world—just as, by the way, the world mistreated Him. I love you because Jesus, knowing all your shame, found you worthy to die for."

"I don't believe that."

"You don't believe that he died for you? Or you don't believe you are worthy?"

She looked away. It was a look of pain, but quickly morphed to anger. She hissed, "Go. Take your money and get out now." She added, "Before I call Isaac."

Ellison sighed. She had diverted every strike he'd thrown. He knew at this point he wasn't going to convince her. His shoulders slumped beneath the weight of his failure. "Fine, but at least take my card." He set a small business card on the table. It read "Mead Mountain Church" and had the address. He said, "I wrote my personal cell number on the back. If there's ever anything I can do, if you need anything at all, you can call day or night."

"Sure. Whatever," she snapped, as the money disappeared back into Ellison's wallet.

He stood up to leave, but on his way to the door he felt a light thump against the back of his head. It wasn't hard for him to figure out that it had been the card he had just given her, crumpled up and thrown at him.

Before he could turn around completely, he heard her shouting, "Don't judge me! I do this for my son. I'm here for *him*. So I don't need your lectures or your... sermons."

Ellison put up his hands, palms forward. He said, "No judgment. Just thought you might need some hel—"

Before he could finish, she erupted again. "Oh I get it. 'Need help?' That's why you picked me, huh? You saw a pathetic, aging day-stripper, past her prime, the most pathetic girl in the whole place! How dare you! I don't need your help."

Ellison shook his head slowly. "Your age has nothing to do with this," he explained. "But what didn't escape my notice was that while other girls chose names like *Desire* or *Ecstasy,* you chose the name Poison. *Poison!* So, yes—you're right—I thought you might've been able to use some help."

Poison stood up and rushed him. She stuck her face right in his. It astonished him to see a woman rise to such heights of anger so fast. Her arms were away from her body, drawn back tensely like she wanted to strike him, but her hands were not yet in fists. In a full-throated scream, she said, "You don't know what you're talking about! My name *is* Poison! You don't know me!" He could sense her breath on his face, along with some warm spittle and the stench of Tequila. She continued aggressively, "So, I don't need your stuck-up, judgmental... come in here all high and mighty... self-righteous, sanctimonious... telling me... " She was unable to form a complete sentence.

Watching the way she erupted, he knew. He knew more about her than she'd ever meant to show. He understood the bubbling caldron of rage that lurked, every hour of her day, thinly veiled beneath the veneer—skin like tissue paper—of a fully functioning adult.

Ellison had a choice to make: advance or retreat.

He chose the wrong one. He shouted, "It's Your Love." She had been ranting without pause, so he had to yell just to throw out a verbal speed bump. "It's Your Love!"

"What?" she finally asked.

He continued, *"That's* why I picked you. I saw your face. I saw your face while dancing to 'It's Your Love,' and I could tell that you were... " Her eyes burned into him and they both waited anxiously to see what his next word would be. "... *yearning.*"

Without a warning, before he had time to see it, he felt a hard palm across his face. It hit him with so much force it spun his head around. Three more blows hit him on the side of his head, then his ear, then the back of his skull, before he even had a chance to put up a hand in defense.

It was too late anyway. He felt a much stronger arm around the back of his neck, bending his whole body over. *Isaac.* The bouncer had heard all the screaming and found their room in time to witness her attack. Siding with the female, and assuming her wrath was well-provoked and well-deserved, the burly man forced the hapless sermonizer into a headlock and dragged him out of the room.

Ellison was in no position to see what was happening. The bright sunlight that burst through the back door was the first usable information his brain received.

With just a twist of the waist, and a jut of his hip, Isaac effortlessly threw Ellison off his feet—bouncing and rolling—onto the ground.

"Pastor, you're not going to believe this," said Brandon Davies. "There's a group of reporters out front and they claim they're here to see you." It was obvious to both people in the room with him—Pastor Riley Ellison and Ashley McAllister—that when Brandon had said, *you're not going to believe this,* it had been a test to see how Ellison would respond.

Brandon and Ashley turned to see Ellison's face. Just as they had feared, there was no surprise in their pastor's countenance whatsoever. Knowing he wouldn't be believed, he feigned, "Reporters? Whatever could they want with me?"

When Pastor Ellison stepped out onto the lawn of Mead Mountain Church, he was still wearing his red windbreaker. Fresh scars from where Poison's nails had cut him that morning were visible on his face. Bloody scrapes could be seen on his hands and he walked with a slight limp—the logical result of a forty-nine-year-old man being thrown across a strip club parking lot. Every painful step he took reminded him of how immediately the bouncer had intervened on behalf of the woman; it delighted Ellison to remember that chivalry still lives.

Trying his best to walk casually, he made his way to the reporters and said, "Welcome. Welcome. Please step this way." Mead Mountain Church lay on the northern tip of seven acres of land. He led the reporters past the gazebo where Ellison performed weddings, and onto a large field where the church put on open-air concerts and held Easter egg hunts. "Just a little farther," he assured them. "I have already determined the place where you will have the best vantage. If we hurry, we can beat the rain." Pastor Ellison stopped short just before reaching a towering, twenty-foot white cross. The Pacific Ocean could be seen in the distance, and right beside it, a clear shot of Mead Mountain.

Ellison turned to face the press. "I'd like to thank all of you for coming out. I promised you a newsworthy announcement and I hope you will see I have no intention of wasting your time.

"Many of you might already know me. My name is Pastor Riley Ellison." Ellison was being humble; they all knew the prominent pastor well. "I have led Mead Mountain Church for twenty-four years. Just recently I have felt called by God to do something... that I wouldn't myself have considered advisable." Ellison cleared his throat. "But I have always endeavored to be a faithful servant of God, and as such, I will trust that He knows what He's doing.

"In Matthew 17:20, the Bible tells us, 'If you have faith as small as a mustard seed, you can say to this mountain, "Move from here to there," and it will move. Nothing will be impossible for you.'" Ellison paused the way veteran preachers often do after quoting Scripture.

The reporters' faces all looked as if they were waiting for him to return to the twenty-first century.

He obliged. "So for better or for worse, I'd like to invite you back to join me, right here at this very spot, two weeks from today, because on Thursday, January 16, I will ask this majestic mountain behind us, Mead Mountain, the eponymous symbol of my church, to move."

The reporters all laughed. The camera men peeked out from behind their cameras and looked to each other, puzzled.

"So... are there... um... any questions?" Ellison asked clumsily.

"Are you serious?" the first reporter shot. "Is this some sort of stunt?"

"No, sir. It's just as I said and nothing more. I will ask the mountain to move, at which time, according to the promises revealed by Holy

Scriptures, the mountain will move. I imagine it will fall into the ocean."

The next reporter to speak was Andrew Crenshaw. He said, "Forgive me, but I can already hear the objections of our readership who are going to question whether this is a stunt. Can you address their concerns?"

Ellison repeated, "Again, it's no stunt. I am 100 percent serious. I have chosen every word advisedly, and in two weeks, in this very spot, I'll make good on all of them."

"What are your motivations?" a reporter asked. "What do you stand to gain?"

"My motivations are to follow the will of God. I don't stand to gain anything, personally."

"Did you actually see God? Where was He when He told you to do this?" asked a young reporter with an impudent sneer.

"No, sir. He did not choose to present Himself to me. I heard His will in my head and my heart."

"Did you happen to hear this late Tuesday night?" the young reporter asked.

Ellison paused. It only took a second for him to remember that Tuesday night had been New Year's Eve. He chuckled and said, "No, sir. I don't drink."

"Are you sure it was God you heard?" another reporter asked.

"Yes, ma'am. As sure as I've ever been."

"Are you trying to make a statement against global warming?" injected Andrew Crenshaw.

"Um... " Ellison had to admit, he wasn't prepared for a question like that. "How do you mean?"

"Well, as I'm sure you know, Mayor Fowler renamed this mountain back in 1987 in honor of Senator Mead and his work."

"Ah," Ellison nodded. "Yes, it was back in 1988, of course, because he was running for reelection. Does anyone know what Mead Mountain's name was before that?"

No one volunteered.

"It wasn't widely used, but its official name was La Gracia de Dios. *The Grace of God.* Spanish explorers saw it first, so they got to name it. So, you can see, I am no more trying to symbolically crumble, topple, or in any way repudiate Benjamin Mead than I am the grace of God."

"Have you ever met Senator Mead?" pressed Andrew Crenshaw.

"We've met on numerous occasions; I can't say we're friends," Ellison said brusquely.

"Do you believe in global warming?" asked Andrew Crenshaw.

"I don't see how that's relevant."

"Then, why *did* you pick Mead Mountain?"

"I didn't." Ellison looked back at the mountain. "I'm kind of bummed, actually, because I like to hike this mountain; I'm really going to miss it."

The press laughed.

Ellison continued, "And the truth is, I'll be lowering my own property value... but the Lord works in mysterious ways."

The press laughed again. Andrew Crenshaw noticed that within the length of two lines, Ellison was able to turn the press from definitely laughing *at* him, to possibly laughing *with* him. He was impressed by his skill.

"Do you really believe the mountain will move?" asked Crenshaw.

"This would be kind of silly if I didn't believe it," said Ellison.

"That didn't answer my question."

"The Bible tells us that it will."

"I'm sorry, Pastor, but that still didn't answer my question. Do you believe—personally believe—the mountain will move?"

Ellison looked straight at Andrew Crenshaw and said, "Yes, I believe it will move."

"Pastor Ellison, if you do believe you have the power—the *God-given* power—to move mountains, why don't you ask it to move right here, right now? Why wait?"

"That part was actually my idea." Ellison stopped looking only at Andrew and returned to judiciously sweeping his eyes from camera to camera. "I want to start a national dialog. I want to create news that the media can't choose to ignore. It has come to my attention that there are those who want to make it taboo to ever discuss Jesus Christ." He looked across the faces of the press and laughed amiably, "I won't name any names." His smile was casual and his wink so effortless no one was certain they really saw it. "But I think as January 16 approaches, you will find it hard not to talk about the Bible. I want people to ask questions. I want people to choose sides. I want people to go on record as the ones who believe it will move and the ones who believe it will not."

Pastor Ellison felt one of the first raindrops nick the side of his ear. He said, "Now, if there are no more questions, I would like to ask the faithful among you to bow your heads with me in a moment of prayer." Pastor Ellison waited for any questions, then bowed his head. He prayed, "Dear Lord, thank You for the fine men and women of the media, whom You have called to this venerable profession. Please bless them, especially in the weeks to follow, with the wisdom and courage required to carry the heavy burden of such an essential responsibility. We ask that we at Mead Mountain Church be given the strength to conduct ourselves in such a way that our actions may reflect Your light, and that we may reach those in need of Your presence in their lives. We hope that my actions in the weeks to follow are pleasing in Your sight, and will serve only to glorify Your name. This we pray in the holy name of Jesus. Amen."

Pastor Ellison, with his head bowed and eyes closed, was unable to see that he was the only one praying.

When Pastor Ellison returned to his office after the press conference, all eyes were on him. The air was thick and he felt more scrutinized than he had been while in front of the press. Brandon Davies and Ashley McAllister were there, as well as his music director and youth pastor. None of them were in chairs. All of them stood with their arms folded. Brandon Davies was leaning against the edge of Ellison's desk. It looked, to Ellison, like he had just walked into an intervention.

Brandon Davies was the first to speak. "I wish you would have told us."

"So you could've talked me out of it?" shot Ellison.

"No. No, we respect what you are trying to do, but... "

"But what?"

Brandon looked to his colleagues for help. No one jumped in. "We just wish you would have told us," he repeated.

"Would you have tried to talk me out of it?" asked Ellison.

No one answered, but there was a slight sense of relief in the room. They all knew the question Ellison wasn't asking: "Do you think it won't move?" They also knew the reason he wasn't asking. He didn't want to hear their answers.

Brandon Davies pushed forward anyway and said, "I wonder if perhaps that passage was meant to be metaphorical."

Ellison did not admonish him; he simply nodded. "There are a lot of great people who interpret parts of the Bible as metaphorical. And why not? When God actually became flesh, we found him speaking almost exclusively in symbolism and parables. But I obviously read that passage literally." Ellison smiled. It was the easy smile of a man who was completely humble. He said, "I guess we're going to find out in two weeks."

Everyone in the room looked at their feet and shuffled for a few moments more. Finally, Ashley McAllister asked, "Why? Why did you do it?"

Ellison shrugged. "God asked me to."

No one said a word.

"God told me to ask the mountain to move," Ellison insisted.

"Did He tell you to call the press?" Ashley challenged.

"Umm... " Ellison equivocated.

Before Ellison could form an answer, Brandon injected, "Did you ask God why?"

"Of course."

"Did He answer?

Ellison nodded, "I heard the words, 'For the sake of a great nation.' Well, isn't that what we've been praying for? For God to heal America? 'For the sake of a great nation.' That told me that this miracle must be felt nationwide. And *nationwide* means we need the press, doesn't it?"

"I've got news for you, Pastor," Brandon informed him. "Thanks to your public status, this news is going to be worldwide."

"Even better! God has a plan here and he wants the whole world to see it. I suppose He's tired of me reaching only one person at a time. I know I am."

"Pastor Ellison," spoke the music director. "Your ministry—which by the way already is worldwide—baptizes over a hundred people a month."

Ellison smiled. "It's still not enough. For every one we reach, there are thousands we don't. Those are thousands of souls that could be saved. Those are thousands of lives that don't know Jesus, and that... Ashley, don't cry. Why do you tremble?"

Ashley McAllister hadn't truly been crying until the moment that Ellison uttered the word *cry*. That one syllable served as a starter's pistol and sent the tears she'd been holding back racing down each cheek.

Ellison looked at the rest of his staff; all their faces expressed the same trepidation. "Guys, don't look so glum! Just imagine what will happen two weeks from now. When that mountain moves, even the hardest skeptic will have to explain what happened, and their hearts will be softened, and they will consider answers that they never in their lives thought they would consider.

"I'm not deluding myself. I know there are those who will always refuse to accept it, but there will be many who ask questions they never would've otherwise asked, and there will be ears opened that would've otherwise remained closed. On the day that mountain moves, even those who had been quick to talk will suddenly be quick to listen."

All the glum faces remained. No one had shown any intention of lightening up. Brandon Davies decided to name what no one was naming. He said, "And if it *doesn't* move, their eyes and ears will be shut off from the truth forever. You will make a laughingstock of not just this church, but all churches and all Christians everywhere. You will sully not just your good name and reputation, but *His*. You won't hurt the Bible, or its message, or God's truths, of course; but you will level a crushing blow to the church here on earth. If it doesn't move, you will be the man who single-handedly destroys Christianity as we know it."

Riley Ellison swallowed hard. Before he could respond, they were interrupted by a knock at the door.

"Not now," shouted Brandon Davies.

"Come in!" yelled Pastor Ellison.

A young man walked in with a notebook and digital camera. He said, "Excuse me, folks. I hope I'm not interrupting."

Brandon Davies sighed quietly, but forced a pleasant face. He said, "No, sir. How can we be of service?"

The reporter answered Davies, but maintained eye contact only with Ellison. "Well, my name is Andrew Crenshaw. I'm a reporter with the *Times*." Andrew Crenshaw was also acting humble; everyone in the room knew who he was. "I just got off the phone with the bossman. He thinks there's a story here."

"Good," said Ellison.

"Yeah, uh... he wants to do a few different articles on you—many, in fact. So, we were hoping I could tag along with you for the next two weeks, be your shadow. That is, as much as our schedules can line up... and as long as you permit it."

The request was on the table and the whole room was silent. There were three people in the room who were hoping the answer would be *no*:

Brandon Davies, Andrew Crenshaw, and Pastor Ellison.

Brandon Davies breathed deep for strength.

Andrew Crenshaw stood uncomfortably waiting for an answer.

Finally, Ellison said, "Sure." He looked consolingly at Brandon Davies, and at Andrew Crenshaw as well. He quipped, "I guess if Jesus wasn't too good to hang out with tax collectors, I'm not too good to hang out with a reporter."

"Eh-heh," Andrew Crenshaw forced a fake, tense laugh. It wasn't really a laugh as much as it was the reporter just saying the words, *eh-heh*. He added unconvincingly, "This is going to be great."

Chapter Two

January 3—Thirteen Days left

Pastor Ellison was at home when his phone rang. It was Andrew Crenshaw.

"I'm so sorry to have to do this to you; I know we were scheduled to have a face-to-face today, but my bossman called and he needs 1,500 words, pronto."

"Breaking news, huh? Well, that's okay. I guess I can take a rain check."

"Actually Pastor, if it's okay with you, I was hoping we could do it after. I could be there by 7:00."

The reporter had been originally slated to meet Ellison at 6:00. "You can write 1,500 words before 7:00?"

"Yes, sir, my editor wants it online by 6:30. News travels fast these days. We try to keep up."

"So you hear about stuff before anyone else?" Ellison asked.

"I guess."

"Well, tell me!" he demanded boisterously.

Andrew Crenshaw laughed at his playfulness. "We're not supposed to."

"Aww, c'mon. I've never been the first to hear anything. I could make all my neighbors crazy jealous."

"All right," Andrew gave in. "Shanté and Elemeno-P are having a baby."

"Oh... okay. I don't know who they are, but it still feels cool to be in the loop."

"Well, if you don't know who they are, that may be evidence that you're not in the loop."

"*Wasn't* in the loop," Ellison playfully protested.

"So, 7:00 is good, then?" Andrew was enjoying the pastor's goodwill, but could feel the deadline looming.

"Yes, sir. See you at 7:00, sir."

When Andrew Crenshaw finally drove to Ellison's home in the rain, he thought he had the wrong address. It was a midsized home, smaller even than his. It wasn't the place he expected to be occupied by someone as famous as Riley Ellison, a man who ran a church with over twenty thousand members, a man whose book had sold a staggering thirty million copies worldwide.

He was checking the info again on his phone when he saw Pastor Ellison step out of his front door and wave cordially. The pastor's wife joined him on the porch and opened a cheerful, flower-print umbrella. They walked together under the umbrella to Andrew Crenshaw's car. The pastor still had a slight limp.

"Welcome," Ellison said over the sound of the rain. "This is my wife, Deborah."

Andrew Crenshaw smiled and reached to shake Deborah's hand. Pastor Ellison stepped out of the way and Deborah positioned the umbrella so it would cover her and Andrew, and no longer her husband.

"It's a pleasure to meet you," Deborah said. "You look just like your father!"

"Well, that's meant to be a compliment, I hope."

Deborah laughed warmly. "Yes," she smiled, "it was. Let's get inside."

The three of them headed to the house with that same formation: Deborah and Andrew under the protection of the umbrella, Riley surviving a little rain.

Once inside, Deborah held out her hands to accept Andrew Crenshaw's coat. Pastor Ellison knocked a few drops off the sleeves of his red windbreaker, but kept it on.

As Riley showed Andrew to the kitchen table, he noticed that the kitchen was spotless. The air smelled of floor wax, combined with the lingering smell of a roast which had been slow-cooking all day.

Andrew glanced at Deborah. The voice in his head reflexively echoed the attitude that had been dinned into him at college: *nineteen-fifties housewife*. Only, he wasn't fully sure if the accusation was supposed to be derisive, or how.

Deborah interrupted these thoughts by asking him what he cared to drink.

"Water, please," he said simply.

Right off the bat, Ellison said, "You know, we have something in common. My father was an atheist, just like yours."

"That's surprising," said Andrew.

"Yeah. He had grown up Christian, of course, because everyone around him was Christian. Then one day he asked himself, 'Why am I a Christian?' and he had no answer. He was a Christian because his marriage depended on it. Having friends depended on it. His job, he believed, depended on it. Everyone expected him to be Christian, so when everyone was bowing their heads, he had always just gone with the flow. But he started to think it was shameful for someone to make such an important decision based on what other people were doing."

"That sounds admirable," Andrew Crenshaw said.

Deborah returned with Andrew's water and a tall glass of iced tea for her husband, then intentionally made herself scarce.

Ellison continued, "So, one night he asked my mother, 'Why do we believe in God?' You know what she told him?"

"What?"

"You're going to love this; she said, 'Because people who don't believe in God are wicked.'"

The reporter laughed. He said, "Yeah, I've met people who think like that."

"Well sure, so have I. One of them, apparently, was my mother," Ellison confessed frankly, but without a hint of condemnation. He smiled and shrugged and said, "It's not the most winsome way to bring people the Gospel. It's not quite the approach we like to take at Mead Mountain Church, in case you're wondering."

Andrew laughed. "That's the kind of thing you just have to respond to with, *bless your heart.*"

Ellison laughed. "You know about *bless your heart*? I'm surprised to hear that particular colloquialism has made it into your cocktail parties and uptown charity events."

"Certainly not!" Andrew feigned indignation, matching Ellison's sarcasm step for step. "You know, I must've picked it up when I wandered into that tractor pull by mistake."

Ellison laughed out loud. He said, "Andrew, I think I'm going to like you."

Hailey's heart contracted when she heard the garage door. She wished she were somewhere else. She wished she was already in the bedroom, pretending to be asleep. But most importantly, she wished Abigail had been asleep, or at least not in her arms.

They both were in the kitchen. Hailey had been pacing the house because it was the only thing that kept the newborn from crying. Abigail wasn't crying now, so Hailey listened intently for any sound that might identify whether her husband was coming home drunk.

She heard the car door open. She heard him step out. She heard him slam the car door closed—a little harder than usual, but inconclusive. She heard him remember to lower the garage door—that one gave her hope. The next sound was a hand attempting to turn the knob, followed by the shuffling of keys in order to unlock it, then finally those same keys, along with her hope, crashing to the floor.

She exhaled the breath she had been holding. Her spine straightened. The release from suspense brought some catharsis, but it was quickly washed away in a sea of pallid dread. The crash of the keys was followed by a litany of cursing as he bent down to pick them up. The cursing didn't bode well, but at that point she already knew the type of evening she was in for.

"Hello, Colton," she did her best to sound casual.

"What's *she* still doing up?" he snapped.

"She was crying."

"Let her cry."

"We can't just let her cry."

"That's what they say you're supposed to do."

"She's too young for that. We're supposed to wait until she's at least four months."

"What makes you the expert?"

"That's what the Internet said."

"The Internet," he huffed, then immediately went to the cupboard where he kept his whiskey. He grabbed his last bottle, Wild Turkey, then began to hunt for a clean glass.

"Haven't you had enough to drink already?"

"Well, I don't know; let's see." He turned to look at her. The dark bags under her eyes were from 103 nights straight without a full night's sleep. The misshapen stomach came from carrying the baby for over nine months, and the disheveled hair came from having no one worth fixing it for. He studied her for a second, then cruelly said, "No, I guess I haven't."

She turned to walk away.

"Don't walk away from me."

"What do you want?"

"I said, don't walk away from me!" he said louder.

"Don't shout around the baby."

"That wasn't shouting! You call that shouting?"

She stood there sullen. Finally, the baby began to cry again.

"Shut her up. You can't shut her up?"

"She won't take her bottle."

"She probably has to burp."

"She doesn't have to burp."

"Did you try?"

"She doesn't have to burp."

"Did you try?"

"Yes."

"Try again."

Colton put the glass down on the counter. He slowly poured the potion until it filled half the glass. His eyes watched it like it was gold in a panhandler's tray.

His euphoric stare was cut short by Abigail, who had picked the wrong moment to kick her crying up a notch.

Hailey could feel her heart pounding. She wanted to turn and leave, but fear wouldn't let her. She bounced the baby frantically, shushing directly into her ear the way the nurse showed her. She felt trapped. She knew that Abigail's crying would set off his rage, but she knew walking away from him would set it off too. Her only hope was to get Abigail, *somehow*, to stop crying.

She positioned Abigail's little head on her shoulder and began to pat her back, trying to burp her.

"You're not doing it right," Colton snapped. "You gotta hit her harder."

"She's fragile."

"You're barely even tapping her. That's not going to do a thing."

Hailey pulled the baby off her shoulder in an effort to move off the subject of burping. She tried to give the baby her bottle, but she wouldn't take it.

"She's not eating because she has to burp. You gotta hit her harder. Didn't you see how the nurse did it?"

Hailey reluctantly turned the baby back around and began to gently pat her back again.

Colton shouted, "What's wrong with you? Didn't you listen to a word I said? You gotta hit her."

Hailey proceeded to pat faster, but not actually harder.

Colton cussed. "Give her to me. I'll show you."

Hailey's blood chilled. "No, I got it."

Colton cussed again. "I said, give her to me."

He reached out to receive the girl, but Hailey's arms only drew her in tighter. She hoped that he wouldn't see it.

He didn't notice the small protective motion, but he did see the fear growing in her eyes.

"I'm not going to hurt her, woman. Give her here."

Hailey just stood there frozen.

"She's my daughter, too!"

Hailey still did not move. She didn't have the courage to outright say, *no*.

The baby began to cry harder.

"Give her here!" the drunk shouted.

"She's crying," Hailey said.

Colton cussed. "She's crying because she needs to be burped. If you can't burp the little monster, you're being cruel."

"You'll hurt her," she finally said.

"*You're* making her cry."

She didn't respond, but slowly took a step in the other direction.

He noticed her retreat and it enraged him. He slammed his drink down on the counter aggressively and marched over to her, holding out his hands to receive the girl.

Hailey's insides began to melt. With him standing so close, she could smell the bourbon. She reflexively turned Abigail away from him.

As she turned, he reached out and grabbed onto the baby.

Hailey shrieked, "You're twisting her foot!"

"I am not!"

"Let go!"

The drunk did let go of the foot, but managed to grab hold of the baby's arm, instead.

"You'll pull her arm out!" Hailey shouted in pure terror. The baby cried harder.

"Let go!" this time Colton shouted it. He had managed to grab enough of the baby that she feared the greater threat to Abigail was fighting him, so she let her baby go.

"There," Colton exclaimed. "My girl too."

The infant continued to scream. Hailey stepped closer to her husband. She could not help the fact that her arms remained outstretched, ready to catch the baby if she fell. "Don't drop her," she didn't mean to blurt out.

"Don't drop her? Would you just shut up!" he shouted over the baby's cry. "Shut up! Shut up both of you!"

Hailey was trembling. Her every action, every mannerism was reserved—and always had to be—fearful above anything of triggering Colton's rage. Her life was like walking through the jungle at the pace of a snail, constantly watching her feet, knowing every turn was rigged with booby traps waiting to be tripped. It wasn't much of a life, living in constant fear, but it was better than the alternative: carelessly tripping the traps.

The baby, however, could not understand this. Abigail screamed directly into the drunk's face, as if she were the master and Colton the most worthless of servant, deserving no respect, no consideration, and no fear. The baby just wanted to be burped; she had no idea she was putting her life on the line.

Hailey saw this and was terrified.

In raw irritation, Colton raised the screaming baby away from his chest. His hands were trembling with rage.

"You can't shake her!" yelled the mother.

"Would you shut up?" he yelled back to her.

Hailey stepped in closer, arms outstretched, hoping at this point that he would *want* to relinquish the baby.

Colton turned the baby away, just as Hailey had done before, bringing the baby close to his chest in the process. Hailey reached in, persistent, so the drunk finally used one arm to shove her away.

It was a violent, angry shove and Hailey fell off her feet and straight into one of their kitchen chairs. The force of her body knocked the chair over and she painfully fell on top of it, then onto the ground.

A wave of pain coursed through her body. This was the point at which, had she been a childless woman, she would have stayed down and sobbed. Instead, she jumped right back up to her feet. Her husband now held the screaming baby in his left arm, and had his right hand cocked back into a fist, ready to strike her if she came any closer.

She froze.

"She just needs to be burped," his voice changed. It was still angry and harsh, but sounded consoling by contrast. "She just needs to be burped, is all." Colton positioned the baby on his shoulder and began to slap the girl's back. The slaps were hard and the sound echoed through her small ribcage like she was a drum.

Hailey moved closer, despite her husband's wishes. "She won't burp while she's crying," she said.

Colton turned away from her and continued to slap the infant's back.

"That's too hard!" she said, being careful not to shout, fearing Colton might try to exact retribution on the baby this time.

He grumbled and cussed and then began to smack Abigail again.

Tears began to flow down Hailey's face, and for a short second, she looked around for a weapon. She hadn't thought it all the way through. She hadn't worked out the logistics of how she could strike her husband to the ground and simultaneously swoop the child to safety, but she knew in that moment she was capable of murder.

Finally, the moment in which Hailey could not stand another second of the pain, the baby burped.

"See?" Colton shouted. Abigail was still crying.

"Fine, now give her back."

"I will in a minute," Colton said. He enjoyed being in control and, although he denied it to himself, he enjoyed being feared.

Colton looked around for Abigail's bottle. He offered the bottle to the baby and she instantly stopped crying. The mother felt some relief. Her heart was still filled with dread, but no longer felt like it would explode.

Colton watched the baby drink her bottle and said, "Just like her daddy." He laughed and looked around for his own bottle. Discovering it on the far side of the table, he placed the baby down on her back in order to reach it.

"You can't leave her on the table!" Hailey snapped.

"I'm not leaving her," Colton snapped back. He leaned over to grab the whiskey bottle with his left hand and shielded the baby from the edge of the table with his right. He kept his right hand in position, ready to catch her, more as a show than anything else. He didn't do it for the sake of the mom, or the baby, but as a gesture; it said, *See? I got her. Stop badgering me.*

Hailey saw this as her chance. Colton had just his right hand between her and her child. It was the same right hand which had thrust her to the floor. It was the same right hand which had knocked her to the floor many times, and worse. But she had no choice. She shot forward without warning and grabbed the baby. She snatched her with so much force, Abigail's tiny hands were unable to keep a hold of her bottle.

The bottle hit the floor with a loud bounce and the drunk realized what was happening too late to stop it. The mother ran the baby down the hall to the nursery, and Colton, furious, ran after. She slammed the door closed and, with a baby in her arms and no light on in the room, struggled to find the lock.

Colton pushed the door open before she had a chance to lock it. Hailey, in fear for her life, and worse, in fear for her baby, pushed the door closed again with all the weight of their bodies, and was able to twist the lock.

Colton felt the knob lock into place. He pounded the door feverishly with his fists.

She said, "I have my phone in here. I'm going to dial 911."

"And tell them what? That I'm drunk in my own home?"

"That you're violent."

"I haven't caused any violence tonight," he mumbled.

She didn't respond.

"You won't do it," he said. "You don't have the guts."

Memories from the last time he'd told her she didn't have the guts— and had been right—invaded her mind, so she used her free hand to pull out her phone. She typed 911 with her thumb and hit SEND.

Before she was able to hear it ringing, Colton shouted through the door. "They'll want to take Abigail away."

She instantly hung up, and slid her phone back into her pocket, defeated and scared.

Abigail no longer had her bottle and so began to cry. Fists continued to rain down on the door. Hailey closed her eyes and bowed her head. After a quick prayer, she opened her eyes and pulled her phone back out.

Pastor Ellison had been talking with Andrew Crenshaw in his kitchen. Andrew Crenshaw was surprised to find himself enjoying his company. From the moment he took the assignment, he began to bone up on all his techniques of how to win trust and induce confessions, but none of them any longer seemed applicable. Pastor Ellison was an open book. He seemed to trust Andrew Crenshaw from the moment he walked to his car to meet him.

Deborah had retired early and the two of them sat in Ellison's kitchen talking as openly as two old friends. They were so wrapped up in the conversation that neither of the two noticed how late it had become.

"So, you remembered that my father was an atheist?" Andrew asked it as a question, but his tone indicated he wasn't surprised. "I guess the whole world remembers."

Ellison smiled. He lowered his voice and said, "That's the news, America. Goodnight."

Andrew Crenshaw's father, David Crenshaw was, for a time, one of America's most respected news anchors. He would end each broadcast of *In the Know* with the signature sign-off, "That's the news, America. Goodnight." That was until the height of his career, in the late 1990s, when he ended his broadcast by announcing out of the blue, "By the way, I just wanted to let the viewers know, I'm an atheist. That's the news, America. Goodnight." After which he was summarily fired.

For a brief period afterwards, "That's the news, America. Goodnight," became the punch line to a joke—an exclamation point punctuating any shocking confession. A gay man might have joked with his friends about coming out to his parents saying, "Mom, Dad, I'm gay. That's the news, America. Goodnight." Or a mischievous husband might have confessed, "I'm having an affair. That's the news, America. Goodnight."

Soon the joke was forgotten, as well as any trace of David Crenshaw's otherwise august legacy.

"But you don't know the whole story," Andrew Crenshaw told Ellison. "His atheism was directly responsible for ending his career, but it may have been indirectly responsible for creating it. All the way back in 1968, he was pretty young, especially for a news anchor, which might have been the reason that *In the Know* had no ratings. He had been with the program for a few years, and there was talk of the network cancelling the show. On Christmas Eve that year, they had asked my father to do a story on the Apollo 8 space mission. They had fresh audio of the astronauts taking turns reading from the Book of Genesis as they watched the sun rise over the moon."

"Oh yes," smiled Ellison, "I've watched that online."

"So my father asked if they could get some of the other talent there to read the story. His reason, he said, was that he was an atheist and thought that maybe a believer could do the story better. Well, as you can imagine his bosses weren't happy. They didn't care about his personal faith so much, but didn't want word getting out that their head news anchor was a heathen, especially not while our nation was at war with the godless Communists.

"So, according to my father, he was invited into the boss's office and severely dressed down. They told him they didn't care what he did on his own time, but unless he wanted to be unemployed, he would keep it to himself. And he still had to do the story.

"So my father did the story, and played the audio, but he ended the broadcast with, 'What a stirring tribute, on the eve of the day commemorating our Savior's birth. That's the news, fellow Christians. Goodnight and God bless.'" Andrew Crenshaw threw up his hands and smiled a wry smile. "That was my father—always irascible, no respect for authority.

"They suspended him for his little stunt, without pay. Two weeks later he was back on the air—and would you believe it? His ratings were higher than ever. They ended up paying him for the time off after all, on the condition that the true sarcastic nature of his comments was never revealed. Middle America was finally embracing my dad. Believing Christians thought they'd found a kindred spirit. For the next few years, he was even invited to host the New Covenant Awards," Andrew laughed jovially. "The poor NCA couldn't understand why he kept turning them down.

"Finally, one day in 1998, my father was having another quarrel with management over some story he wanted to do, but they wouldn't let him."

"What story?"

"It was on the anti-depressant drug, Damitol. My father believed there was a trend of people using it to commit suicide."

"You father ended up victorious on that one. People were using Damitol to kill themselves."

Andrew shrugged. "Well, *Pyrrhic victory*. So anyway, they fought up until the very last second that he was supposed to go on the air. That was the day he ended the broadcast with 'I'm an atheist. That's the news... yadda, yadda,'" Andrew Crenshaw rolled his fingers. "And the rest is history, as was my father's career after that day."

Ellison smiled. "I was watching live that day; I still remember. The truth is, I'd always liked your father—and after what you've told me, I somehow like him even more. I never thought they should've fired him for that."

"Well, thank you."

There was a brief pause of awkward silence as Andrew's mind searched for a new subject with which to fill it. The one rule he had set for himself that night was: *No matter what happens do not bring up the mountain at all.* He said, "Hey, I know." His phrasing betrayed how desperately he wanted a topic, "Why don't you tell me about that string on your finger. I'd assume you were trying to remember something, but you've worn it both days I've seen you."

"Yes," said Ellison. "I'm glad you—" Pastor Ellison's phone buzzed. He seemed a bit shocked as his eyes glanced up at the clock. He asked, "Do you mind if I take a look?"

"Sure, go ahead," Andrew Crenshaw said.

Ellison took one look at the text on his phone and sat up straight in his chair. His eyes took another quick look at the clock and he said, "You got some more time to spend with me tonight?"

"As much as we need," smiled the reporter.

"Great. I'll grab your jacket. We've got to leave right now."

"Open the door," Colton screamed.

Hailey didn't say anything, but Abigail's cries filled the entire hallway.

"Stop messing around and open the door."

There was no answer.

Colton began to pound his fists on the door. It wasn't knocking, it was rage. This made the baby cry harder.

Hailey, who knew there was no point trying to appeal to him using her own feelings, thought she might be able to reach him via the baby. "You're upsetting Abigail."

"Then open the door and I won't have to."

He continued to pound the door. He was calling his wife every dirty word he could think of.

Hailey had once tried to convince herself that the baby would change things. She wanted to believe there was a line her husband would not cross.

That line should have been her personal dignity as a woman, or at least as a human being. That line should have been his love for her. But he'd never shown any respect for those lines.

She wanted the reality where a newborn baby was so precious, such an irrefutable blessing, that it provoked something in him—a wakeup call—causing his knees to crumble and his rage to cease. She imagined the scene where he humbly falls to the ground, thwarted by emotion and asks, "Dear God, what have I become?" She wanted that reality, but it never happened.

If that had been their reality, his behavior would have changed while she was pregnant. For the first few months, he helped measure her waist and he attended all of her sonograms. And even with the mood swings and morning sickness, she was as happy as she'd ever been.

But as her belly continued to expand, the newness wore off and things seemed to fall back into their usual routine. Then one night while drunk, he threw her up against the wall, seven months pregnant.

It should've been a wakeup call for her, not him. It should have told her there was no line he wouldn't cross. There was no symbol, no ideal, no human life, that if in front of him while drunk and raging, he wouldn't bash with his fist. There was nothing he held as sacred.

But still she hoped. The blue eyes of her young child were her last hope: her eyes, her pink flawless cheeks, her complete helplessness and fragility. These were all things that inspired Hailey. These were the earthly things she held most sacred. Surely they would reach him too. Surely he would one day look into his child's eyes and for a second, take pause.

"You're upsetting the baby," she insisted.

"Shut up about the baby. I don't care about that little brat. I hate the baby."

"No you don't," she insisted.

"Whatever," Colton said. He lowered himself down and leaned his back on the door. "Why do you do this to me?" He asked, "Why do you make me like this?"

She didn't answer.

"Hey, Hailey," he called out. His voice was clearly calmer and she could tell he was no longer on his feet. "Hey, sweetheart."

She still didn't answer.

He shouted. "If you don't answer me right now, I'm going to come in and grab that baby and..." he didn't finish. He elbowed the door hard. It hurt, so he began to pound the back of his head against the door. That hurt too, but he liked the way it made him feel, like he could just go crazy. He shouted. "You make me so furious. I'm gonna bash my head through the door."

She said, "Do it."

This made him more furious. He said, "Shut up!"

He turned his ear to the door to listen to her response. There was none.

He said, "Ah, good girl. I said shut up and you did."

He thought that she'd respond to that one, but she didn't.

He continued, "Yeah, that's a good girl who does what she's told. I said shut up and now... she's completely silent."

He waited, but she stayed silent.

"Good!" he yelled. "I want you silent. I'm tired of hearing your stupid voice. It sounds so shrill all the time. I'm tired of your stupid nagging."

He waited. Even the baby had stopped crying.

"You still in there? You haven't escaped out the window, have you? I was only kidding about telling you to shut up. I was just messing with you."

Still silent.

"I'm sorry I said I hate the baby. I don't hate the baby. I love the baby..." He put his ear to the door. "It just cries so much. It just never stops crying."

"She."

"What?"

There was no answer.

"What? Oh, I know it's a *she*! Why'd you have to say that? I was trying to be nice; why'd you have to say that? I know it's a she, you piece of trash. I know it's a she. Why'd you have to say that?"

He staggered to his feet and went back to the kitchen for his bottle of bourbon. It burned going down and he was convinced in that moment in time, it was only making him feel worse, *but what difference would it make?*

He continued to drink as if the objective was no longer *surcease of sorrow*; the objective was merely to continue to swallow. He stumbled back down the hall, but turned into the master bedroom and flopped down on his bed, rubbing his eyes. He knew he could pass out right there if he'd let it happen.

He rolled over and looked at his night stand. He pulled out the top drawer and thumbed the combination to his gun safe. He had to try four times just to punch in his birthday correctly. The safe beeped with each number that he pushed and he knew she could hear the sound. He pulled out his gun and slammed the safe closed—making sure she knew what he was doing.

He ran to the nursery door. "Okay, last chance to open it, or I'm gonna blow off the knob!"

...

"I mean it."

...

"I mean it."

...

He banged on the door using the butt of the gun's handle. He said, "You'd better open this door, or I'm gonna put this gun in my mouth. I didn't mean I was gonna hurt the baby. I'd never hurt the baby. I love the baby. I love both of you. I'm not gonna hurt you. But I think I'm gonna kill myself because I think you'd be better off without me. I don't even remember why we are fighting. Why are we fighting?"

There still was no answer.

"Answer me! Answer me what I said!" He banged with the gun. "Answer what... Answer me what I said!" He banged. "Answer me what I'm saying. Answer me what I'm saying to you."

...

"I'm going to break the door in. I'm going to break the door in, not shoot it. Stand back, 'cause I'm gonna break it in."

...

"I'm going to count to three and break it in."

...

"I'm going to count down from three and break it in."

...

Hailey was frightened. She walked with Abigail to the far side of the room. She turned her back to the door, hoping that if pieces of the doorframe broke off, they would not hit her daughter.

She heard Colton counting:

"Three...

"Two...

"One..."

There was silence. Hailey closed her eyes and bowed her head.

Finally, she heard a loud slam and wood splintering. It was followed by the sound of a door's brass hardware hitting the floor, followed by cussing.

Colton was cussing. He had just heard the sound of his front door being smashed in and was confused about what was going on.

Pastor Ellison rounded the corner to get a view down the hall. The two men spotted each other.

"Well, look who it is," Colton said, both amused and confused. His front door was busted—but he was drunk enough to take that in stride—and to top it off, there was suddenly a pastor in his house. "You have no right to be here," Colton snapped.

"I was invited here by the lady of the house," Ellison said, as Andrew Crenshaw appeared right beside him.

"Lady of the house don't make no rules." Colton stepped into their personal space so aggressively that Andrew Crenshaw staggered a few steps backward. Pastor Ellison did not. Colton could smell the rain on Ellison's clothes. Ellison could smell the alcohol on Colton's breath—bourbon, if his nose was correct. He glanced down at the man's hands to verify his suspicion. In his left hand he carried a bottle of Wild Turkey. In his right hand he carried a revolver.

"That's right!" Colton said as he saw that the pastor saw. He raised the weapon and gave it a mocking jiggle.

"I'm calling the police!" squealed Andrew Crenshaw.

"Relax," said Ellison, putting up a palm in Andrew Crenshaw's direction.

Colton saw Andrew Crenshaw and did a double take. Andrew Crenshaw was accustomed to being recognized, typically at *cocktail parties and uptown charity events*, not usually by gun-wielding drunks.

Colton looked back to Pastor Ellison and said, "Now, y'all two listen up. This ain't Mead Mountain Church, and this ain't no *60 Minutes*. Y'all two don't set the rules 'round here."

It dawned on Andrew Crenshaw that, in his inebriated state, this man confused him with his father, even though his father was dead, and even though the timeline would make no sense at all.

"You set the rules; I see that," said Ellison. It was a sincere statement.

"You're the man of the house. I see that. I respect you and I respect your home. Now, why are you holding a gun?"

Colton narrowed his brow. He didn't show it, but there was a voice in his head telling him he had taken it all too far. He snapped, "It's the only way I can get her to listen."

"Did you try *please*?"

Colton jiggled the gun again. "I want you to leave."

Ellison looked at the closed door beside Colton. He imagined it was locked and he imagined Hailey and Abigail were behind it. He said, "But I'm asking to stay."

The drunk didn't budge.

The pastor added, "Please."

"Why?"

"Just to talk."

"I got nothing to say to you."

"Then you can listen."

"Well, excuse me Mister Pastor, but if you can't tell, I'm in no mood for a sermon."

"No sermon. Just two men enjoying each other's company."

"Three men," Colton corrected him for no other reason than to be obstinate.

Pastor Ellison shook his head. He made a dismissing motion toward Andrew Crenshaw, "No one really enjoys his company; he's with the press."

Colton laughed.

Ellison saw an opening. He said, "You're not really anxious to get back to what you were doing." He motioned to the gun and the locked door. "This wasn't really how you had planned to spend your evening, was it?"

The man looked over at the door. The baby had stopped crying. He couldn't remember why he wanted in there so badly. He asked Ellison, "You got a better idea?"

He didn't. He said, "You set the rules. Why don't you tell us what we should do?"

"Don't try to be smart. Don't try to twist my words around. You won't outsmart me."

"Wouldn't try it."

"Shut up."

"Yes, sir."

"You're being smug."

"No, sir."

"Don't think I don't know. You're no match for me in a battle of wits, just like I'm no match for you at... quoting Scripture." Colton laughed. He continued, "Just like, you're no match for me at a drinking contest and I'm no match for you at... quoting Scripture."

"How 'bout poker then?" said Ellison, amiably.

"You know what..." A sardonic grin crossed his drunken face. "You know what? I think that's a great idea."

Ellison smiled. "Poker?"

"No."

Ellison's smile disappeared as quickly as it had come. His voice almost seemed to crack as he timidly asked, "Quoting Scripture?"

The drunk's smile grew bigger; he was thoroughly enjoying the trap he felt he had just backed the pastor into. He shook his head.

"A drinking contest," Ellison stated, resigned. His eyes were searching. His brain was working on an exit strategy. "Okay, first to pass out loses."

"Now there you go, thinking you can outsmart me again. I obviously have a head start. And you obviously want me unconscious so you can prove to that snake-woman that you're the big hero."

The pastor threw up his hands. "I should've heeded your warning."

"No, you should've left when you had the chance."

The two men watched each other. Ellison wondered where this would go: What price was he willing to pay to best serve Hailey and Abigail? And what were his options? *Of course there would be no drinking contest.*

Ellison looked at the gun, then looked in the direction he imagined would lead to the kitchen. He said, "Why don't you find us some glasses?"

Their bibulous host turned his back on the two of them and headed to the kitchen. Andrew Crenshaw put a gentle hand on Ellison's arm, holding him back. With Colton no longer in the hallway, he whispered urgently to Ellison, "This is our chance to grab the girls and get out."

Ellison nodded his head. He could picture it clearly: by the time Colton would step out of the kitchen they would be halfway out the door. Ellison would inform him they were leaving with the girls and there would be no trouble. Colton wouldn't discharge his firearm. Colton wouldn't even likely lay a finger on them. Ellison knew firsthand the difference the presence of a man can add to a tense situation—a self-assured and uncompromising man, a man acting like a man.

They took two steps toward the locked door and Ellison put a hand on Andrew's arm to stop him. "Then what?" Ellison asked.

"Then she'll be free from him," said Andrew.

"For a night."

Frustrated, Andrew knocked the hand off his arm and hissed, "We have to save the girls!"

Ellison was now picturing something else quite clearly: the countless times he had witnessed Hailey pray for her husband—pray for Colton to stop drinking, pray for him to turn to Christ, and pray, and pray, and pray, and cry on Ellison's sleeve.

Riley looked somberly in the direction of Colton Rucker. He motioned Andrew to follow him. "C'mon," he said in a tone of finality. He sighed. "C'mon... The girls have already been saved."

When the pastor and his sidekick entered Mr. Rucker's kitchen, they saw a rickety card table butted up against the edge of a standard kitchen table. There did happen to be poker chips strewn about the table and Pastor Ellison commended himself on pegging Colton for a poker player, even if he hadn't managed to make the sale. Along with the poker chips were potato chips. A few were in a bowl, but more were on the table, some crushed to bits. The bag from which they came still remained, as did some empty beer bottles. Colton certainly wasn't drinking anything as benign as beer this evening, so Ellison imagined that this scene had been left like this since the weekend.

He knew how hard the mess must've been for Hailey to take, as her pregnancy hormones had been kicking her nesting instincts into overdrive. She must have seen the state of her home as a sign of Colton's contempt for her. Riley couldn't currently disprove that.

Colton was still rummaging through the cupboards and Andrew Crenshaw had already bellied up to the table. Ellison was still considering his next move. He noticed that a chair had been knocked over, so he picked it up from the floor. He positioned it next to the card table, not the main table, and found himself a seat across from it.

When Colton returned with the glasses, he saw Crenshaw at the main table and Ellison at the card table, but thought nothing of it. He took a seat across from Ellison in the chair the pastor had picked up.

"Gum?" Ellison asked as he held out a stick to Colton. The hinge of the folding table leg was pressing slightly into the pastor's leg.

"No," Colton said.

"Suit yourself," Ellison said as he unwrapped the gum and folded it into his own mouth.

"I'd like some gum," said Andrew Crenshaw.

Ellison frowned and said, "That was my last piece."

"Oh... okay."

"I might have some more in the car."

"No it's okay."

"Really? Because you looked disappointed."

"No really, it's okay."

"Would you two shut up?" Colton snapped, irritated by how casually they were yammering on.

Andrew Crenshaw noticed the gun was no longer in Colton's hands. This allowed him to relax quite a bit. He panned the area and discovered it had been left on the kitchen counter.

"Why don't you take off your coat?" Colton asked Ellison.

"I get cold easily," said Ellison.

"Cold blooded."

"I guess."

"Well, this will put some fire in your veins." He raised the bottle of Wild Turkey.

"So they say."

The man's movements were intentionally foreboding, as he set down the glasses—one in front of him, the other in front of Pastor Ellison.

"Shots," Colton blurted as he poured a small amount in the glass before his rival. Pushing the glass closer, he added, "First one to make a face loses."

The pastor looked down at the glass.

Noticing how despondent Ellison suddenly looked, Colton laughed and said, "That face doesn't count."

Ellison shook the gloom face off, smiled and said, "Just thought of a painful memory, that's all."

The man deliberately nudged the glass closer still. Ellison couldn't tell if it was because he wanted the pastor to get on with it, or if perhaps the whiskey was just his recommendation for painful memories.

After another empty moment, the pastor reluctantly slid the glass back across the table, far from himself. He looked at the drunk and said, "If you expect me to take this seriously, you'd better start with more than one finger."

Colton laughed. He doubled the shot and slid the glass back over. He said, "Two fingers, big talker. Now quit stalling!"

Pastor Ellison raised the glass to his lips, then put it back down. He grabbed a discarded napkin from among the trash on the table and used it to deposit his gum, then slid it into his pocket. He said to Andrew Crenshaw, "I should've just given it to you in the first place."

"Well, I don't want it now," laughed Crenshaw.

"Shut up with the gum, already!"

Ellison nodded, resigned. He gazed at the amber elixir on the table, looking through it as one might look through the Hubble Telescope—able to see the history of the universe. He looked at the drunk; there was no one else in the world that Ellison loved more in that moment. He said, "There is only one thing that all deceivers claim to deliver—because there is only one sensation that all mankind seeks. *God.* The name for the contentment, belonging, and unconditional love you seek is God. Many things make that promise, but only He delivers. That hole you are trying to fill with alcohol is really meant for God."

Colton pounded his fist on the table. The glass, for a split second, actually caught some air, but none of it spilled. Ellison thought he might have—as he did in the strip club—just overplayed his hand. He envisioned this ending much the same way, but the man calmed down just as abruptly as he had flared up. He laughed and said, "But I have found god. I found him at the bottom of a bottle, you fool, in the very place y'all said I wouldn't. You fools." He leaned in and set his unsteady gaze on Ellison. "I found a god who welcomes me into his arms, and cradles me in his loving, accepting, euphoric embrace. Say I haven't. Say I haven't!"

Ellison nodded. He said, "You have. You have found a god who entices you with acceptance but ensnares you with rejection, because acceptance is alluring, but rejection is irresistible. You have found a god who comforts you first, then takes off the god mask to reveal a merciless and sadistic devil. Say you haven't."

The drunk did not deny it. He leaned back in his chair, never taking his eyes off Ellison, and released a low growl.

Finally, the pastor lifted the glass. In one controlled swoop, he swigged the entire libation and set the glass back down on the table. He raised his face to the drunk to show clearly: there was no *whiskey face* to be seen. Ellison tried to be a humble man in life, but he was currently guilty of a slight bellicose rise of the chin.

Colton laughed. "Well done," he said. "You surprise me."

Andrew Crenshaw was surprised as well. He wondered if the pastor had forgotten he was a reporter, or by the way he was acting, somehow just forgotten that he was even there. Ellison's eyes were only on Colton. The two men, in fact, seemed to be staring each other down.

But even as his eyes never broke from Colton's stare, his hands were busy investigating the hinge mechanism used by the folding leg of the card table. It had a metal ring that held the two pieces together and stopped the legs from pivoting. Ellison knew the type well; the folding tables they used at the church all had the same basic hinge.

Colton poured himself the same drink and slammed it down without delay. His face, too, was implacable.

He poured the next drink, this time three fingers of whiskey, a respectable amount by anyone's standards.

Pastor Ellison breathed in a deep breath. He said, "Why don't you go first this time. No fair me going first every time."

"You said I made the rules." Colton shrugged flippantly. "I told you not to try to outsmart me. You can't outsmart me."

The pastor covertly pulled a pinch of his gum from out of the napkin and used it to hold the locking mechanism under the table in the unlocked position. He said delphically, "Wouldn't dream of it," then downed the daunting offering.

Again his face was serene.

"Well, I'll be," said the drunk. He quickly poured a drink for himself, anxious to lessen the pastor's accomplishment by repeating it. He sucked it down with no more than a smile. Then the smile turned into a laugh. "I don't know if you've figured this out yet, Pastor, but you're gonna lose!"

Ellison said nothing. Andrew Crenshaw began to rock slightly back and forth.

The man poured the next drink for Ellison, he filled up about three fingers' worth—no more than the last round—then turned the bottle completely over. They all watched as the last drops fell into the glass. Ellison's stomach lurched. He'd been doing his best to game-plan a scenario in which all this could possibly end well. Suddenly, he was up against a contingency he hadn't considered: the bottle was empty.

The drunk continued to hold the bottle stubbornly, desperately giving it a few hard shakes.

"Grab another bottle," Ellison suggested, trying to sound casual.

"Ain't got one," the man snapped. A series of curse words came out of the man's mouth as he frantically shook the bottle, demanding that it produce more than it had to give. Finally, he slammed the bottle down on the table. Both sober men instinctively put up their hands to cover their eyes. The bottle had hit the table with so much force they all reasonably assumed it would break. Somehow it didn't, but that was the least of their problems now.

Colton stomped back into his kitchen and proceeded to open doors and slam them back shut. Pastor Ellison could see his rage boiling and worried that all the ground he had gained while trying to distract him—like a two-year-old from a tantrum—would be lost. The noise from the slamming cabinets must have woken the baby, because over the man's cussing they could hear a distant, but loud, cry.

Colton froze, mid-frenzy. His eyes turned to the direction of the sound. It had informed him—as if for the first time—that they were not alone in the house. He then remembered how this evening had started and he remembered he was supposed to be feeling vengeful. There was hatred in his eyes. He took two perfunctory steps in the direction of the cry, as if summoned by a hypnotic impulse to cause trouble. He glanced over at his gun on the counter.

Ellison had noticed that the books on the bookshelf were all resting at the back of the shelf, like in a home, but the books on the bottom shelf had been pulled to the front, like in a bookstore. Trying to sidetrack him from his current path towards the gun, Ellison yelled, "Where do you hide your alcohol?" He stressed the words extra hard and extra loud, as if trying to rouse a somnambulist, or trying to talk to a foreigner.

It worked and Colton momentarily forgot the gun and the baby. The two visitors watched as he checked behind the bottom row of books on the shelf, the back of the coat closet, and the narrow space behind the refrigerator, hoping to find buried treasure. None was there to be found.

Colton stumbled aimlessly, continuing to mutter profanity. Then his eyes lit up. He turned determinedly to the table in the kitchen, right where they had just been sitting. There was a gray coat thrown over a chair. Colton searched the pockets of the coat and pulled out a large flask.

"Bingo!" exclaimed Ellison, happy to have Colton's attention diverted back to their faceoff.

Colton walked back over, like he hadn't missed a beat and finished pouring Ellison's drink. He poured, hesitated, then poured a little more, hesitated again, then poured a little more.

"Stop!" demanded the reporter. "There is no way that's four fingers!"

The drunk shrugged. "Never said it was."

Colton pushed the monstrosity across the table. The amber color wasn't warm, but somehow cold. It didn't glow, but somehow seemed to swallow light. There was a swirl of a darker color, Burnt Umber, mixed in with the lighter one, a result of the Wild Turkey being topped off with *God knows what*. The pastor's hand moved toward it slowly; he didn't want to touch it.

The baby was still crying. Pastor Ellison pictured the child in his mind. He saw the young woman holding her and imagined their fear.

"We need to up the stakes," the pastor said.

"Were no stakes," said Colton.

"We need some. There's got to be something riding on our little showdown."

"Little late for that," said the drunk. "You should've brought that up when there was a chance of you winning. Makes no difference to talk about it now."

"Why do you make that poor woman lug a baby to my church every week by herself?"

"I thought you weren't gonna to give me a sermon?"

"I'm not. There's a time and place where I do that. I've seen your wife there... but I've never seen you."

The man shrugged. "What difference does it make?"

"I want to make a bet."

"Too late."

"Not too late. If I win, you have to promise me to take Hailey and Abigail to church for the rest of the month."

"Or the rest of the year! Makes no difference." The man pointed at the glass. The three men stared at it gravely. It was oppressive. No one, not even Ellison, believed that he could handle it. Colton said, "Wait a minute. What do I get if I win?"

"What do you want?"

"I want the royalties from your book."

"Too late. I already gave them away," said Ellison. He made a sweeping motion to Colton's middleclass home and added, "Besides, you look like you're doing just fine."

Colton also looked at his home, not the size, but the mess. He said, "But I could sure use a maid."

Ellison laughed.

"How 'bout you just fix my door, then?" Colton suggested.

"Deal," said Ellison. He was going to do *that* either way. "Write it down."

"What?"

With lighting swiftness, almost before Colton could finish the word *what*, Pastor Ellison produced a pen and a piece of scrap paper from the day planner in his pocket. "Write it down. A promise isn't worth much if you can't remember it."

The drunk threw the paper and pen back at the pastor. He said, "Let's just get on with it."

"We will," said Ellison, collecting the tossed items, "just as soon as you write down our new terms. *One year*, I believe you said."

The drunk reluctantly grabbed the pen and paper and scratched out a note.

The pastor looked at Colton's note, then back down at the proffered cocktail. There was no more business left to attend to. There was, in fact, nothing left to do but take the shot. He visualized it in his head, the way great athletes use their minds to encourage their bodies. He could still hear the baby crying. He closed his eyes and silently prayed one of the strangest requests that he'd ever asked of God.

When he opened his eyes, he grabbed the glass with confidence. Instantly the bottom of the glass was aimed towards the heavens and the malevolent concoction poured into the clergyman's mouth. After three large, quick swallows, he slammed the glass triumphantly down on the table. Both his spectators leaned in close.

The pastor's face was tranquil; his eyes were placid.

Andrew Crenshaw could no longer maintain his journalistic neutrality. He slammed his palm down on the wooden table and screamed, "Yes! Yes! Unbelievable. Unbelievable!"

Colton let out a swear word—both angry and impressed. He added, "Man, where'd you learn to drink?"

The pastor didn't answer, he merely slid the man's empty glass closer to him and said, "Fill 'er up, pardner."

Colton poured the drink and set the flask down on the table. It made a sloshing sound, indicating that there was still some alcohol left inside.

Andrew Crenshaw pounced, "No, no... no way. That's not nearly the size of the drink you poured for him."

"Yes, it is."

"Are you joking?" the reporter snapped.

"Fine," Colton grumbled and picked up the flask. He tilted it enough to pour a thin trickle, then tilted it back.

This movement was met with more protests from the reporter. "More! Keep pouring! You know it was more."

"Fine!" the man yelled and turned the flask upside down. Every last drop fell into the glass, all the liquor left in the house. It was clearly not as much as the pastor had to drink, but Ellison wanted to preempt Andrew Crenshaw's protests. "Close enough," he said looking at Andrew Crenshaw. He turned back to Colton and said, "Close enough. Now remember, you can't make a face."

Colton sat looking at the glass. He wore the same disconsolate expression that they had seen on the pastor in the beginning.

"That one doesn't count," said Ellison, chiding.

Colton breathed in deep. It was clear that he was going through the same mental preparation that Ellison had performed, except maybe without the prayer. He said, "Well... my old man used to say, *Here's mud in your eye.* Whatever that means." He reached for the glass, but was interrupted by Ellison.

"Now who's quoting Scripture?"

"What?" Colton paused.

A thin clandestine smile crossed Andrew Crenshaw's lips.

"*Here's mud in your eye...* That's from the Bible," informed Ellison.

"No, it isn't."

"Oh sure, it's in Psalm 161," Ellison's response came fast. He said it with so much casual confidence, it sounded completely believable.

"Huh." The drunk laughed. "Maybe that's where the old lush heard it!"

Colton reached for the glass again, but was interrupted again—this time, by the sound of Ellison and Crenshaw laughing.

"What's so funny?" Colton snapped.

"That's not in the Bible!" Andrew Crenshaw exclaimed.

Ellison leaned back in his chair with a self-satisfied grin. He looked at the drunk and said smugly, "I thought you said I couldn't outsmart you?"

Andrew Crenshaw put his hand over his mouth, suppressing a gasp and suppressing a laugh.

The drunk shot an irate look at Pastor Ellison and groused, "You son of a—"

Pastor Ellison promptly pushed the giant glass of alcohol in his direction and insisted, "Get on with it!"

Colton stood up angrily, grabbed the glass, and downed all its contents. Far worse than simply making a face, he fell into a coughing fit. The glass dropped to the ground and shattered. Colton bent forward with forceful, uncontrollable coughs. Both his hands leaned hard on the card table. His face was solid red and as he coughed, a line of spittle hung suspended from his lips.

Pastor Ellison backed his chair out of the way and used his foot to give the table leg a few taps. Colton continued to cough violently. The force from his weight shook the small table. The force from his hacking breath lifted his scribbled note off the table and onto the floor. The reporter leaned far in the other direction away from the germs and the stench.

The pastor tapped the table leg just a little bit harder. Finally, the leg gave way and the card table fell to its side, the debilitated drunk to follow. The impact with the ground was enough to stop the unstoppable cough, and Colton's hand's shot up to cover his face and hold his head. He remained on the floor, on his side, waiting for the pain to stop. The only proof of life he displayed was the tension in his hands, which looked like they were trying to prevent his head from exploding. Finally, that tension melted and he rolled over prostrate, motionless on the ground.

Andrew Crenshaw watched until he saw all movement stop, then went over to check his pulse.

Pastor Ellison had already located a broom and was sweeping up the broken glass.

Neither man had noticed when Hailey had walked into the room with Abigail, just as neither of them noticed at what point the baby had stopped crying. She glanced over at the body and announced her presence with the toneless question, "Is he dead?"

The pastor grinned when he saw her, put down the dustpan, and rushed over to lift her baby into his arms, just as he did every Sunday. Postponing his answer until he gave Abigail a proper greeting, he finally said, "He's fine. He won't be back up until early afternoon. He won't be in a quarrelsome mood, so if you have the stomach to be nice to him, he'll be nice to you."

She nodded, somberly. "I have the stomach." Her response had a peculiar tone; it was part boast, part shameful confession.

She noticed that the pastor had already gathered the broken glass into their dustpan. She grabbed it off the floor, then opened the cabinet which concealed the trash, and poured the glass in.

Ellison managed to bend over, even with the baby in his arms, and grab the note Colton had written before it got thrown away too. He looked around for his options, then shoved it into the jacket pocket from which Colton had retrieved his flask.

Andrew Crenshaw stepped out of the room to hunt for the brass hardware to the door on the floor of the entryway. It was just a second before he returned, hardware in hand.

Hailey reached for her baby and thanked both of the men for coming. Her eyes paused on Andrew Crenshaw for a second as she tried to remember where she'd seen him before, but concluded that it must have just been at church.

"It's late," said the pastor, a segue to their departure.

"Thanks again," said the lady of the house.

"God bless," said Ellison as he pressed his hand against her shoulder.

On their way out, the men worked together to fix the door. Ellison thought they made a pretty good team.

Andrew Crenshaw asked on their way to Ellison's car, "Doesn't the Bible say not to drink?"

"No, it says not to ged drung." There was a slight, almost imperceptible slur in his words. He already had his car keys in hand, but handed them over to Andrew Crenshaw.

Andrew Crenshaw looked at the keys, then back to the house. "Hey, shouldn't you take his gun?"

"No," said Ellison.

"Why not?"

"Because it doesn't belong to me."

When Andrew Crenshaw finally got home, his girlfriend was already in bed. He tried to sneak into the room extra quietly, but as soon as he rested his wallet on his nightstand he discovered that she hadn't yet fallen asleep.

"Well, you two were up late."

"Yeah. Things took a few surprising turns."

"So, was he a crackpot or what?" Julian didn't bother asking about the turns.

"No," said the reporter. It was the weightiest single word she had heard from him in a long while, only she didn't know what it meant and was too tired to ask.

"Did he try to convert you?" she asked instead.

"No. I didn't even mention I was atheist."

"He didn't ask?"

"No."

Julian didn't ask any more questions and as Andrew situated his covers in the dark, he could tell her breathing had slowed down. He knew it might be his last chance to catch her before she fell asleep, so he asked, "Honey, why are we atheist?"

Even in her groggy, near-slumber state, she was able to answer without missing a beat, "Because people who believe in God are stupid."

The reporter caught a chill. He began to worry that the crackpot was a genius and that he had been trying to convert him the whole time.

Chapter Three

January 4—Twelve days left

"Good evening, America, and welcome to the program. I am Lewis Santos and this is America Today."

The music came on—an allegro piano and a jazz saxophone—and the show's animated graphics spun into position, then dissolved into fast clips of Lewis Santos jumping from an airplane, Lewis Santos running with bulls, Lewis Santos trying to work a blender, and Lewis Santos with a rhesus monkey on his head.

The music faded out and the camera panned the applauding live audience, finally settling on Lewis Santos sitting across from Brandon Davies on two large cushy loveseats.

"Tonight we will be talking to Brandon Davies, one of the head pastors at Mead Mountain Church. As most of you know, the church stirred up controversy earlier this week when its leader and founder promised that he would, on January 16, move a nearby mountain just by asking it to move. Brandon Davies, welcome to the program."

"I appreciate you having me on, Lewis."

"January 16, are you counting down the days to that date?"

"Yes, in fact I bought an app for my phone." The audience laughed as if he had told a joke, so he insisted, "I'm serious." He pulled out his phone to let the camera focus on it. "We have twelve days, two hours, and twenty-three minutes left."

The audience laughed again.

"You seem very excited."

Brandon Davies paused. *Excited* wouldn't have been the word he would've used. He said, "Y- y- yes."

The audience laughed again. Brandon Davies smiled sheepishly.

"So, I have to ask, is this a stunt?"

"No sir. Whatever it is, I can promise you, it is no stunt."

"Are you sure? I mean can you say for sure? We've heard that no one else at the church was even informed about this beforehand."

"Yes, that's true. But I can tell you—I know Riley Ellison very well; I have been with Riley from the beginning and I can tell you, beyond a shadow of a doubt, Pastor Riley Ellison is completely serious."

"And he is—forgive how this sounds—he is completely in charge of all his faculties?"

"Yes, sir. I have never seen him more focused and deliberate."

"Do we have this right? You were his very first parishioner?"

"That is correct."

"So you know the pastor very well."

"I believe that I know him professionally better than anyone."

"And what can you tell us?"

"I can tell you that Riley Ellison is the greatest man I've ever met."

"How did you meet?"

"Now that's a great story. It was back in 1990. I owned a small garage, fixing cars. Pastor Ellison brought his car in just like any other customer. But the check he had used to pay for the repairs had bounced, so—no problem—I called him and he gave me a credit card number instead. The next day I spotted him in my parking lot and stepped out to make sure everything was still all right with the car. He told me yeah, everything's fine, that he'd just come to apologize in person and that he was so sorry he wrote me a bad check. I just thought: *Who does that?*

"I remember the day so well. We stood out in the parking lot talking and his wife got out of the car just to be polite. It was cold that morning, not like it's been here lately, but still cold, especially for Southern California. Pastor Ellison was wearing a windbreaker, like he always does, but his poor wife was shivering.

"Riley said he'd just spent every dime he had on a down payment for a church building. Then he asked if I had a home church and I said no. So he told me I should stop by. I thought about it and asked how many people he was expecting. He said, 'Just you and your family, if you agree to come.'" Brandon Davies laughed. There was a twinkle in his eye as he recounted the memory.

"Well of course, I didn't take that part seriously, but when my wife and I showed up to that small, dilapidated building, we discovered that we were the only ones there!" Brandon Davies laughed again. "So we shook hands with him and his wife, and they invited us to sit on the front row. By that time I was thinking, *This guy's sure nice, but this day is a bust.* I hated to see him fail, but I was pretty sure that we'd be out the door in the next ten minutes. My attitude in that moment was, you know, *Call me when you have an actual church.*

"But instead, he started to talk with us. Our dialog had morphed into his monolog and without us even being aware of it, we found ourselves sitting through a bona fide sermon.

"After the 'service' we shook hands again. He asked me to look out across the chairs and he told me, 'This amazing church holds two-hundred people, yet there were only two seats occupied. Somewhere in the world there is a different kind of building, a metaphorical building, let's call it an anti-church. In that building, they don't offer God's grace; they offer everything from the benign—reality shows and technological gadgets—to the malignant—lust, hatred, pornography, sexual dalliance, envy, hedonism, abortion, every type of evil known to man. This anti-church also holds two-hundred people, but only two of its seats were empty this morning.'

"He looked me in the eye and asked, 'Do you know whose seats those were meant to be?' I said, 'No.' He said, 'Yours.'

"He said, 'They were meant to be your seats, but you were here instead.' Then he swept his arm across the empty church, which by the way, no longer seemed so small, but dauntingly large, and said, 'Each of these empty chairs represents a soul who is disconnected from God. But it's far worse than that. Each of these empty seats represents a Christian who allowed that to happen. Let's not allow that to happen, the two of us. I want you to help build this church. I want you to help fill this building and empty the other.'

"Well, of course I thought that was a bit audacious, considering he didn't even know the first thing about me. *Who am I to fill a church? I'm really only good at fixing cars. Why did he pick me?*

"But then I discovered why. I realized I was no one special to him. I realized that he must've tried the same pitch on everyone he'd meet, and I was the only sucker to go for it. *Who am I?* I thought, *I'm just this guy's sucker.*

"And I have been a sucker for Pastor Ellison ever since.

"And I know that I have monopolized this conversation, but I hope you've discovered that I gave you the dirt that the press has been looking for on the man."

Lewis's eyebrows raised. "No, I guess I didn't notice. What dirt?"

"When his wife was shivering, Pastor Ellison didn't offer her his jacket. I'm telling you, that's the dirt on him, because that's all you'll ever find. And in twenty-four years, that's the single worst thing I've ever seen him do. The guy's just not like other people. Other people have bad moods or bad days. Other people have problems; Ellison never does. He's amazing. The guy's like...*Mister Perfect.*"

Lewis smiled. "You have been a terrific guest and I don't mind you hogging the conversation, because I only really have one question for you: Do you think the mountain will move?"

Brandon Davies had obviously prepared for this question; there was no way he wouldn't have known it was coming. He had rehearsed the answer over and over and over again: *Of course it will move; it is a promise from God.* But now that it was time to give it, just like that, he hesitated. His eyes looked down, and on television it seemed like a long time passed. He said, "If anyone has that kind of faith, it's Pastor Ellison. If anyone can pull this off, it's him."

Pastor Ellison had been watching Brandon's interview live on his phone, blushing slightly despite being alone. He had his feet up on the desk in his office when he heard a knock at the door. He quickly shut off his phone and sat up straight to give the visitor his full attention.

The first thing that struck Ellison was the goodness he saw behind the man's eyes. That was the best word he could think of to describe it—a little bit of kindness, a lot of compassion, honesty, loyalty, just general, garden variety *goodness.* Over the last twenty-four years, Ellison had developed a knack for spotting it in people.

"Pastor Ellison?" Charles asked.

"You can call me Riley," Ellison said with a wide smile as he offered his hand.

"My name is Charles Brandt. It's nice to meet you, sir," said Charles. When Charles shook his hand, his fingers brushed against the elastic cuff of the red windbreaker Ellison was wearing. He saw the few scrapes remaining on Ellison's face from his encounter with Poison. He pointed to the same place on his own face and remarked to Ellison, "I can see that you've been hiking a difficult trail."

The pastor laughed, remembering the scars on his face and where they'd come from. "You have no idea."

Charles's eyes moved from the scars and windbreaker to the geology texts—commingling with theology texts—on Ellison's shelf. "I've heard you love nature."

"And people." Ellison motioned to one of the empty chairs laid out in his office. He said, "Please, have a seat."

They both sat down, separated by a desk of polished mahogany. "Well, I'm one of your parishioners here, and—"

"Oh, wonderful. I'm so sorry we haven't yet met," Ellison said excitedly; he did not mean to interrupt.

"We've just never had the chance. I've only been a member here for a couple of months."

"Wonderful. Do you live around here?"

"South Copeland."

"Oh!" The pastor was struck by the distance Charles had traveled.

"Yes, there are closer churches," Charles correctly interpreted the meaning expressed in Ellison's tone, "but it's okay, 'cause the train drops me off right here." Charles turned to point through the church walls, to the station only two blocks away.

"Well then, let me welcome you belatedly. I hope our Sundays together have been worth your trip."

"They have been..."

"But..."

"Well, I wanted to talk to you about this stunt you are—"

"It's no stunt, Mr. Brandt." This time the interruption had been intentional.

"That's just it..." Charles hesitated. "I respect what you are trying to do, but..."

"I understand; you fear the mountain won't move."

"No. On the contrary. I worry the mountain will move."

"Oh! Well, I guess then *I don't* understand."

"I joined this church because I had heard you were a nature lover. I had even heard you consider yourself somewhat of an amateur geologist."

"Somewhat," Ellison laughed warmly.

"Well then, how can you justify what you are planning? How can you justify the effects it will have on the natural world? Just the imagery alone!" Charles was showing excellent restraint. "You are asking a mountain to crumble. You might as well ask a forest to catch fire. It's the most anti-Earth thing I have ever seen."

"No, sir. Not anti-Earth. Pro-human. Were your parents Christian, Mr. Brandt?"

"My mother was one of the most insanely devout Christian women

I've ever met."

Ellison smiled. "I could tell. I can see her in you."

In the circles in which Charles travelled, he was unaccustomed to people saying they saw the Christian in him. In fact, most of his rock-climbing friends, vegetarian friends, and activist friends—the ones he'd admit it to—were shocked to find out he was Christian at all. Curiosity alone allowed him to get diverted from the point he had been trying to make. He asked, "What makes you say that?"

"Well, like you said, *devotion.*" Ellison looked not at, but into, the man's face. He said, "I can tell that you're anxious to value a cause higher than your own life. I can tell that you understand duty. You're exactly the type of man the world needs now."

"Thanks," Charles mumbled. He wasn't sure how it happened, but at some point his righteous indignation became completely derailed.

"The reason I asked about your folks is because my father died not knowing Christ. I loved my father. Despite the many mistakes he'd made raising me, I loved him." Ellison leaned in closer. "And I love nature. This Earth is a precious gift from God." He spread open his hands. "I can't put it any more powerfully than that. But I want you to be clear about the man sitting across from you. I always want to be clear on this point: if it somehow meant I could go back in time and share the gospel with my father, I would light a forest fire myself." Ellison looked him straight in the eye; he knew how heretical these words were to a man like Charles. "I would personally burn down a million trees just for one opportunity to reach him."

Charles just stared at him. His righteous indignation was back, and with a vengeance. He stood up to leave. He said, "I think this conversation is over."

"Wait!" yelled Pastor Ellison.

When Charles turned around he saw a truly welcoming smile.

Ellison said, "Wait. Please. Sit. I want to know you. If you walk out of my church forever now, you will be breaking my heart."

Charles hesitated.

"Please," Ellison repeated, gesturing toward the empty chair. "The next train doesn't leave for forty-five minutes. Let's talk, one conservationist to another."

The man walked back to his chair. He sat down begrudgingly. "What's there left to talk about?"

"I don't know, the weather? Why's it been so cold lately?"

Charles studied Ellison's face. He couldn't tell if the casual change of topic, which was *not* a change of topic, had been genuine. He answered, "Global warming."

"It's getting *cold* because of global *warming*?"

"Of course," Charles said nonchalantly. He would have left it there, but he thought he detected some confusion, maybe even skepticism on Ellison's face. He said, "The warmer weather melts the ice in the Arctic. The darker water reflects less sunlight than the lighter ice, which creates a high pressure area. The difference in air pressure creates oscillation," Charles made big rotating gestures with his hands. Talking on this subject produced a schoolboy excitement in him. "So, the cold arctic weather is brought down to us."

"Well, okay," said Ellison, agreeably. "Hey, did you notice the curly-Q light bulbs we installed for the office?" Ellison asked with both eyebrows raised. He wasn't hiding—but rather presenting—the fact that it was a cheap ploy for Charles's favor.

"Yes, very impressive," Charles said dryly.

"I'm sure you have a few in your home."

"Of course."

The pastor took a second look at Charles, his drab brown sweater and his full beard—*no, it isn't unruly,* thought Ellison, *very well kempt,* but there seemed to be something feral about it. Ellison looked deep into his kind eyes and asked, "What else can one do to help the environment?"

Charles's eyes popped open. The words erupted up from his diaphragm like he was unable to stop them. "There're *lots* of things you can do!"

"Well, what have you done? That is, besides the light bulbs."

"Well, I recycle."

"Of course."

"And I try to only buy products that are recycled. I take the train to work and have encouraged others to do so. For those who don't, I've organized an office carpool. I also bought a hybrid, but I don't drive it unless it's an absolute necessity. I consolidate my errands and ride my bike whenever possible. Plus, I keep good air in my tires."

"Okay," Ellison nodded gently, "what else?"

"Well, I am a vegetarian. I buy only locally-grown, organic vegetables and I only use a cloth grocery bag. I only drink tap water. I own a low-flow toilet. I use an aerated shower head. I always buy clothing with no dyes and I try to buy hemp products because it requires less water to grow than cotton. I only use biodegradable soaps and cleaning products. I never wash clothes without a full load and I hang all my laundry on a clothes line instead of using the dryer."

"That's quite a list," the pastor said. "You obviou—"

"Oh, there's more," Mr. Brandt interrupted with growing enthusiasm. "My wife and I had a *green wedding* and now we use only cloth diapers for the baby. We use reusable containers in the kitchen so we never use foil or plastic wrap. We use rags to clean up messes, never paper towels. We also buy the unbleached coffee filters. I clean the condenser coils on the refrigerator annually. I insulated my hot water tank and turned its temperature down to 130 degrees, which is enough to kill bacteria. I weatherized our home, sealed all the ducts, doors, and windows. I replaced all the single paned windows with double paned and I replace the AC filter each month. We turn up the thermostat in summer and down in winter, plus we are having solar panels installed. I use a manual reel mower to cut the grass and I only water at night. I turn off the light when leaving the room. Oh, and I have a compost bin in my back yard," Charles added with the perfect tone and diction to indicate that he had finished the list. But Ellison didn't respond.

There was a moment of awkward silence. Charles felt suddenly exposed and inadequate. He quickly added, "I... uh... I don't let the water run while brushing my teeth."

Ellison nodded again. "I can see you understand that every bit helps."

"Yes," Charles nodded along with him, feeling reassured.

"Because you know that if you are not part of the solution you are part of the problem."

"Absolutely," Charles said ardently.

"And, you know that just one person truly can make a difference."

"Yes."

"Have you promoted awareness?"

"I have an environmental blog."

"Have you written to politicians?"

"Of course."

"How about the press?"

"I had an article published on Benjamin Mead's blog last fall."

"Benjamin Mead? Well, you can't get much higher in the

environmentalist world than that."

"I thought you'd be impressed by that. After all, you named your church after him."

"Actually, I named my church after the mountain," Ellison said in the tone of a simple correction, then added, "Plus, I like the alliteration." Getting back on point, he asked Charles, "What else have you done?"

Charles's eyes bulged a little. He wiped his palms along the outside seam of his slacks. At this point, he was pretty sure that Pastor Ellison was only messing with his head, but he still felt compelled to answer the best he could. He said, "Well, um... I have stopped all junk mail coming to the house. And I use latex paint instead of oil-based. I buy in bulk, which means less packaging. I only use rechargeable batteries. I donate my old furniture and clothing. I... I always ask my mechanic to recycle my used motor oil. I only use a laptop computer because it uses less power than a desktop. I only print when I have to and I recycle my toner cartridges. Um... also I have personally planted 378 trees."

Pastor Ellison let out a long sigh. He leaned back in his chair and asked, "Do you feel you have done *enough*?"

Now Charles was certain he was being toyed with, but just couldn't help but lower his eyes. He said, "No, I need to do more."

"I see." Ellison cleared his throat. "And what have you done to hel-"

Charles abruptly cut in. "I know what it is like to be called, called to action, called to service. I know what it's like to look out across a suffering planet. I know what it's like to see so much filth, so much poison, and feel that weight pressing down on you, as if the responsibility to fix all of it falls on my shoulders alone. I look at the problems, which are so enormous, and then I look at my puny arms; I know I am not strong enough. I look at my life and I ask, is there something more I can do? Have I been selfish? Have I been negligent? Was there something I overlooked, or maybe something I was too comfortable, or too proud to see?"

The room went silent. Pastor Ellison watched Charles, who had courageously laid it all out to be judged, who now appeared to be on the verge of tears. Neither man moved. Pastor Ellison was deeply touched by the man's ardor. It reminded him of his early days, building his congregation. A sharp pain bit at his heart and he wondered if his life and his ministry were doing justice to the dreams of that young, wild-eyed pastor.

Charles remained silent. He had said what he had to say. The ball was in Pastor Ellison's court and he had a decision to make. He *had* been messing with him. He wasn't sure now if the question Charles interrupted would still be appropriate, or perhaps more appropriate than ever.

He proceeded, "And what have you done to help the poor?"

Charles's eyes shot back up with a look of utter confusion. "What?"

"Help the poor," Ellison said simply.

"Um..."

Before Charles had time to think, Ellison shot, "What have you done to stem the destructive tide of pornography in our society?"

Charles shook his head slowly. "I haven't done anything."

"What have you done to help stop domestic violence?"

Charles said nothing and shook his head.

"Help keep kids off drugs? Help reduce teenage pregnancies?"

Another headshake.

"Have you done anything to help preserve childhood?" This time Ellison gave no pause for an answer. He pressed on. "It's important to stay informed, Mr. Brandt. Alcohol, drugs, internet porn, bad role models, Hollywood, the music industry, violent video games—don't you see the filth in our children's *social* environment? They can't breathe. Cutting, sexting, cyber bullying, sex parties... Have you done anything to help clean up *that* environment?"

"What can I do about any of that stuff?" Charles asked helplessly.

"Every little bit helps, Charles. One man can make a difference—you know that. And what about crime in the inner-city? Why bother cleaning up the air, when it's not safe for some children to play outside?"

Charles threw up his hands feeling defeated. He had no answer and nothing to offer.

Ellison continued with passion and devotion, matched only by Charles himself, "I've had two important encounters this week. One was with a stripper. She carried with her so much pain, day in and day out, hour after hour, that one need only prick her fragile facade with the tip of a pin to send her into a fit of violent rage. On top of that, she took off her clothes for money. That is real pain. The second was with a raging drunk whose wife had locked herself and her newborn baby girl in a bedroom to avoid his gun-toting rampage. That is real suffering. Do you know what the two have in common?"

"What?" asked Charles somberly.

"The stripper's father was the drunk, and the drunk's mother was the stripper. *Metaphorically*. In other words, it's institutionalized. It's generational pain—the type of pain that can't be fought by a change in light bulbs, the type for which no fashionable cause seems to lend its support."

Charles lowered his eyes.

Ellison's eyes were patient and disarming when he said, "I would love for you to continue to attend our church, but if you are looking to be congratulated every week, this isn't the place for you. My job isn't to pat you on the back; it's to step on your toes. My job is to tell you the things that you need to hear even if you don't want to hear them."

"And you think you're in the position to know what I need to hear?" Charles asked defensively.

"I know exactly what you need to hear. I knew the second you walked in that door. I saw a good, and passionate, and *powerful* man. My heart rejoiced because I saw a once-in-a-lifetime, perfect promoter and defender of God's Word."

Charles looked down. He was somehow shamed by the flattery. He said, "And what do I need to hear?"

"It's a famous old quote actually, one of history's greatest. I have altered it to fit men like you."

The pastor waited. The two men watched each other.

"Okay," Charles said finally, "Lay it on me."

Ellison smiled warmly and said, "All that is necessary for evil to triumph... is for good men to be distracted."

Chapter Four

January 5—Eleven days left
Sunday

"So, it seems like the papers have already made their verdicts." Brandon Davies had been waiting in Pastor Ellison's office with a pile of newspapers on his lap.

"Oh yeah? And what's the verdict?" Ellison feigned optimism.

"See for yourself." Brandon laid the papers out before Ellison one by one. Their headlines read:

> "Pastor Ellison Claims Power to Move Mountains"
> "Mead Mountain Preacher Claims to Talk to God"
> "Pastor Riley Ellison Concocts Shameful Publicity Stunt"

"The actual articles just get worse," said Brandon.

"I guess that's pretty much what you were expecting," said Ellison.

"Well, I wasn't expecting this," Brandon Davies said as he reached to unfold the final paper. Its headline read:

> "Pastor Ellison Can Keep His Cool and Handle His Liquor"

Ellison laughed. "He has a fresh angle on the story!"

"You find this funny?" Brandon Davies challenged.

Ellison offered an insouciant shrug. Picking up the paper, he said, "We've already convinced the choir."

"There's a new Facebook page called *It Will Move*, which already has twenty thousand Likes."

"Oh, that's wonderful."

"But there's also a page called *It Won't Move*. It has over five million Likes."

Ellison flashed a pretend frown. "*It Won't Move,* huh? Well, that could be referring to anything." He smiled.

"An online betting site has given odds on whether or not Mead Mountain will move."

"Really? What are they predicting?"

"They are predicting 93 to 7 that it will *not* move."

Ellison nodded. "Well, narrow is the road that leads to life." He turned his eyes to the newspaper. Laughing, he added, "Remind me I need to buy in."

Brandon Davies didn't laugh. He took a seat in the chair in front of Ellison's desk. He looked at the clock. He tried his best to sound casual when he said, "You know in 1844, there was a group of Christians known as the Millerites." Brandon Davies paused when he saw Pastor Ellison pop his head up. A peculiar smile stretched out across Ellison's lips, but Brandon Davies continued, "Using a passage from the book of Daniel, they believed they had calculated the end times to the day. So, they also believed this information came from God." Ellison put down his paper so he could listen, folding his arms over his chest. Brandon Davies cleared his throat and pressed forward, "Some of them believed it so adamantly that they sold everything they owned and gave away all their money. Some even bought coffins for their own bodies, dug their own graves, and climbed inside. Well, obviously the world did not end that day, and the story is known as the Great Disappointment."

"And?" asked Ellison.

"And..." Brandon proceeded cautiously, but firmly. "And every time I think about that story, I imagine a moment in my head—two of Miller's followers climb out of separate graves and dust themselves off, on a day that they said would never happen. Now the last thing they want to do is make eye contact, but they want to steal a glimpse of the other's face, and they both happen to try to steal it at the same time. And in the morning light, they see a glint in the other man's eyes, betraying they are on the verge of tears, and then they... what?... They shrug, I guess... I guess they just *shrug*."

"What's your point?" Ellison asked.

Brandon Davies's eyes evaded the pastor. He said, "No point," then stood up and left the room.

Pastor Ellison pursed his lips. He said in a stolid monotone, "It's been a pleasure talking to you, Brandon," even though Brandon Davies was already gone.

Ellison checked his phone to see the time, then turned his attention back to the paper.

He heard the sound of his door. Through his peripheral vision, he noticed a long, bright floral skirt and knew it was Ashley McAllister.

"How are things looking out there?" Ellison asked her without looking up. "Did you let Cedric know about the changes I wanted in his set?"

Ashley McAllister said nothing; she simply nodded.

Her personality had been so consistently ebullient over the years that her silence set off alarm bells in his head. He looked up. Both of Ashley's eyes were filled with tears. "What's wrong?"

Ashley McAllister didn't answer at first. Finally, she whimpered, "Pastor." She paused to sniffle. "I think we've got a problem."

"What is it?"

Ashley McAllister still didn't want to answer. She pulled some tissue from the box on his desk and said, "I think you need to see this for yourself."

Pastor Ellison stood up to head to the sanctuary. He left his office without even changing out of his windbreaker and into his blazer. As an afterthought, he quickly stepped back into his office and placed his palms on both sides of Ashley's doleful head and kissed the top of her hair. He said, "It will be okay."

He cut through the hall, rounded the doorway in the choir room, and paused before heading out onto the stage. He could hear the band finishing up. The music director had made the changes he requested.

He already had a sick feeling in his stomach before even opening the door. He had been so caught up with Charles Brandt, with Andrew Crenshaw, and with Hailey and her baby girl that he had nearly forgotten all about Mead Mountain. He pushed through the threshold into the sanctuary.

In the center of the stage, Pastor Ellison put his hand above his eyes to shield the glare of the stage lights. Two bright spotlights from the balcony—at the corners of his vision, 10:00 and 2:00—caused his pupils to contract. Finally, his eyes adjusted enough that he could see his audience, at first just colorless shapes, highlights, and shadows. When his eyes adjusted more he was able to decipher, not just his audience, but his entire predicament. He saw a monochromatic sea of repeating waves of beige, the unobstructed color of the chairs in his sanctuary. It was only in the center section that the painful pattern was broken up by blazers and dresses, colorful women's scarves and striped neckties, by blondes, brunettes, and redheads. But not many.

Now he knew what Ashley McAllister had seen. He woefully scanned the vast empty auditorium. It was the first damage report assessed since he had gone public with the announcement, and it wasn't good. There was only a small fraction of the people who had been there last Sunday. Although his church had over twenty thousand members on its roll, his sanctuary only held five thousand max. For most services it was nearly full. Not today. With hundreds of seats filled, but thousands that were empty, his congregation had been nearly decimated in only one week.

He cleared his throat. It was his modus operandi to burst into his sermon, teeming with energy and the Spirit of God. He liked to piggy back on the excitement produced by the band. Today he stood there slack-jawed for several seconds.

Ellison looked at the string tied to his finger and breathed in strength. He said sincerely, "Thank you for coming."

Pulling himself together, he tried to remember what he had intended to talk about. He had planned his Sunday sermon earlier in the week, but yesterday's interaction with Mr. Brandt, the environmentalist, had caused Ellison to scrap the whole thing.

He knew what he had to say.

"Today I would like to try something different. I would like to take a quick poll. I want everyone here to remember the worst pain you have ever experienced in your entire life. You don't have to replay it in your mind, just identify to yourself what caused it. Do you have it?"

Some people actually answered, "Yes."

"Okay, now raise your hand if it was caused by smog."

No hands were raised.

"No? Okay, then raise your hand if it was caused by an oil spill."

No hands were raised.

"Raise your hand if it was caused by pollution of any kind."

No hands were raised.

Despite the fact that the crowd size was small, Pastor Ellison had failed to notice a woman slip in after the service had already begun, and she was hard not to notice. She wore a small tank top with spaghetti straps and a red leather skirt. She wiped the cold drizzle off both shoulders and found a spot in the back. She sat with her arms crossed, both as a means of protecting herself and to warm up.

It was Poison.

"Raise your hand if it was caused by bullying," Ellison continued, unaware of the congregation's new addition.

No hands were raised.

"Raise your hand if your biggest pain in life was caused by you, or someone else, smoking cigarettes."

No hands were raised.

"Okay, now raise your hand if it was caused by something financial."

This time a few timid hands went up.

Ellison said, "Looks like we have a couple of those." He gave a sympathetic nod. "Okay, you can just pass on the collection plate this week."

People laughed.

This is what church is like? thought Poison in the back. She turned her head for a moment to eye the exit. *What's this guy even talking about?*

He continued, "Now raise your hand if it was caused by a friend."

There were the most hands so far, but still relatively few.

"Finally, raise your hand if your biggest pain in life was caused by garden variety heartache, you loved someone who didn't happen to love you back?"

A quarter of the audience raised their hands.

Ellison smiled. "Sorry ladies and gentlemen, but there's nothing we can do about heartache. That one will always be with us."

Poison stood up to leave, but stopped when a young man caught her eye by standing up in the aisle. A woman on the other side of the aisle had taken her sweater jacket off in the warmth of the sanctuary and hadn't noticed that it fell on the floor. The teenager had—on his own accord—crossed the aisle to pick it up and return it to her. She smiled and thanked him, and the boy returned to his seat, having no idea what effect his single act of kindness just had on someone he'd never met.

The young man wore a freshly-ironed dress shirt. He had starched creases down the length of both his sleeves. A blue tie hung perfectly just past his belt. Poison was amazed by what she saw in him; he appeared to be the exact age of her son, only her son had never ironed a shirt in his life and didn't even know how to tie a tie. And she wasn't certain that her son would stand up to cross an aisle to help someone who was on fire, much less someone who'd dropped a sweater.

She sat back down, more curious than ever to find out just what they did here.

"Now, those of you keeping score at home have probably noticed that the vast majority of you haven't raised your hands yet. So, a lot of you are probably curious to see what the main cause of pain is. But first let me ask you, why does it matter? Why is it important to know? That's an easy one: it's important to know because if we want to change the world, if we really want to help people, then we have to know where to start. If we can't see the real pain in this country, we can't fix it. When people refuse to acknowledge that pain, then they will never be able to change the world for the better.

"In my line of work I see real pain. I can pick up on the signs. I see it in the skinny girl working at the coffee shop with her face all covered in piercings and tattoos peeking out the edges of her clothing. Does she strike anyone here as happy? Like a starving man who throws money back into an altruist's face, she will not take your pity. She announces to the world that she does not want their acceptance. She rejects society long before society has a chance to reject her. I want to help that young lady. I want to tell her that she was never rejected by the only One who matters. I want to tell her that He loves her and finds her worthy to die for.

"I see real pain at daycares when a mother has to peel her crying child off of her so she can go work in a cubicle. There's real pain in the face of that child, but in the face of the mom as well. She spent her whole childhood playing with dolls, pretending they were her babies. Then when she finally has a baby of her own, she drops him off for ten hours a day. And why? To report to a boss who barely knows her name? To make just a few more dollars than she is paying the daycare? She had been lied to all her life. Everyone told her she should have it all—career, fancy car, big house, latest electronics... oh, and a family thrown in. No one told her what priorities she should have planned her life around. There is pain in that mother's life and I want to help her.

"I see it in the street protestor willing to give his life for a cause he can't really define. It's not because he values the cause, it's because he doesn't value his life. He has an amazing, admirable yearning in him that drives him to get involved and take a stand. That passion was meant for God. He wants to belong to something. No one has been able to convince him he belongs to God. He doesn't believe heaven is waiting for him after death, so he foolishly believes in a heaven here on Earth—a Utopia, which could only be instituted by a top-down, intrusive state. I want to help him. I want to tell him to put his faith in God, not in government.

"I see it in the young girl who allows her boyfriend to take a certain type of photo of her with his cell phone and never imagines it will be passed around the entire school. She lets him have what he wants from her because she foolishly thinks she'll receive love in return. I want to help her. I want to tell her she is precious. She is golden.

"I see real pain in the young man addicted to porn. He has an invisible siren around his neck sounding a warning to every female who approaches. It blares in a pitch he cannot hear and in a language he cannot understand. He doesn't even know it's there. Sex becomes all he wants and he begins to hate the women who refuse to sleep with him. So the siren gets louder and the cycle gets deeper. I want to help him. I want to show him the glory of being a man.

"I see real pain in the young girl trying to find love and attention from a porn-addicted generation of boys. She must decide between paying a price she is unwilling to pay, or being passed over in favor of the girls who pay it. I want to help her. I want to tell her that good men do exist and help her learn how to spot them.

"I see real pain in the young boy whose parents are divorcing. The rock he was standing on has just turned to sand. His newfound distrust of his parents' authority leads him to distrust all authority everywhere. He lets go of all the values he grew up with and foolishly concludes he can be successful by making up the rules of life on his own. I want to help him. I want to tell him that to be subjugated to God is liberation and to conform to His Word is nonconformity.

"I know everyone here would love to help these people, but the voices that could help them, don't reach them, and the voices that do reach them, don't help.

"It's heartbreaking. But it becomes more heartbreaking when you realize that all of the things that make up the culture we live in—our movies, music, books, and news—are aimed at attracting *them,* attracting them and producing more of them.

"With all this suffering surrounding us every day, with the pitfalls in life so numerous it's impossible to avoid them all, what are the lessons our children are receiving from the world? Don't litter. Don't smoke. Don't bully. Don't get fat.

"With teenage pregnancies on the rise, out-of-wedlock births on the rise, marriage on the decline, with Internet porn endemic, at a time when the average age for a woman to have her first child is lower than the average age for her to get married, at a time when our popular music is replete with misogyny and profanity and love songs are somehow no longer in style, it's hard for me to believe that there are actually people who think we need to spend time worrying about trans-fats, or recycling, or the Delta Smelt.

"Here's the good news. We don't live under tyranny in America. We are a blessed and affluent nation. Despite what you might hear from exploitative politicians, there is no starvation in this country. Despite what the local news reports, violent crime has been steadily on the decline for forty years. It's true. Polio has been cured. Measles, chickenpox, diphtheria and typhoid all have vaccinations. Smallpox has been completely obliterated from the world, and it's only a matter of time before cancer is cured. At the beginning of the last century, life expectancy was just forty-seven-years-old. Now it's around seventy-eight and still increasing. We are living in the most remarkable age and in the most remarkable country ever known to man. *So why are we so unhappy?*

"We are unhappy for one reason—and now I want you to raise your hand if this describes you—the real pain in this privileged country in which we live is caused by one thing: a person, and it could be yourself, was confronted with a *moral* test and failed."

All the remaining hands went up as well as some of the hands that had previously been raised.

"I don't need to hear the details; I can imagine. There're so many different stories, but they all come back to one thing: real suffering comes from bad morality. Yet, preaching morality has been declared taboo by the gatekeepers of the public discourse. And the voices that could help aren't heard, and the voices that are heard, don't help."

Poison finally got up to leave. This time Pastor Ellison did spot her, but only after her back was turned. He frowned as he wondered who this fleeing guest could be, but it prompted an idea in him.

"That brings me to *my* biggest pain in life." He sighed with genuine sadness and said, "My biggest pain in life is, and has always been, empty seats." He looked at the bleak attendance one more time. "That's why this is a particularly hard message for me to bring to you today. Because... because that skinny girl with the piercings, her seat is right there." Ellison pointed to an empty seat on his right. "And that working mom, her seat's right there." He pointed to his left. "And that protestor, his seat's right there." Each time he pointed to a different empty seat. "And the girl in the photo, that's her seat. The boy addicted to porn, that's his seat in the balcony. The girl looking for love, she's supposed to be down in front. The boy who parents are divorcing, that's his seat. That's his seat." Pastor

Ellison was getting emotional. It wasn't a performance. "I know once surrounded by this many people offering help, willing to listen, willing to take the time, there is no problem that couldn't be fixed. I know with God's grace there's no wound that couldn't be healed. But the seat is empty." He gestured left and right, adding gloomily, "The seats are empty."

Pastor Ellison uncharacteristically, and unprofessionally, turned and walked out. He did not even lead his congregation through a closing prayer. Brandon Davies quickly stepped in to do the job.

Typically, after a sermon, Pastor Ellison would meander through the hallways as everyone was leaving. He tried to shake as many hands as possible and learn as many new names as possible. This time, however, he told himself he had to hurry because he was scheduled to appear on the Jake Dolan Show. He wasn't in that big of a hurry and could have taken twenty minutes to shake hands if he had wanted to. He just didn't feel up to it.

When he bailed out the choir room, he spotted a woman in the hallway pretending to read posts on their bulletin board. She wore a tight leather skirt—the same woman who'd fled just before the end of his sermon. She had her back to him, but he felt certain she was new because he'd never seen any of his congregants dressed like that. On any other day, a new visitor to his church would've had celebrity status, but Ellison passed her by with no eye contact and without saying a word.

"Ain't you gonna say something?" he heard a petulant voice.

He turned around to look the tawdry woman straight in the face. He narrowed his eyes. Poison watched as his lips began to pucker. The pastor either wanted to kiss her, or he could only remember the first letter of her name.

"Poison," she snipped.

"Of course," he smiled. "It's so good to see you!" They were only three feet from his office, so he said, "Why don't you come in and have a seat with me."

Poison looked hesitant. "What for?"

He motioned over his shoulder to the open door through which he was trying to lead her, "A shot of Patron," he said.

Her eyes opened wide as she asked, "Really?"

He was expecting a laugh. He lowered his head when she had responded with so much excitement; it hadn't been his intention to embarrass her. He said, "Not really." They both stood there uncomfortably for a second, before he tried again. "Come on in. Please."

"Can I smoke?"

"Um... sure."

Poison marched into the office like a woman who knew—or imagined—her very presence was offensive somehow, offensive to the books, offensive to the cross that hung on the wall and the framed copy of the United States Constitution, offensive to the photo of the pastor with some baseball player and the framed twenty-dollar bill off to the side of it. She wanted to throw her depravity into the face of the office and the man inside.

This was the first time Ellison actually got to look at Poison's face fully illuminated. Her eyes were crystal blue; he couldn't see that in the darkness of the club. They reminded him of the clear, clean water of a downtown fountain, the kind that, on a hot day, would make a businessman want to forget all his struggles and dive in with his suit still on. There was intelligence behind those eyes, not like the tired pedantry found in the university, but like the fierce cunning found on the battlefield.

Yes, she is beautiful. More beautiful than he had previously realized.

She wasted no time pulling out a cigarette and gave her lighter an imperious flick. "You ain't got no ashtray."

He hadn't thought of that. He passed her the empty coffee cup on his desk. It read "I Hate Mondays." The irony of the sentiment escaped her. She knocked her ashes into it with an aggressive strike of her finger, even though hardly any ashes had built up yet.

"You forgot aimlessness," she accused. She flicked again and added, "You never said you were the pastor."

"What's this about aimlessness?"

"When you were listing things that cause pain, you forgot aimlessness."

A thin smile crossed his lips. He was happy to hear she'd actually been listening. He said, "Aimlessness, oh my, that's a hard one. You're right; I did forget." He waited.

She didn't respond. She eyed the fine furniture as if she resented the elegance. She said, "Why'd you sign up for a whole year?"

Pastor Ellison looked confused for a second, then asked, "Do you mean at the Boys' Club?"

"Yeah, I mean, if you're not into naked girls, why'd you sign up?"

Ellison smiled. He said, "For the record, I'm very into naked girls. I'm crazy for naked girls; I'm just contented with my wife."

"Your wife know you go to strip clubs?"

"Obviously, yes. I'd never go without her blessing."

"She must have a lot of faith in you."

"It's not faith in *me* that guides her."

"She know you spent a thousand dollars?"

Ellison squirmed as if that particular question pressed hard between two of his ribs. He said, "Actually, I haven't... actually... found the right moment to bring that up."

Poison laughed.

"But I think she'll understand. I will look her in the eye and ask her one question: How much is one soul worth to God? What lengths are too far if it means bringing one of His children back to Him?"

Poison was unimpressed. She said, "She's gonna kill you."

Ellison was anxious to steer the conversation back. He asked gently, "Have you been feeling aimless?"

She shook her head. "My son."

"How old is the boy?"

"Just turned sixteen."

"That's a hard age."

"I guess." Poison did her best to sell the idea that, although she drove to the church and sought out his company, then broached the subject, she didn't really want to talk about it. She said, "Hey, how do you get all them teenagers to wear ties and stuff?"

"Oh, well that one's easy."

"How?" she pressed. Her cigarette was primed, held close to her mouth. She was waiting on his answer before she took a drag. It was the first instant where she'd betrayed the fact he had her rapt attention. She wanted to hear some ancient wisdom, some secret knowledge. She wanted to be given a skeleton key that could unlock all the problems with her child.

"We make them," the pastor said, at last.

"So they don't dress up on their own?" Poison was disappointed. She'd been hoping the answer would sound more like a fortune cookie.

Ellison shook his head. "No, that doesn't sound like any teenager I know." He laughed. "So is he getting into trouble?"

"Who?"

"Your boy."

"He's a good boy. Smart. Really smart if he'd apply himself."

"Okay, so how has this aimlessness..." he searched for the right delicate word "*manifested* itself?" Pastor Ellison saw Ashley McAllister's face appear in the small window in his office door. She raised her left hand and tapped her nonexistent watch. Ellison tried to ignore her, but couldn't help pulling out his phone to check the time. He was going to be late. He shifted in his chair and began devising a way he could cut this meeting short.

"My son is going to kill himself," Poison said.

Pastor Ellison sat up and leaned in. He flipped his phone face down. It didn't escape his attention that she said "is going to" as opposed to "wants to" or "might." It indicated a greater willingness on the boy's part, and he feared a greater resignation on the part of the mother. Ellison said, "We can't let that happen. What makes you think he will?"

"His brother Carson did."

"This is very serious." Ellison could feel his heart beat harder. "How long ago did his brother die?"

"I'm sorry I slapped you," Poison said casually. "Sometimes I get..."

"Poison, how long ago did his brother die?"

He could tell Poison resented the question. She didn't want to have to think about that which she had spent so long training herself not to think about. "It wasn't my fault," she snapped. "I'm all alone. I don't know anything about boys. What am I supposed to know about boys? Besides, I'm the one who stayed."

Ellison's voice was soft and steady. He was afraid she would walk out. "No one here is blaming you."

"It was eight months ago."

"That's—"

"No, a year." Poison stared off. She couldn't believe it had been that long. "A year and two months ago," she settled.

His cell phone buzzed. He flipped it over despite knowing what it would say:

Ashley McAllister   12:27 pm
You're going to be late.

Ellison said, "I'm so sorry about your loss, ma'am. Believe me, I am. But it sounds to me like your son is in—What's his name?"

"Tyler."

"It sounds to me like Tyler is in great danger, and—"

"I was hoping maybe you would talk to him."

He again saw the face of Ashley McAllister looking in through the window. She peeked in, then disappeared. Ellison said, "I promise you that I will do all I can, but right now, today, you need to call a crisis center." Ellison immediately turned to rummage through his desk drawer. "They can help him. They will be open on a Sunday; you need to not wait, but do it today. They will evaluate him professionally and if necessary put him in seventy-two hour observation."

"You mean lock him up? He won't go."

"Don't give him a choice." Ellison pulled out a card, circled the number on it, and handed it to Poison. "You have to do it to save his life. Where is he now?"

"He's at home."

"Alone?"

"Y—" She cut herself short before answering. "We don't have the money for that. I was hoping you would talk to him and you could turn him around."

Ashley McAllister stuck her head into the office cautiously. "Pastor," is all she said.

Without looking in her direction, he kept his eyes on Poison. He said, "I'm talking to *you*. I'm trying to turn *you* around. You have to call someone who can observe him. Promise me you will."

Poison didn't answer. She looked crestfallen. Finally, she said, "Okay." The listless way she said it didn't convince him for a second.

"Promise me that you'll get him some help."

"They're going to take him away from me."

"No, they won't. I need you to do this. Will you do it?"

Again she didn't answer. She pushed her cigarette out against the side of the cup and eyed the door. She said, "You're a busy man."

He said, "I'm not going anywhere until you promise me."

She said, "Sure. Sure, yeah."

"Okay, thank you," he told her.

The Jake Dolan Show had sent a limo to pick Pastor Ellison up from his church and drive him to Los Angeles. He rode in the back, restless. He knew Poison had lied to him about calling the crisis center and wondered what he should do. He knew the odds were completely against the boy committing suicide that very day, and rationalized it by telling himself that he had a large, national, cable audience waiting.

After a short mental struggle, Ellison asked the limo driver, who had been nervously checking his watch, "There any chance I could get you to turn this limo around?"

The driver laughed. "No, I hear that all the time."

Ellison was struck by his response. It seemed to indicate that the driver misunderstood his motives for wanting a 180. The limo rolled on, and Ellison stared out the window, filled with shame. In the distance, he could see Mead Mountain.

When they got closer to the Jake Dolan studios, they hit traffic. At first Ellison thought this was an unfortunate coincidence, and unusual for a Sunday, but he saw people on foot, to their left and right, all heading in the same direction they were. He finally realized what was happening. He said, "I feel like I'm heading to a concert. Are all these people coming to see Jake Dolan?"

"Yes."

He watched the people clutching their jackets, enduring the cold. "Are there always this many?"

"Always."

"Can his building even hold this many?"

The driver checked his watch. He said, "No. None of these people here will make the cut off; they just don't know it yet."

"How sad," said Ellison.

The driver didn't know whether Ellison meant it was sad that they wouldn't get in or sad they wanted in so badly. He said, "Every Sunday."

Ellison pushed the button to raise the divider between him and the driver and quickly changed out of his windbreaker and into his blazer. When they were close enough to catch a glimpse of the studio, he saw a line of people that stretched out around the block. He remembered his description to Davies of an *anti-church*. If ever he had wanted a real life exemplar of that concept, he was seeing it now.

When they made it inside, a young hipster armed with a clipboard met Ellison at the door and introduced himself as Felix. Felix wore all black, including his black ear piece.

"How are you today?" Ellison asked.

"Running behind," said Felix as he rushed Ellison straight to the makeup chair.

The young lady who did his makeup had to work double-time, but she seemed undaunted by the pressure. She was polite and professional and chipper. When the clipboard man walked away, she leaned in close to Pastor Ellison and whispered. "I'm a Christian."

Ellison was struck by the way she glanced over her shoulder. It reminded him of the stories he always heard about dissidents in Soviet Russia, where parents would fear that even their children would hear. He whispered back, "That's wonderful. Why are we whispering?"

She said, "Have you ever actually *watched* the Jake Dolan Show?"

"Yes."

"Have you watched it recently?"

"No."

"Half his shows lately have been about you!"

He laughed. "That's okay. Half my sermons are about him!"

Ellison could hear that the show had already started. The distant sound of Jake Dolan's monolog could be heard reverberating against the walls, interspersed with laughter and applause from his audience.

"Pastor, I respect what you're trying to do, but..." she hesitated.

"But what?"

"But you shouldn't have come onto this show."

"If your objective is to heal the sick, sometimes you have to go to the leper colonies."

The lady shook her head. She said, "I understand trying to get your message to the other side. I understand talking to one's enemies, but—"

"They're not my enemies."

"Fine, maybe your *opponents* then. I understand all that, but what's the point if no one will even listen? What's the point if all they do is mock?

These people sure do believe that you're *their* enemy, just remember that."

He said, "Well, then I'll just have to show them otherwise."

She had no response to that. In their shared silence, they could make out the distinct words from Jake Dolan, "Pastor Ellison claims that with faith the size of a mustard seed, he can move a mountain... I don't think faith the size of a mountain could move a mustard seed!"

The audience laughed.

"I don't know, maybe he should've started with something like a molehill."

They laughed again.

"I mean this is the type of guy who sends money to deposed Nigerian Princes."

The audience laughed even harder.

"It's not Pastor Ellison's fault, though. I have recently learned that the ancient Greek word for *mountain* can also refer to one's bowels. But... um... you don't need faith for those to move. I will say that after that time I drank the water in Mexico, this atheist actually found himself praying. I will spare you the details, but just tell you... *God is good, my friends. God is good!*"

The hairstylist rolled her eyes and shook her head. "It always comes back to excrement with him," she sighed, hating her job. She finished with the makeup, pulled the tree skirt off Ellison's chest and said somberly, "Good luck."

Ellison smiled confidently and said, "God Bless."

When they returned from the commercials, the band bumpered them back in and the camera zoomed in on Jake Dolan's face. He said, "Our first guest truly needs no introduction..." he paused for effect. "... at least not with this audience." They laughed. "Pastor Riley Ellison is here with us tonight." When Jake Dolan heard the stray boos, he added, "And he's a good sport, so let's all give him a Jake Dolan show welcome!" he called out as the band played and he stood up.

As Ellison stepped stridently onto the stage, the crowd began to boo. There was so much booing that Dolan wished he hadn't phrased it as a "Jake Dolan show welcome."

Ellison and Dolan shook hands in the center of the stage. When they made their way to their seats, the booing had finally quieted, so Jake Dolan turned to his audience and chastised them, "C'mon, now, that's not nice." No one knew—possibly not even Jake Dolan—if he was being facetious.

The audience laughed anyway.

"It's no problem," Ellison put up a hand to hamper Jake Dolan's rebuke. "I knew what I'd be walking into. I'm happy to be here."

"Okay," Dolan said turning back to Ellison, "So let's talk. Let's *reason together.*"

Ellison smiled at the Biblical reference. "You're trying to butter me up now!"

Jake Dolan laughed. He said, "Enjoy it while you can."

The audience laughed at the ominous warning.

"Yes, sir."

"Actually, I've been rather nervous meeting you." Dolan turned to his audience, "No, I really have."

"Really, why's that?"

"Well, I'm afraid that you might be the one to convert me to Christianity." The audience laughed and Dolan continued with perfect dryness. "Many have tried before—all of them failed—but I just think *you'll* be the one to tell me that one little thing I just haven't thought of yet. After all, we just heard from one of your head pastors that you are perfect."

Ellison tilted his head back, thunderstruck. He scrunched his brow and looked at the studio around him as if he had walked on the wrong stage. He said incredulously, "Wait a minute, you're—You're *not* a Christian?"

Dolan smiled politely. Ellison had matched his dry sarcasm expertly, and it took all Dolan's strength not to laugh out loud. He didn't want to hand Ellison any victory this early in the interview. Moving on, he said, "So, you've told the press that you're going to move a mountain."

"Yes, sir."

"And you say that it is God who is telling you to do this?"

The audience laughed.

"Yes, sir."

"So... why are you doing this?" Leading up to this moment, Jake Dolan had planned on asking Ellison, flippantly, "What are you thinking?" or "What on earth's the matter with you?" but when he came face to face with the very affable and polite pastor, the line ended up being only "Why are you doing this?" The audience laughed as if he actually had used one of the more aggressive lines.

Ellison drew in a long breath. "I'm doing it because deep in my heart I know that good conquers evil. Christ rose from the dead. I see a suffering world that needs saving and I know that Jesus is the way to salvation. I see problems that are impossible to solve, and pain that is impossible to heal, but I know through Him all things are possible."

"Okay, *Pastor,* I'm so glad you got your message out. You feel better now that my audience heard that?" he snipped.

"I do." Ellison smiled.

"Okay, but I can hear what my viewers are all yelling at their TV sets. They're saying, 'What do you know about suffering? *Mister Perfect*, what could you possibly know about real pain?'"

The audience applauded wildly. It was the type of applause heard when a boxer delivers the first solid blow in round one.

Pastor Ellison didn't wait for their applause to die down. He pointed to his shoulder. "You see this shoulder? You know how many alcoholics have cried—*literally*—on this shoulder? Because I do. Forty-Seven. Do you see this phone?" He pulled out the phone from his jacket pocket. "Do you know how many phone calls I get in the middle of the night from men who are going through a painful divorce, or women whose men have left them, or wives whose husbands have cheated on them? An average of two a week, more around the holidays. And I don't mind. Helping people makes me lose sleep, but not helping them would make me lose more." Ellison put his phone back in his pocket, then held out his hands. "You see these hands? These hands have had the privilege of holding the hands of women who have been raped, children who have been abused, men who have been abandoned, teens who are contemplating suicide, of drug addicts, of sex addicts, of manic-depressives, of borderlines, of people who cut themselves, of porn addicts, of porn stars, of strippers, of prostitutes, of murderers, of thieves, of gang bangers.

"I can tell you a lot about suffering, because I meet the wretched where they are; that's the only way to help them. I find them curled up behind the garbage, shivering, dirty and hungry. The alley is dark like you'd expect, it's cold like you expect, but it's not secluded; the thing you may not expect to discover about this alley is the parade passing by."

"What parade?"

"*Your* parade. They get to watch your parade. The wretched get to read the signs promoting slogans that don't help. They get to see the faces of the do-gooders, all those who are so anxious to help and so anxious to save the world, but who are afraid to step into the alley.

"And that's honestly why I need your help," Ellison continued. "I'm exhausted frankly. I want to help as many people as I can, but it's exhausting walking against the parade. I'm not loud enough. I'm not bold enough. I'm short on charisma. So, honestly, I've come to ask for your help."

"My help?"

"Yes! Of course. Because, you see, these people I mentioned who are suffering... I think you care about them too."

The audience was completely silent.

Dolan looked off. He raised his head in order to bring it down forcefully in an affirmative nod, just as a man draws his arm back preparing to throw a ball.

The nod was cut off and Dolan's face remained perfectly uncommitted. He said, "But won't the mountain take care of all that?" The audience laughed. Dolan hadn't said much and the people were impatient for a laugh line. "Why would you need my help when you've got *God's* help?" The audience laughed again. They were indulging deeply now in what they'd come here to see. "After the mountain moves, won't we all be in the streets shouting Hosanna and banging our tambourines?"

Pastor Ellison looked down. When the laughter quieted, he said solemnly, "No." He smiled and added, "I'm actually no longer sure what difference it will make, if any."

"See, that's interesting. How could it possibly make no difference?"

"Because you can't reason people out of that which they weren't reasoned into. Most of the time, people just believe what they are comfortable believing. They arrive at the conclusion first, then look only for specific arguments that support it, and no further."

Jake Dolan perked up. "That's the exact line I use against Christians!"

The audience laughed.

"That might be where I got it." Ellison said it so affably that he drew a few unauthorized laughs from the well-trained audience. He asked Dolan, "So what about you? What will you believe when the mountain moves?"

"I won't believe anything because it won't move."

The audience laughed.

"Well, *if* it did?"

"Well, what will you do when it doesn't?"

"I asked you first."

"If it did, I would probably start repenting of my sins, immediately." The audience laughed although Dolan wasn't joking.

"You mean that?"

"Well of course. If you ask a mountain to move... in the name of Jesus..."

The audience laughed at the name Jesus the way a more mature audience would laugh at the word *fart*. It embarrassed Jake Dolan, who had already decided he would be cordial. Dolan was an intelligent man who could put hijinks aside, but what he was discovering he could not do was escape his own audience. He continued despite the laughter, "... and then lo and behold, the mountain actually moved. Well I don't know how anyone could deny Christianity after that."

"Now that's interesting," Ellison repeated Dolan's line. He added, "You'd have to quit this show of course."

"I imagine I would. Keep in mind, I don't think it will move, but I think it would be too momentous to just ignore."

"Well you still haven't said it."

"Said what?"

"If the mountain moves, I, Jake Dolan will believe in God."

"If the mountain moves, I, Jake Dolan will believe in God," Jake Dolan parroted back to him, then added, "And quit this show." Ellison noticed it was the first thing Jake Dolan said to which the audience failed to respond at all. They were eerily silent. Jake Dolan put up his hand to hamper any independent thoughts his audience might have been thinking. He said, "No really, I can tell you that I personally would believe." He was puffed up with his open-mindedness, but only Ellison could see it. "And I can say that with such certainty because I know it won't move."

The audience fell back in line and did what the applause sign told them to do.

"Now you never answered me, what will you do when it doesn't move?"

"Okay, I guess, *if* it doesn't move, I'd have to give up on God and close down my church." Ellison added, "I can say that because I know it will."

"You will? You'll give up your church?"

"Yes."

"What about your book?"

"I'll kill it. I'll take it off the market."

"What about the members of your church? What will you tell them?"

Dolan seemed to want to push this point, so Ellison leveled with him, "Listen, I'm dug in here, you can see that. If this mountain doesn't move, you won't have to worry about Riley Ellison anymore. You won't have to worry about what I say to anyone, because no one, *no one,* will be listening. If this mountain doesn't move, I will sully not only my good name, but—" He hadn't realized he was repeating the lines Brandon Davies had planted in his head. His voice nearly cracked when he considered the gravity of what it meant. "—but His." Something about saying it out loud with his own voice made Ellison more deeply appreciate the solemnity. Out of a sense of duty, he made himself repeat the whole thought, "I will be the man who single-handedly destroys Christianity as we know it."

"And you will personally forsake God?"

It took one deep breath for him to regain control of his voice. He said sincerely, "I think I have faith the size of a mustard seed. People around the entire world believe I have faith the size of a mustard seed. So if the mountain doesn't move, I will have—" He didn't mean to but he stalled again. "—not that it's my goal. I believe the promises of Scripture. But if somehow the mountain doesn't move..."

"You will have disproved the Bible." Jake Dolan finished for him.

"I will have disproved *one part* of the Bible."

"But that's problematic."

"It is."

"And you will personally forsake God?" Dolan pressed again.

"I think I'd have to."

"So no matter what happens, this time on January 17, we'll see eye to eye on religion!"

Ellison laughed. He thought about it. "Now, that *would* take a miracle!"

Chapter Five

January 6—Ten days left

The strip club was dark. Stepping into the caliginous club from the bright sunlight was too perfectly symbolic to escape Pastor Ellison's attention. The woman at the front counter smiled at him and asked for twenty dollars, but he just presented his VIP card. Ellison noted the strange psychological phenomenon—the club was anathema to everything he valued most sacred, yet it still felt good to flash the card and be waved through.

He tried his best to check the stages for Poison without letting any of the sights there enter into his memory. She wasn't on stage. He felt some thin, feminine fingers trace an affectionate line across his shoulders and back. He turned to see the source of this affection, but the source had stepped playfully in the opposite direction of his turn, eluding him for a moment more.

He heard a woman's voice saying, "Just look what we have here!"

Ellison quickly turned the other way and caught a sight of Ecstasy with her fingers seductively stroking his arm. He was surprised to find that she wasn't a woman, but just a girl. *Just a child.* He tried to think back to when he was a teenager, he didn't remember girls looking so young—or so pretty for that matter. He couldn't believe that the bedizened young beauty in front of him was possibly eighteen yet.

"Hi, sexy, you looking for some company or what?" Ecstasy said.

Pain struck Ellison's heart—that old familiar feeling of abject helplessness returned to him. It was the shared emotion that Charles Brandt had expressed so poignantly, "I look at the problems, which are so enormous, and then I look at my puny arms; I know I am not strong enough." He struggled in that second to find a logical reason why he should be seeking out Poison at all. Could he be certain that she needed help more than this pintsized seductress before his eyes?

Ecstasy still waited for a response.

Ellison deftly said, "Uh..."

They heard an unwelcoming voice behind them. "What are you doing here?"

Ellison turned to see Poison glowering at him. She took her eyes off him just long enough to shoot the same menacing expression at Ecstasy, who rolled her eyes but quickly made herself scarce.

"I came to apologize," Ellison said. "Can we head to the back and talk?"

"No. Get out of here."

"I'm sorry that I didn't listen to you. I'm sorry I didn't make more time for you."

"I don't want you coming here."

"Did you call the center?"

"No." Her eyes averted. "I'm going to do it today." She said it with the same insincere emptiness as her first promise.

"I'd like to talk to him. I'd like to help."

"You had your chance for that."

"Can we go see him now?"

"I'm working."

"Can't you take a break?"

"My shift ends at five."

"I'll be waiting outside."

"No. We can't be seen leaving with clientele." She sighed. "Do you know where Bowman Street is?"

"Sure."

"I'm at the Bowman Point apartments there on the corner. Apartment 115."

"I'll be waiting there for you."

Pastor Ellison waited in his car. He kept the engine running so he could run the heat on full blast. He watched the doorway that led to her corner apartment as if he were on a stakeout. He was worried the capricious woman would, for some reason, try to back out.

Only one window in their apartment faced the side parking lot. Through the glass he saw a few empty beer bottles collected on the windowsill next to the back of a couple of picture frames. He imagined that was Poison's room—not because a wayward sixteen-year-old boy wouldn't have the alcohol, but wouldn't have the picture frames.

Under the bush by the front door was a large pile of mixed white and tan cigarette butts. Ellison figured one brand was Poison's and the other was Tyler's.

At 5:30, she still had not shown.

At 5:45, Pastor Ellison was surprised when he saw the door to the apartment opening from the inside. He sat up taller and tried to rouse his mind from its daydreaming. He saw a young man step out, wearing a long black coat. His hair was long and shaggy, but his goatee was thin and wiry. His eyes were successfully hidden behind his long black bangs. He was around sixteen years old, and he looked aimless.

Ellison already knew what he had stepped out there to do. The boy even *looked* like he smelled of smoke. Still undercover, the pastor watched Tyler's face, what he could actually see of it. He loved him. He remembered the pains of adolescence—the type of pain that you could drown in, and so many do. He knew what happens to people who have to go through that alone, with no guidance. The boy finished his cigarette and tossed the tan butt into the bushes.

But he isn't alone; he has his mother. He thought about how, for at least one moment in time, the mother reached out on the boy's behalf; she wouldn't cry out for herself, but she cried out for him.

He was thinking about how that small, aging, combustible stripper—who was so afraid of anyone regarding her as pathetic—was a bona fide hero, when he heard someone pounding on his window.

"Get out your stupid car," she yelled at him.

Pastor Ellison was a little bit surprised to see Poison wearing a pale purple set of hospital scrubs, but it wasn't very hard for him to figure out why.

The apartment was littered with dirty dishes and discarded clothes. When they walked through the door, they could hear music blaring from one of the bedrooms. The mom walked to the door and tried to open it, but it was locked. She knocked. "Tyler?" she called, but the music didn't turn off. "Tyler, there's someone here who'd like to talk to you." The music still didn't stop. "Tyler?" she asked again, but got no response.

"Tyler!" barked Ellison. He didn't mean to, but he subconsciously forced his voice an octave lower than usual. It worked and they heard the music switch off. There was a click that came from the lock, but no one opened the door.

Pastor Ellison tried the knob and entered the room. He surveyed his surroundings like a doctor getting his first chance to examine a sick patient. He could smell incense, which really meant that he could smell pot. That wasn't good news, but he could have already guessed that much.

The walls were covered with posters from various musical groups. Not one of them looked like they'd be good role models for an errant and intemperate youth. Not one of them looked like they sang about anything other than sex. The posters weren't encouraging, but could've been worse; he didn't see any raised fists, or images of Guy Fawkes. An aimless soul was one step closer to being saved than one invested in a destructive aim.

The pastor would have liked to see at least one book on the shelf, but the absence of books also meant the absence of Hitchens or Dawkins, or any other such purveyors of misery.

The worst things he spotted in the room were a couple of DVDs released by Jake Dolan. Ellison never underestimated the power of ridicule. No one wants to be laughed at and only the strong can stand up against it. The meanest people, therefore, will attract the weakest converts.

The thing that Ellison was most afraid of was his older brother's suicide. The pastor knew the best way to get someone to do something is to show them someone else doing it. He decided he better show this kid someone who is strong, confident, and loving. He said, "Pleased to meet you, Tyler. I'm Pastor Riley Ellison."

The boy was lying supine on the bed, slack like a stoner. His eyes were cloaked, hiding in darkness. He didn't shake the pastor's hand, but his body did tense up, defensively. He looked at his mother, then at the pastor, then at his mother. He shot her an indignant look. Something in the boy's mind really did understand the gravity of that moment. He knew for the first time that he would not have an unobstructed slide into ruin—the kind his mother had allowed his brother to have—and he resented it.

"What's Mister Perfect doing here?" the boy snapped at his mother.

From the look on Poison's face, she clearly didn't understand the reference. Ellison instantly concluded that Poison never kept up with the news, but her son did. This meant that the boy actually knew more about the man standing in his room than the one who had brought him.

"Your mother is concerned about you. She loves you and we want to help."

The boy didn't move. His face turned beet red, not from embarrassment, but from anger. The pastor could recognize the color; it was the type of anger he only ever found in someone he was trying to help.

Ellison said, "I don't believe there is any pain on Earth that hurts as much as a parent losing a child."

"You leave my brother out of this."

"I wasn't talking about your brother; I was talking about you."

"She hasn't lost me."

"What about your father?" Ellison was very quick to amend, "I mean your heavenly Father; has He lost you?"

"What? Go away, dude."

"I came here to tell you just one thing: God loves you. He loves you in ways that you could never imagine. He loves you with a perfect love that knows no bounds. He loves you and he wants to be in your life. When His child doesn't know Him, He aches for that child. He yearns for that child. Because when a soul is separated from God, it hurts Him just as much as when a mother loses her son."

Tyler breathed in deep. He had been postponing the need to take this man seriously at all. He had been hoping he would go away. Finally, he said, "Listen, man, you're just talking gibberish to me. I don't go in for all that Bible stuff, so find another field to plant your *crazy tree*."

Ellison laughed. The kid was colorful. He said warmly, "I'm here to help. Are you in need of help?"

"No."

"We're all in need of some help."

"You don't get it! There's no way you can help me." The boy challenged him, "There is nothing you can offer me. You can't promise me heaven; I don't believe in heaven. You can't offer me God; I don't believe in Him."

"There is something I can offer you..."

"Try it."

"... something that you will believe, one sentence which, as soon as you hear it, you will instantly recognize it for what it is: truth."

Tyler laughed. "Go ahead. Hit me with your best shot!"

"None of this, your life, my life, these people, this world, is *it*."

Tyler waited.

Pastor Ellison pressed forward. His voice raised slightly in insistence, a tone that mocked any opposition to a statement so obvious, "It isn't it! It's not the point. It's not all there is. You were right when you said that school doesn't matter. You were right when you said your grades don't matter." Tyler wasn't expecting a pastor to say these things. "You were right when you said money doesn't matter." Ellison had never actually heard Tyler say any of this, though Tyler mistakenly assumed he'd received the information from his mother. "They don't matter, Tyler. Not ultimately. A part of you has tuned into that. But I wonder if you have yet discovered what actually does matter."

Ellison stayed silent. He would not say another word until Tyler said something first.

Tyler stood up to leave. He mumbled, "This is whack!"

Pastor Ellison knew not to press it further. Tyler wasn't a battle that would be won today. He was there only to make a connection and, believe it or not, he felt he'd made it. A heavy hand at that point was only liable to break it. As Tyler was stepping around the pastor to leave, Ellison placed his card on the boy's dresser. He said, "This is my church. I'm there all week, not just on Sundays. My cell number's on the back."

Before Tyler had reached the door, he impetuously turned back to look Ellison in the face. He stepped forward aggressively and ranted, "I tell you what? I've got an idea. Would you like to hear my idea?" the boy taunted. He mockingly lifted his face upward and said, "Hey, God, if You're really there, show me a sign." Tyler looked around. Nothing at all in their immediate environment had changed.

Ellison stood quietly, patiently enduring the child's theatrics.

"Seriously, dude," Tyler continued, still addressing God. "I'll believe in You, if You show me a sign." He laughed scornfully and looked at Ellison. "So much for your God!"

Ellison silently shook his head. "It doesn't work that way."

"Are you kidding me? I thought you said He loved me. I thought you said that losing a soul to Him is as painful as a mother losing a child. Well, what kind of mother would let her child die if she had the chance to stop it? So, let me ask again, all-powerful God—You can do something to show me You exist. Then You don't have to lose me! Just show me a sign!"

Again the boy looked around melodramatically.

Ellison's face was patient and understanding, like he was trying to correct a child who had miscalculated a very complex math problem. He repeated, "It doesn't work that way."

"No! No!" Tyler shouted, pointing. "No, that isn't fair. I won't let you get away with that, because you know who told me it *does* work that way? You know where I got that idea from? From you! You told me it works that way; remember *Mead Mountain*? I got that idea from you!"

The words hit the pastor like a slap to the face. The proud role of veteran teacher slipped through his fingers and Pastor Ellison truly had no answer. He, for the first time in his entire career, couldn't think of anything effective to say. He'd been completely bested by this pot-smoking twerp. He mumbled, "I hope you receive the sign you're asking for."

"Well, I won't hold my breath," the boy huffed as he walked out the door. From the parking lot, they could hear the rev of a motorcycle. The engine sounded badly in need of repair, but from the sound of it, worked well enough to speed through the parking lot and out of earshot.

Chapter Six

January 7—Nine days left

June Rucker opened her eyes. The clock read 6:47. It was the exact same time she first looked at the clock the morning before, and the morning before that.

Same time. Same bed. Same beeping monitor. Same tubes hooked up to my body. Her hopes that one day she would wake up anywhere on Earth besides that hospice ward were dwindling. An old, attenuated hand reached to turn on the lamp and June could scarcely believe it was her own.

Her compact was right where she had left it, so she grabbed it and flipped it open. She started to apply her eyeliner, the same way she did everyday—careful not to wear it *old lady style*. Then she brushed her lashes with dark mascara, before applying lipstick and conservatively applying a hint of blush.

She had no reason to believe that anyone would be in to see her today; the overwhelming odds were against it. Anyone would have forgiven her for not getting made up just to *literally* lie in bed all day. But she might not have forgiven herself.

She had just turned on the radio to listen to the news when she heard footsteps. She couldn't see who was coming, but when she saw that pair of old sneakers, she knew. It was her son, Colton Rucker.

Colton was sober. He had shaved and at least made some attempt to fix his hair. If Pastor Ellison could have seen him now, he would've scarcely believed this was the same man who'd challenged him to a lively drinking contest just a few nights before.

He drew back the curtain and swooshed in close for a warm hug. He presented her with a box of chocolates and pulled a stool up to the side of her bed.

"Colton, I wasn't expecting you today."

"I was in the neighborhood."

"With chocolates?"

Colton laughed. "Yeah, that's why I was in the neighborhood."

She smiled and reached over to turn the radio off.

He said, "Glad to see you're enjoying the radio."

"Oh yes!" she said, humoring his self-serving remark. She added,

"You're a good boy, Colton."

"I'm thirty-seven," Colton laughed.

June looked at her son. No, he wasn't thirty-seven; he was still a boy. He was still reaching up to hold her hand in the church parking lot. He was still tugging persistently at her apron, wanting to be picked up.

She looked at the radio. "Speaking of good boys..." Her voice was young and strong. "Have you heard about this pastor who says he will move a mountain?"

"Yes, ma'am, I've heard."

She smiled. "What a courageous man. I really respect what he's doing, but—Oh, I just wish he wouldn't wait so long."

"Really, why's that?" His mind pieced it together a moment too late; now he wished he hadn't asked.

"So I could be around to see it."

"You'll be around," he shot back reflexively.

"We need more men like him," she said.

Colton didn't respond. He was having a hard time staying mad at Pastor Ellison after two strange women knocked on his door yesterday with buckets of cleaning supplies and said, "We heard that you two have your hands full with a baby. We're hoping you'd allow us to clean your house."

"Yeah, he's all right." Colton smiled contemplatively. "Hailey attends his congregation."

"What was that?" Sometimes Colton would forget his aged and ailing mother was so hard of hearing.

He repeated louder, "Hailey and I attend his congregation."

"Really?" Her eyes lit up. "Have you spent much time with him?"

Few, desaturated memories of their last encounter remained in Colton's head. He said, "Yeah, we hung out last week and did some shots."

"Oh Colton!" his mom laughed. "You shouldn't joke."

This time Colton was wise enough not to ask for clarification. He knew exactly why she said he "shouldn't joke." He wondered if he could move on from the mess he'd just made without a lecture.

"You know it's in your blood," she quickly added.

Here it comes.

"You know your father never had a single vice. Do you know that man flossed his teeth every day?"

"You've mentioned it."

Tears unpredictably filled June's eyes. She had been able to talk about her husband without crying for many years. She had offered her son this same niggling admonition with dry eyes countless times, but today was inexplicably different. "Then he started drinking and just couldn't stop." She used the back of her knuckle to wipe the tears. "Your father was a great man. He was a great man; I just hope you can remember that far back. It was the alcohol that changed him. You can't judge a whole life just on a few years of weakness."

Colton felt horrible that he had just been acting dismissive; it was not only bad manners, it was bad cover. He grabbed her hand. He looked into her eyes and said, "Mom, I'm never going to drink. Don't you know what Hailey would do to me if she caught me drinking?" He laughed.

"You have a little girl to look after, now."

"I have two little girls to look after. I know that."

"You taking those sweet girls to church?"

"Yes ma'am. Mead Mountain Church, every Sunday."

"Did you—" her mind was sparked. She began to ask if he had heard about that pastor who promised to move a mountain. "Oh," she patted his hand, "that's right. You're a good boy, Colton."

"I'm thirty-seven."

She let out a long sigh, ignoring his response. She said, "Oh... I sure hope I live to see that mountain move."

Dallas stood on the corner of Fifth and Oak. She hated trying to work in this type of weather. The only warm clothes she had covered too much of her body to attract any clients. As a result, she was not dressed in warm clothes.

She noticed a certain Toyota Corolla. She knew this car had already passed by three times before. She smiled because she knew she had a bite. The driver had been casing the block, scanning for cops, and trying to get his courage up. She knew this life too well; nothing surprised her anymore.

She waited for the taillights. Then the reverse lights. She approached the passenger-side window, but the driver had parked and stepped out of the car. He didn't seem to mind the fact that it was raining. He shook her hand, which was a little odd.

"What's your name?" he asked.

"Dallas," she told him.

"So, are you, uh, working tonight?" he asked clumsily.

"Trying to. You looking for some company?"

"Actually, ma'am, I was looking for a prostitute."

She laughed, although she couldn't tell if he was kidding. She said, "You got a place?"

"I have a room at the Four Seasons, just down the street. I can drive us."

"It'll cost you."

"How much?"

"It's two hundred for an hour, six hundred for the whole night."

Pastor Ellison's heart broke. Ethically speaking, selling one's self for five million dollars was no more virtuous than selling one's self for five dollars, but there was still a part of Ellison that wished she'd said, "all the money in the world," or "prove yourself to me," or "prove your love for me," or even, "respect," or "love," or best of all, "marriage." But she said two hundred dollars.

"I think I'm going to have to go for the full night. How long do you think you can stay awake?"

She laughed, again not sure if it was a joke. "You're funny. Let's go."

There was no conversation in the car. Pastor Ellison turned on the heat for Dallas, and Dallas indolently helped herself to his stereo. She couldn't help but notice all his presets were set to Christian Rock, gospel stations, and Christian talk radio. She scanned the dial and found some Hip Hop.

Pastor Ellison couldn't help but think about Poison. He said, "Doesn't it bother you that this genre of music is so disrespectful to women?"

In lieu of an answer, she flippantly scoffed, "Genre?"

After that she clammed up.

Ellison wanted to continue to try to break the ice, so he asked, "So, why's it been so cold lately? I thought it was supposed to be sunny in these parts year-round."

Dallas stared out the window vacuously. She had no reaction. She made no motion that indicated she had even heard him. Finally, without turning her head to the pastor, she said, "It's global warming."

They didn't say another word until they got to his room.

Inside the room, she asked, "So what are you into?"

"What's on the menu?"

She said, "Well, some of my clients like..." She described a variety of sex acts. For most of it, Pastor Ellison could follow along, although there were a few new slang phrases he'd never heard before.

His cheeks flushed red. He said, "I don't want you to do any of that." He pulled out six hundreds, then reached back in and pulled out seven. "I'm going to pay you for the night, but instead of... what you usually do, I want you to listen to me tell you about Jesus Christ."

Dallas's eyes bulged large. She was wrong about having no surprises left.

He reiterated, "Six hundred for the night, plus a small tip."

"Wait. Is this for real?"

"Completely for real."

"What's your game?"

"No game."

"Is this a joke?"

"No joke."

She looked at the money. She picked it up and held it between her finger and thumb. Finally she put it back down and said, "No, I don't think so."

"I'm completely serious. No tricks."

"I don't think so," she repeated.

Ellison was nonplused. "So, wait, are you really telling me that you would rather..." He tried to repeat some of the slang terms, not certain that he got them right. "You'd rather do *that* than talk about Jesus?"

"You don't even know what that is."

"I'm pretty sure I could guess."

She shrugged. "It's part of the job."

"It doesn't have to be, not tonight."

"Yeah, I'm going to go," she said as she grabbed her purse.

Ellison was becoming more distraught. "What I have to tell you could change your entire life, *or* it'd be just some quick cash, but you'd get to keep your clothes on. So why not? Why not?"

"I don't know. It's... *weird*." She got up and walked out the door.

He opened his door and called after her, "At least let me drive you back?"

She gave him a look that said, *Are you kidding?* Her hand made a sweeping gesture presenting the luxurious hotel. She said, "I've got work to do."

Chapter Seven

January 8—Eight days left

The next time Andrew Crenshaw was able to meet with Pastor Ellison, it was in his office. There was something welcoming about the church. Sitting in Ellison's office, he really felt at home. However, he was a little surprised to detect the faint trace of cigarette smoke that still hung in the air.

Andrew saw a chessboard off to the side of the room, where it appeared a game had been interrupted. Only, there was a thin layer of dust on the pieces. He also saw the framed twenty and the geology texts on his shelf. He was trying to decide which to ask about first. He said, "So, how long have you been interested in geology?"

"Oh, many years now. My commitment to God has led to a fascination with His creation. I'm aware that it usually happens in the reverse order."

"Reverse order?"

"Sometimes when people commune with nature, they find God."

"Oh," Andrew nodded. He added, "But sometimes, when people really love nature, it leads them away from God."

Ellison smiled at his keen observation. "This is true, but those are typically the ones who claim to love nature and never step outside."

Andrew laughed. He turned his head west, eyeing the mountain in his mind. He said to the pastor, "I respect what you are trying to do, but... don't you think that it's crazy?"

Ellison smiled. His voice rose to a comical pitch. "Oh yeah, I think it's crazy. I'm going to ask a mountain to move and it will move. That's crazy." He rubbed his head pantomiming a stress migraine.

Andrew laughed. "Okay, just so we're clear." With Ellison's hand on his forehead, Andrew noticed the string around his finger again. He said, "So, you never told me about the string on your finger."

"Oh yes, I guess I forgot!" Ellison smiled proudly.

Andrew actually said the words, "Buh Dum Bum."

Ellison smiled. "Well, yes, you were right. I am trying to always remember something. I'm trying to remember Christ loved me enough to suffer and die for me. And because of his sacrifice I will live in the presence of God forever."

Andrew Crenshaw gave an odd chuckle. He questioned, "Are you really in danger of forgetting that?"

"Oh yes. Very serious danger. I seem to forget it all the time."

"How could you forget something like that?"

"How could I?"

"Right, how could you?"

"How could any of us?" injected Ellison.

"Well, how could we?

Ellison enunciated each word slowly, "How could we?" He gave a resigned nod. His tone seemed to indicate they had resolved a long deliberation in which Andrew wasn't sure he even participated.

Andrew laughed impatiently. He insisted, "I am the one asking you. How could you forget that? It doesn't seem like a thing a person would forget."

"Do you want to know my favorite part of the Bible? It's when the Israelites made a golden calf. There they were in the desert; God had just led them out of slavery; God had parted the Red Sea so they could pass; God had provided them manna from heaven; and then after all that, *after all that,* the second Moses turns his back, they break God's commandments."

"Why?" Mostly Crenshaw asked because he knew it was the response Ellison wanted.

"Because we are human. Because denying God seems to be the very thing we are most specifically equipped to do. So, we learn that Christ died for us; He stood in our place and paid the price for our sins. That's extraordinary! We learn we're going to live forever; what could be bigger news than that? The feeling of gratitude overwhelms us, then what do we do? We sing a couple of praise hymns, recite a few lines of Scripture... and then return to our lives and forget."

"Even you?"

"Even me." Ellison nodded. "How could we forget something like that?" Ellison asked one last time and shrugged. "On the other hand, how could we *not* forget? How could we remember something that every sensation, every breath, every second of this corporeal world of illusion is designed to make us forget? This world takes its toll... and the cost of living is usually our faith.

"But it's important that we do remember, because our moments are not divided up between pleasure and pain, but between faith and doubt. Joy is the abundance of faith and sorrow is the lack thereof. Think about it; how could it not be so? When we truly accept the idea of eternal life, even for as little as our finite minds can grasp eternity, then why should we ever despair about anything? Because we forget. We turn away."

Andrew raised his eyebrow and nodded his head. He sat for a pensive moment and then asked aggressively, "When do I get to see the dirt on you?"

"Dirt?" Ellison smiled.

"When do I get to see the skeletons in your closet? Or would you really have me believe that you're Mister Perfect?" There was a hostility in Andrew's tone, running afoul of his growing affection for the pastor.

Ellison laughed, ignoring the tone. "Yeah, we've been giving Davies a hard time about that remark around here. I think he was guilty of a little hyperbole."

"I don't. I think he meant every word," Andrew's tone only grew colder. "I saw his interview and, well... he's headed for a hard time. Because I've looked up to men before. I've found heroes before and... " He trailed off. "Right now Brandon Davies actually believes you're the man you appear to be. He thinks you're the real deal."

"And you don't?" There was no defensiveness in Pastor Ellison's voice.

"I never believe that anyone is as they seem."

"How awful."

"Well, occupational hazard."

"Yes, I can imagine."

The silence was beckoning Ellison to raise a new subject. Andrew Crenshaw gave every indication that he didn't want to talk about it, but Ellison knew a handy trick to make sure; he simply said to himself, *Wait. Shut up and wait.*

Sure enough, Andrew had more to say after all. He said, "My father interviewed Benjamin Mead once. This was toward the end of his news career. I had already decided that I wanted a career in news, so I asked if I could tag along. I didn't know who *Congressman* Mead was, but he was favored for the California seat in the US Senate, so that seemed interesting enough."

"That was a long time ago."

"Yeah, I was seventeen years old," Andrew confirmed. "So this was before his first term in the Senate."

"And before he won his Nobel Prize," added Ellison.

"So anyway, they both sit down on some fancy set and they turn the cameras on. I don't remember everything that was said, but I do remember thinking, *I've never seen anyone treat my father with such disrespect.* He was impudent and just plain *rude.* So when the interview was over, and the snake left, I asked my father, 'Why'd you let him get away with that? He can't treat you that way.' You know what my father said? He looked me in the eye and said, 'Son, he is a great man.'"

Pastor Ellison whistled the word, "Whew!"

"Yeah, and when they'd finally aired the interview, the station had edited out all the rude stuff. They just took out a pair of scissors and cut around it."

"What'd your Dad say about that?"

"Take a guess."

"Politics," said Ellison.

Andrew nodded. "I decided right then and there I would never allow myself to consider anyone a 'great man.' I decided to never look up to anyone because all people do is let you down. As soon as you think you've discovered real virtue in this world, they'll do something to spit on your high hopes, and you'll find out they've just been edited the whole time."

Ellison let out another whistle. He asked, "What about your father?"

"What about him?"

"Well, he was clearly wrong on Benjamin Mead. And, if you don't mind me saying so, it's no secret I think he was wrong on God; I doubt his wisdom, not his probity. He was surely someone who wouldn't spit on your respect for him. He was the real deal."

"Yeah," Andrew gave a tepid nod. "Yeah, you're right."

Andrew Crenshaw's cell phone buzzed. He looked down to read the lengthy text in silence. Finally, he looked up and said gloomily, "Gotta go."

"More breaking news?" Ellison smiled.

This time Andrew made no attempts to hide the news from him; it was more grist for his mill. He said, "Our California Attorney General is claiming Governor Norwood appointed her in exchange for sex."

Ellison just rubbed his forehead.

Andrew Crenshaw lifted his phone gently, as if he were making a silent toast to his own jaded worldview. He turned to leave.

Chapter Eight

January 9—Seven days left

Pastor Ellison was back on the streets. The only upside to the drizzling weather was that it made it easier to spot the prostitutes. It was a tough night for those whose jobs depended on them being bare. He had just circled his car three times when he pulled up next to a young lady underdressed on the corner.

She approached his car and he got out to shake her hand.

The handshake made her smile, and it was a smile that deeply touched Riley Ellison. He saw great intelligence behind her eyes, but what struck him most was what he didn't see.

So many girls in *the life* wore their destitution behind their eyes. It was a silent howling for dreams long forgotten. It pained, but never discouraged, Ellison to see it; Jesus could always cure destitution.

This young lady before him, however, showed nothing of the sort, and it thrilled Ellison to think she may be new to this game. Perhaps the life she once dreamed of had not yet been forgotten. Perhaps her mind was not yet haunted by the type of *Nightmare Man* that Poison tried daily to forget.

It thrilled Ellison to imagine what she could become—lifted up from the mire—and the blessings her life would bestow onto others.

The feeling so overpowered Ellison that he had to resist expressing all the thoughts that were flooding his mind. Finally, he focused on the one sentiment that would not tip his hand too soon. He said, "You're beautiful."

She attempted a coquettish laugh, but it came out overly-staged.

The laugh grated on Ellison, and he felt like he couldn't wait another second for the moment when he could explain to her the exact meaning of *You're beautiful.* What *he* meant when he said it. And what Jesus meant.

He asked, "So, are you, uh, working tonight?"

"You looking for some company?"

"Actually, ma'am, I was looking for a prostitute." He thought he was just so funny.

"Really?"

"Yes, I was hoping you could quote me a price for the whole night back at my place."

"Your place?" she asked impishly. "How about my place?"

Ellison wasn't expecting that. He asked curiously, "Where's your place?"

She said, "County Jail."

There was a brief empty second in which neither of them moved. An ironic smile crossed Ellison's lips. He smiled because there was nothing else left to do.

The lady pulled out her handcuffs and proceeded to say, "You have the right to remain silent. Anything you choose to say, can and will be used against you in a court of law." An unmarked car from down the street pulled toward them. The driver rolled down the window and placed a flashing red and blue light on the roof.

Within seconds, they had cuffed Pastor Ellison and lowered his head into the back seat.

It was beginning to rain harder as the arresting officer delivered Pastor Ellison in handcuffs from the police cruiser to the receiving area of the San Diego County jail. Once inside, Ellison was led over to a gray cement wall and asked to stand behind a yellow line painted on the floor. There, another officer—in a mechanical, assembly line fashion—removed his handcuffs and asked him to place his feet on two painted footprints.

"Do you have any knives, blades, or needles on your person?" Officer Gonzales asked.

"No, sir," said Pastor Ellison.

This was the first time that Officer Gonzales looked straight at Ellison's face. There was a pause in his movements and a change in his eyes, but he showed no emotion. He said, "I need you to extend your arms out to the side for me."

"Yes, sir," Ellison said.

When Ellison extended his arms, Gonzales stepped forward to Ellison's side of the yellow line. He frisked him and removed his cell phone, car keys, and a single business card. He turned the phone off and slid the possessions into a manila envelope.

The officer then returned to the other side of the yellow line and ordered, "Please remove your belt, your shoe laces, and your jacket."

Pastor Ellison lowered himself down to the floor. It took some doing to remove his laces, which had been in place since he first bought the shoes. Then he stood up and removed his belt. He handed both to the officer and waited.

Officer Gonzales noticed that he had stopped moving, so he repeated. "I also need you to remove your jacket at this time, please."

"Sir, if it's all the same, I'd like to keep my jacket. I have poor blood circulation and I get very cold."

"I'm sorry, sir, I need you to remove your jacket."

Pastor Ellison didn't move. His expressions were morose when he asked out of desperation, "Isn't there someone I could talk to? Or maybe-"

"I need you to remove your jacket, sir; you don't want to be seen as non-compliant."

"Oh, I'm not being non-compliant. I just—"

The officer was beginning to get frustrated. He insisted, "I need the jacket, Pastor." The word *Pastor* came out of his mouth involuntarily. He had not been playing for effect, but somehow the tacit admission that he knew who Ellison was had stopped the debate.

Ellison sighed. He said sincerely, "Yes, sir," and proceeded to remove his red windbreaker. The cuffs of the windbreaker were elastic, so they each had to be pulled off by the opposite hand, lest the jacket be turned inside out. Ellison's movements were slow when he did this. Officer Gonzales stood by impassively and waited.

Once the jacket had been removed, Ellison extended it grimly to the officer. Officer Gonzales's formerly staunch expression changed quickly to unrestrained shock. He whispered the word, "Unbelievable."

Underneath Ellison's jacket, he had been wearing only a short-sleeved t-shirt, so he was forced to stand before the officer with both arms bare—a sight that for twenty-four years had only been witnessed by his wife. The officer blinked, incredulously, as if something were wrong with his eyes. Pastor Ellison's arms were covered wrist-to-shoulder with tattoos. Gonzales saw tribal symbols, Chinese characters, skulls, snakes, and naked women. He saw the image of Che Guevara and what was obviously a red Communist star peeking out from under his sleeve. He didn't mean to stare.

Pastor Ellison had no choice but to stand there patiently while Officer Gonzales got an eyeful. Finally, the officer handed the jacket straight back, looked over his shoulder and whispered. "I think it might be okay, Pastor, just this once."

"God bless you," the pastor said as he quickly re-donned the jacket.

Tyler felt like he couldn't take it anymore. Hidden on the top shelf of his closet was a bottle of Maker's Mark that he'd talked his friend's older brother into buying. He didn't want to open it because he was unsure where his mother went or when she would be home. But his eyes wouldn't leave the closet door.

It had been a particularly long week for Tyler. Wyatt had informed his mother that the strip club would be doing renovations and rudely told her not to return until he called her. She told Tyler that the hospital had cut her hours for the whole week because of some new regulation. Tyler pretended to believe her obvious lie, but not before he had a little fun with her.

"What new regulation?"

"Some new healthcare law; I don't understand how it works."

"Well, what did they tell you?"

"They just told me to take some time off."

"You didn't ask why?"

"They said 'cuz of the new regulation!" she finally said exasperated and escaped to her room, slamming the door.

Lie or no lie, he still had to deal with her being home all week, which meant he had to actually attend school for the entire week—every class.

He told himself it had been a bad week, but he couldn't really remember a good one. He felt tired. He was tired of being depressed. He was tired of being tired. He was tired of thinking all the time. He was tired of people. He wanted to put both his eyes out. He wasn't sure why, but he wanted to be blind. He wished his hands didn't work. He wanted to break both of his hands so that when his mother came home, she would find his hands smashed. He wished that he were crippled. He wished he had autism. He wanted someone to take care of him. He wanted someone to applaud when he actually tied his own shoe. He wanted to find a rope and tie it tight around his head right at his eyes, so tight that his eyes would bleed, so that when his mother came home, she would find him flat on the ground, bleeding from the eyes.

You're losing it. You're going crazy from prolonged depression. It's too late now; you've been sad for too long.

His eyes, for just a moment, left the closet and panned over to the card

Pastor Ellison had left. He pulled out his cell phone and before he knew what he was doing, he found himself with the card in his left hand and his phone in his right.

When he hit send, a voice in his head tried to get him to level with himself. *This is a cry for help.* But he ignored it.

The call went straight to Ellison's voicemail.

In disgust, he hit *END CALL.* Tyler was thinking about their last meeting, the time he had stumped him, the time he had thrown the pastor's own stupid publicity stunt right in his face. *Of course he won't answer.* Tyler, in his adolescent narcissism, imagined that the pastor was screening his calls just to avoid having to talk to him. *I guess I won; that was easy.*

Tyler was angry. He was angry that the pastor wasn't the worthy opponent he'd hoped for. He hadn't wanted to win, but he refused to throw the game. He wanted to believe, but he didn't want to pretend. He didn't want to be one of those who faked belief so effectively that he might one day fool himself. He wanted a father who loved him, but he did not want it bad enough to make one up.

He grabbed his phone and impatiently dialed the pastor's number again. Straight to voice mail. He hung up, but then dialed again. This time he listened.

"This is Pastor Riley Ellison. I'm sorry I missed your call. Please leave a message and I'll return your call as soon as possible. Thank you and have a blessed day. If this is an emergency, hang up and dial 911. For those otherwise in need of help, you will find someone anxious to speak to you at the church crisis line; call—"

Tyler quickly hung up the phone. *Just what kind of weirdoes does this guy hand out his card to?*

He noticed that the icon for his phone's battery was in the red, so he plugged it into its charger. He waited to watch the icon change to make sure it was charging.

Finally, Tyler decided he couldn't wait anymore. He told himself there was a good chance his mom wouldn't even be back until morning. He walked to his closet to fetch the whiskey. He had to stand on his math book to reach the back of the top shelf. Without the benefit of sight, he felt around for the bottle he'd left.

It's not there! He panicked. He feared his mother had found it, confiscated it, and probably drank it herself. He needed to get taller, so he found another text book. He reached his fingers all the way to the back. He touched what felt like a cord of some kind, old junk that cluttered his closet. He stood on his tippy-toes. His fingertips touched what felt like round smooth glass. His heart sang.

He managed to pull the bottle down and stepped off the books. But he was curious about something: *What was that cord?* He stepped back onto the books and reached to grab it. The cord was wound tight and tied with a twist tie. When Tyler grabbed it, he felt some resistance on one end. The cord was plugged into something, which slid off the shelf and fell onto the carpet. Tyler saw a bouncing black gadget and realized right away what it was. It was his brother's old video camera. He could still remember the Christmas when their mother had given it to him, but just barely.

He wanted to see if it still worked so he tried to plug it in behind his night stand. The outlet was full so he unplugged his phone charger. When the camera turned on, he discovered to his amazement that it was filled with old videos of Carson. They were mostly just videos of him drinking, a couple of parties, and Carson and his friends talking about stupid stuff. He scrolled through the clips and found one with just Carson. He turned the volume up on the camera's little speaker.

His brother looked young. The clip was filmed a few years before he killed himself. He was obviously drunk, which is probably why he decided to film himself in the first place. Carson said, "I'm tired. I'm so tired of all the BS. I'm tired of feeling so lonely. I'm tired of feeling... ineffective. I want to... I just want people to see me. I imagine that I'm in the middle of a giant coliseum and all the chairs are filled. Tens of thousands of people are there and they are all watching me. And I just curl up and cry, with everyone watching. I just... I just want people to see my pain. I don't know why. Because maybe if they could see it, then maybe it would matter. Because if they could see it, then maybe then it would... matter. Maybe then... But no one sees it. So it's just *pain*. It doesn't *do* anything. It just hurts. But if it just did something. If it moved. If there was some effect, something that people could see with their eyes. Then it would be more than just pain, then it'd be... I don't know... then it'd be real."

I'm my brother. Oh my God, I'm my brother. We're the same person. We have the same pain.

Watching the video, Tyler opened the Maker's Mark and drank straight from the bottle. Coincidentally, it was the same time that Carson unscrewed the cap of his bottle and took a swig.

Creepy.

Only, his brother was drinking Jack Daniels, but *close enough.*

Carson poured some into the shot glass in front of him. He said, "I've discovered a secret," he slurred as he pulled out a large pharmaceutical bottle and set it on the table. The resolution on cameras back then was not good enough for Tyler to see the bottle's label, but it had a thin blue stripe at the top.

His brother blathered on, "You see, alcohol is a depressant." He paused to spill the pale yellow pills from the bottle onto his desk. He grabbed one and held it up to the light and then put it aside. He said, "But anti-depressants are... anti-depressants." He laughed at his inadvertent tautology and continued to grab individual pills, hold them up to the light, then place them aside. "So when you have one force pulling you one way, and another force pulling you another way... everything in the middle gets torn in half." He held one more yellow pill to the light, then smiled. He said, "I'm fixin' to get torn in half, ladies and gentlemen. I'm fixin' to get torn in half."

He pressed one side of the pill with his thumb and carefully removed the pill's gelatin casing from itself. He then took both halves and dumped their contents into his Jack Daniels. The white powder falling onto the brown liquid provided such contrast that even the antediluvian technology had been able to pick it up.

Carson smiled mirthlessly and used his pinky to stir.

Tyler paused the video. He knew that his mother probably hadn't organized the medicine cabinet even once since this video was taken. He ran to his mother's bathroom to investigate. It didn't take long for him to find a white bottle of the same size in the back. He checked the label; it had that same blue single stripe. He read the label: *Damitol.*

Tyler said a cuss word, excited and scared.

He brought the bottle back to his room and tossed the camera to the floor to clear some space. He opened the pill bottle. It was nearly full. Without having a purpose to do so—other than just to be dramatic—he dumped the entire thing onto his nightstand. The pills were pale yellow.

He looked around for his glass and remembered he didn't have one. He'd been drinking straight out of the bottle. He got up to run to the kitchen, but he heard his mother's keys. He heard the deadbolt releasing and the front door opening. She was home.

Instead of opening the door, he reached to lock it. He turned out his lights and made his way in the dark to the side of his bed. He lowered his body, not to the edge of the mattress, but to the ground. He sat on the floor by his nightstand, leaning his back on the bed, and listened.

He took a long slow drink from his bottle, acutely aware of the faint sloshing sound it made, trying to keep his movements slow so that it remained only faint.

He thought he heard his mom in the kitchen, but he couldn't be sure. The rain picked up again outside, and it masked her exact whereabouts. He waited to hear something unmistakable, and finally heard the microwave. He knew that if she was heating up food, she would do one of two things: She would take her food into her bedroom, which he hoped for because she would soon go to sleep, or she would turn on the TV out there and be up all night.

He anxiously waited, dreading to hear the sound of the television. At last, he heard her bedroom door as it closed shut behind her.

Pastor Ellison was handed off to an officer whose job it was to get his fingerprints. She said, "I didn't expect to see you here tonight, Mister Perfect, although I can't say I'm surprised."

"I respect what you do here, officer," the pastor said. He could tell by the way she was manhandling his fingers that she wasn't a fan. "What's your name?" he asked although he could clearly read it on her badge. Officer Felicia Jones.

"We're not here to chat," said Officer Jones.

"Okay," Ellison said, but then asked, "Why aren't you surprised?" She had been reluctant to talk, but he knew this opening would be too tempting for her.

Felicia Jones gave a snarky laugh and said, "Let's just say I've known my share of hypocrites."

"I'm sorry," Ellison said. "I wish I could apologize for other people. For as little as I represent all Christianity, I'd like to apologize for every Christian who has ever hurt you."

"Who said they hurt me?" the woman snapped. She added, "And I don't know why you're still wearing that jacket, but you're not going to be allowed to keep it on."

Pastor Ellison lowered his eyes. The lady saw his aversion to removing the jacket, although she could've never guessed the cause. There was a strange glee in her eyes as she waited for him to take it off. Once she saw the tattoos, she laughed out loud and scoffed, "Typical."

Next he was sent to a holding cell where he was to wait for his opportunity to make a phone call.

The holding cell was a large room, empty of any furniture. The walls, floor, and ceiling were made of bare concrete. It was lit by strips of florescent lights, with half the tubes burnt out, and one of them flickering. There was only one door leading in or out, and it contained the room's only window.

The place seemed to be divided into two groups: sitters and standers. The sitters curled up in different variations of the fetal position and looked terminally uncomfortable. The standers seemed to be completely at home and in the mood to socialize.

Ellison found a seat on the ground, mainly because his legs were tired. Once he was able to settle in, he noticed a third group: liers. They lay on the floor, mainly because they were unconscious.

Some men were sober, others were not. Some men had shirts, others did not. Getting arrested—much like the ashes of Pompeii—served as a snapshot of their daily lives.

The ones who were socializing separated themselves primarily by race. A large group of blacks had congregated to Ellison's right. There was a smaller group of Latinos to his left. Most of the conversation, which could be heard throughout the room, consisted of men comparing their prison stories.

One black man in particular was busy describing the stretch he did at county. He was reminiscing with fondness about the daily torment he and his fellow inmates put one of the white prisoners through. As he described the stupid human tricks they would force him under threat of coercion to perform, the crowd around him laughed.

The pastor looked over at the only other white man in the holding cell. His sphinx-like expression was nearly perfect. The only hint that he wasn't hard of hearing was the obvious effort it took him to maintain such a poker face.

Finally, the pastor spoke up. He said, "That's nothing you should brag about." He not only spoke up, but he stood up, and as casually as if he were addressing a group at a dinner party, he walked over to join the black man's circle.

The man's dark eyes studied Ellison—his graying hair and sleeve tattoos. Pastor Ellison was aware that, even with his tattoos, there was nothing intimidating about him—a middle-aged white guy with a round face and a look of *bonhomie*.

The black men clustered in around him. The man responded, "Nonya' bidness, pops."

Ellison saw the steely way the man was eyeballing him. He looked from face to face—he even turned to glance at the men close behind him—they all had that same expression. Ellison's voice was steady when he said, "I'm just trying to offer some help."

"Oh I see what's up," the man said. "You care 'bout him 'cause he's white."

"No," said the pastor. "No, the only person in the world I care about in this moment is you."

The man sniffed. "You don't know me, man."

"Not specifically, but I do know one thing about you. I understand one thing about you that apparently even you don't understand."

"What's that?"

"The God who created the world, the God who causes the sun to rise, the God who knows the number of hairs on your head, the most awesome power in the universe, loves you enough to give up his Son for you. Your Savior is my Savior and He suffered and died out of indefatigable love for you." The pastor spread his arms. "What else is so important for me to know after that?"

Everyone in the holding cell heard the heavy door open when Officer Gonzales stuck his head in. He had been worried about Pastor Ellison and was watching the whole scene unfold through the door's small window. "Is there a problem here?" he asked forcefully as he eyed the circle of men that aggressively surrounded Ellison.

Ellison answered before anyone else had the chance. "No problem, sir. Just having a conversation."

"Okay," said Gonzales. He could tell by Ellison's voice that he meant it. He added, "You're okay then, Pastor?"

"Never better," said Ellison.

He could tell by the faces in front of him that their attitude had changed the second the guard had addressed him as *Pastor*, although a few of the eyes took a second glance at his tattoos. Ellison asked the man, "You go to church?"

"Yeah."

Ellison had meant to ask only the man in front of him, but he noticed a few more heads in the crowd nod as well.

"Every Sunday?"

"Yeah," the man said, plus there were more nods.

"A lot of you, huh?"

"Yeah," a few more people answered audibly.

"Well, then I think maybe you guys need to clean out your ears."

"What'd chew say?" the man snapped and the group closed in tighter.

"I don't know what you men have done to find yourselves in here, but from what I've heard from you, it sounds like you've been on this road for a while. You're not living up to the amazing plan God had in store for your life; you're not showing the proper gratitude to a Man who suffered and died in your place; and you're not respecting yourselves the way a son of God, and heir to His kingdom should be respected."

The man stepped closer, nose to nose with the pastor. His anger ticked up, in part due to what the pastor was saying, but in greater part due to the fact that he had no quick retort. For him, violence had always been the answer when words failed him.

Ellison noticed that his eyeballs were glazed over and the shape of his pupils seemed noncommittal. This was Ellison's first moment of physical fear, because he didn't believe the man he was talking to was sober. He was surely on something, but Ellison had no idea what. He said, "You can beat the crap out of me, but it won't change the fact that I'm right, and that you are wasting the precious gift of life, a gift given to you by God."

"Man, what's it to you?"

"It is everything to me. Like I told you, the only person in the world I care about right now is you. Because I spend my life wanting to emulate Jesus Christ. Because I try to love you the way Christ loves you." The entire time they had been talking, both men had been looking straight into each other's eyes. Ellison added, "I love you and I know God has a purpose for your life."

The man looked away.

Ellison panned the room. Not one of the men still had eyes on him. He turned back to his surly interlocutor and added, "You and I have something in common."

"Oh yeah? What's that?" the man sassed, turning to look Ellison in the eyes once again.

"Our first love," declared Ellison, but then expounded, "We both can remember the moment when it first clicked."

"You talking about God?"

Ellison smiled. "He's usually all I ever talk about. I'm talking about that moment of prayer when we felt like we could touch the truth—hold it in our hands—and we knew, all this selfish misery was just a ruse, and that there's an ineffable beauty just waiting to be discovered."

The man scoffed and shook his head. He said, "I don't know what you're even sayin'."

"I'm talking about prayer, and I think a part of you does know what I'm saying." Pastor Ellison spoke very slowly; it wasn't the hurried pace of crafty rhetoric, but the painstaking pace of wise instruction. "I don't mean the childish prayers that we so often recited from memory. I'm talking about that moment, down on your knees, or sitting in a pew, when we talked to God in our heads... shared every secret and confessed every shame... and knew there was someone who heard... someone who was listening... and someone who cared."

The man didn't answer, but his eyes darted high and to his right, as if seeing a distant and forgotten memory. The small muscles around those eyes softened. His cold, hard, menacing expression, his stock-in-trade in the life of a thug, melted away.

Ellison reached out and put his hand on the man's shoulder. He asked, "What's your name?"

"DeShawn."

"DeShawn, will you pray with me?"

He nodded.

Ellison left his hand on DeShawn's shoulder, but turned his head to the room. He said, "I'd like to invite all of you here to join me in prayer." Most men bowed their heads. Ellison was a bit surprised to feel a few hands on his own shoulders and back.

He bowed his head.

"Dear Lord, thank You for the opportunity You have given me tonight to spend time with these Christians. Please help us to face life's challenges without fear. When the stress and the pain become unbearable, please help us to see Your greater plan behind this earthly veil, and to keep in our minds that for as much as we suffer, Christ suffered worse. As much humiliation as we face, Christ faced worse. If there is anyone in this cell struggling with addiction, Lord, please help his burdens be lightened. Help him to get the help he needs. Help him to find his strength in You. Those among us with past hurts, help us to let go of our anger. And for those of us mired in dark confusion, who just can't seem to find the path to success in life, remind our hearts that victory had already been won at the moment Jesus rolled the stone away and stepped free from his tomb. Help us to glorify You, the author of victory, in every choice we make. This we pray, in Christ's holy name, Jesus. Amen."

The men around the room said, "Amen."

Movement beyond the window in the heavy door caught Ellison's eye. Through the small window two of the guards had been watching, Officer Gonzales and Officer Jones—the one who let him keep his jacket, and the one who took it away.

He watched on, inspired.

She turned away, embittered.

Tyler's mother had retired to her room; he would not be disturbed for the rest of the night. He continued to drink slowly on the ground. What seemed like hours passed and he found it somehow menacing to drink in the dark—emblematic of his brooding misery and the depth of emotion that made him so special.

The rain clouds parted momentarily and moonlight came creeping in through his window. It illuminated the pale yellow sea of Damitol, now level with his eyes. Tyler didn't want to be torn in half. *It obviously didn't help my brother, and I am my brother. Nothing at all helped my brother, and I am my brother, so nothing at all will help me. My brother is dead and I am him. So I am dead. I cannot kill myself. I have been dead for nearly two years.*

He liked the way that sounded, so he opened the drawer of his night stand and pulled out his notebook. It was where he liked to record his brooding and his angst. He flipped through his old ramblings to find the first blank page and tried to remember how he had just said it in his head. He wrote:

> I am dead. I am my brother. And he is dead. When he killed himself, he killed me. But, I am him, so I killed me. You cannot stop me from killing myself, Mister Perfect, because I already have. You cannot stop me, Mother, because I am already dead.

Tyler stopped when it dawned on him just what he was truly writing. *This is a suicide note.* The feeling was so strong he felt he had to whisper it out loud. "This is a suicide note." He tore out the page and ripped it into little pieces. For something this important, what he had wasn't good enough. He tried again:

> I am dead. It all ends now. I could've been great. I could've been a superhero. You never took me to the park. You never loved me. You only ever cared about Carson. But I was here, and now you will finally see me. I could've been king of the universe.

This is stupid. Tyler looked down at his note, then tore it out too. He wanted there to be a note, but he couldn't come up with anything that could capture the drama and the... and the... *significance. The sheer significance.*

He began to tear that paper into smaller and smaller pieces, watching intently, fascinated by the simple thrill of destruction. As he relished each slow tear, he remembered the words of his brother. "I'm fixin' to get torn in half."

Tyler didn't want to be torn in half. He only wanted the pain to stop and for it never to come back.

"I only want the pain to stop," he whispered.

Even without a note, Tyler used the knife edge of his right hand to slide some pills over to his left hand—what appeared to be about a half dozen. He shoved them into his mouth and swallowed them with his whiskey. It was pretty easy to do, so the next time he swallowed more. He blocked out the realization of what he was doing by making a game of it, seeing how many he could swallow at once.

He overdid it and began to cough. He did his best to suppress it, grabbing a pillow to put over his face. When he was finally able to stop, he froze and watched for any light to come on from under his door. He didn't move for a long time. There was a still, tranquil break from the rhythm of the rain. Finally, he heard a distant snoring. His mother was asleep.

It was then that he looked over to see that there was only one mouthful of Damitol left. It was then that it became real to him. He tried to stand up, but he staggered. He realized that he was more drunk than he had ever been in his life. With great effort, he forced his body to rise up and walk to the door. He put his hand on the door knob, but did not turn it. He rested his head against the door frame and he stopped to breathe.

There was only one, small lucid sliver in his mind that was clear on why he had stood up in the first place: He wanted to go wake his mother. He was going to tell her what he had just done and ask her to take him to the hospital to get his stomach pumped. He considered it, now with his full focus. He was scared.

With a new determination, he turned the knob in order to go find his mother, but it was locked.

The door was locked from his side, so it wasn't enough to physically stop him. But it was enough to derail his mind's last waning vestige of sanity. He turned from the door entirely. He sat down on his bed and slid the last mouthful of Damitol into his hands. With movements that were measured and deliberate, he swallowed them with his Maker's Mark, then lowered himself on the floor to wait for death.

He felt sad. The teenage angst had left him and he felt sad. He remembered the time that he and his brother had played on the beach, building sand castles. He thought about them skipping rocks, and he thought about Christmas morning. He missed Carson.

Tyler knew that his mother would find his body in the morning, but he had no idea how he felt about that. He felt sorry for her, but only for a second. He also thought it would serve her right. He loved her and he hated her, and he wished overwhelming emotion was enough to base a life around.

Despite the fact that it was now the middle of the night, he decided to try Pastor Ellison's cell one more time. Again it went straight to voicemail, so Tyler hung up, typed out a text and hit SEND.

It might have been the effects of taking a nearly full bottle of the world's most powerful anti-depressant all at once, but he thought he heard his brother's voice. It was faint and he couldn't make out what he was saying, but it was definitely his brother's voice and it was trying to tell him something. Tyler put the speaker end of the phone to his ear but it was silent. He was confused.

"Carson?" Tyler whispered. He searched the room. He saw a small blinking green light. It was his brother's video camera. But that made no sense because he'd shut that off a long time ago.

He flipped open the display screen and saw his brother talking straight into the lens and therefore straight at him. The Jack Daniels and the bottle of Damitol were gone from the footage, and Carson seemed bathed in a strange phantasmal light. Carson said, "I just wanted to tell you how much I love you, Bro. I wanted to tell you how sorry I am. It was selfish what I did. I never once stopped to think about the pain it would cause you or Mom. I wanted to tell you that I'm sorry but I guess it's too late."

Tears were streaming down Tyler's cheeks. He said, "It's not too late."

Carson shook his head somberly. "Listen, Bro. There're only two things you need to know right now. I love you, and don't be afraid." He looked straight at Tyler and repeated, "I love you; don't be afraid."

The video went to static.

The camera dropped from Tyler's trembling hands. He laid his body down across the floor. He felt connected to an everlasting love. He felt that the pain had stopped and that it would never be back. He closed his eyes, knowing he would never open them again, and he was not afraid.

The wind blew the clouds and the moonlight retreated from his room, leaving him alone in total darkness.

Chapter Nine

January 10—Six days left

Once Pastor Ellison's handcuffs were removed, the first thing he did was hug his wife. He was translating the various features of her face, a strange marital exegesis. The eyebrow raised a nanometer, such a small amount it took twenty-six years of marriage to spot, was *I told you so.* The tension in her jaw was *Why can't you stick to sermons and potluck picnics like other pastors?* The twinkle of hope in her eye was *Maybe now you've learned your lesson.* But the smile on her face was *I love you unconditionally, and I'm so glad you're all right.*

He whispered in her ear, "I love you, too."

The free side of the jail looked not unlike a lobby in a hospital. There was a counter enclosed in glass in front of them and floor to ceiling windows behind them. Officer Gonzales was behind the glass. He slid Ellison his red windbreaker, along with a manila envelope containing the personal possessions that he had taken. Ellison quickly covered up.

"I want to thank you for taking such good care of my husband," Deborah told him. She hadn't heard any specifics yet, but offered up Gonzales the respect she believed all police officers deserve.

"Yes, ma'am," the officer said.

"This man really looked out for me last night," said Ellison to his wife, but loud enough for the cop to hear.

The officer did not respond. He said, "I guess they're here for you," pointing to a mob of press approaching the outside windows. "Would you like me to disperse them for you?"

"No, sir, it's all right. In fact, I think it'd be wise to try and clear some of this story up," Ellison said. He could feel his wife elbow him.

Ellison turned to leave, but he heard a firm voice call out, "Pastor, wait."

He turned to show Gonzales he was listening.

The cop said, "I respect what you are trying to do."

"But?" said Ellison.

The officer shrugged. "No *but.* I really respect what you are trying to do."

Ellison smiled. "Thank you, sir," he said warmly.

As he and his wife walked toward the revolving door that led to the street, Pastor Ellison was preparing what he would say to the reporters just beyond the glass. He opened the manila envelope and found his phone, his keys, and a business card for the church with his number on the back. His face showed panic, and he searched the rest of the bag.

His wife saw his panic and held out his wedding ring that she had been carrying. Her voice was tiresome when she said, "You took it off for the ruse."

"Oh." Ellison forced a laugh. He saw that same complicated face from his wife, except the *unconditional love* part of her smile was a little less apparent.

With a low, monotone voice she added, "Oh, and I saw the Visa bill, by the way."

"Oh," Ellison repeated guiltily. He'd been waiting for the just perfect moment to bring up a certain $1,000 charge. This clearly wasn't it. He looked her in the eye and said, "How much is one soul worth to God? What lengths are too far if it means bringing one of His children back to Him?" He then turned to sweep his hand across the surroundings, a gesture that represented the arrest, the bail money, and the entire night. He realized that his prepared plea contained even more weight than when he had prepared it. Maybe it was the perfect timing after all.

Deborah cleared her throat. It sounded suspiciously like a growl. She said, "Whatever."

Ellison grinned. He turned his phone on as they walked through the revolving door. Once on the other side, Ellison stopped, his wife beside him, smiled at the press and said, "I'd like to make a statement please." He felt his phone pulse, still in his hand. He checked it reflexively and saw his missed calls and messages. They were displayed in reverse order, newest first:

        (619) 555-4217   2:49 am
        this id my notr tell god im sorry

        Missed Call
        (619) 555-4217 (4)   2:47 am

Turning back to the press he blurted, "I'm sorry; I have to go."

A roar resulted from the press as they began to hurl their questions.

Mrs. Ellison's face showed shocked—no one had to be married to her to see that.

Pastor Ellison pulled his wife by the hand and led her to the parking lot. A few of the reporters fruitlessly followed them out, but most saw clearly that it wouldn't be worth the effort.

Once inside his wife's car, before even starting the engine, Ellison frantically selected the unlabeled number and returned the call. He said out loud, "C'mon, c'mon... Pick up, Tyler. Pick up."

There could be no answer.

It was no use.

The call was sent to a phone, which lay only two feet from the aimless boy's body, already dead.

When Andrew Crenshaw showed up late for work, his cell ringer was turned off. His head was throbbing so he had driven the whole way without even listening to the radio. Jean Hanson and Lester Brady were cutting up outside his office. The sound of raucous laughter was preventing most of the people in the building from getting any real work done. Andrew searched for a way to enter his office without going near them, but short of parachuting in through the outside window, he couldn't think of any. He knew that type of laughter well. It wasn't the joyful sound of celebration, but the impertinent sound of childish mockery.

"What are you laughing at?" he foolishly asked.

"We're laughing at your boy."

"My... boy?"

"Ellison. He got caught with a prostitute," Lester Brady laughed.

"Well no, he got arrested on charges of soliciting prostitution," Jean Hanson corrected, at least trying to maintain some journalistic standards of accuracy.

Lester Brady said, "Whatever," the same time Andrew awkwardly questioned, "He... what?"

"Happened late last night. When you didn't show this morning, we figured maybe you were with him."

They both laughed again. But it was a boisterous laughter far out of sync with the proportion of the joke.

"Yeah, we thought about giving Douglas some bail money for you."

They laughed obnoxiously, as if they were at a Jake Dolan show.

Andrew said nothing. He was still trying to make sense of it.

"Wasn't he supposed to be your story? Why weren't you with him?"

"He told me he'd be spending time with his wife."

The men both laughed so hard it could be heard throughout the building.

"He probably told her he was going to be with you."

"I should head over there. Where is he?"

"Not out yet... I don't think. We sent Douglas. You won't get in to see him anyway."

"Hey, what's his wife like? Is she hot?" Brady asked.

Andrew shrugged. "She's... beautiful." He remembered the smell of the roast and added, "She's perfect."

"Yeah, I'll bet. These guys really hack me off. They come and apologize to their supporters, make some big speech about integrity or something. All the while their wives are standing right next to them. And guess what? They don't leave them. You know why? 'Cause the money!" The laughter in his eyes had switched to bitterness.

"What money?" asked Andrew.

"You're thinking of politicians," Jean Hanson said. "That's not how the pastors do it. You wait and see. He'll probably come out crying to the press, all sobbing, calling himself a sinner. Then probably blame the whole thing on Satan. I bet he'll call the mountain thing off. Wait and see."

"What money?" Andrew repeated to Brady.

"His book!" Brady snapped. "Thirty million copies? That's *what money.*"

"He didn't keep that money. He gave it away."

Andrew saw Lester Brady's face. He could see that he was at a loss, maybe even impressed, but not for long. He said, "That just makes it worse!"

"How's that make it worse?" asked Jean Hanson.

"Because he's a hypocrite. They all are. He gives his money away so that he can feel like a big shot. That's the same reason he sleeps with whores. He wants to feel bigger than he is. It's *all* prostitution. And he wants to make *us* think he's bigger than he is, but we're not buying it. Am I right?"

Andrew looked like he could cry. He said, "Yeah, no. No, you're right."

"There is no such thing as a great man. I learned that from you, Andrew. This is just more proof."

Andrew nodded, dyspeptically. "More proof."

Andrew had to get away. He felt a strong aversion to their very presence. Their twittering laughter grated on him. He made up an excuse to escape to his office.

In his office, he pulled his chair up close to his desk. He placed his head in his hands. He had to steady himself, brace for impact. He had been able to suspend the malicious news, quarantine it before it was allowed entry into his brain. Now he had to accept it. He had to let it in and let it destroy his naïve fantasy.

He told himself he shouldn't be mad at the guys he worked with. *Those guys were right. How come I felt so disgusted with them?* He let the news in. He accepted the fact that he'd been fooled. After a few quiet moments he realized why he had been so mad at those guys. It was displaced anger that was really meant for himself. *I was the one who was taken in. I should be mad at me. They at least had the good sense to mock the phony pastor; I just stood there slack-jawed like reality had gotten in the way of my schoolgirl crush. How pathetic!*

He pulled out his phone to text Pastor Ellison. He typed:

Why?

Pastor Ellison drove as fast as he could, even through the parking lot. Deborah Ellison continued to dial Tyler's number, and even tried sending a few texts. She looked down excitedly when she felt it pulse in her hand. But, it only read:

Andrew Crenshaw   9:23 am
Why?

Ellison double parked behind a line of cars and told his wife, "Let's go."

"Not me," she said. "I think it'd be better with just you."

"You're right," he said and ran to the door.

When Poison answered the door, she could see the panicked look on Ellison's face. "Where's Tyler?" he snapped.

Poison answered quickly, "He's at school."

Ellison pushed his way into the apartment and ran to Tyler's door. He checked the knob, but it wouldn't budge. "It's locked from the inside," he said.

"Tyler?" Poison screamed as she slammed her palm against the door. Ellison pulled her hands out of the way and slammed the door open with his shoulder.

They both found Tyler's body on the floor beside the bed. Ellison instinctively put his own body in front of the mother's, as if the shock was an oncoming city bus and he was trying to shield her from the blow. He reached to her shoulders in order to turn her away.

Poison let out a scream—it was a guttural shriek of terror and pain. It was the exact same cry she had made when she discovered Carson's body.

The scream was so loud that Deborah heard it from outside the building. She put her hand to her mouth and prayed.

The scream was so loud, it caused Tyler's head to snap up. He opened his eyes in panic, observing the two in his room with disbelief. He frantically pushed away from them with his feet, duck-crawling backward until he backed into his nightstand.

When he did this, he accidentally kicked the whiskey bottle, which was still open, and spilled some of its contents onto the floor. There wasn't much left to spill.

His mother switched rather quickly from fright to indignation. She accused, "You've been in here drinking?"

Pastor Ellison was more concerned with the boy's physical condition. He saw no sign of vomiting, and no sign of any pills. The boy didn't appear to be in pain, and was obviously able to move. He looked around the room for any knives or blades, but couldn't see any. Plus, there were no visible cuts on either arm, nor any blood on his shirt.

The boy's face still showed utter bewilderment. He looked at the two of them as if they were apparitions.

"You've been drinking?" the mom repeated. "And why aren't you at school?"

The boy appeared to be in too much shock to answer.

Pastor Ellison stepped forward and said, "Why did you send me this text?" He held out his phone toward the boy.

Tyler just shook his head. He had never seen that text before in his life. *Or have I?*

"Is this your number?"

Tyler squinted at the number, but didn't answer.

Poison took a quick look at it and confessed, "That's his number."

Pieces of the night were coming back to Tyler. He saw the torn scraps of paper on the floor and the old video camera that had been dropped by the nightstand. He could feel the Damitol bottle pressing against the small of his back, and was happy it was out of sight. He had a slight headache, but otherwise felt fine.

But there was one rather large detail he couldn't explain and he stared around the room incredulously.

"Aren't you going to say anything?" his mom asked as they waited for him to speak.

There was too much going on in his head to speak, and in the silence they all could hear the TV Poison had just been watching in the other room.

Ellison sat down on the bed in order to figure all this out. He was happy to see Tyler alive, but was confused.

In the stillness of the room, the TV seemed to grow in volume and they heard a female voice:

> Pastor Riley Ellison arrested for soliciting prostitution. Your local news is next.

They both turned to look at him. *Oh yeah.* He had nearly forgotten about that. He put up both hands to stymie their accusations, but before he had a chance, Poison said, "How could you?"

"No, listen, my wife's out in the car," he managed to say, but that didn't sufficiently cover it.

"And you betrayed her?" snapped Poison.

It was the first time that the boy's face changed from shock; now it showed disappointment. He remembered what he had been thinking the night before: he just wanted Pastor Ellison to be perfect, so that he could follow him.

Ellison said, "Wait, wait, wait, wait, wait. I was trying to talk to a prostitute so I could convert her to Christ."

Poison laughed like it was a flimsy excuse.

"I was. I was going to pay her for her time, just like a call girl. But instead of sex, I was going to try to reach her."

Poison just kept her arms folded. She wasn't hearing it. Every destructive emotion she had ever felt about men, most of them well-founded, came flooding to mind.

Pastor Ellison couldn't believe the bad timing. He had come there anxious to help save a life. "Wait. Wait. Wait," he continued to insist. He realized why she of all people should believe his story. He said, "Listen, my money for her time! You know I'm not lying. It was the exact same approach I tried with you at the strip club!"

All motion ceased. The room became three degrees colder. They both looked at the boy, and then turned to look at each other. She had the same look in her eyes as she did just before she once beat the crap out of him.

"I'm sorry," he said quickly. "I'm sorry. I made a mess of this. I'd better go." Then he slipped out the door.

The air in the newsroom felt urgent and irritable. It carried the smell of coffee and toner. Nancy Fuller looked for some sort of receptionist desk, or someone who could help her. No one there seemed anxious to apply for that job.

Nancy felt so out of place. She could feel her palms sweating and her throat was getting dry.

She timidly approached a desk near the front. Lester Brady had his face partially hidden behind a monitor. He glanced up when he saw a figure approach his desk, didn't recognize her, then immediately turned his face back to the screen.

Nancy Fuller moved closer, but Lester Brady continued to type. Finally, she mumbled, "Excuse me... Excuse me..."

Brady leaned his head to peer around the monitor, but his hands remained primed over the keys and his chair didn't slide an inch, despite being on wheels. "Yes?" he asked.

"I am looking for Andrew Crenshaw. Can you help me?"

"Is he expecting you?"

Nancy Fuller swallowed. "No. I have information he will want regarding Pastor Ellison."

When she had mentioned the name Pastor Ellison, she saw Brady's eyes pan her up and down. He was trying to determine whether she might be a prostitute. Nancy pulled her jacket closed tighter.

"Hold on." The man's hands finally left his keyboard when he picked up the phone on his desk and stabbed a few buttons. "Crenshaw, you've got some woman here to see you. Says she has information on Ellison."

When the man hung up the phone, he rudely turned his face back to his computer without another word to the nervous girl.

"I guess I'll wait here then," she said. There was no cutting sarcasm in her voice.

After a short but uncomfortable wait, Andrew Crenshaw came out from his office. He greeted her warmly and asked that she come on back.

"Thank you for taking time to speak with me today," she began as soon as they were alone. "I am very anxious to talk with you."

"About what?"

"About this," she said as she placed a copy of their paper on his desk. It was folded to Andrew Crenshaw's article from the previous morning. It was titled, "Pastor Ellison's String Theory."

Andrew Crenshaw glanced at the paper, then looked over to her hands. He noticed that she, too, had a string tied to her finger. "I'm listening."

"I don't think you understand the man about whom you write."

"You've come to give me the dirt on Ellison?"

The woman laughed.

Andrew Crenshaw smiled.

"No," she said, "just the opposite. I want to tell you just how he changed my life."

"Let me guess, he converted you to Christianity." Andrew Crenshaw's voice was patient enough. He did not stop to reflect how this exact type of conversation would have grated on him just ten days ago.

"No," she said. "Not exactly. I was born and raised Christian. In fact, I was once so on fire for the Lord that one day when I was twelve, I tied a string around my finger. No one told me to do it; I just thought it was a neat idea at the time. My parents asked me what I was trying to remember. I said, 'Jesus loves me.' That made them so happy that I decided to wear the string every day.

"Pretty soon, everyone started to ask me what I was trying to remember. I was a social butterfly back then, so I liked the attention. I liked telling them, 'I want to remember Jesus loves me.' While wearing the string everyone, who wouldn't have known otherwise, knew that I was Christian. They knew what I stood for and where my heart belonged.

"But then I got older, I became a teenager. I became interested in things like clothes, makeup and boys. Then one day, I just stopped wearing the string. I never meant to stop, I just took it off to shower and forgot to put it back on.

"When I entered puberty and the boys around me did also, the wrong type of guys no longer knew what I stood for. And by the time I got to college, I didn't know either.

"Long story short, I found myself getting out of my car in front of a Planned Parenthood. The little girl, once so devoted to Christ, was long gone and I was up against a problem I was unprepared to face on my own.

"To cut across the parking lot, I had to walk past a small group of agitators carrying signs. A belligerent man was yelling some nonsense in my face. He made me uncomfortable, but I noticed he made the woman there picketing with him uncomfortable as well. I kept my head down as I walked, staying as far away from them as I possibly could. But something caught my eye: the young woman had a string tied around her finger.

"I was almost to the front door before I decided to turn around. I walked straight over to the entire group, put my palm up toward the belligerent man and told him to shut up. I asked the woman in the resulting silence, 'Why do you have a string around your finger?' She said, 'I want to remember something.' I couldn't believe it. I asked, breathlessly, 'What?' She said, 'I want to remember that I'm precious. I am a sacred child of God and He loved me enough to give up His Son for me.'

"Tears filled my eyes. I asked where she got that idea. She said she had heard it from her pastor.

"Well you can imagine I was anxious to speak to this pastor. I showed up unannounced to his church," Nancy laughed, "a lot like I did here today, and asked why he had a string around his finger, and more importantly, where he got that idea. He told me to sit down, then he spoke of a young girl he ran into with her mother at a grocery store—a young girl, maybe twelve years old, a social butterfly, filled with a child-like faith in God and a fearless love of people. He had asked her what she was trying to remember and she told him, 'I want to remember Jesus loves me.'" Nancy laughed and wiped tears from her face. "Well, of course it was me, but I wanted to make sure. 'How long ago was that?' I asked. 'About seven years now,' he told me. The math was right. I didn't remember us ever meeting. I was asked that same question by so many people. Plus, you have to know, he wasn't *the* Riley Ellison at the time.

"I started to cry again, as you can see I have a habit of doing." She laughed nervously. "When I told him I was that little girl, Pastor Ellison's eyes lit up. He said, 'Well, I have to thank you.' Then he spread his hands out to the massive building and said, 'You have built this church.' He told me about his small church, his dilapidated building, and his two-hundred members. He said that he mentioned the string idea during just one of his sermons and immediately after, most of his congregation started wearing strings on their fingers.

"Apparently, wearing the strings had changed their lives. All of a sudden, people knew where they stood. They had a perfect excuse to talk openly about Jesus. People who never knew their commitment to Christ, suddenly knew. And other people suddenly opened up to them. People who had worked together for years suddenly were discussing their faith, when they hadn't felt open to before. As a result, his church expanded exponentially. God went viral. Soon, strings tied around fingers were everywhere and thousands of people were telling total strangers about what Christ had done in their lives.

"One of those strangers, ironically, ended up being me.

"I sat in Ellison's chair, nineteen years old, completely humbled. He spoke passionately about the ministries that the expansion of his church had allowed him to begin: outreach to addicts, food and housing for poor around the world, and a pregnancy resource center. Well, of course that last one perked my ears up. 'What do they do there?' I asked. 'They help girls in need. They provide money for medical bills associated with pregnancy, they drive women to their sonograms, and help line up adoptions. And for the women who need it, they even bring them food, clean their homes, and hold their hands.'

"Well of course I started crying again. But Ellison mistook my tears for something else. He joyously insisted. 'You made all that possible. You helped all those people.'

"'Not me,' I said. 'A twelve-year-old girl who never once had to struggle in life. She did it. Not me.' I really broke down then. I began to weep uncontrollably, right there in his office. He stood up from his chair, walked over to where I was sitting, and squeezed both my hands.

"That September, I gave birth to the baby I was carrying. The church had helped me line up a nice Christian family to adopt him. I asked them only two things. I said, 'Please name the boy Riley, and please help him to *always remember* Jesus.'

"Now I am a member of the church that I once upon a time, unknowingly, helped to create. I've been married for fifteen years and my daughter is twelve. She's a social butterfly. And with every smile I see on her face, which brings me so much joy, I think of the joy precious little Riley has brought to those deserving parents through the years, and I think of the people who helped me bring him into the world, and I think of all the people in his life who he will help, and I think of how actions have reactions and how the good deeds we do, the brave good deeds, often outlive us."

"Wow," said Andrew Crenshaw. He had been hanging on her every word. He leaned back in his chair and asked, "Why did it stop?"

"Why did what stop?"

"I haven't seen any strings on the hands of any of his congregation. I haven't seen any strings on anyone except you and the pastor."

Nancy Fuller looked down. She said, "A man from Ellison's church walked into his office wearing a string wrapped around his finger. His secretary asked him about it and he told her about Jesus Christ. She claimed to be offended, and when later that year one of her coworkers was promoted above her, she claimed it was religious discrimination that prevented the promotion from going to her. She sued.

"Eventually the lawsuit was thrown out, but by then the company had already changed its policy to forbid 'proselytizing.' Other companies, and even public schools, had heard of the lawsuit—and others like it—and they all followed suit. In an extreme case, one insurance company even tried outlawing cross necklaces. That was challenged in court, so they dropped it. But I am told that their employee handbook, to this day, prohibits strings around fingers.

"God was resoundingly rejected from the public square. And it all seemed to happen overnight. All the good Christians, even from Ellison's crowd, got tired of having to take it off, then put it back on. They all gave up on the idea when it had been made too difficult. So the good deed I once did, while braver than I even am today, the good deed that returned to me and saved the life of my son, Riley, was finally snuffed out."

Andrew looked down. It had been a tough morning for him.

She said kindly, "Well, that's my story. I felt that God wanted me to come here to tell it."

Andrew laughed, not sure if she was kidding. "Yeah, and I suppose God wants me to print every word?"

"Possibly," she said. "All I know is he sent me here to you."

Andrew looked down again.

When Nancy Fuller left, one more connection in his mind finally came together. There was a reason why he had been so repulsed by his nattering colleagues before. They all had accepted the same news—that someone truly exceptional had fallen from greatness and fallen from grace—the difference, and what truly disgusted Andrew, was that they seemed overjoyed by it.

When Andrew Crenshaw arrived at the church, he saw a small group of protestors that had gathered in the front lawn of the church. He wasn't sure what they were protesting exactly—all their signs just read "hypocrite"—Pastor Ellison's whole existence, maybe.

There was a man in sandals and a brown corduroy jacket, a few sizes too small. There was a woman with a large knit hat covering birds-nest hair. There was another man hiding behind a feral beard and black, thick-framed glasses. His fingers were covered with rings and he gestured with them as he talked incessantly about "haters" and his hatred for them.

Andrew Crenshaw thought about coining a new term. When he looked at the motley protestors a thought came to his head: *they were a group only Pastor Ellison could love.*

There was one girl there, however, who seemed out of place. She wore an oversized man's dress blazer. Andrew Crenshaw didn't know what to make of her.

A group of Andrew's fellow newsmen, and their cameras, had descended on the sententious assembly. Andrew Crenshaw couldn't help but notice that the reporters outnumbered the protestors, but he knew it wouldn't look that way in the footage tonight.

Andrew drove his car around and entered through the back door. Before entering the church, he took a good contemplative look at the face of Mead Mountain.

When he rounded the corner through the open door to Ellison's office, he noticed the pastor jump slightly.

Andrew Crenshaw exaggerated his wave and said, "Just me."

Ellison stood up and extended a warm handshake.

"You were expecting me," Andrew Crenshaw said, half question, half statement.

"Of course. You just caught me deep in thought is all."

"Well, I imagine you have a lot to think about."

Ellison laughed at his understatement. He asked, "Do you know an effective way to shut your brain off?"

"Yes, but you wouldn't like it."

"Try me." It was Ellison's habit of assuming the best about people which led him to press the seemingly vice-free reporter.

The reporter cleared his throat. He pulled out a pad of paper and a voice recorder and said, "Actually, I've found sharing my problems in intimate detail with the press to be very cathartic."

Ellison laughed again. "Smooth."

Andrew smiled guiltily. He said, "Well, I'm a pro."

Both men waited for the other.

Andrew Crenshaw cleared his throat again. Finally, he said, "Well, what's on your mind, Pastor?"

"Actually, I was pondering the implications of the hypostatic union."

Andrew laughed. "That's not really the story on everyone's mind."

"No?"

"No, not exactly." There was another moment of silence. Andrew Crenshaw wasn't sure why he wanted Ellison to be the one to bring up the prostitution; it was probably just because he had grown used to the pastor shooting straight with him. He said, "I take it you saw the protesters?"

"It's not the first time this place has been targeted for that," Ellison said with a voice that was both dismissing and proud.

Andrew Crenshaw's eyes glanced to the old-fashioned circular coat rack, where he was used to seeing either Ellison's red windbreaker or his blazer. Ellison had the windbreaker on, but there was no blazer in sight. He said, "I take it you have been out there to see them?"

Noticing the connection Andrew had just made, Ellison said, "Yes. The poor girl was wearing just a spaghetti shirt. She must've forgotten all about this crazy cold front and left home without a jacket. Or it's possible, if she lives around here, that she just doesn't own a jacket. I know a lot of people here who've never owned a heavy coat." As Ellison talked he pressed the palms of both hands against the warm sides of his coffee mug.

"What did you say to her?"

Ellison shrugged. "I said, 'You're cold. Please, take my jacket.'"

"What'd she say?"

"Well, she said, 'I'm not cold.'"

Andrew laughed.

"I said, 'You're shivering."

Andrew laughed again. He was enjoying the deadpan voice in which Ellison told the story.

"So I said fine and left the jacket on the ground in case she changed her mind."

"You left the jacket on the ground?"

"Well, there was no other place for it."

"Then you walked away?" Andrew now wondered if he would ever see the jacket again.

"Well, I did at first, but then I was struck with an analogy. I turned back around and told her, 'This jacket is a lot like salvation. Jesus saw that you were cold, shivering, and suffering, so He brought you a jacket. The only thing He cannot do is make you put it on.' It wasn't my intention to preach. Too predictable! I just couldn't seem to help myself. But then I got back to my office—and if you really want the truth about what was on my mind, this is it—I was mad at myself for my careless words. I didn't even realize that my little analogy had cast myself in the role of Christ."

Andrew Crenshaw smiled.

Ellison added, "Well, at least there were no press there, yet."

"Would it make you feel better to know that the girl finally accepted the jacket?"

Ellison's eyes lit up. It clearly did make him feel better. He had been so caught up in metaphorical meaning, his chest seemed to swell and his face seemed to flush as if he had found out the girl had just been saved. He said, "See, you never know how your actions will affect people."

Andrew Crenshaw saw an opening and was tired of waiting. He asked, "What about your actions last night?"

Ellison mouthed the words *"Last night..."* Andrew Crenshaw was shocked to see that he didn't understand immediately. Finally, he said, "Oh yes, my rendezvous with a police lady."

"Yes, *that* last night."

Ellison proceeded to tell him the story, the real story, just as he had intended to do with the crowd of reporters outside the jail, before Tyler's text had whisked him away. He told him about his routine assignations with prostitutes and how he was only ever trying to spread the Word of God.

"Why didn't you just give that phony excuse to the press?" Andrew smirked.

"I was about to, but I discovered, in what was possibly the worst timing ever, I missed a text."

"A text?"

Ellison told him about the text, the suicidal boy, and how he had been trying to help the mother, "a stripper, who by the way, I first reached out to using the same approach, offering the same *weird* barter."

As he spoke he could see the muscles in Andrew Crenshaw's face loosen, soften. His shoulders lowered a nearly imperceptible amount. Andrew Crenshaw noticed it too. He was surprised by how this entire assignment was ending up nothing like he thought it would be.

When Ellison finished, Andrew Crenshaw said, "Okay, I'll take that story to my editor. I'm afraid people have already made up their minds, though."

"Me too," Ellison said, regretfully. "However, what's most important to me, Mr. Crenshaw, is that you believe me."

Andrew squirmed a bit under Pastor Ellison's direct glance. He said, "It's important that we, in the press, try to remain neutral."

Ellison smiled. He could imagine all the times Andrew had used that line to evade letting the subjects of his reports know he didn't trust, respect, or even like them; this time it was obvious he had just used it to conceal from Ellison how much he did.

Andrew added, "It will be more believable, of course, if I could talk with one of the prostitutes you've... encountered."

"I'm sure I can't stop you," said Ellison.

"Well, do you remember the names of any of them?"

"No, but I'm sure they'll remember me." Pastor Ellison spread his hands out. "I've propositioned just about every prostitute on this side of the city by now."

Andrew sniffed. He said, "I'm gonna do you a favor and leave that quote out of my article."

Ellison laughed.

"Okay, will you give me the names of the boy and the stripper?"

"No," said Ellison.

"I didn't think so. How about the name of the strip club then?"

"No," he shook his head. "Sorry."

"You're not giving me much to work with here."

"I gave you the truth; that's enough. Now, let's talk about something else."

Andrew Crenshaw put down his pad and stretched out his legs. He said, "Let's talk about coffee." He motioned over the pastor's shoulder, "Is this pot fresh?"

"By all means..." Ellison jumped to his feet. He looked around for a second and then began to rummage through the top shelf of his bookshelf. Finally, he produced an old coffee mug.

When Ellison stepped toward the pot, Andrew Crenshaw protested, "Oh, I can pour it."

"Nonsense. How do you take it?"

"Black is fine."

When Ellison handed him the coffee, Andrew couldn't help but notice that the cup read, "Mardi Gras 1999." The idea of Pastor Ellison roaming New Orleans, prospecting for lost souls made Andrew smile. The year on the cup made him think he must have been up to his tricks for a while.

"You know, it's pure arrogance," Riley said when he saw his friend pondering the cup. "People often say that I'm humble. I guess now we have proof that I'm not."

"How do you mean?"

"I knew this young seminary student once. For some reason he looked up to me, so he came to me with this idea of entering into the lions' den. He wanted to go to the strippers, naked and all, and preach Jesus to them—pay for their time if he had to. I rebuked him. I told him it was a foolish idea and to never let his mind entertain it again."

"You thought he had other motivations for such a mission."

"No, I knew his intentions were pure. 'But you're underestimating the devil,' I told him. 'To walk right onto his turf, and offer up your bare chest to the most devastating weapon he has at his disposal... it's foolish.' I looked him in the eye and simply said, 'He'll win. You'll lose.' Truly, the only way you can win a fight like that is to never have to fight it."

"And then you did it without him."

"Like I said, *arrogance.*"

"So how have you won..." He held up the cup to show the date. "... all these years? Or has the devil bested you?"

Riley shook his head. He said, "Before I leave the house. I kneel down and pray with my wife. I confess to God that I am vulnerable to such temptations, and I ask for His protection."

"I don't know; that sounds pretty humble to me."

"No," Riley insisted. "A humble man would respect the risk. A wise and humble man wouldn't go in the first place."

Andrew tried to take a sip, but it was still too hot. He said, "Hey, weren't you once named in a poll *The Most Humble Man in America?*"

Ellison looked back at Andrew genuinely confused. His eyes were searching. "No... no, that was Mason Kessler." There was a new sparkle in Riley's eyes just saying the name.

"Oh yeah, Stone Kessler. I love that guy."

"So do I," Riley said a bit too proudly.

"Do you know him?"

"Yes," Riley anxiously grabbed their picture from off his shelf and handed it to Andrew. "He's actually the man who converted me to Christ."

"Really? For some reason I thought you've always been Christian. Wasn't your mother Christian?"

Riley shrugged. "She tried her best with me."

"Wait a minute." The picture had sparked a memory in Andrew. "Stone Kessler? I thought I heard you converted him."

Ellison laughed. He said, "Yeah. I first heard that rumor ten years ago, and no matter how many times I try to put it to bed, it seems to keep reawakening. But check our ages—the timeline doesn't fit. Remember his performance in the 1982 World Series? That was his first time to publicly thank God."

"Kind of made it a habit after that point," injected Andrew Crenshaw.

Ellison laughed at his understatement. He said, "I was seventeen years old years old in 1982."

"Well, so much for that rumor. I'll make a note of it in my column."

"Thanks." His tone was humoring. Andrew Crenshaw was beginning to think Ellison didn't share his enthusiasm for the power of his column.

"So, how did you two meet then?"

Ellison laughed joyously. "It could've only been God's grace. I was just some kid—no connections, no bestseller—not the type who hobnobs with major league, celebrity athletes. I only had two interests: baseball and socialism." The pastor added, laughing, "You see? I've always wanted to save the world. And of course I was atheist, but more like *Christian-hater*. I spent most of my day inside my head contemplating how stupid one would have to be to call themselves Christian; you know, 'tobacco-chewing, knuckle-dragging, banjo-picking, troglodytes...' that sort of tripe.

I guess it made me feel smarter myself. I was yet to feel any real contentment in life, but I got that self-satisfied feeling that comes with looking down on others, and with nothing to compare it to, I called myself happy.

"But in 1982, a week after the World Series, when the name Mason Kessler was on everyone's lips, when some sports writer had given him the moniker *Stone Mason* for the first time, when the best highlight reel from a single game still played in our minds, at the apex of his heroism, especially around here, he did a press conference and told his story for the first time. He said he'd been a drunk. He described his aimlessness and emptiness and I knew, possibly for the first time, I wasn't happy. I knew he was describing me.

"But then he told me and the world about his relationship with Christ. He said it was through God's power that he could do the phenomenal things he did out on that field, but more than that, he said it was God's power that allowed him to rise from the misery he'd been in. He said that the distance he'd traveled and the work he had done to overcome alcoholism and self-hatred was a feat that made Major League Baseball look easy. Then he looked into the camera and he quoted Philippians 4:13—*I can do all things through Christ who strengthens me.*

"And I wept. I cried and I didn't know why."

"You were seventeen."

Ellison could tell by the special way that Andrew Crenshaw had said it that he had made a small assumption, so he said, "But I wasn't converted that day."

"But it was the first step?"

Ellison's head kind of swiveled. He said, "Eh... not really. I just wiped the tears from my face and tried not to think of what had inspired them. Actually, I was able to just blame it all on the alcohol."

"You were drinking?"

"I was drunk. I was living in my parent's home, had my bedroom door barricaded by my dresser, and I was drunk."

"So, when did... "

"Flash forward four years, not much had changed. Mason Kessler was still at the height of his game, and I was still mired in misery, claiming I was happy, happy enough."

"And Stone Kessler was back in the World Series."

Ellison nodded. "You know your baseball," he said admiringly, and added, "Only this year, he lost."

"He *caused* his team to lose," injected Andrew Crenshaw, who having received kudos, was anxious to show off more.

"Yes, that he did." The pastor shrugged, "But I still loved him, despite his mistakes, despite incessant preaching—what could I do? He was a sensational player!" Ellison smiled. "So one night about a week later, the great California legend, Mason Kessler—" Ellison said the name like it was gilded in gold—"the Christian soldier, armed with a message so inspiring that it could bring a hardened young atheist to tears, *Mason Kessler,* walked into a bar and ordered a double shot of Crown."

Andrew Crenshaw shot up in his chair, nearly spilling his coffee. This was clearly a bit of baseball history that he had never heard. "Are you serious?"

Ellison didn't answer directly; he said, "And the young, naive, self-absorbed, socialist bartender poured it for him."

"It was you?"

"Yes."

"You poured *Stone Kessler* a shot of Crown?" Andrew Crenshaw exclaimed.

"A *double* shot of Crown," Ellison corrected. "I hadn't recognized him. He was wearing a hat and large sunglasses. Plus, you have to imagine the type of bar we were in—a rundown dive named Tequila Mockingbird—the only type that would've hired the likes of me. This was the last place on earth that one would expect to see a Hall of Famer."

"That's why he picked it."

"Yes. But I hadn't figured that out yet, so I just slid him the drink he ordered and told him the price. He slid me a twenty and said, 'Keep the change.' That was his mistake. That's where he slipped up. That was God. It was the first time I felt *something's wrong.* I took a better look at the guy and it hit me in a flash—that double take that anyone feels when meeting a celebrity, the surreal realization that they actually exist outside of a screen. That flash was followed by a second flash—the words he'd been saying for four years, the foundation he set up, the millions of dollars he'd raised for charity, the tears that he made me cry. It all hit me as he raised his glass toward his mouth, so I shot forward and grabbed his wrist."

"You grabbed Stone Mason Kessler's wrist?" Andrew Crenshaw was thoroughly enjoying this story.

"Yes. I was twenty-one. He turned his face to me and said, 'What do you think you're doing, son?' I nodded to the drink and I said, 'What the fudge do you think *you're* doing?' only I didn't say *fudge*. He set the glass down and said, 'This is none of your business, my friend.' I didn't respond. Neither of us said anything for the next moment, but the panes of his sunglasses were still aimed at me, and I still had my hand gripped hard on his wrist. That's the first time I noticed my reflection. He had those reflective type of shades that were popular at the time, especially among celebrities wishing to remain incognito. I saw my reflection, and thought: *Who am I?* I was a dumb, Marxist kid with no special talent, no education, no prospects, no future, and there I was clutching the wrist of a muscle-bound, multi-millionaire, world-famous, Hall of Fame great. I just felt: *Who am I?*

"I let go of his wrist and grabbed onto the glass. He tugged on the glass and I tugged back. I knew that if this were to come down to a contest of masculinity, he'd win handily. But there was a voice in me, telling me not to let go. Inside my head, where everything was usually muddled and chaotic, suddenly it was clear. I loved Mason Kessler, and because I loved him, I wanted him nowhere near the life I was living. In that clarity, I saw how much I hated myself. I had never sought a change because my wretched life was good enough for the likes of me... but not for him.

"He continued to glare at me, a hidden, hard, intimidating stare. He could see fear in my eyes—I was about to cry—and I was shaking like a leaf on a tree. I think that was God, too. Mason saw my shaking. He saw the fear I had, standing up *against* my personal hero. It must have touched him somehow. He saw that despite all that fear, I still wouldn't let go.

"Finally he let go and stormed out of the bar. A week later he showed up at the bar again, still disguised. He said he wasn't there to order a drink. He wanted to find me; he wanted to thank me. I felt special and I got his autograph. A full month later, he showed up again, this time with no hat and no glasses. All he said was, 'We should talk.'

"And we did talk. He showed me that anything not good enough for him should not be good enough for me. He shared with me the gospel and asked me to invite Jesus into my heart.

"I had pulled a thorn from the paw of a lion. That one decision—the first worthwhile thing I'd ever done—changed my entire life."

Tyler checked his phone. It was still dead, despite having been plugged in all day. When he followed the charger cord back behind his night stand, he discovered that it wasn't plugged in after all. He walked it over to a new outlet and plugged it in. As soon as it turned on, he noticed that he had seventeen missed calls. All from the same number, all minutes apart. He also had three texts. They read:

You are precious.

You are sacred.

You are a child of God.

Chapter Ten

January 11—Five days left

When Pastor Ellison pulled up to the church, he was overwhelmed by emotion at just the sight of Mead Mountain. To top it off, he spotted a rundown motorcycle out front. It made him hurry his pace a little. He greeted Ashley McAllister in the hallway and she said, "There's a young man here to see you. I hope you don't mind, I told him he could wait in your office."

When he opened the door to his office, he saw Tyler sitting with his elbows in and his head hunched over. He looked like a schoolboy waiting to enter the principal's office. His eyes, what the pastor could see of them, were bloodshot. Ellison imagined that he had spent the night drinking again. He said, "Hello, Tyler. I'm happy to see you."

All that Tyler said was, "Hey."

Ellison made his way over to his chair behind the desk. He could already see that Tyler wasn't going to be forthcoming.

"You drove your bike over here in the rain?"

Tyler shrugged it off, like it was no big deal.

"I see. Does your mom know that you're here?"

Tyler shook his head.

"She still mad?"

"At you?" Tyler asked.

"Yeah."

Tyler laughed and Ellison felt one sheet of ice melt between them. He said, "One summer, at a pool party, my brother started choking on a hotdog. Everyone looked to my mom to perform the Heimlich Maneuver, but she didn't know how. I ended up being the one to do it, even though I was only eleven. So, yeah, we pretty much knew she wasn't a nurse after that."

Ellison laughed as he pictured Poison lying and changing into scrubs for nearly five years, while her children played along. There was something strangely touching about it. He asked, "So she never knew you knew?"

"She does now!" snapped Tyler. He added a sarcastic, "Thanks a lot!"

Ellison laughed.

Tyler smiled warmly and said, "Man, I talked to her; we worked it all out."

"That's good," Ellison said. "You know, your mom's a hero. Whatever other mistakes she has made, she cares about you and is trying the best she can to help you. That's a hero in my book."

Tyler smiled slightly, trying to conceal how much the words meant to him.

"So, then... what brings you by?" Ellison asked.

"What matters?" Tyler asked, even before Ellison was finished.

"What matters?"

"You told me my grades didn't matter and stuff."

"Oh yeah."

"So what matters?"

"Well, the simple answer is, everything we choose to do or say matters."

Tyler's face showed a little irritation. He was looking for something more specific, a shortcut that would let him bypass all the drudgery, a royal road to life. He was also hoping it would *sound* wise, perhaps even worthy of a bumper sticker.

Pastor Ellison continued, "And, more precisely, what we choose matters in only two regards: Is it pleasing to God? And does it strengthen our faith in Jesus Christ? What matters is that I love you, and you love me." Pastor Ellison made a serving motion with his palm. "That's all that matters."

The boy smiled briefly. It appeared to have been prompted by the world's smallest devotion to etiquette. But after a quick second, his expression faded back into a numb emptiness. It was the same look the boy had always been chained to, but today Pastor Ellison saw something new. It took his years of experience in trying to preach to the lost for him to see: the new look in Tyler's eyes was openness. There had been a reason he drove his motorcycle to the church in the rain. There was something that the boy needed from him.

"So, who's black?" The boy motioned toward the chessboard, evasively changing the subject.

"You want to know who is black?"

"Who's black?"

"Stone Kessler."

"The baseball player?" Tyler's eyes darted to the photo of Ellison and

Kessler on the shelf. He must've had a pretty good look at the place while he was waiting.

Ellison nodded. "We go back a long time. He moved to Eureka when he retired, but we see each other every couple of years.

"Eight years ago we were playing chess. I was white and he was black. I guess you see how it turned out; the game is two moves away from being all over. 'Check' I told him, then watched him stare at the board, trying to come up with a plan that could keep him from his fate. Finally, I said, ominously, 'There's nothing you can do.' All he said was, 'Hold on.' What could I do? I held on. Ten minutes later, he was still studying the board. Ten minutes after that, he was *still* studying the board. 'This is the type of tenacity that wins ballgames,' I said flippantly. He just shushed me. After a few more minutes I said, 'Wow, you really, *really* can't stand to lose.' He said, 'Shut up.'"

The boy laughed.

So did Ellison. "In my own church he told me to shut up. I checked my watch and realized that he had a plane to catch, and that, instead of the scintillating conversation we usually had—pondering the eternal mystery and grandeur of God—we were going to spend our last minutes together in silence, while he checked every possible piece for every possible move. Finally, he said, 'Leave this here. Don't touch it.' Well, he only makes it to town every few years! But what could I do? It was Mason Kessler. This man changed my entire life. So I left it out." Ellison laughed, "But every time he's been back since, he comes up with an excuse not to finish!"

Tyler took another look at the board.

"He's seen hard times," the pastor said pensively. "It was God who lifted him up from the path he was on. *I* have also seen hard times." Ellison stood up and walked toward the board. "I know what it's like when you feel you can't move, can't win. I know what it's like when your mind travels and re-travels the same path, trying to find a way out. You start with your queen, here." He touched the queen. "And you try every option. Every possible option, then every counter move. When that doesn't work you try your rook. Then your knight, your bishop, all your pawns, then you just try to get your king out of the way. And none of it works. Do you know what you do then?"

Without missing a beat, the boy answered, "You try your queen again."

It was exactly what Ellison was going to say. He was happy to have made the connection, but his heart broke; he never liked to see anyone understand suffering so well. He nodded, "And again and again and again and again. And you wake up each morning knowing you have nothing to look forward to other than your stupid brain—which you can't turn off—reexamining the same useless moves... because you *don't want to lose.*"

"But you've lost!" the boy snapped. He gestured to the chessboard, "Black has lost! There are no moves!"

"Oh, but there is one. Hand your life over to God. With Him, anything is possible. God reaches down and grabs you, lifts you up and carries you in his hand." When Ellison said this, he grabbed the black king and lifted him out of check. "And when God lifts you high above it, you look down at your life as we are looking at the chessboard now. And everything you thought was your life, was just a game. And all the things you thought were your problems don't seem so significant anymore. You cease being the pieces and become the player... no, you realize that you had been the player all along. There is a whole world that matters, that is important, but when you are down in the game, you think the game is all there is."

Ellison smiled because he received the perfect response from a listening teenager: silence. He went to put the black king back on the board and spotted a large pharmaceutical bottle down by Tyler's feet.

Tyler's eyes shot to his eyes and he knew he had seen it. "I did try to kill myself," the boy said abruptly.

Ellison lowered himself into his seat. "You did? How?"

Tyler reached down and grabbed the empty pharmaceutical bottle. He said, "I swallowed a whole bottle of pills."

"This is very serious," said Ellison, receiving the bottle. He looked at the label. *Damitol.* He immediately asked, *"This* bottle?"

"Yes."

"You swallowed an entire bottle of Damitol?"

"Yes."

"Last Thursday night?"

"Yes. The night I sent you that text."

The pastor leaned back. He made a sad face, a sad but knowing face.

Tyler correctly interpreted the expression. He shouted, "I'm not lying! I swallowed every last one of them."

Pastor Ellison sighed. He tapped the Damitol label. He said, "Tyler, I remember when this stuff came out. They were barely able to get it approved. It is one of the most controversial drugs on the market. It's nicknamed the *Suicide Pill*, Tyler! Now listen, I've tried to make myself very clear. I want to help you. I'm prepared to bend over backward to help you. What do you gain by coming in here and..." He tried not to used the word *lying*. "...prevaricating like this?"

"I'm not lying!" Tyler shouted.

"Tyler, if you swallowed a whole bottle of Damitol, there's simply no way you'd be sitting in front of me right now."

"It happened!" Tyler was still shouting.

"You'd be dead!" Tyler was only partially surprised when Ellison shouted back.

"I swallowed those pills," Tyler then added a word not typically heard in churches.

"Then how are you still alive?"

"God did it!" Tyler shouted. When he said that, two pools of tears formed spontaneously in his eyes. "He lifted me up out of checkmate."

That was the moment that Ellison realized Tyler's bloodshot eyes had not been from alcohol this time; Tyler had been crying all morning. The pastor's lips parted slightly, but he did not speak.

"I asked God for a sign, remember? I asked God to show me a sign and He eventually did. He just did it on His own timing, I guess. You may not believe me, but I know what happened. I swallowed all those pills, thought I was slipping into death, and woke up fine the next day, with no more than just a slight hangover from the alcohol."

Pastor Ellison was considering all that had happened. It had cost him a thousand dollars in order for him to talk with Tyler's mother in private. He was remembering now how close he had come to simply walking away. He didn't because he heard a voice in his head, as clear as a bell. That voice asked only one question: *How much is one soul worth to God?* The voice hadn't been for Poison; the voice was referring to Tyler.

As he considered the gravity of it, both his hands raised slowly to his mouth. His fingers stroked the freshly shaven side of his cheek while he marveled at God's grace.

Finally, Ellison lowered his hands and said, "I'm very sorry I didn't believe you, Tyler." He chuckled disarmingly, "Ya gotta admit it's unbelievable!"

"You do believe me?"

"Yes."

"I wonder because it only happened three days later."

Ellison laughed. "One thing I've learned: God's timing is not our timing."

"And you do think it was God?"

He spread his hands. "I can't think of any other explanation."

"So there is no other explanation? Is there a way that someone could swallow a whole bottle of Damitol and live?"

"And not even go to the hospital?"

The boy shook his head.

"And not even have a tummy ache?"

He shook his head again.

Pastor Ellison thought about this. He had made up his mind to shoot straight with this kid, so he really thought about it. He said, "No. No, it would take a miracle."

Poison hadn't been to work since the day Wyatt told her to stay home during remodeling. She had been waiting for someone to call her, but no one had called. She was beginning to run out of money, so she drove to the club to see what was going on.

She was surprised to see the parking lot full of cars. When she walked through the front doors, she noticed that the lights were set to the same level as usual, the open sign was on, and nothing in the lobby at least seemed to have been remodeled.

She spotted Isaac working the door. Isaac had always been good to her, so despite the fact that Ecstasy and Desire were hovering around him, Poison walked over to talk to him. She asked, "What's everyone doing here?"

"What are *you* doing here?" snapped Desire before Isaac had a chance to speak.

Poison ignored her and spoke straight to Isaac, "Wyatt was supposed to call me when we reopened."

"Wyatt?" laughed Ecstasy. "Wyatt's gone. You don't know what you're talking about."

"You'll have to talk to the Cap'n," Isaac gently informed her.

"What about Mr. Holloway?" asked Poison. "Who's *the Captain*?"

"The Cap'n!" Ecstasy said, obnoxiously.

"Cap... n?" asked Poison, "As in Crunch?"

"You're an idiot," laughed Desire.

Poison's face started to redden. She knew how much Ecstasy and Desire hated her and she wanted to get away from them, so she just turned and walked straight into the club. No one tried to stop her. Desire just made a sound like she was coughing up phlegm.

"Whatever," Poison shouted back. As she entered the main club, it was dark, so dark that she couldn't see a single person. It was only because she had worked there for more than half her life that she was able to find her way to the back office without her eyes having to adjust.

She entered without knocking. The lights were on in the office, as usual, but the furniture was different. She found a man with his feet up on a large desk. He was a heavy-set man in his late forties. The extra weight on his round face made his eyes look even more beady than they might have otherwise. There was a trail of sweat down each side of his face, despite the A/C being on full blast. There were patches of red dirt on his worn out jeans. The desk looked sturdy enough, but past its prime. Poison imagined someone had discovered the desk in the basement of an old school building slated for demolition. She could not imagine where anyone would have found the man.

"Who are you?" Poison snapped.

"Who are you?" he rebutted.

"I work here."

"Waitress?"

"Dancer," she stressed.

He looked at her face, but Poison could tell he was looking at her wrinkles. He looked away to spit some tobacco juice into an empty can of Coors. "What's your name?"

"Poison."

"Oh, *you're* Poison." He laughed condescendingly. "Now it makes sense."

She could feel her anger escalate. She didn't like people talking about her behind her back. She began angrily, "Who ar—" She stopped abruptly. She knew who he was, the type of guy who would give himself a nickname. He was *Cap'n*, obviously. But she didn't know what that meant to her employment. The anger grew and she felt like she wanted to snap, it was her dire financial straits alone that restrained her. She couldn't dare take the chance of offending this guy, just in case her worse fear ended up true: Her job depended on this creep named Cap'n.

"I thought we sent you packing," he said.

"Packing?"

"Listen... Poison. I don't know if you failed to notice, but this place is under new management. We're going for a new image here and I'm afraid you just don't fit in."

She looked at the dilapidated desk and the dilapidated man. She wanted to snap, "What image?" It took everything in her to keep her fists from balling. She asked, "Where is Mr. Holloway?"

The man laughed again. She interpreted his laughter to mean, *Silly child.* He said, "He's gone! He's dead. Six feet under."

"What about Junior?" She must've been desperate; Wyatt hated her— but at least he treated her better than this snake. At least Wyatt knew that she actually worked there.

"Wyatt inherited the place and sold it to me."

"But..." She had nothing.

"Don't you get it? It's over. You're too old. We've got no room here for a shopworn day-dancer. Go away now. Go do whatever it is that washed-up strippers do."

"I've worked here for twenty years."

"That's the problem."

"I have nowhere else to go."

"That's not my concern."

She felt an unstoppable tidal wave of rage heading straight to the shore. It was coming to clobber this rude wretch and she could already picture what would happen when it did. Only, at the last second she threw her own body in its path, bearing the brunt herself, shielding the wretch. When the unstoppable force of her rage collided with the immovable love for her son, the pressure forced her eyes shut tight.

She stood there and trembled for a moment, then finally opened her eyes. They were completely wet with tears. She cried, "Please?" The tears streamed down her face.

Cap'n just laughed.

"Please, I need this job. I have a son." She continued to cry.

He said, "Oh... this is pathetic."

"Please."

"You're pathetic."

"I need the money."

"Just look at you! No one wants you. Oh, wait! I have an idea."

"What?" Her heart actually felt some hope.

"Come back when you're nineteen." He laughed.

She struggled to control her face. She didn't want to show him any more tears, and she couldn't do or say to him what she really wanted.

"No wait," he laughed. "I really do have an idea."

She didn't answer. Tears slowly began to leak again from her eyes, even as he laughed all the while.

"I said I have an idea," he said threateningly, suddenly no longer laughing.

"What's your idea?" she complied, her voice as pleasant as she could muster.

"If you can prove to me that you've still got it, I'll let you stay."

"You will?" she asked.

"Of course."

"Okay..." she said cautiously, "So... I'll go get changed." She turned to leave.

"Not out there," he said, laughing.

She turned back around. This was the first time she discovered the true source of his mocking laughter: he was drunk.

"Why don't you dance for me?" He rolled back his chair and slowly drew his knees apart, presenting his lap.

"What?"

"You said you're a dancer. I want a dance. I need to check out the merchandise before I can put it on the shelf."

She could feel her jaw flex so tight, she thought her bicuspids were going to crack. "There's no music," she said.

"This job ain't about music, honey."

Poison hesitated.

"What's the big deal?" he asked. "It's part of the job."

She tried to keep her mind from thinking about anything but Tyler. "Fine." She took off her shirt robotically, then went to unhook her bra."

"Not over there!" he snapped, patting his knee.

She grabbed her shirt and thought about running out of the room.

"No, keep that off."

She forced herself to walk closer to him. She was overcome by the stale smell of beer.

She reached to undo her pants. He grabbed her wrist.

"Not so quickly," he said. "You've got to move a little. Dance."

She began to move. Her knees were between his knees. All the lights were on in the room.

As she danced, she closed her eyes.

It was late May, 1997.

"Do you know what I want?" asked the boy. He was young and strong, tall and good looking. His wavy hair and facial features had a boyish quality, but his irrepressible confidence was manly.

The girl was defenseless against that confidence, the way he seemed in control of every situation, the way that every movement of his body and every word out of his mouth seemed so effortless. "What do you want?" She knew in that second she would have given him anything that he asked for, anything at all.

"I want a dance," he said.

"But there's no music," she said.

"Dancing isn't about music," he said.

"Oh, it isn't, huh? What's it about then?"

He grabbed her arm and pulled her body close to his. Without waiting for her permission, he began to lead her in a music-less dance. He said, "Dance just one dance with me, and then you can tell me what it's about."

He tried to lead, but within a few moments, their dance steps morphed into gentle swaying. They were two young romantics, swaying and holding each other. She slowly lowered her head onto his muscular shoulder. And just when she thought she couldn't be happier, she heard music.

He had snuck his remote control out of his pocket and powered on his CD-changer in the corner of the room. The perfect disc was already in there and he selected *track three*. It was Tim McGraw's brand new song "It's Your Love."

Sweet music filled the room and he pulled her into him so tight, she had little room left to breathe.

She felt protected. It was the type of protection she never received from her parents. It was the protection that was long overdue, and she knew in her heart it would last forever. She finally knew what it meant to be pampered, cradled, and treasured, and she would never let go. And neither would he.

When the song came to an end, she was crying. She didn't move her head because she didn't want him to see her tears. He didn't try to get her to move; he already knew she was crying. He asked, while still holding her, "So, now what you do think dancing is all about?"

She pulled him closer. Her cheek was to his shoulder, her eyes peering out into a dark room. She didn't answer him, but asked a question of her own, "Do you think I'm pretty?"

He abruptly stepped away from her. She had no choice but to look at him now. Her eyes and cheeks were wet and she had never felt so vulnerable in all her life. He looked down from his towering heights and she knew that the next words out of his mouth would change her life: either give her poor trembling legs the strength to continue to stand, or scar her young heart beyond recognition. She wished she had never asked.

He said, "You are the prettiest girl I've ever met." They were the only eight words he'd ever told her that were true.

That night as she lay in bed beside him, the first time she had ever lain down with a man, she reflected on her life. *I am truly fortunate to be so pretty.* She wasn't trying to fixate on it, but it felt really good. She knew she was lucky. She knew that all her girlfriends wanted a shot with him, and she was the one who got him. *It isn't fair... but life's not fair. It doesn't mean I'm a better person; it just means I'm lucky. I have something of value.* She smiled. *It's going to win me everything I want out of life. It just means I'm lucky.*

Three years later, she gave birth to her second son, and the wavy-haired man was nowhere to be found.

Poison felt the man put his hand on her naked thigh and she snapped out of her trance. She inhaled the smell of Skoal on his breath and the cigarette smoke on his clothes. She saw the shapeless contempt in his eyes. She saw the tightness of his jaw and the three-day stubble on his disgusting face.

She brought her right hand down onto that face with all her might.

She went crazy on him.

She used her left hand to grab his long, matted hair. Her right hand formed a fist and she began to pound his face with everything in her. She focused all her anger; it was finally her chance to hurt the man who humiliated her, who betrayed her, and who no longer found her pretty.

A series of swear words flew out of her mouth with all the volume she could muster. She secretly knew it was a cry for help—Isaac. She had the advantage of surprise, but she knew she'd be in trouble once the man's shock wore off. Isaac was her only hope of survival.

The Cap'n was finally able to stand up and grab her arms, but she continued to struggle. His hands were too strong to break free. She began to try to kick him, but he flung her away from him. Her body flew tumbling across the top of the desk and onto the floor. He stood up in a fit of rage.

Isaac opened the door to the office. When the bouncer had thrown Pastor Ellison out, he had instinctively sided with the woman, but this time the man was his employer, and no one was sure what Isaac would do. Not even him.

The Cap'n took a step to round the desk and descend on her, but thought twice since he had to factor in the bouncer's presence. Isaac was a large muscle-bound piece of unknown data in the equation.

There was blood running from the coward's lips when he yelled, "Get this trash out of here!"

Before Isaac had time to respond, Poison had grabbed her shirt and pants off the floor and ran out the door. She fell for the first few steps, and her flailing retreat became a combination of running and crawling.

Ecstasy and Desire had been talking idly when Poison stumbled hysterically back through the foyer. In only her bra and panties, with her clothes hugged tight to her chest, she pushed open the front door and ran out into the rain. Her frantic sobs were so loud they could be heard over the Hip Hop music.

Ecstasy and Desire laughed uncontrollably, unable to see their own future.

The rain had only begun to fall harder, so Pastor Ellison told Tyler he would drive him home. He promised to have someone deliver the bike just as soon as the rain stopped.

As they drove through the parking lot, Tyler was surprised to see his mother's car was there. It didn't seem like the pastor noticed it, so Tyler didn't mention it.

When he walked to his front door alone, he could already hear his mother inside. She was sobbing. He turned the doorknob just enough to crack open the door, then waved bye to Ellison. When he entered the apartment, he found his mother curled up on her bed, her back against the headboard, her knees drawn up into the fetal position, protecting her.

Her face panicked a little when she saw that he'd come home, but it was too late to hide. She half expected him to scuttle off to his room, or maybe even make some wisecrack. He didn't. Instead, he rushed over to her side and asked gently, "Mom, what's the matter?" He put his arm around her to comfort her. His affection seemed so loving and kind.

She didn't answer. She grabbed onto him, clinging to his arm, drawing him closer. His embrace only made her cry harder.

He said, "Mom, whatever this is, it doesn't matter. It doesn't matter, Mom. It doesn't matter," he repeated as she cried. "None of it matters," he insisted.

Tyler liked Pastor Ellison's chess analogy, but wondered what it was actually supposed to look like in the real world. He could accept that he was supposed to act in a manner pleasing to God, but wasn't sure what it was God wanted him to do.

His mother continued to cry. Tyler was impressed and amazed by just how much he only wanted for her to stop. He pulled her close and spoke softly into her ear, "All that matters is that I love you and you love me."

His words entered her head like a fantasy analgesic, the kind you would buy from a mysterious medicine man selling potions from the back of a cart. Her crying stopped and her nose cleared, and for a second, she just held onto her baby boy and breathed.

He hadn't told her that he loved her since the funeral, and she realized that she didn't tell him nearly enough. She said, "I love you, Tyler. I love you so much! You are all that matters to me. You are all that I have. I love you and I'm so scared of losing you."

"You don't have to worry about that anymore."

"I'm sorry I've been a bad mother for so long."

He said, "Pastor Ellison told me you were a hero."

She smiled. "I'm no hero. I have no idea how to raise you right."

"Well... I guess we'll just figure it out together."

Chapter Eleven

January 12—Four days left
Sunday

Sunday morning, Ellison was haunted by the feeling he felt the previous week when he walked out into the sanctuary and discovered it was nearly empty. He breathed deep and asked God for strength. *It has never been my congregation; it has always been God's. As long as I am endeavoring to do His will, He will provide.*

The silence in his office was jarring his nerves. "Is the band ever going to start?"

"Actually, there is no band," said Ashley McAllister.

"What do you mean?"

Ashley didn't hear any aggression or hostility in Ellison's voice—nor had she ever—but she still felt the overweening urge to crawl into a hole. She said, "Only Clifton Wagner has shown up."

"What do you mean?" asked Ellison. "Where are the others?"

"We've been unable to reach them." She gave a sad, consoling look. "We believe they are probably at home sick," she said unconvincingly.

"Wow," said Ellison in disbelief. "You mean we have a sanctuary full of people and just a one-man worship team?"

Her countenance sunk even further. She said, "N— uh— N—" then sighed. In desperation, she looked to Brandon Davies.

Brandon Davies had nothing more to offer than a comforting hand on the shoulder—and *that* he shared with Ashley. Unlike her, Brandon wasn't feeling all that anxious to comfort their head pastor.

Ellison finally let Ashley off the hook. He nodded in sad acceptance. He remembered how he had mentioned to Brandon Davies just one week ago how they had already convinced the choir. *Could things really be unraveling so quickly?* He asked, "What instrument does Clifton Wagner play?"

This time Brandon answered. "Tambourine. Cedric just brought him on a few months ago."

They saw the concern in Ellison's eyes. It made Ashley spiral into compassion, and Brandon spiral into irritation.

It wasn't his intention to pile on, but Brandon Davies had something he felt he needed to say. He said, "The Bible does say that those with faith can move mountains, but I've been thinking of another part: the part where Satan tempts Jesus in the wilderness."

Pastor Ellison raised one eyebrow.

Ashley McAllister hurried out of the room.

Ellison obviously knew where Davies was going, but Davies resolved that he would actually say the words he felt Ellison needed to hear. "Christ quoted Deuteronomy and said, 'Do not put the Lord your God to the test.'"

Ellison nodded. He smiled, it contained zero traces of *smirk*. He was thinking about how the non-religious mechanic he met twenty-four years ago could have become such a wise follower of Christ. He said warmly, "By the way, I hadn't asked many random people to be my first members; you were wrong. I had only approached you. I thought I saw goodness and brilliance in you, and I was right."

Brandon Davies smiled. These words filled his chest and he could feel his cheeks start to redden, but he would not allow himself to be diverted. He said boldly, "I think you are tempting God, and I'm afraid as punishment He will withdraw His favor from this country. I'm afraid the result will be more empty seats in your church and in churches around the world."

Ellison's face was stone. Brandon's words had touched him and he sat imagining the unimaginable.

Brandon couldn't stand to see Pastor Ellison—who had brought hope to so many—look hopeless, but still he would not let him off the hook. He had thrown his gauntlet down and he would force Ellison to give an accounting.

Neither man said a word and Brandon's mind grew obsessed with demanding an answer. He resolved that they would sit there in that silent, lifeless church for as long as it took, but Riley *will* answer him.

Finally, the silence was broken, not by Pastor Ellison, but by the gentle strumming of an acoustic guitar. Ellison's head popped up. He listened intently to the first few notes. Without another word, he rose from his seat and walked to Brandon Davies.

Ellison placed a gentle hand on the side of Brandon's face. The gesture—so strangely intimate—reminded Brandon that Riley was his friend, his pastor, and his beloved mentor. He had just been viewing him like an adversary. Emotions flooded his chest and Brandon's eyes began to tear up. His wet, frightened eyes met with Riley's, and Riley no longer looked hopeless at all. Ellison's eyes contained that old familiar look Brandon had always seen in them, and that he had properly identified a long time ago: *faith.*

Brandon Davies knew that the only answer he would ever get—and perhaps ever need—he had just received.

Ellison left the room. He wasted no time cutting through the choir room and through the back door of the sanctuary, where the music was coming from.

From the back of the stage, he watched Clifton Wagner play, absorbed in his sweet music. The young man apparently was proficient at more than just the tambourine. Pastor Ellison wondered how Cedric could have overlooked so much raw talent. He tried to recognize the song, but he had never heard it before. Clifton sang:

> I went to tell the train conductor,
> But I didn't have a prayer.
> I went to tell the old pawn broker,
> But she said she didn't care.
> I went to tell it on the mountain,
> But the mountain wasn't there.

It was then Ellison realized that Clifton Wagner must have penned this song himself. He smiled broadly.

> I went to tell the haggard hobo,
> But he spit in my face.
> I went to tell the lonely schoolboy,
> He said get out of this place.
> I went to tell it on the mountain,
> It was gone without a trace.

The music picked up and Clifton really laid into the strings.

> You decide. You decide.
> There's a pastor and a mountain just a-gonna collide.
> Choose a side. Swallow your pride.
> Mead Mountain's the only thing that God'll let slide.

Finally, the music switched back for the final verse.

> I went to tell a pretty waitress,
> But she treated me wrong.
> I went to tell a loony landlord,
> He said I didn't belong.
> I couldn't *Go Tell it on the Mountain,*
> Because the mountain was gone.

Delighted by the boy's talent and creativity, Pastor Ellison still could not help but notice in his peripherals—the chairs were far more empty even than last time. Only, now—with the splendid music playing—he didn't seem so daunted.

He saw Hailey Rucker with her baby girl and he remembered how dedicated she was to Christ. Could he ever consider her precious soul to be *not enough?*

Nancy Fuller was there with her daughter. She still had a string tied to her finger, and now so did her girl. Ellison marveled, *Just twelve and so much courage! Was this enough? Of course it was.*

He saw Andrew Crenshaw. *Andrew Crenshaw?* He noticed that he was sitting with a row of reporters. *For a second, I got my hopes up!*

He noticed the reporters had also set up cameras. He had originally invited them to film and report on his sermons, but prior to his arrest, no one had taken him up on it. Now, suddenly, the press was more numerous than the actual parishioners. Seeing the cameras, Ellison realized that although this was the smallest number of people to which he had preached in decades, it might also be the largest.

Clifton strummed out the last few notes, and everyone turned to Ellison, all watching and waiting.

Ellison grabbed Clifton as he tried to exit the stage and pulled him in for a hug. "That was beautiful," he said. "I'm so proud of you."

Alone on stage, he looked over at the press—*his largest audience ever.* He reconsidered, positing the question in his mind: *Of what use is media exposure if they will only cut around the message, use only a few lines that are the most controversial, or the most scripturally impotent?*

It was with that in mind that he decided, once again, to scrap the sermon he had prepared and improvise a new one. He finally spoke, "We live in a fallen world. Not one of us can reach the high standards of virtue that God has set for us, not one. The good news is that His son, Jesus Christ has—out of love for us—stepped in to make up for the gap. He alone paid the price for our sins. He suffered and died in our place, then He rose again. Evil lost. God won. And now through Christ, we are promised that same victory over death. God bless you all. Thank you for coming."

Pastor Ellison turned and walked out.

After Brandon Davies had wrapped up history's shortest sermon with a closing prayer, he found Pastor Ellison alone in his office.

"That was a pretty quick sermon," Brandon said, provocatively.

"Well, I figured: back to basics."

"Back to basics," nodded Brandon.

Ellison turned his full attention to Brandon Davies. "Brandon, I'm sorry I cut us short before, what you were saying is—"

Brandon put up a hand. "Never mind what I was saying."

"I... I... know that you've been a little... upset."

Brandon laughed, seemingly at the word *upset,* as if the word alone were somehow preposterous. "Speaking of that, you know what happened to me on the way into church today? I got a speeding ticket." Brandon answered his own question without giving Ellison a chance to respond.

Ellison noticed the tense way Brandon was standing. He motioned to the chair on the other side of his desk. He said, "Well, that can certainly be upsetting."

"Can it?" Brandon Davies paused to give Ellison time to think about that, then finally sat down.

"I... guess." Ellison answered slowly like he feared stepping into a trap.

"Well now, suppose I knew that the Creator and Master of all the universe loves me—*me*—enough to give up his only begotten Son? Not only that, but he says I am to be like his adopted son, and I will live forever in paradise with Him."

"Okay."

"Well then if I knew that, I wouldn't get so mad over a ticket, would I?"

"Well—" Ellison began to answer, but was interrupted.

"But I did get mad. So, what does that mean about me?"

"It means you don't know it," said Ellison, but was quick to add specifically, "Is that what you're going to say?"

"It means I don't know it!" Brandon Davies furrowed his brow. "Now suppose that my son was captured by the North Koreans, or something, and I knew they were going to put him into a POW camp and probably torture him for years. How hard would I fight to keep him out of that camp?"

"Until your very last breath."

"Yes, I think so. But now answer me honestly: What if my son came to me and told me he was atheist? How hard would I fight to keep him out of eternal Hell?"

"You would still—"

Brandon Davies interrupted again, "Would I fight more or less hard than I would to keep him out of North Korea? More or less hard?"

Pastor Ellison looked down. "Less hard."

"Right. So the only logical conclusion is that I don't really believe it. The only logical corollary is that I lack even a modicum of faith."

"There you go using logic." Ellison smiled casually, but it didn't seem to faze Brandon Davies.

"About 70 percent of this country calls themselves Christian, right?"

"It's something like that."

"But less than 4 percent call themselves homosexual."

"Okay."

"And yet a man in the media could insult Christians and keep his job, but if that same man insulted homosexuals, he would surely lose it."

"Yeah, most likely."

"Because more people in that 70 percent of Christians would stand up for homosexuals than would stand up even for other Christians."

"Most likely."

"I'm beginning to think we never once had 70 percent. I mean, *where are the Christians?* Why, if there are so many of us, are we the ones who are pushed around? The truth is, we were never in the majority, *never*, not even in America, at least not in my lifetime. Whatever glorious anomaly may have once existed in this country, it's over. We are now a country that resembles your first sermon: two seats filled, and rows of pews empty."

Ellison nodded. He said consolingly, "I find comfort in the fact that the Bible described the human condition as being just that way: 'Wide is the gate and broad is the road that leads to destruction, and many enter through it. But small is the gate and narrow the road that leads to life, and only a few find it.'"

Brandon Davies thought about that. He said, "I'm not finding much comfort at all these days."

"Oh, Brandon."

"I told you that you would be the man who decimates Christianity as we know it."

"Um, you said destroyed," laughed Ellison.

Brandon Davies continued, bereft of humor, "But now I think you're just the man who revealed it. You didn't cause anyone to lose faith, but I think you've single-handedly proved to people how little they ever had. And I'm afraid one of those people is me."

Ellison sighed sweetly. He hated to see Brandon Davies worry. "I want you to see something," he said, then slowly opened his drawer. He rummaged around for a brief moment, then pulled out a tiny Ziploc bag. It was the type of super-small bag that was usually only used to sell cocaine, but this bag had no drugs in it. All it contained was a very small seed. Ellison handed it to Brandon Davies.

"What's this?" asked Brandon Davies.

"That," said Ellison, "is a mustard seed. I ordered it off the Internet." He laughed. "Keep in mind I like to study geology, not botany."

Brandon Davies held the bag close to his eye, to really get a look at the minuscule seed. "You know, Deborah probably already had some in the kitchen."

"Oh." Ellison laughed. "I hadn't told her yet. The first thing I did after God spoke to me, before I talked to anyone, was order that seed. I guess I just wanted to see it. I wanted to visualize it."

"It's smaller than I expected."

"Do you believe what the Bible says is true?"

"Yes. I think so."

"Do you believe that I have faith equal to that tiny seed?"

Brandon Davies grumbled. "It depends. I mean, I don't know what the conversion rate is between feelings and seeds."

Ellison laughed.

"I'm being serious!" said Brandon. "Right now, I'm not sure anyone, anyone has even this much faith, that's my point."

"I'm not asking you about *anyone, anyone*. I'm asking you about *me*. Do I have this much faith?" He grabbed the mustard seed and held it up.

Brandon Davies slowly—reluctantly—nodded. He saw that Ellison had considered this conversation closed, so he quickly asked, "But what about *me*?"

For the past ten days, Pastor Ellison hadn't shown much concern over Brandon Davies's crisis of faith. It wasn't because he didn't love him, but because he loved him so much and knew his character. "You?" He tossed Brandon Davies the tiny Ziploc for him to keep and said blithely, "Oh, *you*? You'll come back around when the mountain moves."

Pastor Ellison acted tough around Davies, but as soon as he was gone, he rolled his chair over to his computer. He opened his e-mail and selected Mason Kessler from his address book.

After Mason Kessler had retired from professional baseball, he dedicated his life, and his fortune, to philanthropic work done in the name of Jesus Christ.

He opened athletic centers in inner cities, where he brought great athletes in to mentor underprivileged kids. He visited cancer wards and helped raise money for a cure. He allied with the USO and raised money for the families of fallen heroes. There was no other athlete or country music star who was invited to attend more military funerals—by posthumous requests of warriors themselves. He attended every one of them.

He was recognized by the NCA as their Man of the Year in 2002 and again in 2011. He was once named by a Gallup poll to be the second most admired man in America, after Elemeno-P.

Despite all this, Pastor Ellison never once tried to bank on his friend's good name. But in light of all that was going on, and with Brandon Davies's dire warning still echoing in his ears, he decided to write Mason Kessler an e-mail.

It read simply, "I think I'm in over my head. I could use some help handling the PR. Perhaps you could come stay with me and Deborah for a few days, and maybe we could make a few appearances together. Tell me what you think."

Hailey Rucker was trying to read the Bible. She wanted to find comfort and solace from God's Word as she had so many times before, but she couldn't concentrate. There was too much on her mind.

He will never quit drinking, her mind repeated.

Colton had come home drunk again. Fortunately, this time, Abigail was sleeping soundly in her crib. That was the only fact that allowed Hailey to keep it together, while he continued to drink in the other room. She knew Colton wouldn't bother either of them. She knew if they both could just stay quiet, he would forget they were even home.

He will never quit drinking. She was going over her problems in her head, like a chess player who had lost the game. She ran over the same futile options again and again, just hoping to discover something she had missed before.

She couldn't help but think about Marc Hogan. Melissa Hogan was her best friend growing up and Marc was her older brother. Although he had been the misfit in their small town, Hailey had found his geekiness cute. He was tall and lanky. He never liked to leave his room, and he preferred books to football. While in high school, Marc had come up with a new type of Internet search engine back when most boys in his class hardly knew what the Internet was. Six years later one of his behemoth competitors bought all his designs, just to dismantle them. It had left Marc independently wealthy at the age of twenty-four.

The first thing he did with his wealth was show up on Hailey's doorstep driving a shiny new silver Bentley convertible. Hailey squealed at the sight of the car, the way only a nineteen-year-old girl could. He showed her pictures of his new property on Molokai Island—"You own this place?"—and of the beach—"In your own backyard?"—and of the sunset—"Outside your window every night?" With each new picture, she continued to work herself into a frenzy, which finally escalated with her declaration: "Marc, you are the luckiest man alive!"

"And I want to make you the luckiest girl alive!" He blurted with reckless joy.

"What?" She was stunned.

"Come with me. Come be with me in Molokai. I want to take you away from here. I want us to get married."

The excitement left her eyes. She lowered the photo she had been holding. She informed him simply, "I'm with Colton now."

The absence of any reaction on Marc's face indicated that he had already known about their relationship. He repeated, "Come with me to

Molokai, Hailey. It's paradise on earth."

She touched the cross necklace that Colton had bought her. It had been Colton who had first helped bring her to Christ. "Colton's a good man," she mumbled simply.

Marc grabbed the photos from her lap, held them up pleadingly and said, "It all can be yours. You can be the luckiest girl alive."

Hailey looked back down at the photographs. It was clear she was considering it. Finally, she looked back up and said, "But I already am the luckiest girl alive."

Hailey had a new appreciation for Colton after that. She had a new measuring stick. She had put Colton's love for her up against riches, and the love had won. She understood for the first time that to be so gently loved was a fate better than paradise.

When she saw Colton that evening, she ran to him, jumped into his arms, and planted a long, wet kiss on his lips. When she finally gave him a chance to breathe, he asked, "What was that for?"

"That's for being a good man. That's for being worthy."

"Worthy of what?"

"Just worthy."

She didn't tell him about the proposal she turned down, and he didn't tell her that he had just put a down-payment on a ring. They were engaged a week later and were married that spring in the little white church at the center of town.

When Colton's job brought them to the big city, he started drinking. The stress was too much for him, and Hailey believed he'd never gotten over his father's death. She'd always imagined that losing a parent you hate must be just as hard as losing one you love. And from the guilt and confusion she saw in Colton, she imagined it might be harder.

Then the alcohol changed him. She tried hard never to think of Marc Hogan or the measuring stick again.

She still loved Colton—the Colton that was still left, the Colton that the whiskey hadn't yet corroded away. But love wasn't enough. She knew that she couldn't raise her girl in that home. She owed it to her baby to get as far away from him as possible. She knew that Abigail's life probably even depended on it—her happiness, certainly, but possibly even her very life.

But where could I go? A small town girl with no skills and no more than a high school education? And who will look after Abigail while I'm at work? How could I raise my daughter without a father? Next came a thought she was a little surprised to think: *What would happen to Colton?* It must have been an old habit from having taken care of him for so long.

She knew he would surely die—either from drunk driving, alcohol poisoning, or if he continued down the path he was on, by his own hand.

I could never leave him; he would die. But she had to. She couldn't raise her precious girl around such a drunk. Hailey knew the way he treated her was the way he would one day treat Abigail. She couldn't let that happen. She had no other choice, no good options.

She imagined him dying, saving her the cost and stigma of divorce. She imagined a knock on the door from a police officer, or a call from the hospital, or simply walking into a room and finding his body. She pretended to ask herself how she would feel, but secretly she knew—free.

She quickly pushed these thoughts out of her head.

She was trapped. She repeated in her head, *I am trapped. I am trapped. I am trapped.*

She had to, at all costs, get Colton to quit drinking. She prayed to God every hour, on some days, many times an hour. It was always the same prayer. "Dear God, please help my Colton to stop drinking. Please bring my worthy man back to me."

But she had lost hope. *He will never quit drinking.* She had gone full circle.

If he can quit drinking, things can go back to how they used to be.

He will never quit drinking.

I can't leave him.

I can't stay.

I can't kill him.

If only I could get him to quit drinking.

Oh yeah... He will never quit drinking.

I am trapped.

Her mind repeated the steps, round and round, full circle, making a well-worn path in her brain, crowding all other thoughts—even the Word of God—out of her mind.

The sound of her door flying open broke her train of thought.

It was Colton. "Where'd you hide my keys?"

"I didn't," she said unconvincingly.

Colton swore. "I'm not playing this game. Where'd you hide them?"

"I didn't. You probably lost them."

"I put them on the table."

"They probably fell to the floor."

"They're not on the floor."

"You don't need to go anywhere. It's raining and you're too drunk to drive."

"You hid them."

"I didn't."

Colton looked at the clock, frustrated. "Listen woman, they stop selling in fifteen minutes."

"You won't make it anyway."

Colton swore again.

She foolishly added, "My clock says you have twelve minutes."

Colton started cussing up a storm. In one long sweep, he knocked everything that had been piled on the dresser onto the floor.

"You'll wake the baby!" she cried out.

"Where are they?" he barked as he pulled every drawer from the dresser and threw its contents onto the floor.

She worried about the noise waking the baby, so she snapped, "They're not in here."

Colton froze. He hadn't been certain, before that moment, that she had actually hidden them. He ran to the side of her bed and cocked his fist back menacingly.

There was nothing about the way he advanced on her that indicated it was just a threat, so Hailey quickly turned her head to brace for impact. In the same motion, she pulled her Bible in close over her heart. She screamed frantically, "I can last five minutes."

"What?" he stopped, fist still aimed at her.

"In five minutes, it will be too late anyway. I won't tell you, even if you beat me for five minutes."

This made his rage ramp up more. He tore the Bible from her chest with both hands and threw it on the floor. He wrapped his hands around her neck and screamed, "You fool. I'm not going to beat you for five minutes. I'm going to beat you for an hour, even after it's too late, just because you'll have deserved it."

Hailey spat, "But you'll still be out of alcohol!"

With that, he drew back his right fist again and shouted, "Last chance! Tell me where they are."

Hailey said nothing. She didn't put up a hand to protect herself. She just closed her eyes and waited.

Colton groaned. "Last chance!"

She still didn't move. She wasn't calling his bluff; she didn't believe he was bluffing. There was no doubt in her head he would probably hit her for the next hour, but she wouldn't tell him where she'd hid his keys.

She waited. When no blows came, she opened one eye to look at him. He was still holding her by the throat, still had his hand cocked back. His face was red with anger. His eyes were glossy and empty of humanity.

A puckish smile curled his lips and he let her go. Faking a laugh, he said, "I figured it out. You little minx. You're so clever." He turned to walk out of the room, still talking. "You hid them in the last place you expected me to look... the baby's crib."

"No!" she cried as she jumped to her feet. By the time she reached him, he already had his hand on the knob to Abigail's room. She grabbed his arm forcefully. "No, they're not in there."

"I think they are." She knew he didn't really think they were there. She knew that he just wanted to barge in there drunk and ransack her crib just to show her, just to win.

He forced his hand back to the knob. She knew he had no time to waste, and therefore no time to negotiate and no time to consider his actions. He looked back at her ominously for one last second.

"They're in your gray coat pocket!" she blurted out.

Colton instantly turned and ran for his coat. She followed on his heels, pleading, "Wait... wait... "

Once he was in the kitchen, he scanned the area. She instantly reached to grab the jacket before he could, but he was able to catch it a split second later and snatch it from her small hands. He stuck his hand in the pocket and grabbed the keys. The speed with which he did so caused a small tear of scratch paper to fall from the pocket and flutter to the ground.

Curiosity provoked him to bend and pick it up. It appeared to be a note. It was written on a page from a day planner. He unfolded it and was amazed to find it was written in his own handwriting. It read "I will take Hailey and Abigail to church on Sundays." Colton stared at it confused. He sat down on one of the chairs and reread it.

His eyes darted to the spot where Pastor Ellison had been sitting, and Hailey knew it had just come back to him. He hadn't taken her. Two Sundays had past. Pastor Ellison had won that night and Colton had welched on a bet.

Colton's eyes looked sad. It looked to Hailey like they were on the verge of tears, but they always kind of looked that way while he was drinking. She watched him sit motionless, staring at the note. Finally, she reached out to gently stroke the hair on the back of his head. She laced her finger through his hair and lovingly caressed his neck.

After another second, he slowly crumpled the note and tossed it into the trashcan. He frowned, looking down at his watch, he said, "It's too late to go anyway. I don't need to drink any more tonight." Without looking into her eyes, he added, "I'm tired. I think I should just crash."

Hailey grabbed his hand and pulled it. She said, "Let's go. You'll feel better by the afternoon."

Chapter Twelve

January 13—Three days left

Tyler's life had completely changed. Even the air felt different. He felt lighter. He had a new type of energy, one that his life had been sorely missing. It was hope. The things he used to care about didn't seem important now. His old friends seemed out of step with his burgeoning new identity.

With the passion of a new convert, Tyler had tied a string around his finger, just like Pastor Ellison. He'd seen it on Ellison's finger and had read about its meaning in some article he found online. So, Tyler had made up his mind that he would wear it and explain it to everyone he sees. He had been the recipient of God's miracle; of all the people in the world who were lost, God chose to spare him; God saved his life—why would he ever keep all that a secret?

But when the time came and a boy in the hall after first period asked him, "What's with the string? You trying to remember something?" all Tyler said was, "Oh... just some homework I have due today." The boy laughed at him, "Dude, I just set a reminder in my phone."

The string didn't remain even until lunch.

Tyler looked down at his naked finger now. He felt ashamed. He didn't know why it'd been so hard. *Are people really as bad as that? Or is it just me? God saved my life and this is how I repay him?*

Tyler threw his book bag down in his room and plopped down on his bed. He replayed that night in his head.

It was the first time he really thought about the glowing footage of his brother speaking directly to him. He didn't know what to make of that. *Was it a vision from God? Was it a message from Carson via God? Was it a hallucination brought on by the Damitol? Or was it as simple as a dream?*

He thought it probably wasn't a dream because he hadn't passed out yet, but he could have been dreaming that he hadn't passed out yet. He decided that he'd check the tape. He didn't really expect to find the glowing part still on the tape, but he wanted to be sure.

The video had been paused at the part where he first stopped it. He hit play. He saw nothing mysterious, nothing new, no strange auras, just a corporeal adolescent blathering on and on while drunk.

Tyler was struck by how different he felt watching Carson now, as opposed to that night. That night he felt like he and his brother were so simpatico. He felt like he was walking through the same quicksand that sank his brother. *But now...* now he still felt the echoes. The things his brother was describing didn't feel foreign, but they didn't feel so daunting either. Tyler couldn't remember what about his pain he had found so quixotic.

He was awe-struck that one change could affect his life so profoundly, that one new ingredient could change the entire recipe. The ingredient was God, of course, but more specifically to Tyler, it was *hope*. He had been given a way to fight. He had been shown a clear path out of the quagmire his life had been in.

As he watched his brother, he no longer looked up to him. The things he said were no longer the poetry from a deep-feeling sage; they were the ramblings of a drunk teenager trying to sound dramatic. He felt a greater love for his brother than he had ever felt before, but it only added up to greater sympathy. Any feeling of younger-sibling awe was gone.

On the video, his brother continued to drink. He repeated the same routine with the pills about a half dozen times. Each time he cycled through numerous pills, checking them against the light, then putting them in a separate pile. Tyler had no idea what that was about. Each time, he would stop with what he somehow deemed to be a worthy pill, break it open and pour it into his drink. Tyler noticed that once done with it, he would put the pill back together and add it to the same separate pile.

He wished he could go back in time to speak to his brother. He felt like he had real answers to give him. He felt like if he just had a chance to talk with him, armed with this new tool, this new Truth, he could actually save his brother's life. The ideas made him happy, sad, proud, and humbled all at the same time.

He watched his brother finish what was in the glass, slide the separate pile back into the container, and close the lid. Carson reached past the side of the camera and the video ended. Tyler just thought, *What a waste! What a waste of a life that was precious, sacred, and belonged to God.*

He turned off the camera and brought it in tight against his chest.

Wait a minute! He almost missed it. He immediately turned on the camera and replayed the video. He advanced it to the end, and paid closer attention. He really did see what he thought he saw: his brother slid the discard pile back into the same bottle. Tyler gasped as he figured out what that meant: that's why he was holding up the pills to the light; he was checking to see which pills he had already emptied the time—or times—before. By Tyler's count it seemed like he had to try nine or ten that were empty before he found one that was full. If that same percentage held true for the whole bottle, then there was only about 10 percent of the pills that had contained any medicine at all, and that was *if* the moment on this very old video had been the last time Carson had done this same routine.

It wasn't God at all!

He didn't swallow a bottle of potent pharmaceuticals; he swallowed a bottle of hollow gel caps. Tyler could feel his face burning. He felt a weight re-settle on his shoulders and a knot re-tighten in his chest. He felt the cold, sharp claws of a demon reach into his chest and pull out, not his heart, but his *hope*. It had bonded to his heart and his ribs, his muscles and his lungs. Now they were all being torn open. It was hard for him to breathe.

It wasn't God at all! It wasn't God at all! It wasn't God at all! he kept repeating. *It wasn't a sign. What a fool I was.* He said a swear word and threw the video camera across the room. He fell to his knees. The inescapable pain that he had escaped was suddenly back. He sobbed openly. He embraced his pain like an estranged cellmate, the face he hated most in the world, but a face he knew. He felt like he wanted to blind himself.

Andrew Crenshaw shook the raindrops from his hair as he walked through the door. This was the fourth strip club he had visited today. He saw two people behind the counter, idly talking—a scantily clad young girl, who looked like she might have been picked up at a strip club supply store, and a muscle-bound black man, who despite his intimidating physique, had a friendly face.

Andrew Crenshaw approached the man. "Excuse me, I was wondering if you could tell me if you've seen this gentleman around here recently?"

Isaac looked at the photo, then looked at Andrew Crenshaw. He couldn't have specifically identified what about Andrew Crenshaw's face allowed him to know he was not a cop, but somehow *cop* never entered his mind. He handed the photo back and said, "We don't talk about those things."

Andrew Crenshaw politely extended the photo back again, but Isaac didn't receive it. He said, "Ah, but if you hadn't seen him, you just would have said no."

"You can assume what you want," Isaac said, "But, I'm not—"

Isaac was interrupted when Ecstasy snatched the photo from Andrew Crenshaw's fingers. She said, "Ah, I know that guy! That's that old dude that Poison went off on."

"I said, we don't talk about those things," insisted Isaac, turning to Ecstasy.

Andrew Crenshaw took one step closer to the girl, further from the man. He asked, "Someone yelled at him?"

"No, she let him have it." Ecstasy looked to Isaac—after all it was from him that she'd actually heard the whole story—but Isaac now said nothing.

"She hit him? Who's this girl?"

"Poison."

"What's Poison's real name?"

"I don't know. She says it's Poison."

Andrew Crenshaw eyed the door leading into the club. "Is she here, now?"

"Naw, she got fired."

"Do you know where I could find her?"

"Why do you want to find her?" Isaac interjected.

"I'm a reporter. I've been doing a story on this man." He grabbed the photo back from Ecstasy. "You may have seen him in the news; he's the pastor who claims he will move a mountain."

Both their faces were blank.

"You also might have heard of him because he was arrested on prostitution solicitation charges."

"Oh yeah, that's that big shot preacher caught paying for sex," said Ecstasy.

"Yeah, okay," said the bouncer, nodding.

"Well, he says he didn't do it and I believe him. I also believe this lady, Poison, and her son can help me confirm it."

"How?" pushed Isaac.

"Pastor Ellison had been trying to help them. He was with them immediately after the arrest."

The girl said nothing.

Isaac snatched the photo of Ellison out of Andrew's hand one last time. He remembered that day very well. He hadn't known at the time that the man he was throwing out on his butt was a pastor; that was a first for him. Andrew Crenshaw noticed the way he seemed to study Ellison's face, as if he was trying to detect his humanity. Isaac was asking himself whether or not this was a good man, whether or not the prostitution charges were true, and whether or not he might have been actually trying to help Poison that day, and he was looking for these answers in Ellison's eyes. Finally, he said, "We have her address in one of our files. I'll go find it for you."

Chapter Thirteen

January 14—Two days left

When Tyler walked into Pastor Ellison's office carrying an old video camera, the first thing Ellison asked was, "Aren't you supposed to be in school?"

Tyler wasn't expecting this. His eyes tried their best to retreat even farther behind their cover of hair. He said, "Um... no. We let out early for a pep rally."

"On a Tuesday?"

"Yeah. Look, I need to talk to you." Tyler was getting frustrated.

"You need to talk to me after school hours," Ellison pushed.

Tyler slammed the camera down on Ellison's desk and insisted, "Dude, this is important!"

Ellison could see the desperation on the young man's face. He said, "Yes, sir, how can I help?"

Tyler played the video for him, pointed out the empty pills and explained the events of that fateful night.

Ellison took it all in. He sat silently looking at the back of the camera for a long time, tape on pause, staring at a life cut short. Finally, he said, "Come with me..." Ellison stood up to walk out of his office and the heartsick boy stood up to follow.

Ellison led him down the hall, then out to the parking lot, past the gazebo and through the field. When they'd almost reached the giant white cross, Ellison stopped and presented Mead Mountain to the boy.

"That's the one, huh?" asked Tyler. Tyler had never bothered to really look at the mountain.

"Yes, sir, that's the one. Is it beautiful?"

The boy kind of shrugged. He said, "Yeah."

"Look again. Is it beautiful? Is it glorious? Is it majestic?"

The boy really looked. He smiled. "Yes, it's... amazing."

"Was that mountain created by God?"

The boy didn't answer; his brow narrowed.

Pastor Ellison preempted any answer that might have been forthcoming and continued, "... or is that mountain a result of a shift in our tectonic plates?"

The boy looked at his feet. It was the first time he saw in Tyler something that he had often seen among his young parishioners: respect. The boy didn't answer because he was afraid to say the wrong thing in front of Ellison.

Ellison smiled. He kept talking in order to let Tyler off the hook. He said, "The correct answer is *C: both*. I happen to love geology, so I am fully capable of telling you, using science, exactly how that mountain was made. But that answer doesn't tell us how to live, or what to live for. That answer doesn't tell us what happens to us after we die. That answer doesn't promise perfect justice in the universe, and doesn't comfort us when we fear. That answer doesn't tell you the one thing I want most for you to understand..."

"What's that?" Tyler asked.

"That *you*, far more than a silly mountain, are glorious, majestic and... amazing."

The boy laughed, mostly because he felt uncomfortable. He said, "You forgot beautiful."

Ellison laughed hard from his belly. He said, "Well... you could use a haircut."

The boy smiled and tossed some off the hair from his eyes, which immediately fell right back.

Ellison stepped closer to the boy. His voice was gentle when he asked, "Is it possible that God invented *seismic pressure*, and He invented *tectonic plates*, and then He used the force of His tectonic plates to make this mountain appear just the way He wanted it?"

This time Ellison was not going to let the boy off the hook. He was going to wait until the boy answered. Finally, the boy said, "Sure, I guess... if He's God and all."

"And then isn't it also possible that God knew those pills were empty when He let you find this video? You could've hidden that alcohol anywhere. Isn't it possible that God knew you would find the camera on that shelf when He spoke quietly to your heart and told you, *top shelf, closet*. Isn't it possible for someone who is *God and all* to pull all these coincidences together to give you the sign that you asked for?"

Tyler nodded.

"Now you have a decision to make, because faith must always be just that: a decision. You have all the evidence you need to know that God had nothing at all to do with saving your life. But you have something else too.

You have ambiguity. You have just enough wiggle room in the evidence to *believe*. So, the choice is yours. It was either a random series of happy accidents, or part of a heavenly plan and glorious mystery. It's your choice."

The boy smiled a fresh, clean, hopeful smile. And for the first time since infancy, Tyler was truly beautiful.

When Tyler left, Ellison went immediately to check his e-mail. He didn't find what he was hoping for, so he checked his phone. Nothing.

Ellison knew he had to hurry home to pack.

For the first twenty-four hours after Pastor Ellison had e-mailed Stone Mason Kessler, he did not receive a response at all, despite the fact that Ellison had put the word *URGENT* in the subject line of his e-mail. When Ellison finally did receive a reply, all it contained was one line:

I'm sorry. I cannot help you on this one.

Ellison had immediately picked up his phone to call him, despite it being almost midnight. As it was ringing, Ellison wondered why he didn't just call in the first place. When it went to Mason Kessler's voicemail, Ellison figured the aging great had gone to bed. Ellison's message was as terse as Mason Kessler's e-mail. He said, "Hey, it's Riley. Give me a call."

Ellison couldn't silence the alarm bells in his head. He showed the one-line e-mail to his wife, who took one look at it and said, "Something's wrong. That's not like Mason at all."

"No, it isn't," Riley said gravely.

"The man's never turned down a request for help in his whole life." Riley immediately hopped on the Internet to buy a plane ticket.

He tried calling two more times in the morning, but received no answer. He sent him a text that read, *There's nothing you can't talk to me about. There is nothing we can't overcome with God.*

When he got home after talking to Tyler, he had just enough time to finish packing. He was mostly done when his wife scrutinized the contents of his carryon bag, "What are you taking that for?" She noticed that the framed twenty that usually hung on the wall in Ellison's office was now wedged between two shirts.

"Just thought it might help to bring up old times."

"You think he's drinking again?" It was the fear that lurked behind their conversations, but it had gone unsaid.

Ellison shrugged. "I don't know what's happening. I just want to be ready."

"You'll be ready," she said supportively. "Do you have your tickets?" she asked, mothering him the way she liked to do.

"Yes."

"Do you know the gate?"

Reflexively, Pastor Ellison opened his mouth to say, "Yes," but realized that he didn't know the gate after all. "No," he told her, "I guess I don't know the gate."

"I'll look it up for you," she said sweetly.

"Thanks, babe."

Ellison was trying to go through his mental checklist when he heard his wife gasp from the other room. "Sweetheart!" she yelled. "You need to come see this." There was noticeable tension in her voice.

When Deborah had gone to check the gate number, her internet browser took her to her home page, on which she saw the lead news story:

Mason Kessler Admits to Affair

"Oh God," said Pastor Ellison. It wasn't idle use of the Lord's name. It had been a genuine quick prayer.

Deborah read from the article:

> When Channel 6 Eureka came to Mason Kessler with unsavory photographs of him and Miss Doreen Howell, the retired athlete confessed to having a six-month affair with the young lady he had hired to help ghostwrite his biography. With his wife beside him, he announced at a press conference that rumors of the affair were true and he apologized for the pain he might have caused his fans worldwide. Kessler claims to have already cut off the affair and had already informed his wife. The two of them plan to remain together and work it out.

Deborah frowned and said to Riley, "He wasn't refusing to help you;

he was trying to protect you. I guess he figured that any association with him would only make things harder for you."

"It will," Ellison said dryly.

"You still want to get on that plane?" she asked although she knew the answer.

"Now more than ever," he said.

His wife checked the time on her monitor. She sighed and said, "We need to get going."

After trudging his way through security, Ellison made his way through the airport to find his gate. He noticed that the woman walking several feet in front of him was wearing a t-shirt with a line drawing of a mountain crumbling. At the top it read "Mead Mountain." At the bottom it read "I have faith!"

Ellison smiled. He felt a gentle gratitude warm his face. He wanted to thank the woman, but she had not seen him and she was too far ahead. In his mind he said, *That was fast. God bless capitalism.*

Ellison noticed that as he walked, faces in the oncoming foot traffic would often do a double take. It would start with the same small pause—a moment of uncertainty followed by either a scowl of disapproval, or a warm smile of hope. A few people reached out their hands and gave him a quick pat on the shoulder or back. Not wanting to hold him up in his travels, they would pass and just say "God bless you," or "I believe."

The woman immediately in front of him was walking with an eight-year-old boy. She saw enough people reacting to the man behind her that she finally had to give in to the curiosity. She wrenched her head around a full 180 degrees, not sure if she would even know whatever pseudo-celebrity she'd discover.

She did know him. She slowed her pace and turned her body in order to say hello and shake his hand. Then she kept walking. After a few seconds she turned her head back again and said, "I respect what you're trying to do, but... you don't really think it will move do you?"

"I do," he said quickly.

The lady turned back and kept walking, saying as she turned, "Well let's hope you're right."

The two of them must have found their gate, because at a certain point, they both turned right while Ellison continued forward. The lady grabbed the boy's hand to guide him. Only the boy turned his head one last time. He looked up at the pastor and said, "*I* think it will move."

When Ellison landed in Eureka, he found a taxi and gave the cabbie the address. Instead of promptly hitting the gas as one might expect from a cab driver, he paused, leaned back, and with the tone of an inquisitor asked, "What business do you have there?"

The two men looked into the other's eyes via the rearview mirror.

The look of surprise and confusion was evident on Ellison's face so the cabbie confirmed, "Yeah, I know whose house that is; but how do you know it?"

"We're old friends."

"Uh-huh, I suppose you want an autograph, or maybe you've got a sob story and are going to hit him up for money, or maybe you're that broad's husband and you think you've got a score to settle."

The cabbie had evidently heard about the affair, so Ellison explained patiently. "I heard my friend got into some trouble. I've come to offer whatever help I have to offer."

The cabbie took one more look in his rearview then quickly spun around so he could look Ellison straight in the face. He said, "Hey, you're that pastor, aren't you?"

There had been nothing about the tone of the cabbie's discovery that would indicate whether or not he was a supporter. He seemed to want to keep ne'er-do-wells away from Mason Kessler's home, and Ellison appreciated that at least. "Yes," said Ellison. "I'm that pastor."

"We'll I'll be," the man said. "I guess that explains it." He pushed on the gas, repeating the phrase, "Well, I'll be," and adding again, "I guess that explains it."

When Ellison arrived at Mason Kessler's door, the news had broken only three hours prior. Mason Kessler opened the door and the two looked at each other. Mason Kessler said, "What took you so long?" then they embraced.

Ellison heard two dainty footsteps enter the foyer. He looked over from Mason's shoulder to spot his wife. She looked just as beautiful as she had the last time he saw her, only there was now a hint of red in the corners of her eyes. Ellison could tell that she'd been crying for many days, perhaps weeks, straight.

"Nicole," Ellison said as he pulled her into a kind hug.

Nicole returned his hug. It was the first moment that the distant news story about the affair felt real, because there in the entryway of her and Mason's home, Nicole actually said nothing at all.

Mason suggested that it might be easier if the men talked in private, so he led Ellison with his suitcase into the spare bedroom.

"You ever feel like a phony?" Mason Kessler asked Ellison once they were alone.

The guileless pastor pondered what the real answer to this question was, then pondered what he was *supposed* to answer. Finally, he just told the truth. "No."

Mason pressed on regardless. "Do you remember when I hit that grand slam?"

Pastor Ellison had found a chair on the side of the room, but his friend was pacing frantically. He had all the energy of a great athlete, or a troubled soul. Or both.

"The whole world remembers when you hit that grand slam," Ellison assured him.

Ellison had no idea what made Mason wince like he was in pain. "That's my point," Mason said. "The world loved me. I have played and replayed that moment in my mind. I knew the second the ball left that bat. I knew the second that sound hit my ears. *Homerun. I just won the World Series.* And in that moment, I didn't feel success, victory, or accomplishment. I felt *love.* I felt love from the entire world. But it was the greatest kind of love, because none of them knew me."

"That's the worst kind of love," Ellison insisted.

Mason just gravely shook his head.

"Because it's meaningless," Ellison explained.

"It's the *best* kind because it's meaningless. I was *Stone Kessler.* They loved who I was as Stone, and nothing else mattered. They didn't know who I was as Mason and they didn't care. They didn't care what type of husband I was, what type of friend, what type of son, what type of brother, what type of father. They were blind to my failings. All they wanted me to do was hit a ball... and *hit a ball* I could do better than anyone. So, as time went on, all I ever wanted to be was Stone Kessler, not Mason. "

"I understand."

"I love my wife. You know I love my wife."

"Nicole is an amazing woman."

Mason Kessler nodded sadly. "But she knows me as Mason. Doreen

Howell only knows me as Stone."

"I understand," said Ellison.

Mason Kessler continued, knowing that Ellison did *not* understand. "Every woman in the world thinks I'm perfect, except one." He left the next second empty, hoping Ellison could possibly get it. He wanted to convey the weight of what he was saying and the pain it caused to press down on his heart. "Everyone idealizes me, except for the one person in the world who I want most to idealize me. She doesn't."

"She doesn't idealize you. But she loves you despite your flaws," insisted Ellison.

Mason Kessler nodded. "She does. God help her; she somehow does. But that's not the way I want to be loved. I want to be loved the way I was in October of '82."

Pastor Ellison nodded pensively. He said, "The heart is a deceptive organ."

Kessler tilted his head away. It was a flippant gesture that seemed to say, "Yeah, yeah."

Ellison looked around the guest room. The first thing he noticed was how poorly the bed was made, from this he knew that it had been Mason who made it, not his wife. From this he knew that Mason had been sleeping in it. That wasn't altogether surprising, considering, but what he saw next disturbed him more. He saw that all the books on the shelf had been pushed to the back of the shelf, but all those on bottom had been slid to the front. He said, "You're drinking again?"

"That's none of your business."

"My friend."

"What?" Mason reflexively looked at Ellison in confusion.

"This is none of your business, *my friend*—that's what you told me that first night." Mason Kessler looked away again. "A few weeks later you came into my life and changed everything, turned my head around, and saved my soul. Now, did you do all that just so that I would love you?"

Mason Kessler threw up his hand. "It worked."

"Yeah, it worked. I'm crazy about you. There is no one in the world I love more in this very moment than you."

"That's *my* old line," shot Kessler.

"Was it really just a line?"

Pastor Ellison gave Kessler a chance to respond, but he didn't take it. His eyes remained unreachable.

"Now hold on," insisted Ellison. "Before we get carried away, let me tell you about the Mason I know, the Mason I idealize. You used to tell me that your greatest joy came from drawing closer to God. How else can you explain the tireless work you have done to serve His children, *to feed His sheep*? How else can you explain the literally tens of millions of dollars that you've given away? You wanted to grow closer to Christ by emulating Him. I know you. I know Mason. You didn't do all that just to be loved."

"Riley, what if I did?"

Ellison had nothing to say. He shook his head. His voice made these sounds: "Uh... ih... eh... "

Mason continued. "It was all a lie. You don't know me. You don't know Mason, because I never let you know him. His greatest joy did not come from Jesus Christ. His greatest joy... *My* greatest joy came from winning ballgames and from getting drunk. My greatest joy comes from lying down with that young woman and being touched not like a husband, but like a Hall of Famer. No matter how much I prayed, how hard I worked, how many years I spent serving the Lord, the one thing that never left me—never once—was my insatiable appetite for sin. That's who I am." He noticed Ellison's look of anguish. He knew he was hurting his friend with this confession. He pushed on anyway. "That other stuff was just a persona I played."

"Well, you played it well," said Ellison, still unconvinced.

"Yes, and I played it as long as I could. I thought that if I ran hard enough, I could steal a base. But now I see it was a lie. Perhaps *all* of it was."

"Look at all the good you've done! You're telling me all that was just a persona?"

Kessler shrugged. "Possibly."

"All lies?"

"Possibly."

"Well then... keep lying. Keep on lying. I have never seen so much good brought to this world as when Mason Kessler lies! Those young boys who you mentored, who against all odds and the cards stacked against them were able to avoid drugs and gangs, and many of them find their way to Christ—they don't care that you were faking. The sick children whose lives you helped save and the families who you helped to support after their loved ones died fighting for the rest of us—none of them care that you were faking. Keep on faking!"

"I can't."

"Why not?"

"Not after two weeks ago!" The statement was shouted. Mason Kessler just threw a hard fastball, and if Ellison wasn't mistaken, he threw it right at the pastor's head.

"What happened two weeks ago?" Ellison asked cautiously.

Kessler stopped pacing. He turned to look at Ellison. His face was calcified and graceless. He said, "You know what happened two weeks ago, *Pastor*."

"You mean..."

Mason Kessler nodded. "You told the press—without talking to your old friend first, by the way—that you would tell a mountain to move, and that the mountain would move. And you told everyone to choose sides. Well, I prayed on it, and I prayed on it. I asked God what would happen and how I should feel about it... and I received no answer.

"Then one afternoon, I found myself lying next to Doreen. We had just made love. My cell phone buzzed and I saw my wife had just texted me. She said, 'I'm sorry that you've been so stressed. I hope you are having a great time today,' because she thought I was playing golf. And yet, with all this going on, my mind was on *you*... and your stupid mountain. And the only moral issue that I was struggling with was how I could trick myself into believing the mountain would move. Finally, I realized I couldn't. Not even I, who had been faking for so long, could fake my way through that one. I knew right in that moment the mountain would not move. I knew that I had no faith and had been living a lie. And I had been living it my whole life."

Mason Kessler looked out the window because it was easier than looking Ellison in the eye. He saw a car pull up to his curb, followed by another one coming from a different direction. He didn't have to wonder what was going on; he had seen enough press in his lifetime. He heard his cell phone ring, followed by Ellison's.

What he didn't know was the cabbie, who had once acted so protective, had snapped a picture on his phone of the two men hugging in the open doorway. He had innocently uploaded it immediately to his wall. The post had gone viral fast enough to be picked up by the AP, who promptly added the headline, *The Adulterous Leading the Adulterous?*

"Vultures," snapped Mason as he silenced his phone. He turned to Ellison and spoke not as to an inside party, but the type of intruder the cabbie had expected him to be. He said curtly, "You don't want to deal with this. I'll distract them. Nicole can drive you back to the airport."

"No, I came all this way, and I think we need to—"

"No, Riley," Mason Kessler said firmly. "You need to go."

Pastor Ellison was restless on the plane ride home. He kept thinking of the dismal expressions on Mason Kessler's face. It was the same countenance he had first seen from him twenty-eight years ago in a seedy bar. He kept thinking about the bottom shelf of books. Ellison did not mention it to Mason Kessler, but he had noticed one of those books was *Love the Sinner,* Pastor Ellison's own best-seller, a book for which Mason Kessler himself had written the foreword.

But more haunting than any of that were the words Mason Kessler had said about the mountain. *Could it be that my little stunt actually ends up costing souls, not saving them?* He thought about Tyler and his mother. *Could I really accept winning those two, if it meant losing Mason Kessler? Is that a trade I'd really be willing to make?* He wondered if all souls were equal in God's sight. He'd always imagined God has the paradoxical power of loving all his children more than the rest. *But Mason Kessler? For those two.* He stressed the words again in his mind, *those two.*

He instantly wanted to correct the way he had been thinking. His mind rushed to the reserve of Christ-like love he had always tried to carry in his heart, but for the first time since he became a Christian, Pastor Ellison found that reserve empty. He repeated in his mind, *Mason Kessler for those two?*

Had I been too proud? Had I sought to boast? Had this whole stunt just been a way to serve myself? He could not live with the idea that he had placed a stumbling block in the way of Mason Kessler's faith, Mason Kessler, the man who had saved him. *Could it be true that I pulled a thorn out of a lion's paw, only to later push him into a thorn bush?*

When Ellison's taxi finally dropped him off at the front of his home, he saw a reporter waiting out in the street. It was more than he could bear. He lashed, "This is ridiculous. If you would've called my office, your call would've been returned. You don't need to disturb my home and my wife."

The reporter did not respond, but like a jack-in-the-box, sprung into action with the questions he had been going over in his mind while waiting. "Is it true that you visited the home of Mason Kessler?"

"Mason Kessler and I have been friends rather publicly for decades; this is hardly news."

"Did you two discuss his affair?"

"This is ridiculous," Ellison said as he turned his back on the reporter.

"Did you discuss the prostitution?" The question was lobbed at the retreating pastor's back.

Ellison said nothing.

The reporter waited in the street, just past the curb, while Ellison headed toward his home. He had almost reached the front door, when the reporter shouted one final question, "Do you have a comment on his doping scandal?"

Ellison froze in his tracks. He turned to the reporter. His face was merciless, graceless. Ellison had loved the stripper. He had loved the drunk. He had loved the prostitute. He had loved the gang-bangers in jail. He could find no love for this reporter. He hissed, "That's a lie! Stone Kessler has never taken steroids in his life." Ellison took a few steps closer to him.

"The Inquirer broke the story." The reporter's voice was firm and projecting. "Mason Kessler had confessed it to his mistress in their... intimate moments. She had confessed it to the tabloid... a little less intimately." He looked down at his pad. "Reportedly they had slipped a hundred grand into her bank account."

"It's impossible."

"From 1978 to 1983 is what he had told Ms. Howell."

"Well, that's before he was Christian," Ellison responded a bit too quickly.

"No, sir. That would include the famous 1982 World Series; that was the year he first came out thanking God for his win." The young reporter couldn't help himself; he added, "Turns out it wasn't God's power at all, but... something else."

Pastor Ellison turned to head inside.

The address that Andrew Crenshaw had received from Isaac led him to the Bowman Point apartments on Bowman Street. He knocked on door 115.

Maybe it was all his years of being a reporter, but as soon as Poison opened the door, he knew he was in the right place. He said, "Excuse me, ma'am, for showing up uninvited and unannounced."

Poison's face was irritated and standoffish. From the moment he called her *ma'am*, she assumed he was selling something.

"My name is Andrew Crenshaw and I'm a reporter with the Times. Pastor Ellison is a friend of mine, and—"

"Pastor Ellison?" her face changed when she heard the name.

Andrew Crenshaw had a basic plan of what he would say before he even stepped foot onto her mat, but none of his outlines contained the phrase, "Pastor Ellison is a friend of mine." Those words just slipped out that way.

"Yes, ma'am, and I've been working with him to clear up some facts regarding his recent arrest. I was hoping that we could sit down and chat."

"What would I have to do with that? I'm not a prostitute." Poison folded her arms across her chest.

"No, ma'am. The pastor claims that the reason he could make no statement to the press is because he rushed to this apartment."

Poison lowered her eyes. "He gave you our address?"

"No, ma'am. I was able to acquire that from an outside party."

"Outside party? You been snooping around about me?"

Andrew Crenshaw noticed that her left hand, which still held the door, drew it closed just a little more.

"I'm just trying to help out Pastor Ellison. Now is it true that he reached out to you and your son?"

Poison nodded. Her face softened a bit and the door opened a bit.

Andrew repeated, "I was hoping that we could sit down and chat."

Poison looked over her shoulder back into her apartment. "Now?"

"If at all possible."

"Hold on," she said abruptly and slammed the door closed.

Andrew Crenshaw waited patiently on the porch. He looked out over the parking lot. It was another chilly day. He noticed a pile of cigarette butts beneath the hedges. He waited so long that he began to doubt she was coming back. *She had said hold on, right?* He began to question if he'd heard her correctly.

Finally, he heard the door open behind him. She said nothing, but stepped aside, giving him room to enter.

The apartment looked impeccable. The floors had obviously been freshly vacuumed; he could still see the lines the vacuum's wheels had left in the carpet. The shelves contained nothing but photographs of her and two boys. They had obviously been freshly dusted; he could still smell the Pledge. He had not been waiting outside long enough for her to do all of these things; the apartment had obviously been clean before he ever even knocked. He wondered what the wait had been about.

"Come. We can sit in the kitchen," she said.

When they both sat down, he realized she was wearing more makeup than when he first saw her.

"What can I tell you about Pastor Ellison?" she asked.

"Well if you've got time, why don't we start at the beginning?"

She did. She told him about how he came to the club and left his card. She left out Tim McGraw. She left out the part where she hit him. She told him about Carson's death and how she had come to ask for the pastor's help. She told him about the miracle, how Tyler had tried to kill himself but suffered no effect. She told him how he had tested God right in the pastor's face. She did not tell him about the video or empty gel caps, because Tyler hadn't told her that part.

Andrew Crenshaw asked, "You believe it was a miracle, a sign from God."

"Yes, I do," she smiled. "Can you believe that God would drop everything, just to help an ex-stripper and her son?"

Andrew chose to assume the question was rhetorical. He asked, "How long have you been a... dancer?"

"I *had* been a stripper most my life. I started at sixteen."

"Sixteen? How on earth did that happen?"

"That's not relevant to your article."

"No, I guess it isn't. Well... uh—"

"My mother was addicted to heroin... I found out. I knew about the pot. I knew about the speed, knew about the coke. I didn't know when she started the heroin. One day, she walked into my room without knocking. I screamed at her to get out because I was dressing, but she didn't care. She said, 'I need you to move out.' I told her I had no place to go, and she said she couldn't afford to keep me. At that point I knew she had picked drugs over me. She said, 'I want you out by Sunday,' then left my room.

"I was panicked. I didn't have anywhere else to go; I was sixteen. That Friday night, I came home at five in the morning. Of course my mother was still up. I barged into *her* room without knocking. When she looked at me, her eyes were devoid of brain activity and she appeared to be watching me, unaware that I was able to watch back. I remember thinking, *This must be what the television sees*. I laid a tall stack of twenties, fives, and ones on her table, over $700 worth. 'What's this?' she asked me. 'This month's rent,' I said. 'Now you can afford to keep me.'

"After a while though, I couldn't afford to keep her. She kept asking me to borrow money. When I stopped giving it to her, she stole it."

"That's horrible. Did she realize that her daughter was stripping to get her drug money?"

"Of course. She once stole over $20,000 hidden in a shoebox in the back of my closet. Where else could I have made that kind of money? I was sixteen." She corrected, "Seventeen by that point. Either way, she knew I wasn't working for Microsoft. She didn't care. I found a better place to hide my money, course then she just beat me 'til I told her where it was hidden."

"How long did this go on?"

"About a year and a half. Until I met Derek."

"Who is Derek?"

Poison turned her head sharply. She spat, "That's not relevant to your article."

"Okay, I underst—"

But again she interrupted, "Derek was my savior."

It was the most interestingly amalgamated tone of voice Andrew Crenshaw had ever heard. Along with her complex face, she conveyed bitterness, fondness, shame, pride, pain, joy, regret and relief—all wrapped up in just one name. She shook her head. It was obvious that she would say no more about him.

She said, "But I continued stripping. I continued the same lifestyle. The whole time I thought I was rebelling against my mother, but that makes no sense. I was, in fact, building my life, painstakingly, brick by brick, as a monument to her—her ways, her values, her hatreds. I thought I was such a free thinker, but I had become exactly what every statistic said I would be."

Andrew Crenshaw's eyes looked down. Poison had assumed that as a reporter he had seen it all, and could not figure out why her words seemed to sting him in a deep, personal way.

"How many people read your paper?" she asked.

"A lot."

"Is it just here in town?"

"No, we have subscribers all over the country. Plus, we're on the Internet."

"Can I say a word to my mother, in case she reads your article?"

"Sure. Anything you'd like."

"Tell her I finally left her. I finally rebelled. Tell her I am happy now, despite her. Tell her I've found answers. Answers that you could never provide..." Poison hadn't noticed that she switched pronouns. "Answers to questions you were too selfish and too weak to ever even hear. Growing up, you never even knew I existed, but I won't have to *burden* you anymore. You never loved me. You were never even there to love me. Even when you were there, you weren't there. You never loved me. You never hugged me, or kissed me, or held me in your arms. You never noticed that everything I ever did was only to please you. *You!* But you never noticed. You never cared about a thing I did, or even questioned if I was happy." Her tears ran through the freshly applied mascara and pulled two dark and harrowing streaks down her cheeks. "But you no longer have to worry about me. I am happy now, in spite of you."

Andrew Crenshaw stabbed away at his keyboard. It was one of those splendid moments in which words flowed from him effortlessly, and every word was sincere and steadfast and perfect. He told the story of Ellison's arrest—the real story. He told the story of why he had inadvertently avoided the press. He told the story of his interview with a stripper named Poison. He typed on in wild abandon, not even pausing to save the file— *power surge be damned!*

He came to a part of the article that he himself hadn't expected. He typed:

> I listened to the lachrymose woman detailing her mother's failures and that's when it hit me; I realized she wasn't talking about her mother... she was talking about my father.

He sat and stared at the screen. He had never told a single soul, yet he had just put it in an article that would potentially be read by countless thousands. He quickly hit *SAVE*.

His fingers remained poised, primed over the keyboard, lightly touching the home keys. The cursor blinked like a schoolyard punk, triple-dog daring him.

Andrew Crenshaw had not moved for a long time, and the house had been completely silent, so the sound of his phone made him jump. It was a text. He looked at the face of his cell phone. He didn't recognize the number, but easily figured out from context who it was. It read, *Please don't write all that stuff I told you to tell my mom.*

He had already decided not to include the details of her personal message. He unlocked his phone and began to type a text in return, when it buzzed again in his hand. Poison's second text read, *Just tell her I forgive her.*

The words hit Andrew Crenshaw like cold water in the face. He replied, *Are you sure?*

He waited for a response, but he didn't get one. He returned to his keyboard and began to type. Words flowed out of him without effort as he wrote:

> And when I watched her breakdown into a torrent of tears, I wasn't seeing a broken woman, I was seeing a broken man. I was seeing everything in me, which had never been more eloquently summed up than by her wild, maudlin sobs, the tissue held firm to her nose and the rivers of mascara running down both cheeks.

Andrew Crenshaw's bottom lids began to fill with tears. He felt the weight of his childhood bearing down on him, and all the doors he had barricaded closed had just burst open. But all these old emotions felt somehow new. It was as if there was a new filter in his heart, straining out the muck and leaving only nuggets of gold.

> My father, newsman David Crenshaw, was a self-absorbed drug user, and a profoundly bad dad. It feels good to say. It is a fact that I have spent my life denying. I was denying the truth—watching old reels of my father and pretending that the man the world knew was the man that I knew—and denying the pain. And my latest act of denial came last

year, when my career hit a few bumps and I had no wife, no parents, and no God to turn to; I turned to the needle. My father's poison. The only solution he'd ever taught me. The only faithful navigator through the vicissitudes of life.

He rose from his desk to find some tissues. He found some in a purple box with flowers. Julian had bought them before she'd moved out. *Bless her heart.* For the first time in the week since he broke up with her, he missed her.

He checked his phone to see if Poison had texted back. It still read, *Just tell her I forgive her.*

He returned to his office chair before his keyboard, sat down, then quickly stood back up and began to pace. He felt overcome with a raw, new energy; it was exhilarating, and tear-soaked, and caffeinated, and liberating. He checked his phone. *Just tell her I forgive her.*

Finally, he returned to his chair. He typed:

> But I have recently found a new answer. I discovered that the hole I was trying to fill with heroin was really meant for God. The false promises of fulfillment and acceptance from these deceivers—drugs for me, alcohol and attention from men for Poison—are nothing more than lies. I learned that from Pastor Ellison on the very first night I spent with him. I have learned more from him in the days that followed than I had ever learned from my own father.
>
> The Pastor Riley Ellison that he shows to the world is the same Pastor Riley Ellison he shows to his family. It is the only Riley Ellison. He is only one man, not two. The selfless servant who gives his life to help people, who loves us as Christ loves us, is real. The licentious lothario who hypocritically solicits prostitutes is not. There is one Pastor Ellison and he changed my entire life.
>
> Pastor Riley Ellison is a great man. Pastor Ellison is the real deal.

Andrew Crenshaw stopped typing. He looked at his screen and for the first time in his life felt the power of words. It was the power once wielded by Martin Luther King, Jr., Thomas Jefferson, and the apostle Paul— the world-changing power of words written and words read. He typed:

> I humbly

He had to pause because he was overcome with emotion. He hit the back space eight times and then started again.

> I humbly

Again he deleted it. He looked over to his shelf and through his tear-blurred vision saw a picture of his father. *Or perhaps it isn't my father at all, perhaps it is just David Crenshaw, the trusted name in news, David Crenshaw, the American icon.* Ironically he was posing for a photo with Commander Frank Borman.

Andrew Crenshaw picked up the photo and gently lowered it into a drawer. He paused for a second, looking at the photo, hearing only the rain. Finally, he closed the drawer on the photo and on his past.

He wiped the tears off his face, and tried a third time.

> I humbly confess that I can't do this on my own. I'm in over my head. I need a Savior. I need Christ to do for me what he has done for Poison. All my walls are down. All the grand artifices I hid behind have been transparent the whole time. I am shivering, and lost, and pining, and suffering, now for all the world to see. I yearned for a father; I have a new Father. I was seeking an anchor—an *Anchor*—that David Crenshaw never was. I want my readers to know that I, Andrew Crenshaw, am at long last a Christian.

> That's the news, America. Goodnight.

Chapter Fourteen

January 15—One day left

"I want you to see something." Andrew Crenshaw was carrying a slim leather satchel. He pulled out a folder and set it on Ellison's kitchen table. From out that folder, he produced two crisp white sheets of printer paper. He said, "It's the article I turned in to my editor. I hope you don't mind; I went behind your back to talk to Poison. I'd like to say that I'm sorry I did, but I am not."

"It's okay. I knew you were a reporter when I agreed to let you hang out with me."

"Yes, but that's not why I'm not sorry. The truth is, meeting with Poison changed my life. The last two weeks have changed my life. I heard about how you helped her. It's amazing what you did for her and her boy. Now, I want you to read how you've helped me. Please read the article."

Ellison handed it back, stoically. "I've already read it."

"No, you haven't," Andrew Crenshaw said as he pushed the paper back, insisting.

Ellison looked perplexed. He began to read.

The whole time Andrew Crenshaw watched the pastor's eyes, he could not help but have a déjà vu. He remembered the day he handed his first ever editorial to his father. He had watched the old anchor's face, desperate for a hint of approval, fearing the slightest twitch of his facial muscles that would indicate anything less. For some reason, the words echoed through his head, *Is it good enough, Father? Can I become a newsman, just like you?*

Ellison's face showed a hint of impatience as he scanned the words he had already read—the words he had clearly told Andrew Crenshaw he had read. But his eyebrows perked up as he discovered new stuff. As he reached the last few lines, his jaw even dropped. He drew in a long breath, making his shoulders and chest rise in such a swell that conveyed surprise, disbelief, and sweet ecstasy.

He said, "You submitted this to your editor?"

"Yes."

"But this isn't what was printed?"

"No, it isn't."

"And it's all true?"

"Every word."

"You've accepted Christ into your heart?" Ellison asked again, still having a hard time accepting the words he had read.

"Yes, sir."

Ellison put his hand over his mouth. His eyes appeared to be on the verge of tears. He slowly lowered his hand to reveal a radiant smile. He put his other hand on Andrew's shoulder, and the two of them remained in that position for a long time.

The gesture felt so sincere. It conveyed a feeling of permanence that Andrew Crenshaw's life had been sorely lacking.

Ellison reached to hug him and Andrew Crenshaw felt awash in unconditional love. When Ellison finally let go, he caught sight of Andrew Crenshaw wiping a few tears from his eyes.

Andrew quickly stowed the folder and printout back into his bag, so he could have something else to focus on. "It's simple," he said. "I asked myself why I was atheist, and I did not have an answer. I realized that I had become what I was expected to be." Andrew Crenshaw laughed. "And you know the whole time I thought I was such a free thinker—son of an atheist, from a family of newsmen, *ivory*-league educated. Raised on the *left* coast—but I'd become exactly what every statistic said I would be."

"So what's the story with your editor? How come this masterpiece did not go to print?"

"Well, I'm as shocked as you are. When I turned the piece in I knew... well, I knew its power. I figured I'd be receiving a frenzied phone call, or curt e-mail, or something... and yet it never came. I waited and I waited, until finally the deadline passed. I figured that they had nixed the whole spot without telling me, or they had printed it as is. I never imagined that they had taken every little bit that mentioned Christ out of my story."

Ellison's eyes narrowed. He said, bemused, "They left the part in where you confessed to being an addict—they let their readers all discover that fact—but they took the part out where you confessed to becoming a Christian."

"Yes. I picked up on that too."

"Did you call them on it?"

"Yes, as soon as I saw the hatchet job they'd done to my work, I marched straight into my editor's office and demanded an explanation."

"What did he tell you?"

"He said that he didn't care what I did on my own time, but unless I wanted to be unemployed, I would keep it to myself." Andrew Crenshaw sighed. "I had been still living in my father's world. I never saw that the tides had turned. In my mind, I was always protesting the inquisition, or the crusades, or the Salem witch hunts, none of which had anything to do with the world we live in, or even the country or century we live in. I never saw the witch hunt happening right under my nose, and in my own paper."

"Did you tell them you'd stay quiet?"

"Yes." Andrew shrugged guiltily. "It all took me by surprise. I hadn't expected to give up my career on a random Wednesday." His phone rang. Andrew Crenshaw looked at the phone and grimaced. He said, "Well, speak of the devil."

Ellison laughed.

"I'm sorry; I have to take this," Andrew said to Ellison. "Hello," he said to the phone. He looked at his watch and said, "No. Not busy. Have time." He pulled out his pen and pointed to a napkin on the table. Ellison quickly handed it to him.

"... uh huh... uh huh..."

Andrew Crenshaw wrote down *1,000 words.*

"... uh huh..."

He wrote down 7:00.

Ellison looked at his own watch. It was 4:49.

"What about?" Andrew asked the phone.

Within a few seconds, Ellison saw his face change. He began to write *Mas—* but stopped. His hand immediately crumbled the napkin and hid it from Ellison's sight. He turned his body away from Ellison, blinking frantically, but not quickly enough to prevent the pastor from seeing the new tears that had formed.

The last words he said, breathlessly, were, "Okay, I'm on it."

He hung up the phone.

The reporter remained with his back to Ellison for a few moments. Ellison could see his shoulders move as he drew in two long breaths. When he finally turned to Ellison, he said nothing, but moved to grab his stuff.

"Breaking news, again?" Ellison asked, intentionally leaving it vague.

"I'm sorry, but I have to go," Andrew said, even more vaguely.

"It doesn't look good," Ellison pressed.

"It's not," the reporter said.

"Well, if ya gotta go, ya gotta go," Ellison said standing up.

Andrew Crenshaw froze. He was already on his feet. His left foot remained planted, but his right foot took small steps out of the room, back to the center, then out again. Finally, as it appeared the mental struggle was resolved, he turned completely to walk out.

Ellison called to him. "Andrew Crenshaw!" When Andrew turned around, Ellison spread his arms, palms up, and smiled. His smile was warm-hearted, and in the moments before impending bad news, courageous. He said, "You can tell me."

Andrew didn't move and didn't speak.

Pastor Ellison pulled a chair farther out from the table. He said, "Why don't you come back, for just a moment, and have a seat."

Andrew Crenshaw returned and quickly sat down. He held his satchel in front of his chest, protecting him. He said, "Maybe you'd better have a seat as well."

When they were both sitting, he continued. "It's better that you hear it from me I suppose. I don't want you to have to read it from my article. There was a car accident..." His entire career was in breaking news, and most of it bad, but he never once had to *break news* to a person and not a laptop. "It was fatal. Mason Kessler is dead. Toxicology reports have not yet confirmed whether or not he had been drinking. I'm sorry."

Chapter Fifteen

January 16

Brandon Davies checked the app on his phone. It read:

00 days: 00 hours: 05 minutes: 26 seconds

He and Ashley McAllister stood at the front of a massive crowd. Pastor Ellison had very cryptically asked both of them to "Wait outside with the people." They were shivering. It surprisingly wasn't raining, but no one expected it to be this cold.

Brandon had spent the last two weeks wondering what Pastor Ellison would be like in the minutes leading up to the main event. He had seen the pastor on days when the light from his eyes could rival the sun, when every word of his sermon would fall into place and he felt locked in an embrace with the Creator and all of creation. It was as if Ellison's favorite emotion in all of life was to be overwhelmed. Pastor Ellison was overwhelmed by God's grace, overwhelmed by the promise of eternal life, overwhelmed by the sacrifice Jesus had made, overwhelmed to have a place where he belonged, to know it, and to be standing in that exact spot. Like a house cat sprawled out in a sunbeam, Pastor Ellison would luxuriate in the everlasting glory of God.

But all that was before yesterday. In the hours since Kessler's death, Ellison had not been the same. The light had left his eyes, and Brandon Davies questioned if there remained any traces of the radiant and effusive man he had known for twenty-four years, the man who epitomized the love of God.

He checked his app:

00 days: 00 hours: 03 minutes: 46 seconds

He imagined the pastor should be stepping out of the church at any time now.

Brandon Davies couldn't believe the size of the crowd. He searched for faces he could recognize. Andrew Crenshaw was there. Although officially he was there on business, Brandon Davies knew he would've been there no matter what. Hailey and her new baby girl were there, but not Colton Rucker. He looked around for Poison and her son, but he couldn't see them. He did catch sight of Nancy Fuller. She had tied a string around every finger, just for luck.

How cute, Brandon smiled. He noticed that many people were treating the occasion like a festival or carnival. He saw a few people wearing the same t-shirt that Ellison had seen in the airport. It read "Mead Mountain. I have faith!" He saw other shirts that simply read "It will move." But he also saw t-shirts from the other side; they displayed a tiny caricature of Pastor Ellison attempting to move a large rubber tree plant. The caption read "He's got high hopes." People were so proud of their t-shirts that they had bundled up in many layers and stretched the t-shirts over top.

Members of their congregation—their old congregation that they hadn't seen in two weeks—were also there. And more people where continuing to flood in.

The press was gathered in the exact spot that Ellison had originally instructed them to stand. Ellison had arranged for a makeshift stage to be erected. The stage only stood a foot tall, but it provided a landing ground, as well as the perfect angle to capture the mountain.

While some in the crowd were treating the occasion like a party, others were more reverent. They wanted to see God's miracle. They had come from far and wide, anxious to witness the first overt show of force from God in two millennia.

There were people from all over the globe, followers of Christ, many of whom appeared to be counted among the world's poor. Some had sold almost everything they owned just to be there. Mead Mountain Church had become a place of pilgrimage. They'd come to see something biblical.

He spotted a group of school kids. They all wore white shirts with black ties. Their skin was darker than any complexion Brandon Davies had ever seen. He assumed they were from Africa and wondered what wealthy philanthropist had arranged for their long journey.

Beside the twenty-foot white cross, there was a long line of small homemade crosses, plaques, signs, and flowers. There were photos of Pastor Ellison lined with garlands, handwritten notes from children, and stuffed teddy bears.

There was an area where people had pushed their loved ones in on wheelchairs, or even carried them on simple, third-world stretchers. Some were missing legs, some were missing arms, some were missing both.

They were hoping for more miracles than one. There were blind men and women who hoped to see. There were strange shouts and loud babbling from those clearly inflicted with one mental illness or another. There were people struggling with cancer, Alzheimer's, Parkinson's, autism, senility, Tourrette's, and schizophrenia.

There were people who brought their babies and people who brought their grandparents. Many carried crosses and crucifixes; some carried photographs of relatives that had passed on.

There were people who were crying already, people who kept making the sign of the cross, and people who had been bowed with their foreheads to the frozen ground the entire time.

There were protestors, anxious to soak up some of the media attention for their own cherished causes. Brandon Davies saw different groups carrying rainbow triangles, Venus symbols, hammer and sickles, Guy Fawkes masks, and swastikas. He saw an American flag hung upside down and a dummy made to look like Pastor Ellison with a noose around its neck.

One particular group of malcontents, believing they were social justice warriors, hung an enormous banner between two street lamps. It was in the opposite direction of the mountain, but no one in the crowd was able to miss it. It read: STOP HATE.

Brandon opened the Twitter app on his phone. Some unknown supporter had created a hashtag for the event which was now trending number one. Tweets were coming in, many per second, from all over the world. They were all asking the mountain to move. The idea was that they would all lend their voices, and their faith, to Pastor Ellison's. It was heartening for Brandon Davies to see.

He looked up to see some commotion where the press stood. The crowd seemed to be parting to let someone through. The reporters had congregated to one spot and Brandon Davies could hear loud voices overlapping each other. He stood on his tippy toes to try to catch sight of what was going on. Finally, he spotted a man with his arm up, trying to shield a woman from the cameras and questions. It took him a moment to realize who they were. It was Mason Kessler's wife and son. They had made their way to the front of the crowd, anxious to see what would happen, like everyone else.

The press finally left them alone once they were satisfied they'd be making no statement and answering no questions. Brandon Davies stared at them. He wondered if he should go over there, but he never really knew them that well and had no idea what he would say. He just shook his head. *God help us if this thing doesn't move. God help us.*

He reopened his countdown app. It had reached zero at some point when he wasn't watching. The display read:

00 days: 00 hours: 00 minutes: 00 seconds
KA-BOOM

Brandon didn't know why it said "Ka-boom." He had never used this app before. He suddenly wished he had picked a different one. He couldn't help looking down again.

KA-BOOM

It filled him with a strange foreboding. It gave him one more reason, besides the cold, to shiver.

The crowd must have noticed that it was past time, too, because their idle chatter tapered off and they became as quiet as a golf game. Even the rowdy protestors were silent.

Brandon would never have thought a crowd that size could possibly have been quiet enough to hear the squeak of the church's front door in the distance, but it was. Ten thousand faces turned to see. It was Ellison and his wife. Brandon Davies was not sure when Deborah had joined him, but they both walked toward the crowd, their steps in unison. Deborah linked her arm on his and Brandon Davies had never seen her look so beautiful. The two of them reminded him of a young couple, newly married, exiting a chapel.

The crowd closed in tight around them. The protestors shouted straight in their faces, while the faithful all rushed in for a chance to touch their clothing. The Ellisons walked on, unfazed by the bedlam.

When they reached the stage, Pastor Ellison turned to face the cameras. Deborah kissed him gently on the cheek, then found a spot to stand over by Mason Kessler's wife. She turned to watch her husband, like the rest of the entire world. And another hush fell over the crowd.

Pastor Ellison was carrying the black king in his pocket. He addressed the crowd, "God bless you all."

There was no applause, no boos, no murmuring—just the sound of ten thousand people holding their breath.

"I invited you all here because I have been called by God to ask this mountain to move." He gestured to the mountain, and for the first time that day, looked over at it himself. His eyes narrowed and he felt a cold rock in his gut. He couldn't believe what he saw. Some adventurous hoodlums had climbed the mountain overnight and defaced it. In enormous, white block-letters, the graffiti on the face of Mead Mountain read:

GOD IS DEAD.

Pastor Ellison paused. He had never once since his conversion to Christianity let the detractors get to him. He had passed undaunted by the image of him being hanged, and the insults being shouted at his wife, yet somehow seeing that message in those crisp, white letters disturbed him. It deeply disturbed him.

He was visibly stunned. His cheeks were ashen and his lips were blue. He couldn't remember what he had prepared to say. He didn't feel like an instrument of God. He didn't feel like a wise prophet of biblical proportions.

Before the moment he heard of Mason Kessler's death, he hadn't once considered the possibility that the mountain wouldn't move. He was certainly picturing that outcome now. *I will be the man who single-handedly destroys Christianity as we know it. I will be launched to the status of most significant man in the twenty-first century, overnight.* It was never his intention to get his name in history books, but he knew the moment would be studied for hundreds of years, like the moment Martin Luther nailed demands on the door of the Church of Wittenberg, the first shot on the Old North Bridge, and the assassination of Archduke Ferdinand, all rolled up together. It would be the start of something big, and in this case, something monstrous. It would not be the first domino to fall, but it would move the cause of atheism forward a thousand years. Not just atheism; it would be a boon to every aberrant cause proposed by the type of miscreants who were currently lynching him in effigy. It would advance America a quantum leap forward along the dark path which pastors, for centuries, had warned she was ultimately heading.

He wished the cameras would go away. He wished he and his wife could escape to a private island to live out the rest of their lives alone, and let the rest of the world, literally, go to hell.

He reflexively looked to the string on his finger. Moments like this were what it was for—and had always been for—to help him remember what he, a flawed sinner, would so easily forget.

But the string wasn't there.

He tried to remember exactly when he had forgotten to put it back on. He couldn't. Sometime between the moment he had heard about Mason Kessler's death and this moment that he was in, he had forgotten all about the string. He wasn't even sure where it was.

The cameras were still rolling. He stood there looking like a frightened fool. The only thing that moved was the mist that formed on every labored breath he exhaled.

Finally, his wife rushed over to support him. She pulled him into a strong embrace and spoke directly in his ear. "You have a job to do. You were called by God to do it. Nothing else matters." Her words were encouraging, but firm.

He pulled out of the hug so that he could look her in the eye. He said, "It won't move. What have I done?"

"It will move. It's a promise from God."

"I can't do it."

"You were chosen by God."

"He made a mistake. I can't. Not me."

Pastor Ellison felt another hand pull on his shoulder. It was Brandon Davies. He turned Riley to face him. He held the tip of his index finger pressed against the tip of his thumb. He appeared to be holding nothing. With his other hand he turned Ellison's palm up and dropped what he had been pinching into the pastor's hand. It was the mustard seed.

Riley pulled the tiny seed up to his face. It was so small.

Deborah saw the seed and understood. She looked up at her husband and said, "It's okay to doubt." She pointed at the seed. "Do you have this much faith left in your heart? Do you have this much of Christ's love still lingering in your broken heart?"

Pastor Ellison nodded slowly.

They both took their cue and returned to the crowd.

Ellison stood before the people, once again, alone. He saw the eyes watching him. And, what is more, he saw their suffering, their real pain. He wanted to reach them. He felt like he had answers to give. They had never been a secret. He imagined a world in which lost and pining people desperately seek real answers, but those who are in the know stubbornly keep it all to themselves. *That* world might actually make sense, but that somehow isn't the real world. Ellison looked out to see the real world, well represented by the crowd before him, in which the possessors of the truth are desperate to give it away, and the lost and the pining are defiantly reluctant to receive it.

He had his chance to reach them now. He remembered the answer God had given him: *For the sake of a great nation.* He remembered one of his favorite quotes, which he repeated before every sermon, instructing him: *Words from the heart, enter the heart.*

He said, "I know what it's like to hurt. I know what it's like to feel like you don't matter. I know what loneliness—real loneliness—feels like. I know what it's like to feel unloved. I know what it's like to look at your life and feel that the problems you face are bigger, stronger, and more impenetrable than this mountain.

"But I also know what it's like to close your eyes in prayer, open them, and discover that the mountain is gone, inexplicably gone. Vanished without a trace. I know from where we draw the power to move the immovable.

"So when God told me that He would move this mountain, I didn't blink. I didn't doubt He could do it because I've seen Him move mountains, insurmountable mountains, bigger than this one.

"It's no secret. I am talking about Jesus Christ." He flashed a mischievous grin, then turned to the mountain. The camera zoomed in on the side of Ellison's face; beyond the pastor's profile was the inviolate strength of Mead Mountain. It was the perfect shot. Ellison said, "I can do all things through Christ, who strengthens me."

The cameras all zoomed in just a bit tighter. Nancy Fuller bowed her head in prayer. Hailey's arms drew tighter around Baby Abigail. Brandon and Ashley held their breath. Andrew Crenshaw noticed that his own hands were trembling.

Ellison spoke. "By God's eternal power, and by the passion of Christ, and the blood of our Savior, according to the promise He has made, I now command you, Mead Mountain, to crumble!" His stentorian demand echoed off the side of the granite ridge, returning to the pastor's ears and the microphones of the press, undistorted, but unanswered.

"By the power of Christ, I command you, mountain, to move from our sight!" he repeated, calmly.

They waited. Ashley and Brandon looked at each other. Brandon wished he had never expressed his doubts to Ellison out loud, not once. Hailey Rucker began to cry. Deborah Ellison had her head bowed and could feel a number of hands pressed against her shoulders and back. Despite the cold, Andrew Crenshaw had to wipe the sweat from his temple.

Ellison heard something comforting and familiar: jumbled whispering. It was the sound that could be heard during worship at Mead Mountain Church on any given Sunday, the sound of hundreds of separate overlapping prayers.

Still the mountain didn't move.

He spoke again, "God, it's me, your humble servant. I am asking you, in Christ's name, to move this mountain."

Nothing happened.

"Please, God. Please, hear my prayer. Search my heart. I believe in You. I have faith in Your power. Move this mountain, God."

Nothing moved. The cameras rolled on.

"Has my work been displeasing to You God? Have I been arrogant? Have I been vain? I ask You now to move this mountain, not for me, but for your church, for a desperate and ailing land, and *for the sake of a great nation*. Move this mountain, Lord."

Thousands of people turned their faces away from him and watched only the mountain. A few of the cameramen even zoomed in so tight on the mountain that it cropped Ellison's face out of the picture. Other networks showed it in a split-screen.

But the mountain didn't budge.

"Please God. Please. Please. God, move this mountain, if it be Thy will, move it only for your glory."

Nothing happened.

"Not for my glory, but for Yours."

His wife ran over to his side and handed him a black and gold Bible. He clutched the Bible against his heart. "By Your Holy Word, Your sacred promise, please move this mountain from our sight."

Nothing happened so he stepped down off the stage and got down on his knees. He said, "Please, God, who can count the grains of sand, whose words can calm the storm on the sea, who taught the very stars to shine, please let it be that this mountain crumbles into the ocean."

Ellison could hear that the crowd was no longer silent. People were sobbing. Some of them even howled so loud it sounded like demons being tortured in Hell. Others laughed, throwing out taunts and curse words.

And the mountain remained.

"Please God, remove Mead Mountain from our sight."

The welter of wailing increased; the din of laughter increased; but the mountain didn't move.

He tried the exact words from the New International Version, "Move from here to there."

He tried the King James translation, "Remove hence from yonder place."

He even tried the Ancient Greek, "Μεταβα ένθεν έκεί."

Each word of Scripture puffed in white smoke from his mouth, but did nothing more.

Ellison dropped his elbows to the ground in a deep, suppliant kneel. The frozen dirt chilled him. The cameras had to zoom out drastically if they wanted to still contain him in the shot. Ellison realized in that moment, that he had been praying with his eyes open. He placed his forehead to the Bible and shut his eyes tight in propitiation.

In his mind he could feel the eyes on him: his wife, Mason Kessler's wife, Andrew Crenshaw, Brandon Davies, Haley Rucker, and the great cloud of witnesses.

He cast off every weight that hindered his mind. He pleaded, "My sweet Lord, always faithful, my precious Jesus, the name above all names, glorious mystery, all-powerful God, hear my prayer. Hear the longing of a stricken world; hear the prayers of your desperate children. Bring us the hope we need. Fill us with Your grace. If it be Thy will, move this mountain, Lord."

Ellison raised his head slowly and opened his eyes, hoping to—as he had described it—see the immoveable mountain vanished into thin air.

But it was still there. Still there. Mocking him.

"Please, Oh, Please. Lord..." Ellison paused.

The last thing he wanted to do was make eye contact with Brandon Davies, but he wanted to steal a glimpse of his face. And in the overcast light, they both could see a glint in the other man's eyes, betraying they were on the verge of tears. And they just *shrugged*.

The greatly disappointed pastor had no words left.

The mustard seed slipped through his fingers.

"Have I wronged you, God? Have I..." His mind was searching. He looked over to the giant white cross and said, "My God, my God, why has Thou—" He didn't finish. He could feel his wife's hand on his back. She crouched down beside him and began to pull him to his feet. She wrapped both arms around his waist, and walked him, like a wounded soldier, back to the door of the church. They again had to pass the mocking atheists and the heartbroken faithful. They passed the howling demons and the laughing demons. They passed the row of crosses. They passed the lynched dummy with Riley's face. Someone had just lit it on fire.

Deborah Ellison drew her hobbled husband, a *laughingstock*, across the threshold and then closed and locked the door of Mead Mountain Church.

Chapter Sixteen

Poison and Tyler had been watching the coverage live. They hadn't said a word to each other since the moment it was clear the mountain wouldn't move. They watched on as Ellison continued to grovel with God, and the knot in Tyler's chest grew tight.

Finally, the network switched to a commercial. It played dinky music as a woman in ballet slippers danced through a wheat field. The commercial was for Damitol. Tyler clicked it off fiercely.

It was only then that they both realized what a balm the television noise had been. They were now left wallowing in a heavy, thick, sepulchral silence. Finally, the boy turned to his mother and said, "Well..."

"Well what?" she snapped.

He turned his eyes away. "Just *well.*"

Poison knew what he was doing. He was doing what she had always hoped he would do. He was looking to her for guidance. He was, for one brief ill-advised moment, viewing her as a parental figure with wisdom and life experience. But she was out of her depth. She spat. "There is no *well.* No *well* about it. We were scammed; that's all. I bet all he was ever after was money. So typical."

"Wait," Tyler injected confused. "Did he ask you for *money?*"

"We were scammed!" insisted Poison. "He manipulated us, just like-" She stopped herself abruptly.

Tyler turned to look at her. He asked, "Just like all men?"

Poison looked away. She looked out across her apartment. The dishes were done. The clothes were picked up. The place had been looking better than it did on the day she moved in. Her boy was on the small couch with her. She couldn't remember the last time they just sat together—just sat together—so close.

When she had failed to respond, Tyler got up to leave. Her lips tightened and she was fighting back tears. She shook her head and mumbled, "Better that we found out now." She repeated the words like a woman who had called off her engagement, but was still longing for the union that she knew would not work, "Better to find out now."

No one had been left in the room to hear her words.

Andrew Crenshaw had just arrived home. He had driven home with the radio on extra loud—music from a random channel. As he entered into his kitchen from the garage, he could still hear the garage door lowering, the last remaining distraction before he had to face the impending silence.

The first thing he thought, once he re-granted his brain permission to think, was that he was lonely. The house felt empty and interminably quiet. He was all alone.

His phone buzzed when his boss texted him.

I need 1000 words by 5:00.

He checked his watch. It said 4:07. He hurried to his computer, propelled only by duty and habit. *More like wishful thinking.* He knew that he would not have 1,000 concrete words to say on the subject. He couldn't make any sense of it in his head.

He jiggled his mouse to wake up his computer. His word processor was already open and he was looking at—in front of his very eyes—a one-thousand-word story about the mountain. He had cheated and written it in advance. The only problem was he had written a version in which the mountain moved.

He read his own words, his opus, by far the greatest thing he had ever written, replete with Jeffersonian eloquence, detailing the excitement, the wonder, and the indelible *victory* surrounding the moment when a trillion tons of stone slid into the ocean before throngs of the cheering faithful. It felt so surreal to him now. He couldn't imagine that mere hours ago he had so much faith. He tried to relate to the man who he had been just that morning and he couldn't. It was as if he was waking from a dream and what had made perfect sense in the dream, made sense no longer.

Andrew Crenshaw read the optimistic report again and again and again, hoping with each read it might reveal greater truth, or somehow blot out the last ninety minutes of his life. He was overcome with a stronger emotion than he had ever felt. He wanted the story, not reality, to be real. He wanted to live in his words. For a man raised by atheists, the idea of intentionally deluding himself felt adorned in thorns; he didn't want to touch it. He said it out loud, just to ameliorate his mind to such an apocryphal confession, "I *want* to delude myself." He wondered if he could do it. He wondered if, before the mountain failed to move, he had been doing just that. He wondered if he was alone in that fact.

He deleted the file.

It was now after 4:30. Opening a new page, he was greeted by the bedeviling cursor. He typed, "I was duped by Pastor Ellison."

About half an hour later, his phone buzzed with another text. It was 5:05 and his editor was, no doubt, asking for the story. All Andrew Crenshaw had written so far was, "I was duped by Pastor Ellison." His head was leaning hard against his left hand. He had been there for so long that his arm had fallen completely asleep. He tossed the phone aside with his right.

After another minute, the phone, half-buried in a messy desk, began to ring. Andrew Crenshaw didn't have to check, but accidently saw the number when he grabbed the phone to silence it. It was his editor, of course. He threw the phone across the room.

He had been staring at the words, "I was duped by Pastor Ellison," for so long that the words no longer made sense. The first to go had been "duped." *That's a strange word to begin with.* Soon even "I", "was", and "by" no longer seemed to connect with any intelligible concept in his mind. The only words left were "Pastor Ellison."

Pastor Ellison. Pastor Ellison. Pastor Ellison. He knew those two words would never leave him—a wound that wouldn't heal. Those two words burned white-hot in his head.

He had foolishly let his guard down. It was naïve to think he'd found someone to look up to. Now he found himself back where he had always been: hating his father. He hated his father more than ever, only *his father* had a new face and a new name.

Since he was back where he'd always been, he decided to do what he'd always done.

He slid open the bottom drawer of his desk, where he kept his heroin.

Officer Gonzales came home from a long shift helping keep the city safe. He had been working all night, but he had seen the footage. Officer Felicia Jones had pulled up the video of Ellison's genuflecting and there was a cluster of cops hovering around her monitor for the next few hours.

When he stepped foot inside his home, he could tell by which lights were left on that his wife had already gone to bed. He tried to be quiet as he hung his car keys on the hook she had setup for them. He entered his bedroom as quietly as possible and began the daunting task of trying to change out of his uniform in the dark.

"Just turn on the bathroom light; I'm awake," he heard the pile of bedding say.

Gonzales said nothing, but he did turn on the light.

"You okay?" is all she asked him.

"Yeah, I'm okay."

As soon as he was ready, he turned off the light and made his way to the bed in the dark.

"Do you want to say a prayer?" she asked. It was clear from her tone that she had asked out of habit. It was a stimulus response to the light being turned out, and had nothing at all to do with the news of the day.

The room was filled with dark silence. She could hear the profound quality of her husband's suffering communicated in that silence.

Finally, he said, "Not tonight, dear," and rolled over.

She placed a hand on his back. It felt as if she had just been holding hot coffee in a paper cup. The warmth comforted him. She raised her head to say something, but then rested it right back down.

The next day, the print edition of the *Times* ran with the front page headline: *He Can Do ALMOST All Things Through Christ*. Another paper mocked Ellison's supplication with the remark, "He tried everything but *Simon Says*." The first clip of Ellison's pleading that made it to the Internet had racked up fifty million hits overnight. The churches that supported Ellison all ran to change the messages they had on their marquises. The newspapers that did not support him were all coming up with different ways to say "I told you so."

It was early afternoon and Colton Rucker had already forgotten about what had happened the day before. He had heard about Pastor Ellison's embarrassing display, and Hailey had decided to sleep in Abigail's room that night. He cared a little bit about the news, but none of it felt more relevant to him even than that night's poker game.

He had promised his mother he would come to see her the next day he had off. When he arrived, the curtain that surrounded her bed was completely closed, which was unusual, but it didn't cause him any alarm. He cracked open the curtain and called out, "Good morning!"

Pain struck his heart.

He quickly rushed down to his mother's side. "Mom, what is it? How are you? Are you okay?"

June Rucker's pallid, wizened face stared back at him, without a hint of makeup.

"No," she said. "Not okay." She tried to smile. She touched a moribund hand to the side of Colton's face. She said, "My precious Colton! You look so much like your father."

Colton didn't know what to say. He stuttered, "Do you... uh... should I get a nurse in here?"

"Nothing they can do for me, darling. I'm dying."

"Now?"

"Soon."

Colton had instantly forgotten about his poker game.

"Today?" he asked.

June breathed deep. She said tonelessly, "Not today."

"What's going on?"

"I just feel it."

"I can stay with you all weekend. I don't work again until Monday."

"No, you have a baby to look after."

"She'll be fine."

"No, Colton, I won't allow it."

"I think I should stay."

June smiled. "I'll have the nurses throw you out if I have to."

"Mom."

"Can we please talk about something else?"

The two of them sat still, sharing a silent moment, completely aware that it would probably be one of their last.

Colton examined the room. "What happened to the radio I brought you?"

"The damn thing quit working."

"Mom! I believe that's the first time I've ever heard you say a bad word."

"You heard some on the day you were born, you just don't remember."

Colton laughed.

She said, "I figured since I don't have much time left, I'd give cursing another try."

"How was it?"

She shrugged. "Overrated." June looked at the empty spot where her radio had been, and her eyes suddenly lit up. She said, "When was your pastor supposed to move that mountain?"

She couldn't understand why her son's eyes instantly darted away. He said, "That was yesterday."

June's eyes began to fill with tears. She said, "Did you see it? Were you there?"

"Um... I watched it on TV."

She smacked his hand. "You should've been there. Something like that!"

"Well, we had the baby, so... it was just too cold out."

"Was it..." She paused. She wanted to ask if it was magnificent, but she chose a phrasing that was simply more honest. She asked timidly, "Did it... did it move?"

Colton breathed in sharply through his nose. His entire torso expanded. He sat up tall and said, "Yes. Yes, of course it moved."

A tear formed so quickly in her eye that it skipped the intermediate step of pooling in her eyelid, but rather jumped recklessly down onto her cheek. She asked, "Was it magnificent?"

He nodded. "It was God's miracle."

Tears continued to flow down her face, feverishly. Her jaw began to quiver. She said, "I'm going home. I'm going home, aren't I? I'm coming home to Him."

He said, questioningly, "Mom, you've always known that."

She smiled. She attempted to wipe the tears from her face, but there were too many. She said, "Yes, I've always known it, but now I *know* it." She leaned her head back and looked towards the beckoning heavens, and added, "Praise God! Praise God! Praise God!"

Five hours later and three drinks into the night, Colton Rucker was sitting around a poker game with his buddies, with his mother's words, "Praise God," still ringing in his ears. The baby was sleeping and Hailey was pretending to.

A voice in Colton's head was singing a song he wasn't even clear how he knew, "Rise and shine and give God your glory, glory."

"You guys see the footage of that pastor?" one of the men asked belligerently.

Colton said nothing. Week after week, Colton would host their poker night and every week he'd hope Wade wouldn't show.

Wade continued after nothing was said. "I was glued to CNN all day. I must've watched that thing twenty times. When they finally took a break from playing it, I hopped onto the Internet to watch it. That's the funniest stuff I've ever seen."

No one in the room responded. One of the men there cleared his throat. He tipped his head toward the player to his left.

Sam saw this gesture toward him and tried to preempt it, "No, by all means, talk. I don't care what any of you say about it."

Wade put both hands up, saying, "Now I'm not making fun of anyone's personal beliefs. I know that Sam here is a Christian. You're still a Christian, right?"

"I said you can say what you like, but I'd rather not talk about it," said Sam.

"D'you hear what Jake Dolan said about it?" Wade continued, ignoring the tension. "He tweeted, 'I ordered my dog, *Remove hence from yonder place*. He just stood there and licked himself.'" Wade laughed and repeated, "Remove hence from yonder place! Too funny. Oh, then Dolan added, 'I guess I lack faith in Dog!'"

No one responded, so Wade felt inspired to make his defense. "I'm not offending anyone."

Sam shrugged. "You're not offending me."

Everyone looked uncomfortable. In the resulting silence, they could hear an inadvertent humming.

"What's that you're humming, maestro?" Wade asked Colton.

"Oh," Colton wasn't aware he had been humming, but he knew full well what song it must have been. He said, "Nothing. Just some commercial I think."

Sam looked at Colton with an amused and accusing smile.

Colton looked at Sam and stated firmly, "It's just some catchy jingle I saw on TV."

Sam nodded, without actually trying to convince Colton he believed him.

"Hey, listen man, listen," Wade said to Sam. His inebriated mind was still fixated on making his case, whether Sam claimed to be offended or not. "Hey, listen. You may be Christian, but you've never asked a mountain to move; am I right? I mean, you may be Christian, but—*come on*—you didn't think that garbage would really work. You didn't think the mountain would move."

"Well—" Sam made a motion to answer, despite being unsure if it had actually been a question, but he was interrupted by Wade again.

"I mean the guy's a total crackpot." Wade's face changed. He turned to Colton and asked, "Hey didn't you tell me once that your wife goes to that church?"

Everyone turned to look at Colton. His mind went to the wrinkled note in his coat pocket. He had tried to throw it away, but something made him fish it out of the trash the next morning. He had felt silly at the time—like the way a misty-eyed romantic keeps a movie stub from a perfect date. He could feel that note now in his back pocket, as if it were radiating heat. "No," he said, "She goes someplace else. Not that guy. I wouldn't let her. That guy's a crackpot."

Down the hall, Hailey stared up at the wall of their bedroom in the dark. She refused to unclench the fist of her right hand. Shadow patterns of leaves danced as the distant street lamp threw them onto the wallpaper from the 1970s. She had been listening to every word from the kitchen. One hand clung to her Bible, while the other hand—clenched in a fist so tight it was beginning to hurt—concealed what she didn't have the strength to face.

The Good News was in her right hand, the bad news in her left.

She repeated in her head the same thing millions across the world had been repeating for the last twenty-four hours, "What are You doing, God? God, what are You doing?"

Finally, she opened her left hand to reveal the pregnancy test that she'd been clutching. It read +.

Chapter Seventeen

When Pastor Ellison arrived to his church parking lot that Sunday, the mobs of press and protestors were long gone. There stubbornly remained a single agitator—one recalcitrant protestor mocking the Word of God and pouring salt in the wounds of Ellison's faith:

Mead Mountain.

Mead Mountain, *never flitting, still is sitting, still is sitting.*

Mead Mountain sat as an intransigent symbol of transience, a gift to all those who ridicule the faithful, a ten-thousand-foot monument to the rise of the new atheists and their quest to uproot a once-strong nation.

It read "God is Dead."

For three days, Pastor Ellison had been asking God to enter his heart, but He hadn't. Hour after hour, down on his knees, elbows to the ground, Pastor Ellison begged God to just speak to him, clear the brambles in his mind, and elucidate the path that he should take. But God had been silent.

For the first time since Mason Kessler had walked into his hole-in-the-wall bar, come to return a favor, God was silent in Ellison's heart.

The words of Mason Kessler's doubt had weighed heavily on his mind. The two of them had once been riding so high, teaching people, reaching souls. There was a feeling that what they were doing was important. There was an eternal significance wrapped around every word Ellison uttered. A hundred people baptized every month. Thirty million books sold. It all felt so immovable. It even felt stronger than Mead Mountain. If one of these two monoliths were to fall, it would've only made sense for it to be the mountain.

He could remember the look Jake Dolan had given him when he said, if the mountain didn't move, he would forsake Christianity. *I'm sorry God; I was so prideful.* Was he now just one of those people he himself had talked about—who just believes what's comfortable, regardless of evidence?

Brandon Davies and Ashley McAllister did not enter his office at any point before his scheduled Sunday sermon. Pastor Ellison had been so despondent after Mason Kessler's death that he had asked to be left alone. They obviously thought that order stood indefinitely. Quite the contrary, Ellison would've been happy to see them, at least just to know he wasn't alone in the building.

He reluctantly headed toward the choir room. There was no music playing at all. He put his ear to the door, but still heard nothing. He'd never once, not even on a Monday morning, experienced his church so silent.

Finally, he heard the gentle strumming of an acoustic guitar. He felt comforted, and knew it must be Clifton Wagner. He remembered the moment, when facing a rapidly shrinking congregation, that Clifton's gift had so inspired him. He felt no such inspiration now.

This was the moment—preceding a sermon—which used to fill Ellison with the spirit of the Lord. But rather than feeling besotted with God's grace, today he felt tired. He was worried about what he'd find on the other side of that door.

Ellison wasn't worried for himself; he had already decided that he would step down as pastor. No matter what else the mountain's obstinacy actually pointed to, the one thing he did learn last Thursday was that he wasn't qualified to lead any church; he was clearly in no position to speak on God's behalf. *No, I'm not worried about myself; I am worried about the body of Christ around the world.* He was worried about the future of the faith.

He knew one thing for sure: the diminished crowd after his announcement, and certainly the one after his arrest, was specific to his church. What was terrifying him now was that he knew the size of his crowd today would be universal. It would be a representative sample, one small drop of blood which would indicate either a healthy or diseased body. What he would discover when he stepped into the sanctuary would likewise be discovered in the church down the street, in the churches in different states, and even different countries, Catholics and Protestants alike.

He breathed a deep breath and gave a meager prayer, then pushed through the threshold that separated him from the final verdict and news of the fate of his once-vibrant church.

Once again, upon entering the sanctuary, his eyes had to adjust. Only no spotlight hit his eyes this time. There weren't any lights on at all. His eyes had to adjust, not because it was so bright, but because it was so dark. Ellison had a group of youth volunteers who had the responsibility to run the spotlights, the stage lights, and the sound system. They had all failed to show up. Not only that, but apparently there was no single person there who even knew where the switch for the main lights were.

His church was shroud in darkness. And every seat was empty.

In the dim light which filtered in through a few stained glass windows, Clifton Wagner sat on a single stool and dutifully strummed his guitar.

The few people within earshot to hear it weren't seated in seats, but clustered in the walkways. Most of the parishioners who had come discovered there were no lights on and left, imagining there would be no sermon. Some of the families, however, bumped into people they knew on the way out, and had been lingering in the aisle talking when Ellison walked in. In his glorious building that held five thousand, a group consisting of no more than two dozen people remained, and them on their feet, not far from the doors.

Under his breath, for the first time since his conversion to Christianity, standing right in the center of his precious church, Pastor Ellison uttered a quiet and involuntary four-letter word. He immediately also mumbled, "May God forgive me..." but it hadn't been referring to the cuss word.

He didn't bother to turn on the lights. There was no activated sound system, but there was no need for Ellison's voice to reach to the back balcony since there was no one there to hear it. He stepped off the stage, where he felt he didn't belong anyway, and spoke to the people.

He said, "I let you all down." He stood tall and projected his voice even firmer. He continued, "I want you to know that this was never a stunt. I legitimately thought God had asked me to try to move that mountain. But I was wrong. I do still believe in God, because He has provided too much real assistance in my life and countless others that I have been blessed enough to witness. But I do not believe I am qualified to speak on His behalf and I no longer believe I am qualified to lead this congregation. May those of you who have supported me please forgive me. May God please forgive me. So, I'm afraid that there's nothing left but to—"

Pastor Ellison was interrupted when he heard a gunshot. His blood ran cold. He dipped his head and panned the room for any hint of where it came from. *No, wait, it wasn't a gunshot.* It was followed by three more loud pops, then silence. The people in the sanctuary looked around confused and frightened. Finally, as their adrenaline was beginning to wane, the windows trembled slightly and they heard a loud roar that seemed to be coming from outside.

Pastor Ellison ran straight for the door, and the remnant of his congregation followed behind. It was a bright, cloudless day. The light from the sky hurt their eyes and they all put their hands up to shade the sun. The first thing Ellison saw—clearly out of the ordinary—was a large cloud of dust, as if a meteor had hit or a bomb had exploded. Despite it being his own property, he experienced a bout of shaky disorientation. The horizon had always been fairly repetitive—the only real landmark he had grown accustomed to seeing was Mead Mountain. But he couldn't see it. At first, it appeared to have been concealed by all the dust, but a strong gust of wind came along to thin the dust, and remove the veil.

Mead Mountain was gone.

Chapter Eighteen

"Colton!" June Rucker exclaimed when he walked through the door. She was sitting up tall in her bed. Her face was florid and radiant, ready to take on the day. Her makeup was expertly applied—not too little, not too much, the perfect blend of beauty and class.

For the second day in a row, Colton was compelled to ask his mother, "What's going on?"

"What do you mean? I feel wonderful."

"That's what I mean. What happened to all your dire predictions?" Colton asked.

June smiled, undaunted. "Only God knows when my time will come. Even the doctors can't tell us anything; you're going to trust a silly old woman?"

Colton laughed and sat down by the bed.

"Besides, I told you not to come today."

"I had to come."

"I'm fine, Colton. You know your mother can be a drama queen sometimes."

"No, it's not that. It's just..." Colton grabbed her hand. "It's just that... the mountain moved."

"I know. Isn't it wonderful?"

"No, I mean it moved. It actually moved!"

"I know." Her tone matched his in incredulity and wonder. His attitude now gave her no reason to expect he had lied to her in the first place, because after all, the news had been recycling in her mind, hitting her again every hour or so, as if being heard for the first time.

"It was a mountain. A mountain! How much do those things weigh? A lot, anyway. I mean, he couldn't have faked that."

"Faked it? Colton!"

"Some people are saying it was an earthquake, but seismologists reported that there was no seismic movement at all, and the press has reported that nothing besides the mountain was damaged."

"Of course he didn't fake it, darling."

"He couldn't have. Even *if* it had been some kind of earthquake, who could ever predict when an earthquake will happen? There's just no way he could've faked it," Colton repeated, even as his mind still searched for a way the pastor could have faked it. He rubbed his eyes with the back of his hand like a child woken early from his nap. "It's cataclysmic!"

He noticed a box made of thin brown cardboard rested on the edge of her nightstand. He asked, "What's this?"

June smiled. She said, "I asked my sister to stop by my place and pick up my old photographs. Would you like to go through them with me?"

Colton eyed the box. Something about the idea suggested a warning. The dark side of his mind instinctively knew to stay away. He said, "No, I think I'd rather not."

"Oh nonsense," she said. "Grab the box and set it right here," she instructed as she sat up taller.

Colton dutifully complied.

The first couple of pictures were relatively benign: Colton unwrapping a toy truck on Christmas morning and Colton beside a lake carrying a fishing pole. Then slowly he began to realize what the dark part of him had wanted to avoid. He saw himself and his parents dressed up in their Sunday best. He hated wearing ties, but his father had forced him to wear one every Sunday growing up. He saw photographs of him on a swing set, in the kids' area beside their old church. He saw photos of him wearing a Cub Scouts uniform. His troop used to meet in the activities room at the church. He saw photographs of his father. He tried to flip by them quickly.

He found a new envelope containing photos his aunt took the day he was honored as an Eagle Scout. His mother saw what he was looking at and sighed fondly. She said, "We were always so proud of your accomplishments."

As he flipped, memories of the day came back to him. It filled him with a second's worth of pride, but it wasn't enough to keep the persistent darkness at bay. He said, "Yeah, Dad always wanted to see me become an Eagle Scout." Then he spat bitterly. "Too bad he couldn't have troubled himself to live long enough."

His mother let out a small stutter. It was the incomprehensible sound of a word being snuffed out before even reaching the first letter. It was the sound one makes when the urge to say something and the wisdom to stay silent are separated by a nanosecond.

Colton heard the sound and he imagined she wanted to protest his bitterness. But, as he looked at more photographs—Colton with his mother, with his aunt, with his scoutmaster, with his best friend at the time—the truth came back to him. He had confused his timeline for a moment. His father *was* still alive when he became an Eagle Scout. He was just functionally dead. He had been less good for Colton than if he had been actually dead.

Tears began to fill Colton's eyes, but he blinked them away.

Then he saw Hailey. She had both arms wrapped around him. Again his timeline had been blurry. *Had he really known her for that long?* She looked so young. She looked so pretty. He had forgotten how excited he used to feel looking at every feature of her face. He had forgotten how he used to lie beside her and trace the tip of his fingers around the edges of her lips, along the hard line of her jaw, and through the locks of her hair.

He brought the photograph up to his face, wishing to go back in time. She was pulling him in so close to her. She looked at the young man in the photo, not at the camera. He had never seen one person look at another with so much love. *Real love! And at the time, perhaps, warranted love.* He asked himself where that little boy had gone. He asked himself where the bright-eyed young man had gone. But he knew the answer. That child was drowning in poison.

In his head he asked, *Dear God, what have I become?*

And again he started to hum without intending to.

June picked up on the song right away and joyously sang along, "Rise and shine and give God your glory, glory."

"You know that song?"

"Rise and shine and..." She clapped. "... and give God your glory, glory." She belted out the words like a woman who would live for a very long time. She said, "Know it? Honey, I used to wake you up with that song every morning."

Colton's face changed. It was searching. That sounded right. He said, "Yeah, I think maybe I remember."

June smiled. She repeated her favorite quote from St. Augustine, which Colton had heard many times: "Vessels long maintain the taste of that which you first pour into them."

Tears began to fill Colton's eyes far faster than he could blink them away.

June added, "Try to remember that with Abigail, okay?" She looked to see his response and spotted him crying.

The tears rolled uncontrollably down each cheek. He was left with no other recourse than to throw his arms around his mother's neck and hug her tight. He exclaimed, "I love you, Mom. I love you so much."

"I love you, too, sweetheart."

Colton said much quieter, "I'm so sorry, Mom."

"Sorry for what, baby?"

Colton didn't answer.

Angelica Morgan was thrilled that she finally got a chance to sit in the front row. Angelica Morgan, a native to Los Angeles, attended the taping of Jake Dolan's show every week, but try as she might, she never seemed to get there early enough to get a great seat. A couple of times she hadn't gotten there early enough to even get in and she remained stuck outside with the hundreds of people who were turned away.

Today there were no such hundreds. It was only ten minutes until show time and there were still empty seats.

Angelica had heard on the radio that Mead Mountain had moved earlier that day and immediately went to YouTube to watch the video. Clifton Wagner had set up his camera in an out-of-the-way spot so he could get good footage when Ellison moved the mountain. When it refused to move, the optimistic boy, whose faith was undaunted, decided to leave his camera there just in case. The hard drive on the camera held eight hours, and for the first time in a long time there was no rain in the forecast, so he just left it there and came back every eight hours to erase the uneventful footage and start it over again.

Clifton Wagner sold the clip to every network. He posted it on YouTube with his original song about Pastor Ellison. The video had a link to a site where he was selling the song for ninety-nine cents. Fifteen million people had watched the video so far, but only 10 percent of those actually decided to buy the song.

Angelica Morgan had watched that clip at least a dozen times. She was certain that it was a hoax, but she couldn't tell how. She just wasn't sure what she thought about it and was waiting for Jake Dolan to tell her.

As time ticked on, members of the audience began to speak with each other. They had heard that the mountain moved and had noticed the empty seats; they asked each other if the two might somehow be related.

There was an eerie feeling among them. The news of the mountain moving was so unsettling. They salivated for Jake Dolan to make them laugh again, to tell them who to mock, and to just make things feel *right* again.

But he didn't come out. Slowly people began to check their watches. The low rumble of the crowd grew louder and Angelica Morgan was becoming filled with anxiety. She checked her watch. It was already ten minutes past the time he was supposed to start. In desperation, she pulled out her phone. She started her television app, and within moments saw Jake Dolan standing on stage, delivering his monolog as if nothing were out of the ordinary. She held the phone up, befuddled, looked at the empty stage in front of her, then at the copacetic comedian rhapsodizing on that very same stage. It took her a second to figure out they were airing a rerun. *But why would that be?*

Her anxiety morphed into full-fledged dread. She stood up impulsively and shouted, "Jake Dolan! Jake Dolan? Come out, Jake... Jake Dolan, we need you!"

There was no answer. The stage seemed cold and unwelcoming. The curtain from which Jake Dolan usually emerged stood now like an impenetrable threshold, concealing the fate of tonight's show, and the fate of Jake Dolan.

Finally, a man slipped through the curtain's crack. It was not Jake Dolan. It was Felix, the black-clad hipster with clipboard and headset. He walked to the front of the stage and shouted, "We regret to inform you there will be no show tonight. We apologize for the inconvenience. Please drive home safely."

No one in the audience heard the apology, nor the last line, which was really a polite way to say *leave*, because they had begun booing so loudly after the first line: "There will be no show tonight."

The hipster scuttled off stage as fast as he could. The crowd continued to shout curses at the empty stage. After another five minutes, the lights in the studio began to turn off one by one.

Colton hadn't been home all day. He said he was going to visit his mom, so Hailey had stayed home with the baby. That was several hours ago.

Hailey paced the floor just imagining where he could be. She had already put Abigail down and had nothing left to do but worry. She worried that he might have been killed in a car accident, but then wondered if that was just an old reflex. She wondered if his safe return was really the absolute blessing that she used to pray for.

Her spirits were lifted by the news that the mountain had moved. It gave her the type of hope she had not felt in a long time—hope that she could possibly cut the Gordian knot of her husband's alcoholism. It was one small change in the repetitive cycle of trying the same things and watching them fail in the same way. It was something new. More than that, it was an act of God.

She heard the garage door.

She drew a long breath in and held it. She heard the car pull into the spot. His radio was on, but turned off when he killed the engine. She heard his left foot touch the ground, then his right. She heard him close the car door. It was a little bit hard, but the sound was still inconclusive. She heard him fumble with his keys.

Then she heard the keys hit the garage floor.

Her heart sank. *Today?* She asked. *On a day like today? He couldn't stay sober for the day of God's miracle?* She could feel the hope torn from her body and in its place was an empty, cold void and the realization that nothing would ever change. She began to sob wildly out loud. She feared waking up Abigail, but she couldn't help it. Her voice wailed out from the knowledge that not even a miracle could save her family. God had come through for Pastor Ellison, but God had neglected her. All her prayers had been in vain.

She heard a knock. That was different. She barely heard it over her sobs. She walked over to turn the knob, her eyes full of tears and her nose stuffed up.

Colton pushed the door out of the way with his foot. His hands were full of bags. He was carrying flowers. He said, "Sorry babe, my hands were so full I dropped my keys. Hey, why are you crying?"

"Are these flowers for me?" she asked as she watched him struggle to place things on the kitchen counter.

"Of course they're for you. Why are you crying?"

"What for?"

"I don't know. Just because I thought you'd like them. Don't you like them?"

She quickly began to rummage through his bags.

Baby clothes.

"Yeah, I just thought those were cute."

Baby books.

"I thought I could start reading to her"

Baby books about Jesus.

"Um, yeah, those were on sale."

And a stuffed animal.

"That one took me all day to find. Watch. You push his belly and he lights up and plays..."

He played Hailey the song and she recognized it.

"My mom used to sing it to me as a baby." His voice shook, despite his best efforts to sound casual.

She threw her arms up around his neck. "Oh Colton!" she yelled and snapped right back into a fit of crying. Only, these were a different type of tears. These were unexpected, inexplicable, inexorable tears of joy. Fearless tears of joy.

He said, "I'm so sorry. Things will be different. I am so sorry."

She held him so tight he had to struggle free. He had to pry her body off of his just to look her in the eyes. He said, "Did you hear the mountain moved?"

She nodded, looking level with his chest, tears covering every inch of her face.

He grabbed her chin to make sure she was looking at his face. He said, "I'm going to quit drinking, okay. No more drinking, I promise."

She turned her eyes away, a reaction to the first hint of fear, the needling voice in her head telling her not to play the fool. She asked, "Can you really do that?"

He said, "All things are possible with God."

Jake Dolan was wearing an ultramarine blue silk robe. It was emblazed with the letters JD. He turned on some music, as his call girl fidgeted with her thumb. Cheryl Fox had been acting funny since she arrived.

He could tell right away that she was going to need to be loosened up. He sat down beside her, so close he was practically on top of her. When he leaned in to kiss her, she actually turned away.

"Kinda' defeats the purpose of an escort," he snapped as he turned her face back toward his.

Again she turned away. "What if there is a hell?" she asked.

"What are you talking about?"

"The mountain moved," she said plainly.

"So what?"

"So that means there is a God; you said so." In time with her challenge, she turned her face back toward him.

He, however, turned his face away. She didn't realize the extent of her betrayal. He had called her up in the first place so he wouldn't have to think about this very topic.

Since he heard the mountain had moved, he could not keep his mind from running over everything. He could not keep his mind from remembering the promise he'd made to Pastor Ellison. The truth was, he was invested in atheism. He was good at it. He made a living at it. It felt good to him. The way that he besmirched any part of the Bible that made no sense—it was easy. Drawing applause just by dropping the words knuckle-dragger, troglodyte, or hater—it was easy. He had a formula and it allowed him not to have to think too hard. He needed those clear lines in his life: sophisticates on one side, simpletons on the other; intellectuals on one side, imbeciles on the other; freethinkers on one side, mindless automatons on the other.

Jake Dolan had a shelf of trophies, not for television or broadcasting, but for arguments he believed he had won. The nostrums he would repeat by rote, and the names of atheist philosophers, scientists, and mathematicians that he liked to drop—they were like glimmering, solid-gold trophies in his mind.

The simple truth was—and he knew this very well—he did not have the strength of character to openly say, "I was wrong, while so many were right. I claimed to be above them all, but I'm not above them." He didn't have the strength of character to say, "My solid-gold trophies have been tin the whole time."

He had a formula and it worked. He spoke of fact, reason, and evidence. It made his chest swell up so full. It felt better than any drug he'd ever discovered. It made him high. But he was now being evicted from his comfortable life. His mind tread and retread any option that could make sense, any option that would allow him to keep his trophies. He would have to ignore the mountain and carry on as if Pastor Ellison never existed.

But no matter what, the *high* was gone. He could never hypnotize his mind to forget Mead Mountain. He couldn't knowingly deceive himself, and at the same time look down on the self-deception of others.

"We're not going to hell," he told her. "Why would we?"

"I'm a prostitute," she said flatly, as if the full meaning of her thoughts were conveyed with just that one word.

Dolan smiled and spread out his hands, presenting, "Who are we hurting? Even if there is a God, why would he care? Who are we hurting?"

She didn't answer.

He stood up from the couch and said, "You know what? I think you need a drink."

She still didn't answer. She remained deep in thought the whole time he was gone. He set her drink down on the end table beside her, quickly swallowing his own.

She didn't take the drink or even look at it. She said, "I used to dream that I'd get married and live in a house..." It sounded as if she trailed off.

"And?"

She looked up meekly. "That's it," she said. "I used to dream that I'd get married and live in a house."

It was clear from Dolan's expression that he wasn't getting it.

She pushed. "The man would be my soul mate. We'd stay together forever; even after death we'd be together."

"Why are you telling me this?"

"That's who we're hurting!" she snapped. "We are hurting my soul mate. I gave up on finding him, but..." She looked down, deflated. "But... maybe he didn't give up on finding me. Maybe he's out there looking for me, and by throwing my life away like this... I'm hurting him. We're hurting him... and we're hurting God."

"We're hurting God?"

"We're interfering with His plan."

"What do you know about God's plan? Really? All that stuff you were just saying about soul mates, and you playing the princess, and you meeting the prince—did you read that in the Bible? No. No, you didn't get that idea from God, you got it from Walt Disney."

Cheryl Fox shrugged. "It's just something I've always believed." He didn't seem impressed by her statement, so she wanted to strengthen it. She said, "It's what I *want* to believe." This time she could tell that he was impressed—more than impressed, her words, to her own surprise, seemed to strike some kind of nerve. She leaned in like she smelled blood in the water and asked pointedly, "What do you *want* to believe?"

He quickly returned to the voice he liked to use to talk down to her, and delivered one of his well-worn favorite lines: "We don't believe things because we want to believe them, we believe things because the evidence requires it."

"Evidence?" she quipped. "He moved a mountain!"

Dolan had no response. He challenged, "So what? Are you going to stop hooking?"

She shot him a nasty look, just over his choice of verb. "Yeah. I think so."

"Why?"

"Because it upsets God's plan."

"... God's plan." He said the last part in near unison with her. "Well, where will you go? What will you do?"

"I don't know. I could get married." She got really quiet. He could tell that she was thinking about it. She looked around at his place, at his giant flat screen, his polished chrome bar, his mind-blowing view. She said, "You love me."

"We're not getting married," he said dryly.

"You've always told me you loved me," she protested.

"You're a prostitute," he said flatly, as if the full meaning of his thoughts were conveyed with just that one word.

She got from the couch, grabbed her purse, and walked out the door.

That night at the police station, Officer Gonzales felt a timid tap on his shoulder. He was surprised when he turned around to see Officer Felicia Jones. She had tapped his shoulder, but didn't appear to have anything she was anxious to say.

He asked, "How's your night going so far?"

"Oh fine," she said. "So... uh... I heard the mountain moved."

"Yes, ma'am, it did."

"That's pretty amazing, huh?"

"Yes, ma'am, it is."

"Hey, um, I was thinking tomorrow I might go see my folks."

"Your parents?"

"Yeah, I haven't seen them in like twenty years."

"They live out of state?"

"No, they live here in town."

"Oh, I see."

"Yeah, I just think it's time. And... uh, I was wondering if maybe you'd want to meet me and drive me over there?" When Officer Gonzales didn't answer, she continued, "I just know I'll probably chicken out on my own."

Officer Gonzales smiled. "It would be my pleasure."

Tyler knocked on his mother's door. The entire apartment was beginning to smell, but he couldn't tell if it was from the trash piling up, or the dishes left in the sink. Poison had been out of work for thirteen days and Tyler wasn't sure if she had left her bedroom, or even her bed, since the day the mountain refused to move.

Poison didn't answer.

"Mom?" he called out. His voice was crisp and strong.

Again there was no answer, so he turned the knob and pushed the door forward. He saw his mother lying in bed. It was the same pose he'd seen her in many times, usually passed out from drinking. Only this time, he knew there was no alcohol in the house. And this time, she had her eyes open.

He looked at those eyes. They did not appear to look back.

"Mom, didn't you hear me?"

She didn't answer. She didn't move.

"Mom, are you dead?" he asked casually.

She still didn't answer.

He stood there studying her. Finally, he said, "The mountain moved."

Her eyes blinked. She groggily raised her head from the pillow and lumbered up into a sitting position. "What?" she asked.

"The mountain moved. It's gone. It fell into the ocean. It's just *gone*. Everyone on the news is talking about it."

"It moved?" she asked weakly. She had lines from the folds in her pillowcase visible on her face and her hair was sticking up at odd angles. "How did it move?"

Tyler looked down. He shrugged bashfully. "Well, God did it."

Poison blinked repeatedly. Her eyes looked high and to the left, at images in her own mind. She didn't respond, so Tyler pressed, "God moved the mountain, just as Pastor Ellison said He would."

The doorbell rang.

"Do you want me to get it?" Tyler asked.

"I got it," Poison said as she called on her languid body to move.

She knew that no one would ring her doorbell like that, unexpectedly in the middle of the day, except maybe Pastor Ellison. But if what Tyler had said was true, it must've been a big day for him. She imagined he would be too busy for the likes of her.

All she could figure was that it was a package, and that by the time she got to the door, the driver would be long gone and whatever it was she'd forgotten she ordered online would be waiting on her doorstep. For this reason, she didn't even bother to try to fix her hair before she opened the door.

It was Ecstasy and Desire.

Poison instantly shot her hand up to her hair, giving it a few quick tosses. Poison was shocked to see them. Her old life at the club seemed so long ago. She didn't even think that these girls knew where she lived.

Ecstasy and Desire had gotten a hold of the same personnel file Isaac had.

They both stood dumbly, each one hoping the other—or even Poison—would speak first. Finally, Ecstasy did. She held out a black garter with a silver skull pendant and said, "Here, you left this at the club."

Poison looked down at the garter with contempt. "Thanks," she struggled to say. "You both came here to give me this?"

Ecstasy and Desire looked at each other. Ecstasy said, "No, ma'am." The *ma'am* caught Poison's attention. "We were wondering if you could..." She had gotten her prepared speech out of order. "Um, we know that you don't like us. But, we were hoping you could..."

Ecstasy had gotten it all messed up, so Desire jumped in. She asked, "You know that pastor, right? The one on the news?"

Poison eyed her two former rivals, former tormenters. She stepped to one side and said, "Please, girls, come on in."

When they stepped inside, they discovered that Tyler had already tied up all the trash and was busily loading the dishwasher.

Poison invited them to sit at the kitchen table. It was the same spot where she had previously confessed her Christianity to Andrew Crenshaw.

They all sat down, and again, no one wanted to talk first. They could hear the continued clinking of dishes and silverware.

Finally, Ecstasy said, "We don't understand what happened. We don't know how the mountain moved." She looked over to Desire for help, but continued on anyway, "Some people are saying that it was a hoax, but can't explain how. What do you think? Did God move the mountain? Do you believe there is a—" Ecstasy stopped when it became apparent that the clinking had suddenly stopped.

They all looked over to Tyler. He was frozen, mid-motion, with a dinner plate still in his gloved hands. His eyes were aimed straight at his mother.

Ecstasy turned back to Poison and finished her question, "Do you believe there is a God?"

Poison saw her son's eyes on her and she noticed something that she didn't ordinarily see: her eyes in his. She remembered the day she had asked his father if she was pretty. This must have been what her eyes had looked like then, suspended in space for one moment in time, breathlessly waiting for the next words to be said.

Poison looked down at the garter she had been absentmindedly fiddling with. It was a symbol that had once promised liberty, but had only ever delivered servitude.

She tossed it into her trashcan, then looked at the young lady and answered her honestly, "I do."

Chapter Nineteen

Riley Ellison was in love.

He drove to his church on Sunday, with the glorious Deborah Ellison by his side. It had been one week since the mountain moved and their joy hadn't even begun to diminish. The sky was clear for the first time in months, and Riley felt the heat radiating from the sun-lit dash. He turned the knob on his AC over from red back to blue.

"Do you want to know the absolute best part?" he said exultantly to his wife. "You never stopped believing in me. Brandon Davies stopped believing in me, I even stopped believing in me. But you always believed in me, and in God. I don't think there was a single second in which you doubted the mountain would move."

The two rode in silence.

He watched her slyly from the corner of his eye.

Deborah cleared her throat. She said casually, "A lot of people out today."

Ellison laughed. He tapped his brake. An unexpected line of cars still separated them and the stop sign. He confirmed bewilderedly, "There *are* a lot of people out today."

As he drove on, he soon found himself stuck in serious traffic, which was unusual for a Sunday. When he noticed that the road of oncoming traffic was empty, he realized that it wasn't any regular traffic jam. It was concert traffic, game day traffic, race weekend traffic, only all those hoards of people weren't headed to a theater, stadium, or track. They were headed to Mead Mountain Church.

As they drew closer the pace of the traffic grew even slower and they started to see people, who had obviously parked blocks away, walking toward the church along the side of the road. When they turned the last corner and were finally able to see the church, they saw a line of people leading to the building that wrapped all the way around the block. They saw crowds of people not even trying to get in, contenting themselves to congregate in the yard. They saw a number of church volunteers who took it upon themselves to help direct the overflow of traffic.

What they did not see was Mead Mountain.

Deborah finally answered him: "Yeah, I never did doubt it would move." Her heart swelled in her chest, as wave after wave of the significance of it all—the missing mountain, the crowds of people—grew steadily bigger in her mind. When the joy grew too much to contain, she began to stomp her feet wildly on the floor boards. Pastor Ellison thought that she was going to explode out of the car. Then finally she did. As soon as they were close enough to make out individual faces in the crowd, she saw her dear friend, Ashley McAllister, and just couldn't take it anymore. Without a word, she threw open the car door and ran full force toward the church and toward the people.

Poor Riley had no choice but to pull his car over—double parked—the best he could, escape out the car, and run after his wife.

Ashley McAllister noticed the Ellisons both running toward her. She began to run too. Next Brandon Davies noticed, then the whole crowd noticed.

Deborah and Ashley met in a jubilant embrace. Then Ashley let go and quickly hugged the pastor. The crowd was gathering tighter around.

Deborah Ellison wrapped her arms around Brandon Davies. And Riley hugged Brandon's wife. Finally, Brandon and Riley turned to face each other, man to man. Brandon put out his hand to shake. He simply said, "You did it."

Ellison shook his hand and told him, "We did it together. It has been you, me, and God from the beginning." Ellison pulled him into a rhapsodic hug.

Brandon began to weep in his arms. He tried to mumble, "You have been such a blessing to my family."

Ellison firmly replied, "You have been such a blessing to this church."

Past members of Ellison's congregation gathered around to greet their pastor once again. None of them were even aware of what had happened to the size of their church in their absence. All of them just thought they had skipped church for a week or two; none of them realized almost everyone else had skipped also.

His heart rejoiced because he knew this was just one church. He knew that the size of this crowd was the size of every crowd in every church, not just down the street, but around the world. He was witnessing a renewed faith in God. He was part of the next Great Awakening.

Andrew Crenshaw was there, as always, but this time Pastor Ellison knew he wasn't there on business. Ellison extended his hand, but Andrew refused it, drawing the pastor in for a hug. He whispered into Ellison's ear,

"I'm going to need a lot of help."

"Count me in," smiled Ellison. Ellison held him close until he felt a long, healing, hopeful breath fill the young man's lungs.

When he finally let go of Crenshaw, Ellison spotted Hailey and Abigail heading his way. It took him a moment to realize the man walking beside them was Colton. He had his hair slicked to both sides of his head, parted right down the middle. He wore a yellow shirt. The sleeves were short, but it had a collar. It looked like it might even have been ironed. It all reminded Ellison of the way some country-boys look when they appear in court.

Pastor Ellison greeted Hailey who was beaming with joy, then extended his hand to Colton and said, "Welcome, sir, it's an honor to have you here today."

Colton affectionately received his hand. "I came to hear more about Psalm 161."

Ellison laughed. "Well, I hadn't planned on covering *that* one today, but for you I can make an exception."

Ellison grabbed Abigail up in his arms like he had done since she was born.

Abigail was smiling and reaching for the pastor's nose when they were approached by one of the new guests.

She said, "Forgive me, but I just wanted to shake your hand, too. You probably don't remember me. We've actually met before."

Colton gathered Abigail from Ellison's arms and gave a departing nod and smile before leading his elated wife through the crowd. Ellison waved to the departing family, then turned back to the new guest. He shook her hand while trying to place where they had met. "I'm sorry, did we meet here at the church?"

"No," she said, "At the corner of Twelfth and Main." It was Cheryl Fox.

"Oh," he said with a wry smile. "Well, then I am *very* glad to have you here. Please, let me introduce you to my wife, Deborah."

Deborah extended her hand, and Cheryl Fox received it with a timid bow. She said, humbly, "You are a very lucky woman."

"Yes, ma'am," beamed Deborah. "I'm very blessed."

Riley saw another figure approaching out of the corner of his eye. It was clear, even from his fuzzy peripheral, that she was dressed respectfully in a long skirt and a high collar. She had been politely waiting until he was done talking to Ms. Fox, and now threw both arms around Ellison's neck.

When he realized it was Poison, Ellison immediately wrenched his head around to search for Tyler. The young man stood just beside his mother wearing dress slacks, a jacket, and tie. His hair had been almost completely chopped off. No more veil. No more hiding.

"Looking sharp!" Pastor Ellison whistled. "I like the tie."

Tyler's arms shot out for his turn to embrace the pastor. He grumbled, "Mom, made me wear it."

"Way to go, Poison," Ellison said

"You can call me Bella," Poison said.

Ellison grinned slyly. "I thought your name was Poison."

"It is," she told him. "My full first name is Belladonna. My mom must've just thought it was funny to name me after a poison." She shook her head and said quietly, "Doesn't matter now."

"Oh... well, I think Bella is a lovely na—"

Before he could finish, his wife butted into the conversation. "Wait, don't you know what *bella donna* means?" Deborah asked Bella.

Bella nodded and confessed, "It's a nightshade, a poisonous flo—"

"No, what it means," Deborah interrupted again. She smiled, taking a second to admire Bella's intrepid face. "Bella donna means *beautiful woman.*"

Bella blushed slightly. She might have known that if she'd ever told anyone her full name.

Deborah pressed, "Looks like your mom probably wasn't trying to be funny after all."

A bitter-sweet release filled Bella's face. "I've been hiding for so long," she whispered as she blinked away a few nascent tears.

"Speaking of beautiful women," Ellison said to Bella proudly, "This is my wife, Deborah."

Her eyes lit up. She looked straight at Deborah and instantly blurted out, "I'm sorry about your Visa bill."

"Oh!" Pastor Ellison jumped in to deflect the topic. "Who have you brought?" He motioned to the two girls waiting patiently.

"These are my..." The hesitation was microscopic. "... friends, Terry and Elaine."

"Thank you so much for coming," said Ellison as he shook their hands. There was no mystery from where Bella knew these two girls. He said, "It is an honor to meet you both."

More and more people began to surround the pastor, all of them anxious to introduce themselves, embrace him, and tell him how much what he did meant to them.

"I hope you don't remember me," one lady said. That one took him a second. It was Officer Felicia Jones. He did not recognize her without her uniform.

Ellison smiled. "No, I am the one," he looked over both shoulders playfully, "who hopes you do not remember."

Officer Felicia Jones smiled. "Your secret's safe with me."

"God bless you," said Ellison.

He looked out across the crowd that had formed a wide radius around him and his wife. It had just become clear that there would be no sermon today. Every congregant, old and new, opted instead to gather in for the chance to greet Riley Ellison and his wife personally. They would be hugging and crying and blessing each other for the rest of the afternoon.

Ellison could not believe what God had done. He looked over at the mountain. *Yep, still gone.*

"What are you growing?" He heard a woman's voice. Ellison turned around to see Nancy Fuller.

Ellison blinked. "I'm not sure what you mean."

"You've got a little sprout growing over there. Did you plant something?"

"Where?" asked Ellison. He felt a strange tingle.

"Right over here, come on."

She led Ellison through the parting crowd, to the spot where he had stepped off the stage on that nerve-wracking and historic day. Pastor Ellison knew what it was before seeing it, but even with the benefit of sight, he could not completely believe it. In the spot where the seed had been dropped, not planted, he saw a small burgeoning mustard plant. It was far bigger than what could imaginably have grown so fast, especially in the frozen ground.

Nancy Fuller stared at the plant and also seemed to be pondering its sudden winter arrival.

"Is it a miracle from God?" she asked.

"The entire universe is a miracle from God... and every new day." Pastor Ellison grabbed her hand to squeeze it affectionately. He could feel the course twine of her string against his palm. He added, "This, however, is just a reminder."

Chapter Twenty

Jake Dolan checked his watch. He was on in ten minutes.

He knew that no one would be bothering him this close to the start of the show—he once called it his "moment of Zen"—*Did I, really?* He was always so full of it. He remembered the way he used to tear the head off any of his crew that would interrupt him during this time. *I was always so mean.*

There'd be no *Zen* forthcoming. His mind was too chaotic.

There was only one option left open to him. An about-face. Join Pastor Ellison and help him to turn the parade around. Throw down his old sign and pick up a new one. He could march to alleviate suffering, even if it meant losing his career, his fans, his wealth, and his identity. A new courage began to stir in his heart. He could discover what it was that always made Christians so irritatingly happy.

Even as he pictured it, he could hear the old *high* calling him back. He doubted he could learn to look up instead of always looking down, accept instead of ridicule, embrace instead of alienate, submit instead of attack. *I can't do it. It's not me.* He could feel the *high* trying to rekindle in his chest, but the news of the mountain kept throwing cold water on it before it could blaze. His mind was now wet to such a kindling and such a blaze. And it always would be.

Curse Pastor Ellison. That man has no idea what he's done to me. He has no idea that he's destroyed a life.

His mind was running over what he was about to do. This would be his last show. He had given his word. He knew his show was doomed now anyway. *Better to do it swiftly. Better to do it by my own hand.*

He had shut out all his writers from working on this week's episode. For the first time in his entire career, he was going to step on stage with nothing on his teleprompter. *No problem... I will just step on stage and...*

His thigh vibrated. He had silenced his cell for the show obviously, but that had always been superfluous because anyone who had his personal number was also very well aware what hours on Sunday evening he would obviously be busy.

When he pulled the phone out to investigate, he saw a text from Pastor Ellison, *the inimitable Riley Ellison*, who obviously *did* know when

Dolan's show would start. The timing could not have been coincidental.

It read:

> My dear Mr. Dolan, I have always admired your intelligence, wit, and charisma. You are one of the most powerful and influential men I have ever met. I know that these qualities will make you one of the world's greatest promoters of God. YOU have the power to turn the parade around. YOU have the power to alleviate real suffering, and to change lives for the better. One of them just might be your own.

He first read the text in his own voice—sarcastic and rude. But then he read it in Ellison's voice, the tone in which it was intended—genuine and sweet. A paroxysm of emotions erupted in him.

An about-face, he told himself. *Throw down your sign and pick up a new one.* He wanted to help the people Ellison wanted to help. For the first time in his life, he saw how much he wanted to.

Dolan considered how his audience would react and a heavy sick feeling overcame him. He hated his audience in that moment, maybe he always had. They were mean. They were the most pathetic group of trained seals—mindless and mean—that had ever been organized under one roof. *Where do we find these people?* he asked, but his new-found courage wouldn't let him get away with pretending not to know. *Simple. We made them... no, I made them. It was me all along.* He hated everything he had ever done in television. He hated everything he had ever done in his life. *Three divorces! Three divorces and yet I publicly mock any Christian or conservative who has an affair.* He tried to count his own affairs... He couldn't.

He saw for the first time all the real suffering that he had caused both publically and privately. He wondered what individual members of his audience might have achieved in life if he—*or someone*—would have encouraged them to do something besides get stoned and laugh at Christians.

He thought maybe he could encourage them now, but it was too late. He knew just what would happen. He would go out there and with all the sincerity that he could muster he would tell them that he wouldn't be doing comedy tonight. He could picture it. He would tell them that he wanted to discuss a very important matter, perhaps the *only* important matter. He would tell them that he believes Jesus is the Savior and that he had welcomed Christ into his heart. Then some idiot on his crew would turn on the applause sign.

Then, we would have a clash on our hands. Then we would see which part of their conditioning would win out. Would they go along with their programming to boo anything remotely religious, or would they be snared by the stimulus response, demanding that they clap at a blinking sign?

He knew Ellison would say not to hate them, but in fact, to love them, and he wondered if he was up to the task. There was so much hatred in his heart. *Maybe I should just go out there, look at the real people, warts and all, and tell them that I love them. That's how I'll start. I'll just say. I love you... all of you.*

Then it hit him—the Zen. At last, order where there had just been chaos. No, it wasn't quite Zen. It was peace. *Peace.* It felt so new. It felt like the answer: love. He understood it would be hard for him, but he felt like he could do it. He had a new tool. Love could change the lives of the suffering people in his audience. They weren't cruel; they were hurting. How did he miss that before? Love could save them. If God could move a mountain, and if God could soften his sclerotic heart, then God could reach them as well.

The kindling in his heart was set ablaze but it wasn't a high; it was contentment. It was belonging. It was peace. He wasn't going to end his show tonight; he was on in twelve million homes! He was going to use the show—his gigantic microphone, his bright national spotlight—he was going to use it to glorify God.

From the corner of his eye, he saw a dark figure approaching. Someone had the courage to disturb him before the show after all. Felix ran up to him and put both his hands on his shoulders. "You can't do it!"

"Do what?"

"The mountain thing—it's a hoax!"

"It can't be." Dolan knocked both Felix's hands off his shoulders.

"It is!" There was a strange excitement that surrounded Felix in that moment. Jake Dolan understood it and it terrified him.

"There was a mountain," Dolan explained condescendingly, as if to a child. "And now it's gone."

"No, that part's real," the assistant explained. "But God didn't do it. God didn't do it!"

Felix's excitement was obviously not rubbing off onto Jake Dolan. In fact, Jake Dolan just checked his watch.

This only made Felix talk faster. "There were cracks in the mountain already," he explained quickly. They both could hear the band starting. "It's just been reported by Benjamin Mead on his blog."

"Benjamin Mead?"

"Yes! The cracks were already there. Senator Mead did the research. Pastor Ellison must have done the same research; by his own admission, he's an amateur geologist. By his own admission!"

"So there were cracks! So what? That doesn't mean that Ellison, or anyone would know when the cracks would break. Does it?"

"No, but he knew what week it would freeze. Last week, historically is the coldest week of the year. That's why he picked it. It doesn't usually freeze around here, but he knew last week it probably would!"

They could hear the band looping the intro music.

"What does a freeze have to do with it?"

"Mead's theory is that because of the record rainfall we've been having, the cracks filled completely up with water, like they never had before. Then extreme cold caused the water inside the cracks to freeze. When water freezes, it expands. The force from the expanding ice cracked the top half of the rock from the bottom half. Leading geologists have investigated the remains of Mead Mountain, and they've confirmed the theory!" Felix's joy was uncontainable. He added, "*Leading geologists. Nobel Prize winners!*"

They could hear stray shouts from people who must have been in attendance last week and now feared another no-show. They were whistling and calling his name.

"Well, God works in mysterious ways," Dolan told Felix sincerely. He hardly understood what he was saying, or what was provoking him to say it. "God sent the rainwater and sent the cold front."

"No, don't you get it? The cold front is a result of climate change. It's never this cold in southern California. It wasn't the work of God; it was the work of *science*. It wasn't God who moved the mountain; it was global warming!"

Finally, a new light fell on Dolan's face. A stagehand had opened the curtain, hoping to nudge Jake Dolan enough for him to actually walk out onto the stage of his own show. The audience looked straight in on him and he had no choice but to stumble feebly out onto the stage.

The spotlights illuminated the confusion on his face.

Jake Dolan was an empty man. He had just had everything from his life ripped from his hands, then just as abruptly and somehow just as painfully, all brought back. Only, he couldn't remember why he had once held onto it so tight.

He stared at his audience. The audience, the cameras, and his crew, all stared at him. He didn't know what to say. He looked at the teleprompter, but it was as empty as he was.

Finally, he held out both hands palms up toward the audience and said, "I love you." Nothing else came to him so he just futilely repeated, "I love you."

There was a voice in his head that said, *Let's face it, you don't know enough about being Christian to ad lib.* He said, "I *love* this audience, because this audience is so well informed. Let's hear it for Pastor Ellison!"

There was no applause.

"Let's hear it for Pastor Ellison," he tried again.

Still no applause.

"Let's hear it for Pastor Ellison, because he almost pulled off the most elaborate hoax of the new millennium!"

The crowd went wild with applause.

"Let's hear it for Benjamin Mead!"

Even more frenzied applause.

Jake Dolan returned to what he knew, a language he could speak, a formula that worked for him. He needed no teleprompter. He said, "You gotta love science. You gotta love science! You know, once upon a time, knowledge of science was a very elite and well-guarded secret. The power of astronomy actually granted people the ability to predict solar eclipses. During this time, learned men used to go to the illiterate, backwards villagers and tell them, 'Unless you all became my slaves, I will ask God to blot out the sun.' The villagers would refuse to listen. That was, of course, until the moment they saw the sun disappear, then they'd immediately begin to tremble in fear.

"Today, we've seen that Pastor Ellison is also a learned man. He is brilliant. We've got to hand it to him—he's brilliant! And almost had me fooled! The only problem is: today nothing is a well guarded secret. Today we have the Internet. Today we can't be fooled." The crowd cheered as if it were a campaign rally. Jake Dolan added, "Well maybe a few toothless, tobacco-drooling, knuckle-dragging troglodytes in the South will be fooled... but they were already Christians to begin with!"

The applause sign blinked and the crowd erupted. The cheering sycophants reminded Jake Dolan why he had once clung to this life, and he felt high once again.

Chapter Twenty-One—The Last Chapter

February 2
Sunday

That next Sunday Pastor Ellison truly did know what to expect. The public mood since the Benjamin Mead article had been raucous. Sides were being chosen and lines were being drawn. Both sides had just recently been led to believe they had delivered the knockout punch. Both sides had to watch their opponents stubbornly rise from the mat against all odds. The zealots from both sides were given fodder for their zeal, while the complacent continued to cling to their complacency—beyond all rationale.

Ellison had spent the week foolishly trying to reverse-engineer God. He wondered what it had all been about.

As he rounded the door to the choir room, he knew what he'd see when he reached the sanctuary. The only thing he didn't expect was to see Brandon Davies waiting for him. He stood in the choir room, right outside the entrance to the sanctuary.

"Brandon," said Riley.

"Riley," said Brandon.

"Whatcha' doing?"

Brandon smiled nervously. He said, "I'm afraid to look out there."

The pastor nodded, "It was a crazy month."

"Yeah, you could say so." He nodded to the sanctuary behind him, smiled and asked, "So, are we going to see six more weeks of Christianity?"

Ellison smiled. "I think we're going to see a lot more than that." He put his hand on the good man's shoulder and said, "Tell you what, let's step out and look together."

Ellison pressed open the door for them.

The amazing thing that they saw was Ellison's old congregation. The amazing thing was that nothing was amazing. After everything that had happened, the size of the congregation had not changed in the end. Nearly five-thousand in attendance, not perceptibly larger nor smaller.

Pastor Ellison knew it was a representative sample, a turnout that was reflected in churches around the world. It was one single drop of blood, indicating that the body was—as always—healthy, but threatened; diseased, but fighting the good fight. He looked at his congregation and saw the world: Every man, woman, and child who had been Christian the morning of January 16, the day he asked the mountain to move, was Christian today. Every man, woman, and child who was not Christian that morning, still wasn't.

Pastor Ellison had heard Benjamin Mead's theory of rainwater filling the natural fissures, freezing, then tearing the mountain apart. He liked it a lot better than some of the websites that said he used dynamite, C-4, or cosmic micro-rays from the sun. He liked it better than the conspiracy theories that accused him of being a member of the Masons, Knights Templar, or the Bilderbergers. He possibly even liked it better than the theories that posited Mead Mountain never even existed in the first place.

Pastor Ellison had put on his geologist hat and considered Mead's theory. He looked at all the evidence, then honestly concluded that what Senator Mead had described was actually what happened. He even confessed this conclusion to the press, but then challenged them. "The only thing about Senator Mead's theory I don't understand is how that makes it less of a miracle. Now people have a decision to make, because faith must always be just that: a decision." He looked into the news camera and said, "You have all the evidence you need to know that God had nothing at all to do with the mountain moving, or for that matter, your own life or the existence of the universe. But you have something else too. You have ambiguity. You have just enough wiggle room in the evidence to *believe*. So, the choice is yours. All of it has either been a random series of happy accidents, or part of a heavenly plan and glorious mystery. It's your choice. But as for me and my house, we will serve the Lord."

Then there was the part about God *asking* Ellison to move the mountain. This unfortunately didn't present much of an obstacle for his detractors; they just claimed the pastor was lying.

In the end, everyone who already called themselves atheist concluded that he was a mendacious geologist, whose knowledge of science gave him a glimpse of the things to come, and who used that knowledge to orchestrate an elaborate hoax. Everyone who already called themselves Christian believed that he was a true prophet and servant of God, who courageously followed His will, and facilitated His miracle.

Everyone who had placed their faith in Christ believed it was the result of God's promise in Scripture being fulfilled. Everyone who had placed their faith in science believed that it was the result of CO_2 emissions and melting polar ice caps.

But why did God tell me to tell it to move in the first place? And what benefit did it actually provide to America?

Sure, his heart rejoiced when he saw Poison—that is Bella—down near the front with her son. Ultimately, they chose Christ, but their conversions had nothing to do with the mountain. Andrew Crenshaw had also chosen God in the end. He still had some hard battles to fight, but he wouldn't have to fight them alone. But Crenshaw—like Poison and Tyler—had first accepted Christ *before* January 16; they did not stubbornly wait for a sign. Pastor Ellison did not need Mead Mountain in order to convert these three; and furthermore, since the mountain's failure to move was their first stumbling block, Ellison might have had an easier go at them without the mountain's involvement at all.

So what had been the point, God?

He looked at the few remaining empty seats. They had always hurt his heart, but now they had proper names affixed to them. He saw two side by side, for Terry and Elaine. After Benjamin Mead's article, they went to beg for their jobs back from Cap'n at the club. Ecstasy and Desire forevermore.

He spotted an empty seat to his left. It was for Cheryl Fox. She had returned to her agency, who said that Jake Dolan had been asking for her.

He saw a seat for Jake Dolan, a man who had the charisma and intelligence to help turn the parade around, but refused.

He saw an empty seat, up in the balcony for Officer Felicia Jones, a dedicated public servant who was strong enough to get past the mistakes of her parents and hurt of her childhood, but just needed a little more to close the deal.

The last empty seat he saw, and perhaps the one that cut him the worst, was next to Hailey Rucker. She sat in the front, as usual, and had coincidentally left an empty seat right beside her. Perhaps it was a symbolic gesture for her own mind—an empty chair, a prayer unanswered, left waiting for the worthy man she'd been aching for, waiting for the day God would ease the pain in her heart, her longsuffering heart, empty and waiting.

And what about America? Must my prayers for this country I so

dearly love remain unanswered? Wasn't this all supposed to be "for the sake of a great nation?" Are we to continue our slide into a nihilist society? Continue to bar Jesus from our once-great institutions? Will we cease to be good, and therefore cease to be great? Are we to lose the very faith that made us exceptional? Have You withdrawn Your favor from this land, and have we lost our last, best hope of Earth?

Pastor Ellison looked up, not toward the ceiling of the church, but toward the heavens above. After being a Christian for twenty-eight years, God still had a way of confounding him. He did things that Ellison just couldn't figure out.

When his eyes lowered, they happened to rest on Hailey Rucker sitting in the front row all alone. Alone in a crowd of five thousand. *But wait.* Ellison noticed something strange. *Where is Baby Abigail? Surely Hailey did not leave her at home alone with that drunk?*

Then he saw a man walking down the aisle, dressed in his day-of-court best, hair slicked straight to both sides. When the man stepped closer, Ellison could see he was carrying a baby in his arms; precious Abigail was resting her little head on Colton's shoulder.

He had just stepped out to change her diaper. That's all. When Colton reached his spot—the empty chair, no longer empty—that Hailey had saved for him, he moved to hand Abigail off to her mother. But Abigail refused to let go. She pushed her mother's hand away giggling and used both arms to grab tight to Colton's neck.

Ellison saw Hailey shrug. If he had read her lips correctly, she had softly said the words, "Daddy's girl."

Ellison's heart filled with the awesome power and wonder of God's grace. He understood now. *How much is one soul worth to God? To what lengths will God go if it means bringing one of His children back to Him?*

It had been about just one person the whole time. It had never been about Ellison's prayers; it was about Hailey's. God had brought her worthy man back, back to her and back to Him. God finally answered Hailey's incessant prayers for her family and He used a mountain to do it.

Ellison felt hope—hope for his congregation, hope for the country, and hope for the world. This is how you heal America; this is how you change the world. Not in big jumps, but small steps. Not with the collective, but the individual. Not the state, but the citizen. Not with the whole parade, but with one family, one man, one Christian.

Who was Colton Rucker that God would devise such a plan just for him? Pastor Ellison mused as he saw Hailey touch her palm to her growing belly.

Simple. He is precious. He is sacred. He is a child of God. Pastor Ellison smiled knowingly. *Colton Rucker will become a great nation.*

THE END

Note to Reader:

I hope you have enjoyed reading my debut novel.

Love the book? Please leave a five-star review on Amazon.

Hate the book? Come find me on Facebook and lets talk about it.

This book was published by Authoritative, a small start-up from Texas, without the assistance of the large New York firms. You can help support this novel, and those to follow, by spreading the word about the work we are doing. Those of you on Facebook, please join my fan page: Facebook.com/AuthorBKDell, and invite your friends to join. Mention this book on your wall and share a link to BKDell.com. If you run a blog, please mention me on your blog. Come find me on Goodreads.com; friend me and click to become a fan. Amazon and Goodreads are the best places to leave a five-star review.

Of course, the most helpful thing you can do is tell your friends and family, face to face, how much you enjoyed this book.

Please visit BKDell.com for updated links to Facebook, Twitter and more.

Please check back often for new titles coming soon!

God bless you!

Now please check out the Eleasha Postscript -->

ELEASHA POSTSCRIPT

The Eleasha Postscript is an additional postscript I add to each of my novels, tailored specifically for my loving wife and her kind heart, although I hope you will enjoy it as well. It is my last chance to make sure the book has a happy ending, and apply a healing salve to any hurt the reader might be left with. Eleasha Postscripts are sometimes Pollyannaish and usually absurd. Pursuant to this, I have even raised characters from the dead before.

~B.K. Dell

"Before we get started, there is one more issue that must be settled," Ellison told his congregation. "I would like to read for you the first post from the world's newest, and I suspect one-day greatest, news website: *The Crenshaw Review*." He glanced at Andrew Crenshaw in the audience and gave a proud nod.

Ellison walked over to his podium and picked up a stack of printer paper. "It is a fine piece of investigative reporting on what really happened the night of Mason Kessler's death. Mr. Crenshaw was able to get the whole story from a firsthand witness, one of the parties involved in the crash. I won't read the entire article; for those who are curious, I suggest you visit the site yourselves, and check back every day for that matter. But for now, I'd like to read this young man's account, exactly as it was given to Mr. Crenshaw."

Ellison raised the page and breathed in deep. He read:

My father and I were driving home on January 14. It was late at night and the weather was rainy, just as it had been for weeks on end. We were on Shady Trail; the papers got that part right at least, but it wasn't Mason Kessler who caused the accident. I caused the accident. In fact, Mason Kessler was not even involved in the accident... at first.

My father and I were returning home after some shopping. I was turning right onto Stonebridge, like I have done countless times before. I always take that turn slowly because I know how dangerous it is. But I guess with the conditions of the road, I just didn't take it slowly enough. Our car began to hydroplane and I felt that sickly feeling I get when my tires relinquish their grip on the pavement. They squealed in panic and my fingernails dug into the steering wheel. I hit the brake, but couldn't prevent our car from careening into the other lane. And in that tremulous moment of powerlessness, we were overcome by a much higher set of headlights barreling down on us.

The impact shattered every window, bent the frame of my small car, and spun us around backward. The flash of the airbags might have saved my life, but the force knocked my father unconscious. When I was first able to raise my head and assess the situation, I saw that my father's head was limp to one side and there was blood beneath his nose. In my frazzled condition I was afraid that the car might explode, like you always see in the movies. I bailed out of the car and ran to my father's side. The door was jammed shut, so I tried to pull him out through the broken window. The angle was all wrong for me to get any leverage, but I tried anyway. All I had was the strength of my arms, and my arms just weren't strong enough.

I started to panic. My hands were shaking and I was crying. I must've been in shock because I felt like I was seconds away from breaking down—either slip into a state of paralysis, or just lose consciousness, or maybe even go insane and never come back. I must've been quite a sight for the man who walked up behind me.

At first I thought he had come from the truck we had run into; maybe that's how the initial news reports got it wrong. I may have told that to someone later. I can't remember.

The man gently moved me aside and began to pull my father out of the car.

I protested. "It's no use. You won't be able to lift him."

The man's voice was calm. His eyes were steady, and steadfast, and sober. All he said was, "I can lift him."

I continued to panic. I think I was rambling, but I don't remember what I was saying. I remember the man looking up to ask me, "Do you know the number for 911?"

It was a joke, meant to calm me down, but it eluded me at the time. I actually had to consider it. "I do," I told him proudly.

"I need you to call them for me. Tell them we are at the corner of Stonebridge and Shady Trail and we need an ambulance."

I was lucid when I pulled out my phone. Having a clear task to perform helped pull me out of my shock. As I spoke to the dispatcher, I was amazed to see the stranger, despite having many years on me, pull my father to safety without effort.

He lowered the limp body down by the side of the road. I knelt beside my father and I could see that he was just beginning to come to.

"What happened?" my father mumbled.

"We were in an accident," I answered. "This man here pulled you out." I turned to motion to the man behind me, but like a phantom—or maybe like an angel—the man was gone.

My eyes searched for him among the wreckage, but the rain was coming down in sheets now and it was too dark to see. Rainwater was pooling on my eyelashes, flooding at intervals into my eyes. I rapidly blinked away the sting and continued to scan for our brave Samaritan. Just as my vision was able to focus, the entire scene was illuminated by oncoming headlights—the road, the trees, the wreckage, and most harrowingly, the form of the man who'd saved us. He and the hobbled man on his arm, the other driver, were limping from the crash through the darkness.

I turned my head away from the impending carnage. For the second time that night I heard the squeal of tires, only this time it was followed by a scream.

Ellison lowered the papers—he, himself, turning from the carnage. The stage lights shined at 10:00 and 2:00, and he looked out across a packed congregation for strength. He raised the papers again and scanned to the end of the story.

The next thing I knew, our rescuer was flat on the street and it was my turn to help him. But there was nothing I could do.

I held his injured body on my lap and was repeatedly thanking him. My father was clear from the wreckage when the third car hit, his life saved by a total stranger. A true hero.

I held him as we heard the first hints of the ambulance. I told him to hang on and that help was on the way. The flashing lights lit up his face once more and I had my first calm moment to really look at him. It was my final surprise of the night. I asked, "Hey, you're Stone Kessler, aren't you?"

"No," the man said. "I'm only Mason," were his last words. I have no idea what he meant by that.

A tear formed in Ellison's eyes and he looked out at the congregation. He said, "I know what he meant by that. He meant that a lifelong deliberation had finally been resolved. He meant he was finally free."

Suddenly he felt a quick bump beneath his feet. Five thousand heads snapped forcefully to one side in unison, as the ground shifted beneath them. They heard what sounded like a fleet of freight trains and Ellison felt the stage he was standing on begin to shake. The congregation anxiously scanned the environment for any clue of what was happening.

The seats trembled beneath them and the frightened congregants reached to grab onto their arm rests and onto each other. Ellison's legs crossed a few times as he tried to remain upright on what felt like a ship on a raging sea.

Over the sound of tremors, a mighty groan rose from the very bedrock itself, as if the earth were bemoaning its growing pains. This noise was met with the sound of glass breaking and a cacophony of screams. Broken pieces of plaster fell from the ceiling, and from the view of the people below, it appeared as though the ceiling itself might be falling.

Everyone's face turned to watch the convulsions of one of the church's support pillars as it fought to remain standing. The realization that they were moments away from being horribly crushed filled their minds and they all began to run.

They could not run very far however, because the spasms of the earth would not allow it. People stumbled into the isle, collided with other people and fell to the ground. Bodies tipped pell-mell over the backs of seats, sending wingtips and pumps into the air.

Hailey Rucker, along with others, immediately saw the futility in running. She curled her body tight around Baby Abigail and Colton leaned in, covering Hailey's body with his own, encircling them both protectively with his arms. He covered Hailey, who covered Abigail, and prayed for Jesus to cover him—the perfect symbolism for a proper family.

The support pillar lost its fight and broke in two. The bottom half fell to the side and the top half fell straight down. Everyone watched with terror as ceiling fell toward them, then stopped. The roof didn't collapse, but merely buckled in a few feet before its weight was transferred to the remaining pillars. A plume of dust burst forth from the crack in the ceiling and descended onto the crowd. Gray dust clung to their sweat and their tears.

The main lights went out in the congregation and a pall of darkness enveloped them. The only lights remaining were the red lights over the exit doors and the two spotlights that lit the stage. But the stage was now empty.

Ellison had run toward the area where the pillar had fallen, searching for injured people.

The weight of the roof pulled at the top of the western wall, causing it to break apart. An avalanche of bricks slid into the sanctuary as most of the wall came tumbling down. Extremely bright sunlight pierced the darkness. Its individual rays were revealed in the thick, eddying fog of dust.

As Ellison frantically hunted for any injured, it took him a moment to notice that the quaking had stopped. The screams had stopped as well. The place was surprisingly quiet. There were no cries of pain or panic, and no indication that anyone was hurt at all.

Ellison shot a glance from person to person, but no one looked back at him. All their faces were turned toward the collapsed wall, toward the sun. He imagined that people should still be rushing for the exits, regardless of whether the shaking had stopped. But they weren't.

Every face was turned to the west. And everyone was silent.

Ellison had intentionally made his way to the area of the church with the most destruction. The rest of the congregation had fled away from the falling bricks. As a result, their pastor now stood in front of them just before the opening left by the missing wall. His shoulders and hair were edge-lit by the raking sunrays and it gave him a heroic aura. But no one saw it. All their eyes were looking past him, out toward the newly-visible sky.

The steps in Ellison's brain happened in the span of far less than a second: the confusion over his church's behavior and the realization that they must be stunned—stunned still and stunned silent—by what they actually were looking at. This confusion, if it had time to be given words might have asked, *Why aren't people panicking? Why aren't they running? And what could possibly require so much attention in a moment like this?* Pastor Ellison turned his head to see for himself.

Behind the pastor, beneath the sky, before the sea, framed by the aperture of the wounded wall, they beheld a glorious gift from heaven. In the exact place where Mead Mountain had stood, they discovered a resplendent peak, a majestic summit, a new mountain.

It was the logical result of two obstreperous tectonic plates butting heads with seismic force. The amateur geologist stepped to a spot atop the rubble and gawked at God's miracle. He no longer feared the church would fall. He knew it would never fall.

The new mountain looked so familiar to him; he tried to remember what Mead Mountain had looked like and he couldn't notice a single difference. The graffiti, of course, was gone. A smile crossed his lips and he said, partially to himself, partially to God, "Now that's funny."

It hadn't occurred to him that he was still mic'd up, and apparently the sound system must have been linked through the same intact circuit as the stage lights, because the entire church heard what Ellison had said and began to laugh.

He turned back to look at the people, the sunlight filling their joyous faces, and he heard God's voice. It was the second time in his life that he had heard the Lord speaking so clearly to his heart. He heard:

Mason Kessler is with Me now and I've given him a good talking to.

Tears filled Ellison's eyes and his sweet sobs filled the giant room. He gathered himself and said. "I think this would be a good time to make an announcement. Starting immediately, our congregation will have a new name." He held up his hand, presenting the new mountain. In a sonorous tone of victory, he declared, "I would like to welcome you all to Mason Mountain Church."

And they all lived happily ever after.

Made in the USA
Lexington, KY
07 June 2017